Exploring Seriality on Screen

This collective book analyzes seriality as a major phenomenon increasingly connecting audiovisual narratives (cinematic films and television series) in the 20th and 21st centuries.

The book historicizes and contextualizes the notion of seriality, combining narratological, aesthetic, industrial, philosophical, and political perspectives, showing how seriality as a paradigm informs media convergence and resides at the core of cinema and television history. By associating theoretical considerations and close readings of specific works, as well as diachronic and synchronic approaches, this volume offers a complex panorama of issues related to seriality including audience engagement, intertextuality and transmediality, cultural legitimacy, authorship, and medium specificity in remakes, adaptations, sequels, and reboots.

Written by a team of international scholars, this book highlights a diversity of methodologies that will be of interest to scholars and doctoral students across disciplinary areas such as media studies, film studies, literature, aesthetics, and cultural studies. It will also interest students attending classes on serial audiovisual narratives and will appeal to fans of the series it addresses, such as *Fargo, Twin Peaks, The Hunger Games, Bates Motel,* and *Sherlock.*

Ariane Hudelet is Professor of Visual Culture at Université de Paris (LARCA/CNRS). After working on film adaptations, she has devoted her most recent research to contemporary TV dramas, from an aesthetic and cultural perspective, and is co-editor of the online journal *TV/Series.*

Anne Crémieux is Professor of American studies at Université Paris 8 – Vincennes-Saint Denis. She has published books, articles and book chapters on the representation of minorities in cinema and television.

Routledge Research in Cultural and Media Studies

Media Cultures in Latin America
Key Concepts and New Debates
Edited by Anna Cristina Pertierra and Juan Francisco Salazar

Cultures of participation
Arts, digital media and cultural institutions
Edited by Birgit Eriksson, Carsten Stage and Bjarki Valtysson

Adapting Endings from Book to Screen
Last Pages, Last Shots
Edited by Armelle Parey and Shannon Wells-Lassagne

Migration, Identity, and Belonging
Defining Borders and Boundaries of the Homeland
Edited by Margaret Franz and Kumarini Silva

Exploring Seriality on Screen
Audiovisual Narratives in Film and Television
Edited by Ariane Hudelet and Anne Crémieux

Locating Imagination in Popular Culture
Place, Tourism and Belonging
Edited by Nicky van Es, Stijn Reijnders, Leonieke Bolderman, and Abby Waysdorf

For more information about this series, please visit: https://www.routledge.com

Exploring Seriality on Screen

Audiovisual Narratives in Film and Television

Edited by
Ariane Hudelet and
Anne Crémieux

LONDON AND NEW YORK

First published 2021
by Routledge
2 Park Square, Milton Park, Abingdon, Oxon OX14 4RN

and by Routledge
52 Vanderbilt Avenue, New York, NY 10017

Routledge is an imprint of the Taylor & Francis Group, an informa business

© 2021 Taylor & Francis

The right of Ariane Hudelet and Anne Crémieux to be identified
as the authors of the editorial material, and of the authors for their
individual chapters, has been asserted in accordance with sections
77 and 78 of the Copyright, Designs and Patents Act 1988.

British Library Cataloguing-in-Publication Data
A catalogue record for this book is available from the British Library

Library of Congress Cataloging-in-Publication Data
A catalog record has been requested for this book

ISBN: 978-0-367-49148-2 (hbk)
ISBN: 978-1-003-04477-2 (ebk)

Typeset in Sabon
by codeMantra

Contents

List of illustrations   vii
Acknowledgments   ix
List of contributors   xi

Introduction: cinematic, televisual, or post-serialities   1
ARIANE HUDELET AND ANNE CRÉMIEUX

PART I
Serial specificities   17

1.1 Opening gambits: cross-media self-reflexivity and audience
    engagement in serial cinema, 1936–2008   19
    ILKA BRASCH AND FELIX BRINKER

1.2 Ensemble storytelling: dramatic television seriality, the
    melodramatic mode, and emotions   37
    E. DEIDRE PRIBRAM

1.3 The cinematic-televisual: rethinking medium specificity in
    television's new Golden Age   53
    C.E. HARRIS

PART II
Marketing seriality   77

2.1 A forgotten episode in the history of Hollywood cinema,
    television, and seriality: the case of the Mirisch Company   79
    PAUL KERR

2.2 Diversions in the *Hunger Games* film series: the fragmented
    narrative of hijacked images   103
    CHLOÉ MONASTEROLO

2.3 Raising Caine: Hollywood remakes of Michael Caine's
    Cockney cycle   122
    AGNIESZKA RASMUS

PART III
Seriality and the cinematic/televisual convergence   137

3.1 The (re)making of a serial killer: replaying, "preplaying,"
    and rewriting Hitchcock's *Psycho* in the series *Bates Motel*   139
    DENNIS TREDY

3.2 *Fargo* (FX, 2014–) and cinema: "just like in the movie"?   159
    SYLVAINE BATAILLE

3.3 Screening dreams: *Twin Peaks*, from the series to the film,
    back again and beyond   177
    SARAH HATCHUEL

PART IV
Meta-serialities   197

4.1 In-between still and moving pictures: series and seriality in
    Stephen Poliakoff's serial drama *Shooting the Past* (1999)   199
    NICOLE CLOAREC

4.2 "The abominable bride": *Sherlock* and seriality   213
    CHRISTOPHE GELLY

4.3 Subject positions and seriality in *The Good Wife*   233
    SAMUEL A. CHAMBERS

    Index   259

Illustrations

Figures

3.1.1 Starting Over: The idyllic shot of Norma Bates (Vera Farmiga) that bookends the entire *Bates Motel* series (S01E01, S05E10) 147

3.1.2 The Gradual Decline of Norman Bates: this chart indicates episodes over all four "prequel" seasons which stage the progressive symptoms of Norman's descent into madness. Higher bars indicate episodes that give more intense focus on that trait 154

4.2.1 The initial stage in the train travel 217

4.2.2 The same image turning around with the Carmichael mansion in the background 218

4.2.3 The superimposition of both images upside down 218

4.2.4 The Carmichael mansion 219

4.2.5 Holmes as a second Jeremy Brett 226

4.2.6 The famous Granada credit sequence 226

4.2.7 The narrative as metafictional 228

4.2.8 21st-century Watson appearing in the 19th-century narrative 230

Table

2.3.1 Theatrical and DVD release dates of Michael Caine's British originals and their Hollywood remakes 128

Acknowledgments

Ariane Hudelet and Anne Crémieux would like to thank the LARCA (Université de Paris/CNRS), CREA (Université Paris Nanterre), and CERILAC (Université de Paris), for their financial and institutional help during the completion of this project.

Our warmest thanks as well to the SERCIA (Société d'étude et de recherche sur les cinémas anglophones) and to the GUEST consortium, which made it possible to organize the 2016 conference on "Cinema and Seriality" that led to this publication.

Contributors

Sylvaine Bataille is Associate Professor of Literature and Film Studies in the English department at the University of Rouen Normandie, France, and a member of the research group ERIAC. Her research interests cover appropriation, adaptation, translation, and reference, with a focus on Shakespearean screen adaptations and drama television series. She has co-edited three issues of the online journal *TV/Series* ("TV Series World-Wide: Changes and Exchanges", 2012; "TV Series Redux (I): TV Series and Intermediality", 2013; "TV Series Redux (II): Cultural, Social and Ideological Representations in TV Series", 2013) and has published several articles on television series such as *Rome, Battlestar Galactica, Sons of Anarchy, Boss,* or *Game of Thrones,* and their reworking of so-called "classical" works.

Ilka Brasch is Assistant Professor in American Studies at Leibniz University, Hannover, Germany. Her monograph *Film Serials and the American Cinema: 1910–1940* was published at Amsterdam University Press in 2018. From 2013 to 2016, she was a member of the Research Unit "Popular Seriality – Aesthetics and Practice," based at the Free University of Berlin. Part of her research on film serials appeared in *Screen* and in *LWU- Literatur in Wissenschaft und Unterricht.*

Felix Brinker is a postdoctoral researcher in the division of American Studies at Leibniz University Hannover, where his current research focuses on late 19th- and early 20th-century periodical culture. His recently completed dissertation engages with the current prominence of super-hero blockbuster film and develops a re-conceptualization of digital-era participatory culture from the vantage point of Marxist theory. His research interests include early 20th-century mass culture, contemporary American film, television, and comics, as well as popular seriality, media studies, and critical theory more generally.

Samuel A. Chambers is Professor of Political Science at Johns Hopkins University, where he teaches political theory, cultural politics, and political economy. He is co-Editor-in-Chief of the journal *Contemporary Political*

Theory and is series co-Editor of Routledge's *Innovators in Political Theory*. He has authored six books and edited four, and published more than thirty journal articles, along with numerous chapters and essays. He has recently published the monograph *There Is No Such Thing as "The Economy": Essays on Capitalist Value* (Punctum, 2018), and the article "Undoing Neoliberalism: *Homo Economicus, Homo Politicus,* and the *Zoon Politikon,*" *Critical Inquiry* 44 (Summer 2018): 706–732.

Nicole Cloarec is Senior Lecturer in English at Rennes 1 University (Univ Rennes, LIDILE-EA 3874, F-35000 Rennes, France). Her research focuses on British and English-speaking cinema and questions related to the cinematic apparatus, transmediality, adaptation, and the documentary. She is a member of the editorial board of *LISA* e-journal and *Film Journal*. Among her most recent publications, she has co-edited *Social Class on British and American Screens* (McFarland, 2016) and "The Specificities of Kitsch in the Cinema of English-Speaking Countries" (*LISA* e-journal, 2017).

Christophe Gelly is Professor of British and American literature and film studies at Université Clermont Auvergne, France. He has worked mainly on film genre, film noir, and adaptation, and has published two book-length studies on Arthur Conan Doyle and Raymond Chandler, and co-edited *Approaches to film and reception theories / Cinéma et théories de la réception - Etudes et panorama critique* in 2012. He edited the issue of *Écrans* devoted to French literary realism and film adaptation (*Ecrans*, n° 5, 2016-1) and co-authored a book-length study of Ang Lee's adaptation of Jane Austen (*Sense and Sensibility*, Atlande, 2015). He focused on comic book and adaptation in *Lovecraft et l'Illustration*, Christophe Gelly and Gilles Menegaldo [eds.], 2017. His current research deals with film theory.

C.E. Harris is a PhD candidate in Cinema and Visual Studies at Université de Paris, affiliated with the Centre d'Études et de Recherches Interdisciplinaires (CERILAC) and the Laboratoire de Recherches sur les Cultures Anglophones (LARCA), and is a laureate of the *Initiatives d'excellence* fellowship of the Université Sorbonne Paris Cité. Currently working on a dissertation on mise-en-scène and spatiality in digital cinema, Harris has taught film courses in the United States and in France, and is interested in film philosophy, aesthetics, formalism, phenomenology, and the phenomena of cinema and audiovisual media, intermediality, and the analogic relationship between science and the arts.

Sarah Hatchuel is Professor of Film and Media studies at the Université Paul-Valéry Montpellier 3. She has written several books on Shakespeare on film (*Shakespeare and the Cleopatra/Caesar Intertext: Sequel, Conflation, Remake,* Fairleigh Dickinson University Press, 2011; *Shakespeare, from Stage to Screen,* Cambridge University Press, 2004; *A Companion* *to the Shakespearean Films of Kenneth Branagh*, Blizzard Publishing, 2000) and on American TV series (*The Leftovers: le troisième côté du miroir*, Playlist Society, 2019; *Rêves et séries américaines: La fabrique d'autres mondes*, Rouge Profond, 2015; *Lost: Fiction Vitale*, PUF, 2013). She co-edits (with Nathalie Vienne-Guerrin) the Shakespeare on Screen collection (PURH/CUP) and co-edits (with Ariane Hudelet) the online journal TV/Series (*http://journals.openedition.org/tvseries/*).

Paul Kerr is Senior Lecturer in Television Production at Middlesex University. He is the author and editor of several academic books (including *The Hollywood Film Industry* and *MTM Quality Television*) and has published articles on television and film. He spent 25 years as a television producer for the British Film Institute, the BBC, and Channel Four, as well as international co-productions. His research interests include documentary, drama documentary, "quality" television, arts programming, the independent production sector in film and television, Hollywood, and international art cinema. He is a former member of the *Screen* editorial board and was a producer-director at October Films from 1999 to 2007. His new book, *Hollywood's Missing Link: How the Mirisch Company Remade Hollywood*, will be published by Bloomsbury in 2021.

Chloé Monasterolo is a PhD candidate specializing in Film Studies at the Université de Toulouse Jean Jaurès, where she teaches classes in film history and analysis. Her dissertation focuses on narrative identity and cultural convergence, taking a specific interest to recent works that experiment with intermediality and transmediality. She has published an article entitled "Le *reboot* de l'apocalypse : la [re]médiation de l'invasion zombie dans *Chroniques des morts-vivants/Diary of the Dead* de George Romero (2008)" in *Médiations apocalyptiques/Imag(in)ing the Apocalypse* (2018), an open access publication of Université de Bretagne Occidentale.

E. Deidre Pribram is Professor in the Communications Department of Molloy College, Long Island, New York. She is, most recently, the author of *A Cultural Approach to Emotional Disorders: Psychological and Aesthetic Interpretations* (Routledge, 2018), *Emotions, Genre, Justice in Film and Television: Detecting Feeling* (Routledge, 2013), and "Melodrama and the Aesthetics of Emotion" in *Melodrama Unbound: Across History, Media, and National Cultures* (Columbia UP, 2018). Her research encompasses cultural emotion studies, film and television studies, gender, and popular culture.

Agnieszka Rasmus teaches in the Institute of English Studies at the University of Łódź, Poland. She is the author of *Filming Shakespeare, from Metatheatre to Metacinema* (Peter Lang, 2008), *Hollywood Remakes of Iconic British Films: Class, Gender and Stardom* (EUP, 2020 forthcoming) and co-editor of *Images of the City* (CSP, 2009), *Against and*

Beyond: Subversion and Transgression in Mass Media, Popular Culture and Performance (CSP, 2012), and a special issue of *Multicultural Shakespeare: Translation, Appropriation and Performance*, vol. 12 (27) "Diversity and Homogeneity: Shakespeare and the Politics of Nation, Class and Gender" (Łódź University Press, 2015).

Dennis Tredy is Associate Professor of American Literature at the Université de Paris 3-Sorbonne Nouvelle and teaches literature and film adaptation at Sciences Po Paris. He is co-founder of the European Society of Jamesian Studies and has published three volumes on Henry James: *Reading Henry James in the Twenty-First Century* (2019), *Henry James and the Poetics of Duplicity* (2014), and *Henry James's Europe: Heritage and Transfer* (2011). In addition, he has published studies on film and television adaptations of the works of Henry James, Edgar Allan Poe, Vladimir Nabokov, and other authors, as well as on literary adaptation and radio adaptation for television, on TV series past and present, and on the representation of American culture, diversity, and counter-culture in the 1950s, 1960s, and 1970s.

Introduction

Cinematic, televisual, or post-serialities[1]

Ariane Hudelet and Anne Crémieux

From its very inception, the cinematographic medium has been intrinsically bound to seriality. Starting with Eadward Muybridge or Etienne-Jules Marey's chronophotographic experiments, or the countless optical toys such as the zoetrope of the phenakitiscope, pre-cinematographic inventions relied on seriality: the rapid succession of a series of still images created the illusion of movement – as if the magic lay in the brief interstice between two images (Aumont 1990; Crary 1990; Mannoni 1995). Powered by the technological prowess materialized in the Lumière brothers' Cinematograph and Thomas Edison's Kinetoscope, cinema soon ventured into storytelling. As cinematographic narratives became more complex, many creators and producers chose to adopt the serial form, in the tradition of the serialized novel of the 19th century. Episodic storytelling on the big screen quickly became popular on both sides of the Atlantic with serial films such as *Arsène Lupin* (1910–1911), *The Perils of Pauline* (1914), or *Fantomas* (1913–1914). Following a story along from one episode to the next, inviting spectators to reconnect with characters after moments of separation, seriality was already meant to enhance a sense of intimacy, emotional attachment, and spectatorial involvement that popular cinema, followed by television and other audiovisual forms, would continue to cultivate up until today.

In fact, today more than ever, the serial form reigns supreme, both culturally and economically, and spreads across media – it has become a "dominant mode of narrative presentation in Western culture – if not in fact the dominant mode" (Hagedorn 1988, 5). With high-budget, high-grossing franchises, *sequels, prequels, remakes,* and other *reboots,* from the *Marvel Cinematic Universe* to *Star Wars,* from *Alien* to *The Hobbit,* seriality is at the heart of mainstream commercial cinema. On television, the serial form acquired full cultural legitimacy and artistic status at the turn of the 21st century – critics and audiences celebrated "the third golden age" of television, also described as "quality," "high end," or "prestige" TV (Feuer, Kerr and Vahimagi 1984, Jancovich and Lyons 2003; McCabe and Akass 2007; Nelson 2007).[2] With the multiplication of channels and the rise of satellite and cable TV in the last decades of the 20th century came the shift from "lowest common denominator" to niche programming, which dominates most serial production on television today (Edgerton 2007; McCabe and Akass 2007; Gray and Lotz, 2012). The multiplication of production models, from networks to cable channels, and to the recent success of "OTT" content (streaming) on VOD platforms (Netflix, Amazon, Hulu, Disney+), has confirmed the age of Peak-TV (Johnson 2018), or the "gilded age" of television[3] where audiences find it hard to keep up with the ever-increasing amount of programs at their disposal and constantly experience the "Fear of Missing Out" (FOMO), leading to what is often considered to be compulsive practices such as binge- or speed-watching.[4] In a context of major technological and economic shifts, formats and norms evolve and mutate fast so that modes of audiovisual production and reception are very different today from what they were 20 or 30 years ago. In the audiovisual realm, the digital turn has led to an increasing convergence in the modes of production and reception of cinema and television (Kipnis 1998; Jenkins 2006; Dwyer 2010). The distinction between the two seems further blurred by the expansion of serial narratives on small and big screens alike, so that a separation based on social and cultural roles becomes debatable, leading to new, all-encompassing non-categories such as "post-television" (Missika 2006; Leverette 2008; Gray and Lotz 2012).

First disregarded critically for its disproportionate use by supposedly inferior genres (crime fiction, animation, melodrama), seriality has become a dominant model independent of cultural hierarchies. A spate of studies from a growing number of critics and academics across disciplines have started to focus on the nature and functions of seriality. For several years now, the impact of episodic shows and films on viewers who devote long hours of their lives to serial fiction has been studied from numerous angles, whether it be narratology (Thomson 2003; Allrath et al. 2005; Guilbert and Lassagne 2014; Esquenazi 2017), film studies (Higgins 2016), media studies (Gitlin 1983; Caldwell 1995; Mittell 2015; Letourneux 2018), or social sciences (Glevarec 2012). As recent studies devoted to the aesthetics of television series suggest (Gray and Lotz 2012; Jacobs and Peacock 2013; Dunleavy 2017), we must now explore the way both cinematic and television series are redefining the very concepts of film, cinema, or television, in order to apprehend the new audiovisual forms of expression in which seriality dominates.

Critical studies have long treated seriality within a specific medium, whether with full-length studies on television seriality[5] for instance, or of Hollywood franchises (Alberse 2015). Series have also often been observed as pop culture productions in the context of cultural studies "less interested in the *seriality of popular forms* than in the *popularity of serial forms*" (Denson 2011). In other words, the form and processes of seriality have tended to matter less than the uses and functions of these mass-produced series in the specific context of their reception. More recently, the phenomenon of seriality itself has become the focus of increasing academic interest that attempts to combine a consideration of the cultural and economic contexts with what is perceived as a form of "quality" worth studying for itself. The expansive and polymorphous nature of the objects of study requires adaptive methodologies that combine macro- and micro-approaches, close readings, and far-reaching theories. Establishing a theory of seriality is indeed a near-impossible task because of the essentially interdisciplinary nature of the field. When trying to pinpoint what could be specific to the serial form, the cultural, artistic, and economic history of each media is staggeringly vast: literature, comics books, films, television, video games, and more are all heterogenous subcategories, "cultural paradigms" (Gaudreault 2008), that must be taken into account because they navigate seriality each in their own way.

In spite or perhaps because of the difficulties listed above, many studies inspired by the general enthusiasm for either TV or cinematic series have attempted to bring out the specific features of seriality across media. After Eco's seminal article on "Innovation and Repetition" (Eco 1994), one of the first full-length attempts to tackle seriality in its diverse manifestations across medias was Jennifer Hayward's *Consuming Pleasures* (1997). In this groundbreaking work, Hayward brought together the serialized novel of the 19th century, the first comics, ads, and *soap operas,* tracing "family resemblances" between serial forms across different media – common inherent features such as complex and intricate plot lines, a large number of characters, plot twists, lack of narrative closure, multiple points of view, narrative clichés, but also, and most importantly perhaps, heightened modes of audience participation and engagement. She points out how audiences develop active strategies of consumption such as collective reading for instance, and attempt to participate in the creative process (Hayward 1997, 5). Most studies of seriality, Hayward's included, also stress the capitalistic, economic framework of serial works, bringing forth the connection between serialized cultural products and a market economy that relies on serialized manufacturing processes – a link conceptualized, decades earlier, by Walter Benjamin (Benjamin 1939). Seriality also represents safe investment in a capitalistic economy, since producers rely on recurring characters, open-ended plotlines, and delayed closure to whet the audience's desire (idem, 2). Serial narratives thus "promote themselves and the medium in which they appear" (Loock 2014). Historically, the continually renewed pleasure of the serial form has returned stable profits and ensured the economic stability of new technologies – whether it be the new, cheap, mass-produced book, periodical publications such as newspapers or magazines, cinematic film, radio, television, or video games (Hayward 1997, 2–3).

The fundamentally commercial nature of seriality shouldn't, however, be the only point of entry into these works, or suffice to disregard them as exploitative lures for alienated audiences. The idea that serial works merely embody a form of mass culture imposed by a hegemonic system of capitalist production in the tradition of the Frankfurt school theory of the culture industry (Adorno and Horkheimer 1944) has been largely undermined by cultural studies and theories of post-modernity. As Hayward points out, beyond the safe investment that seriality represents in a capitalistic logic, there are "the very real pleasures and satisfactions of audiences, [...] the practices surrounding consumption of serial texts," and "the functions such texts may serve for the individual and for the community" (Hayward 1997, 2).

Many more books and journal issues have studied seriality as a phenomenon crossing generic or formal borders. Special issues of academic journals (*Literatur in Wissenschaft und Unterricht* in 2014, *Cahiers de Narratologie*, and *The Velvet LightTrap* in 2016) have focused exclusively on questions related to seriality and serialization. In Germany, an ambitious pluri-annual research project, "Popular Seriality – Aesthetics and Practice," funded by the German Research Foundation between 2010 and 2016, has greatly contributed to the emergence of what can now be called Seriality Studies, with major publications such as *Media of Serial Narrative*, a comprehensive collective work that addresses seriality in diverse forms – the literary serial, video games, cartoons, graphic novels, and digital technologies (Kelleter 2017). In France, Mathieu Letourneux's wide-ranging sociological and historical study of seriality focuses on literature, cinema, comic books, and television, pointing out that the diversity of formats requires the acknowledgment of a "serial pact" (Letourneux 2017, 54) established with the reader, viewer, or gamer, that depends on the nature of the media. For him, the study of seriality requires new methods – shifting from texts to series of texts, from intertexts to architexts, from the assertion of originality to phenomena of convergence or negotiation, from the literary to the textual and from the textual towards the whole of cultural production – with a particular focus on issues of circulation and appropriation, and mixing literary analysis with historical, social, economic, and political angles (Letourneux 2017).

Our volume engages in this ongoing interdisciplinary conversation while limiting the scope of our study to cinema and television so as to focus more specifically on seriality within audiovisual narratives. Studying seriality on the big and small screens allows our authors to fully analyze issues related with medium specificity, and with the evolution of the audiovisual form and industries today. With the digital turn, the process of convergence between cinema and television is technological as well as societal and spiritual (Jones et al. 2000). As David Campany points out, our experience of film, in its broader meaning, is now polymorphous, far from the initial mode of viewing of the original *cinema*, which meant "a big screen, dimmed lighting, rows of seats [...]. Today, [...] the cinema is only one among many contexts in which films are viewed. The large auditorium takes its place alongside television, computer screens, in-flight entertainment, lobbies, shop windows, galleries and mobile phones" (Campany 2007, 16). This "cinematic heterotopia," as Victor Burgin calls this "network of separate but overlapping interfaces and viewing habits" (Burgin 2007, 198), leads many contemporary audiovisual works, whether they be cinematic films, television series, video games, or YouTube uploads, to critically and fruitfully explore their common heritage as well as their distinctive traits.

The hegemony of the serial form in both cinema and television thus leads us to wonder about the persistence or erosion of cultural, industrial, and artistic boundaries. Terminology itself becomes an issue: what do we mean when we use the terms "filmic," "cinematic," or "televisual"? A debate has emerged in academia, the press, and social media over the use of the term "cinematic" to qualify series considered to be artistically superior. Most often, "cinematic" programs are praised for their enhanced visual style – modern technologies have certainly afforded denser visual images and more effective soundtracks – and for developing a more complex audiovisual expression than what is deemed typical for television (Nelson 2007). Others have denounced this use of the term, which they accuse of implying the superiority of a "cinematic" form, and of reinforcing stale cultural hierarchies between cinema and television. For Brett Mills, using "cinematic" as a "positive term when applied to (some) television can only be seen as a reassertion of a hierarchy that sees television as film's poor relation" (Mills 2013, 64). Deborah Jaramillo also radically rejects any use of the term in appreciation of television fiction, which according to her "perpetuates an audio-visual media hierarchy that is hopelessly antiquated" and "implicitly argues that film has a clearly understood essence that can compensate for television's lack thereof" (Jaramillo 2013, 67).

While also trying to stay away from an essentialist approach, other critics have, on the contrary, seen this use of the term as an opportunity to explore the slippery and unstable meaning of the "cinematic," a notion that evolves as it is being used. Elliot Logan, for instance, draws on Stanley Cavell's idea that a "medium is something through which or by means of which something specific gets said or done in particular ways" (Logan 2014, 6). This means that a medium is not defined by its materials but is rather created by the use of its materials, uses that "realize what will give them significance" (Logan 2014, 7). The use of the adjective "cinematic" would thus imply a sort of shared horizon of cinema and television that manifests itself most blatantly in these expansive serial narratives. Today, the "cinematic" exists in the form of increasingly diverse avatars. This expansion of the cinematic beyond its traditional frontiers of the movie theater leads to what Gilles Lipovetsky calls "hypercinema" (Lipovetsky and Serroy 2007) or what Shane Denson and Julia Leyda describe as "post-cinema" (Denson and Leyda 2016).

Ever since television started to be seen as a menace in the 1950s, ominous prophesies of "the death of cinema" have repeatedly flourished, especially with the technological evolutions linked to the digital turn.[6] No doubt the renewed fear of pandemics will also be a major challenge for the preservation of cinema as a collective viewing experience in an enclosed space.

In the past decade, the upcoming "death of television" has also often been predicted – is television going to be replaced with undifferentiated, polymorphous "contents" available via diverse streaming devices? Should we argue that the adjective "televisual" is becoming inadequate in the age of post-television where an increasing part of serial production emanates from sVoD providers (Subscription Video on Demand) such as Netflix, Hulu or Amazon Prime, the new giants of audiovisual production and creation? Or, on the contrary, should we consider that the terms "television" and "televisual" are meant to evolve, and are perfectly able to designate these new forms of non-linear, online content? This televisual inheritance is, for instance, acknowledged in YouTube's name and square-shaped logo, which draws a direct connection to the defunct cathodic tubes of earlier forms of TV-watching. Some go as far as declaring "the end of television" (Missika 2006), whereas other prefer to coin expressions such as "post-television" (Leverette and Ott 2008) or "television after TV" (Spigel 2004), to mark the persistence of the medium while acknowledging the end of at least *some* part of what used to be considered as (linear, broadcast) television. The increasing convergence between the two forms, revealed by a study of audiovisual seriality, shows that "cinema" and "television" must be apprehended as evolving, fluid entities, in need of ever-renewed definitions based on critical observation and reflection.

Beyond issues of terminology, what this debate illustrates is an epistemological choice between convergence and divergence, between intermediality and medium specificity as the most fruitful criteria to approach the serial art form. Should we call for more focus on the audiovisual, aesthetic qualities of the form of TV series (Jacobs and Peacock 2013; Wade and Seitz 2015)? Or should we consider TV series as fundamentally different from movies, not to be judged primarily on aesthetics because such an approach would implicitly disparage the emotional, narrative impact that less visually sophisticated shows may have? (Nussbaum 2014).

By displaying the elasticity of the terms rather than simply picking one side over the other, the authors of this volume investigate the complex aesthetic, cultural, industrial, and economic implications of film and television series. Our 12 chapters analyze the mechanisms, contexts, and consequences of seriality on screen, distinguishing specific features, pointing out historical landmarks and specific narrative strategies, showing how seriality offers a fruitful angle to tackle the common and diverging points between cinema and television, the interplay between narrative invention and marketing strategies, and the increasingly complex processes of remaking, recycling, and rebooting that pervade popular culture. Although the chapters illustrate the great variety of methodologies that can be adopted with regard to seriality, they are connected by recurring themes such as authorship, audience engagement, and media convergence. The link between seriality and the audiovisual form (if we decide to use this generic adjective to gather network and cable television, VOD platforms, and cinema together) logically leads us to consider how this form "overflows" the limitations of both what is traditionally considered cinema and what is traditionally considered television. With increasingly similar modes of production and reception, with actors, directors, and technicians shifting back and forth between cinema and television, and cultural hierarchies fading or shifting along different paradigms, the separation of the two media seems moot. With the role of fan communities increasing, stories get told along myriads of transmedia forms – film, series, video games, ARG – which makes the very notion of series more complex and polymorphous, and raises questions related to the unity or fragmentation of artistic and cultural works. Without pretending to establish any definitive typology of seriality, the four parts of this volume fall under narratological, aesthetic, political, and industrial lines.

Three chapters comprising the first part entitled "**Serial Specificities**" offer theoretical and historical reflections on the nature of seriality itself. They engage with major paradigms in seriality studies: audience participation, the relationship between seriality and affects, and media convergence. They focus on elements brought forward when attempting to delineate the specificity of seriality beyond essentialist conceptions of cinema or television.

Cinematic series are nothing new, as the diachronic, narratological study of **Ilka Brasch** and **Felix Brinker** reminds us. Their chapter contrasts some opening sequences of cinematic serial narratives from the 1930s to some of the 21st century, demonstrating the similar ways in which these openings encourage audience participation. Brasch and Brinker analyze the films' "politics of engagement" – that is, the ways these opening sequences articulate a film's preferred mode of reception. These liminary sequences establish the serial films they introduce both as parts of chronologically told serial narratives and as belonging to more widely sprawling, non-linear transmedial clusters – often referencing comics or other media and making use of their particular aesthetics to self-identify as fragments of a larger series.

The double inclusion of the episode within a particular series and within a larger body of work is also at the heart of **E. Deidre Pribram**'s chapter, which addresses the affinity between TV series and specific genres. To understand seriality in contemporary American television dramas, Pribram refers to two recent movements that are having considerable impact on both cultural theory and film/television studies: first, the "turn to affect" and how it neglects the productivity of emotionality; and second, the argument that contemporary television serials belong to melodrama as a larger narrative mode. She points out that many scholars, while acknowledging televisual seriality's origins in soap operas, pulps, and other "low" genres, rather tend to stress the structural, self-reflexive, and poetic qualities of "narrative complexity" and thus minimize contemporary seriality's links to the melodramatic narrative mode. On the contrary, Pribram argues that the specific traditions of melodrama and its apparent emotional "excesses" tend to connect characters and audience members as human subjects confronted to difficulties and dilemmas inscribed in specific sociocultural contexts. Her chapter shows how this link between seriality and melodrama contributes to the specific form of emotional engagement that characterizes the form.

While the first chapter deals with cinematic seriality and the second with televisual seriality, the third moment of this initial part conceptualizes the links between the two. With the popularization of television series of high production value (such as *Breaking Bad,* AMC 2008–2013, or *Game of Thrones,* HBO 2011–2019), **C.E. Harris** explores the notion of "cinematicity" so often connected with them by questioning the efficiency of the term, including when applied to cinema itself. Harris suggests, however, that the term may help tackle some form of medium specificity for TV series through the prism of what she calls "an aesthetics of time" – she argues that one of the primary criteria that situate certain television series within this category of "cinematic" programs has to do with their repertoire of devices aimed at aestheticizing time, in direct link to seriality and narrative structure, but also to formal devices such as the use of the long take, deliberate contemplative moments of plot lag, a dedication to the episodic and the quotidian within the narrative, or episodes that serve a purely aesthetic function instead of advancing the plot. She also points out how some TV series deliberately position themselves in a cinematic lineage by cultivating and advertising references to high-profile, prestigious cinematic works from Italian neorealism, "slow" cinema, or "New Hollywood."

As pointed out above, seriality picked up at the same time as the industrial revolution and major economic mutations that led to the advent of market economy – the principle of seriality itself guarantees financial returns and produces its own profitable system. The second part of this volume, **"Marketing Seriality,"** thus focuses more broadly on the essential link between seriality and capitalism, and on seriality as a marketing tool to be studied in terms of industrial decisions, transmedia strategies, and the star system.

First, **Paul Kerr's** historical approach reveals the projects and commercial choices of the Mirisch company – a rarely studied film studio active from 1957 to 1974 – and raises our awareness of the major role played by production in the programming of seriality. The Mirisch Company is, as Kerr explains, a "missing link" in Hollywood history. A decade before *Jaws, The Godfather,* and *Star Wars,* it helped re-invent cinematic sequels with *The Magnificent Seven, The Pink Panther,* and *In the Heat of the Night* film series, as means to a long tail strategy. In his minute survey of the landmark productions of this little-known production company, Kerr demonstrates how Mirisch had understood the series format's synergies between film and television long before the term "transmedia" was coined.

Chloé Monasterolo prolongs this focus on industrial strategy in her study of *The Hunger Games* franchise – a perfect example of transmedia marketing that encourages fan participation in the very construction of the storyworld. She uses recent theory on transmedia to sustain her interpretation of the franchise, and draws parallels between the storyworld and the trans-media marketing campaign that accompanied all stages of production. Her analysis of the *polysemy* of the term "diversion," which is central to the *Hunger Games* narrative and marketing strategy, shows how the franchise resorts to techniques – such as the manipulation of images – portrayed in the films as part of dictatorial propaganda. Her chapter analyses how the franchise's construction and exploitation of icons oppose the repetitiveness of seriality to its transforming nature, and how it uses the narrative's serial, fragmented form as a self-reflexive evaluation of contemporary media's involvement in society and cinema.

Finally, **Agnieszka Rasmus** explores another mode of seriality based not on narrative or theme, but on the spectators' engagement with an actor's persona. Her original concept of "seriality of actorship" here relies on the study of several remakes of films in which Michael Caine was the leading actor. His four major iconic roles – *Alfie* and *The Italian Job* in the 1960s, *Get Carter*, and *Sleuth* in the 1970s – were all remade within a short space of time from 1999 to 2007. For Rasmus, this proliferation of remakes of the actor's earlier works cannot be coincidental, especially since Michael Caine himself has embraced many of these remakes, extensively commented on them, and participated in two of them. Rasmus not only studies the adapting/updating/recycling of popular motifs and characters but also more broadly reflects on the "seriality of actorship" based on a repeated engagement with the works of a single star.

The third part is devoted to the ways in which seriality enhances media convergence between cinema and television. Opting for intermedial approaches free of cultural hierarchies, the three chapters focus on case studies, analyzing works that navigate the increasingly fluid frontier between cinema and television by offering televisual ramifications of fictions that started on the big screen (Tredy, Bataille), or vice versa (Hatchuel). All three chapters show how series manage to incorporate the ongoing cross-media dialogue in their very texture, defying issues of authenticity or precedence.

Dennis Tredy first explores the distinctions between a serial and a remake through a close narratological focus on the series *Bates Motel* and its connection with the cinematic series that started with Hitchcock's *Psycho* in 1960. For him, the issue of narrative time is crucial to understanding the specific kind of seriality at hand. Taking on the task of rebooting an entire franchise that was spurred by Hitchcock's seminal horror film *Psycho* (1960), the writers for *Bates Motel* (A&E, 2013–2017) had to find a way to deal with the vast legacy of novel and film sequels, remakes, and lookalikes, a well-established and well-known continuity and mythology, and images from the original film firmly engrained in our collective consciousness. Tredy takes a close look at the methods used by the series' showrunners to embrace the film's seriality while at the same time rerouting it to eventually turn it upon itself. This process involves a highly coordinated reworking of character development and story arcs, creating a complex dialectic of past and present through aesthetics and referentiality, setting up clever games of anticipation, repetition, and deviant replay.

Sylvaine Bataille is concerned with televisual/cinematic intertextuality in Noah Hawley's *Fargo* and its interaction with both actual and fictional cinematic intertexts. Studies of *Fargo* (FX, 2014–) in relation to the Coen brothers' film (1996) and their filmography in general have already been made, but beyond the anecdotal and reverential, Bataille focuses on meaningful instances of reflexivity in the second season, whereby the show comments on its own cinematographic, narrative, and transfictional aspirations. Her chapter takes a close look at episode openings and the inclusion of fake film clips to reconfigure and experiment with its relation with the film *Fargo*, the Coens's filmography, and cinema itself.

Finally, **Sarah Hatchuel** applies a *politique des auteurs* lens on David Lynch's *Twin Peaks* film (*Fire Walk with Me,* 1992) and TV series (ABC, 1990–1991; Showtime, 2017) with an approach that combines narratology, intertextuality, and gender studies, to focus on the myth of the sacrificed movie star and reveal how the series ideologically and narratively interacts with the prequel film. While the *Twin Peaks* series broke with traditional television codes on aesthetic and narrative levels, Lynch's prequel film, *Twin Peaks: Fire Walk with Me* (1992), which dramatizes Laura Palmer's very last days, was innovative in terms of gender representation, as it denounced the mystifying screens created by the original series and its patriarchal ideology. Many series influenced by the seminal show, such as *LOST* (ABC, 2004–2010) or *Carnivàle* (HBO, 2003–2005), have further unfolded Lynch's artistic project by developing, explicating, or diffracting it. Taking these shows into account helps Hatchuel build a unified theory on the *Twin Peaks* matrix (the series and the film), in which the cinematic theme of the sacrificed young female star meets a narrative of dreamlike, parallel worlds, which in the end interrogates the very fabric of fiction.

The last part of this volume, **"Meta-Serialities,"** is devoted to the ways in which seriality manages to produce its own analytical tools in terms of aesthetics, narratology, and politics. These three final chapters demonstrate how, thanks to the gaps opened up by interruptions within the narrative and long duration, serial works produce their own meta-critical discourse that audiences and critics alike can then use to build an interpretative system.

Nicole Cloarec focuses on *Shooting the Past* (BBC2, 1999) the first TV series created by Stephen Poliakoff, a British author of cinema, television, and the theater. *Shooting the Past*, now considered a major breakthrough in his career as one of British television's most acclaimed writers and directors, interrogates seriality on two major levels. First, by questioning the place of authorship with regard to TV series, Cloarec contends that *Shooting the Past* may indeed be construed as a manifesto propounding how serial forms can induce an alternative model of "authored drama" production on television. Second, by exploring how the seriality of still images is inherent to the filmic form, since the system it relies on brings out the still images that lie behind the apparent movement of the moving picture. It is also a significant example of how "high end" television drama has been extending the series-serial narrative. The whole drama is indeed conceived as variations on the notion of series and seriality, playing on episodic and serial effects. It ultimately offers self-reflexive comments on the serial essence of the filmic image itself and on its power to build up a narrative when set in montage.

Christophe Gelly also aims his magnifying glass at a British series to show how Moffat and Gatiss's 21st-century transposition of Doyle, *Sherlock* (BBC1 2010–2017), chooses to break with the principle of modernization, specifically in the episode entitled "The Abominable Bride" (01.01.2016). Gelly argues that, by suddenly shifting the characters and story back to the 19th century – a choice that was strongly criticized by many – the series stereoscopically accentuates its interpretative choices and develops a metanarrative discourse. The confrontation of the two eras and the temporal passages from one to the other shed additional light on the metatextual discourse that had been developed from the start, for instance, about the evolution of gender norms. By deliberately destabilizing diegetic features that distinguish one time frame from the other, the episode also manages to enhance the interpretative uncertainties that connect the different installments of what can be seen as an all-inclusive canon, encompassing Doyle's texts as well as the previous episodes of the show. It also marks a new step towards intimacy and complicity with the fans, notably because the episode insists on narrative interruptions and includes self-referential allusions to the fictionality of the plot. This particular episode allows Gelly to develop the concept of seriality as "assumed discontinuity," emphasizing the relevance of each new reading.

In the volume's concluding chapter, **Samuel Chambers** considers how the specific form of seriality found in network shows allows for a political questioning of norms, normativity, and transgression. Chambers analyzes the US show *The Good Wife* (NBC 2009–2016) through Michel Foucault's understanding of subject positions. The articulation of broad concepts of political theory and queer theory with close readings of specific scenes demonstrates that the evolution of the subject position of main character Alicia Florrick relies on the show's serial structure and form. Indeed, both the initial setup, and the subsequent development brought by the 156 episodes over seven years of broadcast, allow for a subtle exploration of norms, subjectivity, and agency, ultimately staging a powerful subversion of dominant norms of gender and sexuality only possible because of the length and serial structure of the show. Chambers confirms Judith Butler's claims about the political potential of seriality whereby repetition with a difference can produce a challenge to, or subversion of, norms otherwise sustained through repetition. While Chambers makes an argument about *The Good Wife*'s feminist and queer politics, his chapter also stresses the crucial importance of seriality itself to achieve the cultural political work of staging and critiquing normative forces.

Thus, the four parts of this volume prolong ongoing reflections on the nature and modalities of seriality on big and small screens, and suggest paradigms and methods that will continue to grow and change as the serial phenomenon pursues its expansion within and across increasingly interconnected media.

Notes

1 The chapters of this book originate in the 22nd SERCIA conference (Société d'Etudes et de Recherche sur le Cinéma Anglophone) that took place in Paris in September 2016 at Universite de Paris (LARCA and CERILAC research groups), with the collaboration of Paris-Ouest Nanterre University (CREA research group), the Fondation des Etats-Unis (Cité Internationale Universitaire de Paris), and the GUEST consortium. A direct consequence of this is that our authors exclusively focus on American and British series because this conference gathered specialists of cinema, television and media in the English-speaking world.
2 Many of these terms have been subject to criticism for the new cultural hierarchies they establish (see Levine and Newman 2011).
3 The expression "Peak TV" was coined by FX CEO John Landgraf. See Cynthia Littleton, "FX Network's Chief John Landgraf: 'There is Simply Too Much Television'", *Vanity Fair*, 08.07.2015. https://variety.com/2015/tv/news/tca-fx-networks-john-landgraf-wall-street-1201559191/ (accessed 11.27.2018). Since then, Landgraf has expressed his preference for the expression "*gilded age of television*", referring to the deceitfully prosperous and highly inegalitarian period of the late 19th century in the United States. See Adalian, "Forget Peak-TV: FX Boss John Landgraf Says We're Now in the 'Gilded Age' of Television", *Vulture* 08.02.2018. https://www.vulture.com/2018/08/fx-john-landgraf-tca-peak-tv-gilded-age.html (accessed 11.27.2018).
4 The "fear of missing out" is hinted at, ironically, in some series such as *Master of None* (Netflix, 2016-). Binge watching is the watching of a great number of episodes in a row. "Speed-watching" consists in watching series or films on a slightly accelerated pace (20 to 50% faster than normal), which is made possible on YouTube, VLC or Netflix without losing the intelligibility of dialog (Bischoff 2019).
5 See for instance the special issue of *Screen* (57.2, 2016) on television studies, which attempts to map out the fluctuations of mediatic borders and the brings forth the need for theoretical adjustments. See also the special issue of *Art Press 2* on the aesthetics of TV series (Kihm et Zabunyan 2014), and the specialized, peer-reviewed journals *TV/Series* [http://journals.openedition.org/tvseries/] or *Series* [https://series.unibo.it/]. We also notice that ever-more numerous single-authored or edited books dedicated to individual shows are published on both sides of the Atlantic, at publishers such as I.B. Tauris, PUF, or Atlande for instance. A new collection entitled *Screen Serialities* has recently started (Edinburgh University Press) under the direction of Claire Perkins and Constantine Verevis.
6 See for instance Quentin Tarantino declaring the end of cinema at the 2014 Cannes Festival (Saul 2014).

Works Cited

Adorno, Theodor W., and Max Horkheimer. "The Culture Industry: Enlightenment as Mass Deception". 1944. In Max Horkheimer, Theodor W. Adorno, and Gunzelin Noeri (eds.), *Dialectic of Enlightenment*, Stanford, CA: Stanford University Press, 2002. 94–136.

Alberse, Anita. *Blockbusters: Hit-making, Risk-taking and the Big Business of Entertainment*. New York: Henry Holt & Co, 2015.

Allrath, Gaby, Marion Gymnich, and Carola Surkamp, eds. *Narrative Strategies in Television Series*. London: Palgrave Macmillan, 2005.

Aumont, Jacques. *L'Image*. Paris: Nathan, 1990.

Benjamin, Walter. "The Work of Art at the Age of Mechanical Reproduction". 1939. In Hannah Arendt (ed.), *Illuminations*, New York: Schocken Books, 1969. 217–51.

Bischoff, Samuel. "Le speed watching : analyse de la consommation à grande vitesse". *FMC Veille*, March 15, 2017. https://trends.cmf-fmc.ca/fr/le-speed-watching-analyse-de-la-consommation-a-grande-vitesse/ (accessed 06.20.2020).

Caldwell, John Thornton. *Televisuality, Style, Crisis and Authority in American Television*. New Brunswick, NJ: Rutgers, 1995.

Campany, David, ed. *The Cinematic*. London: Whitechapel, 2008.

Crary, Jonathan. *Techniques of the Observer*. Cambridge, MA: MIT Press, 1990.

Denson, Shane. "'To Be Continued…': Seriality and Serialization in Interdisciplinary Perspective". Conference Proceedings of: "What Happens Next: The Mechanics of Serialization. Graduate Conference at the University of Amsterdam, March 25–26, 2011". In *JLT* Online, 06.17.2011. http://www.jltonline.de/index.php/conferences/article/view/346/1004 (accessed 12.20.2018).

Denson, Shane, and Julie Leyda, eds. *Post-Television. Theorizing 21-st Century Film*. Falmer: Reframe Books, 2016. http://reframe.sussex.ac.uk/post-cinema/ (accessed 06.20.2018).

Dunleavy, Trisha. *Complex Serial Drama and Multiplatform Television*. New York: Routledge, 2017.

Dwyer, Tim. *Media Convergence*. New York: McGraw-Hill, 2010.

Eco, Umberto. "Innovation et répétition: entre esthétique moderne et postmoderne", *Réseaux* 68, 1994. 9–26.

Edgerton, Gary. *The Columbia History of American Television*. New York: Columbia University Press, 2007.

Esquenazi, Jean-Pierre. *Éléments pour l'analyse des séries*. Paris: L'Harmattan, 2017.

Gaudreault, André. *Cinéma et attraction : Pour une nouvelle histoire du cinématographe*. Paris: CNRS éditions, 2008.

Gitlin, Todd. *Inside Prime Time*. New York: Pantheon, 1983.

Glévarec, Hervé. *La Sériephilie. Sociologie d'un attachement culturel*. Paris: Ellipses, 2012.

Gray, Jonathan, and Amanda Lotz. *Television Studies*. Cambridge: Polity, 2012.

Guilbert, Georges-Claude, and Shannon Wells-Lassagne, eds. "Television Series and Narratology : New Avenues in Storytelling". *Graat Online* 04.15.2014. http://www.graat.fr/backissuetvnarratology.htm (accessed 01.24.2019).

Feuer, Jane, Paul Kerr, and Tise Vahimagi, eds. *MTM 'Quality Television'*. London: BFI, 1984.

Hagedorn, Roger. "Technology and Economic Exploitation: The Serial as a Form of Narrative Presentation". *Wide Angle* 10.4, 1988. 4–12.

Hayward, Jennifer. *Consuming Pleasures: Active Audiences and Serial Fictions from Dickens to Soap Opera*. Lexington: University Press of Kentucky, 1997.

Higgins, Scott. *Matinee Melodrama: Playing with Formula in the Sound Serial*. New York: Rutgers, 2016.

Jacobs, Jason and Steven Peacock, eds. *Television Aesthetics and Style.* New York: Bloomsbury, 2013.

Jancovich, Mark, and James Lyons, eds. *Quality Popular Television. Cult TV, the Industry and Fans.* London: BFI, 2003.

Jaramillo, Deborah. "Rescuing Television from 'the Cinematic': The Perils of Dismissing Television Style". In Jacobs Jason and Peacock Steven (eds.), *Television Aesthetics and Style,* New York: Bloomsbury, 2013. 67–77.

Jenkins, Henry. *Convergence Culture: Where Old and New Media Collide.* New York: NYU Press, 2006.

Johnson, Derek. *From Networks to Netflix.* New York: Routledge, 2018.

Jones, Stuart Blake, Richard H. Kallenberger, and George D. Cvjetnicanin. *Film into Video: A Guide to Merging the Technologies.* Woburn: Focal Press, 2000.

Kelleter, Frank, ed. *Media of Serial Narrative.* Columbus: Ohio State University Press, 2017.

Kihm, Christophe, and Dork Zabunyan, eds. "Séries télévisées. Formes, fabriques, critiques". *Art Press* 2.32, 2014.

Kipnis, Laura. "Film and Changing Technologies". In John Hill and Pamela Church Gibson (eds.), *The Oxford Guide to Film Studies,* Oxford: Oxford University Press, 1998. 595–611.

Letourneux, Matthieu. *Fictions à la chaîne : littératures sérielles et culture médiatique.* Paris: Seuil, 2017.

Leverette, Marc, Brian L. Ott, and Cara Louise Buckley, eds. *It's Not TV: Watching HBO in the Post-Television Era.* New York: Routledge, 2008.

Levine, Elana, and Michael Z. Newman, eds. *Legitimating Television: Media Convergence and Cultural Status.* New York: Routledge, 2011.

Lipovetsky, Gilles, and Jean Serroy. *L'Ecran Global, Culture-médias et cinéma à l'âge hypermoderne.* Paris: Seuil, 2007.

Logan, Elliot. "The Ending of Mad Men's Fifth Season: Cinema, Serial Television and Moments of Performance". *Critical Studies in Television* 9.3, Autumn 2014. 43–53.

Loock, Kathleen, ed. "Serial Narratives". *Literatur in Wissenschaft und Unterricht* XLVII 1/2, 2014.

Mannoni, Laurent. *Trois siècles de cinéma, de la lanterne magique au cinématographe.* Paris: Réunion des musées nationaux, 1995.

Mc Cabe, Janet, and Kim Akass, eds. *Quality TV: Contemporary American Television and Beyond.* London; New York: IB Tauris, 2007.

Mills, Brett. "What Does It Mean To Call Television Cinematic?". In Jacobs Jason and Peacock Steven (eds.), *Television Aesthetics and Style,* New York: Bloomsbury, 2013. 57–66.

Missika, Jean-Louis. *La Fin de la télévision.* Paris: Seuil, 2006.

Mittell, Jason. *Complex TV: the Poetics of Contemporary Television Storytelling.* New York: New York University Press, 2015.

Nelson, Robin. *State of Play Contemporary "High-End" TV Drama.* Manchester: Manchester University Press, 2007.

Nussbaum, Emily. "Cahiers du Buffy". *New Yorker* 03.28.2014. https://www.newyorker.com/culture/culture-desk/cahiers-du-buffy (accessed 06.20.2020).

Saul, Heather. "Cannes 2014: Quentin Tarantino Declares Cinema Is Dead". *The Independent,* 05.24.2014. http://www.independent.co.uk/arts-entertainment/films/cannes-2014-quentin-tarantino-declares-cinema-is-dead-ahead-of-pulp-fiction-screening-9430049.html (accessed 06.20.2020).

Thompson, Kirstin. *Storytelling in Film and Television*. Cambridge, MA/London: Harvard University Press, 2003.

Screen 57.2, "Situating Television Studies", summer 2016.

SERIES, https://series.unibo.it/

Soulez, Guillaume. *Quand le film nous parle. Rhétorique, cinéma, télévision*. Paris: PUF, 2011.

Spigel, Lynn, and Jan Ollson. *Television after TV: Essays on a Medium in Transition (Console-ing Passions)*. Durham, NC: Duke University Press, 2004.

TV/Series. http://journals.openedition.org/tvseries/.

The Velvet LightTrap #79. "Serials, Seriality, and Serialization". Spring 2017.

Wade, Chris, and Matt Zoller Seitz. "What Does 'Cinematic TV' Really Mean?". Video essay. *Vulture*, 10.21.2015. http://www.vulture.com/2015/10/cinematic-tv-what-does-it-really mean.html (accessed 09.17.2017).

Films and Series Cited

Alfie. Lewis Gilbert, Paramount, 1966.

Arsène Lupin. Michel Carré, 1910–1911; Viggo Larsen, 1910.

Bates Motel. A&E, 2013–2017.

Breaking Bad. AMC, 2008–2013.

Carnivàle. HBO, 2003–2005.

Fantomas. Pierre Souvestre et Marcel Allain, 1913–1914.

Fargo. Joel and Ethan Coen, Polygram, 1996.

Fargo. FX, 2014–.

Game of Thrones. HBO, 2011–2019.

Get Carter. Mike Hodges, MGM, 1971.

Get Carter. Stephen Kay, Warner Bros, 2000.

The Good Wife. CBS, 2009–2016.

The Hobbit. Peter Jackson (1, 2 and 3). Warner Bros Pictures, 2011–2014.

The Hunger Games. Gary Ross (1), Francis Lawrence (2–4). Lionsgate, 2012–2015.

In the Heat of the Night. Norman Jewison. Mirisch, 1967.

The Italian Job. Peter Collinson, Paramount, 1969.

Jaws. Steven Spielberg, Mirisch, 1975

LOST. ABC, 2004–2010.

The Magnificent Seven. John Sturges, Mirisch, 1960.

The Perils of Pauline. Louis Gasnier and Donald Mackenzie, 1914.

The Pink Panther. Blake Edwards, Mirisch, 1963.

Psycho. Alfred Hitchcock, Paramount, 1960.

Sherlock. BBC1, 2010–2017.

Shooting the Past. BBC 2, 1999.

Sleuth. Joseph L. Mankiewicz, 20th Century Fox, 1972.

Twin Peaks. ABC, 1990–1991; Showtime, 2017.

Twin Peaks: Fire Walk with Me. David Lynch, New Line Cinema, 1992.

Part I
Serial specificities

1.1 Opening gambits

Cross-media self-reflexivity and audience engagement in serial cinema, 1936–2008[1]

Ilka Brasch and Felix Brinker

Understood as the practice of re-telling or continuing an already known story in a way that "achieves a dialectic between order and novelty, [...] between scheme and innovation" (Eco 2005, 200), narrative serialization has been at work in American film production at least since the days of early cinema and Edison's unauthorized remakes of Biograph pictures (Forrest and Koos 2002). However, while "cinema has repeated and replayed its own narratives and genres from its very beginnings," as Kathleen Loock and Constantine Verevis note, it was only during the last two decades that film scholars have begun to seriously consider serial phenomena (Loock and Verevis 2012, 2). This new interest informs a number of recent publications that engage with varying serialization practices in Hollywood cinema and beyond – including work on remaking, sequelization, and related phenomena like adaptation, franchising, and transmedia storytelling that can similarly be understood in terms of repetition and variation (Loock and Verevis 2012, 2–3; Kelleter and Loock 2017; Loock 2017).[2] The focus on mainstream contemporary and (post)classical Hollywood cinema has recently been broadened by studies of film serials (see, for example, Barefoot 2011; Higgins 2016; Brasch 2018), a form that has traditionally received less academic attention than other, more self-contained types of narrative film. The recent prominence of research on cinematic serialization furthermore coincides with an increased interest in the topic of popular seriality in general, which is evidenced in a number of studies and collections that examine serial storytelling across multiple media and historical periods (see, for example, Hayward 1997; Kelleter 2012b, 2017; Allen and van den Berg 2014; Mayer 2014; Kelleter and Loock 2017).

In the following, we combine a study of serialized feature films across the second half of the 20th century and into the 21st with a consideration of sound-era film serials to trace approaches to serial storytelling across different filmic forms and over several decades. To parse out continuities but also shifts in cinema's construction of serial narratives, we examine a number of examples from three decades across the 20th and 21st centuries – namely, the film serials *Ace Drummond* and *Radio Patrol* from the 1930s, the 1978 superhero blockbuster *Superman*, and a number of comic book movies from the first decade of the 21st century (including 2004's *Spider-Man 2* and 2008's *The Incredible Hulk*) – and consider how these productions signal their serial character. To do so, we follow David Bordwell's observation that "the viewer tends to base conclusions about the narrational norm upon the earliest portions of the syuzhet" (1985, 151), the story that unfolds. Hence, we turn to the opening sequences of these examples to examine how they propose a preferred mode of audience engagement. We therefore suggest that the very first moments of installments of our case studies all articulate how the respective examples of serial film want to be consumed. We furthermore argue that all of our examples exist at a nexus of two different but closely related types of narrative serialization and therefore delineate two distinct and separate trajectories for serial engagement.

Writing about early 21st-century television, Ivan Askwith uses the term "engagement" as a shorthand for a "range of possible investments (financial, emotional, psychological, social, intellectual) that a [...] [recipient] can make in a media object" (Askwith 2007, 49; Ziegenhagen 2009, 79). Askwith emphasizes that recent television series aim to encourage an active audience behavior beyond the regular viewing of new episodes. To survive and prosper within a competitive media environment, network television dramas like *LOST* (2004–2010) invite a range of activities that contribute to their commercial success, including conversations and discussions on social media, the consumption of tie-in products and spin-off narratives in other media, as well as the participation in fan culture (see 49–50). While Askwith's argument is specific to contemporary television, serial narratives of all media and periods have developed means and devices to ensure such an active and ongoing engagement – the most obvious being the cliffhanger ending, which is meant to ensure continued consumption across the "narrative break" that separates installments and invites the audience to speculate about events to come (Hagedorn 1988, 7; see also Lambert 2009). Through such similar devices, serial narratives practice a "politics of engagement," that is, a particular employment of the serial form (and of the medium in which it appears) that is geared toward pre-structuring and steering consumers' reception practices (cf. Brinker 2015, 305–308). Engagement in this sense is not a stable category, but one that, like serial forms more generally, is impacted by "varying media and medial formats [...]; by the technological, political, and cultural contours of [...] media environments, and by the complex and uneven interactions of authors, audiences, and larger institutional configurations," as Ruth Mayer notes about the principle of popular seriality in general (6). Accordingly, different types of serial cinema aim to solicit multiple forms of audience engagement, which differ considerably from the serial engagement demanded by the television series that Askwith discusses.

On the most basic level, studying engagement means asking for the concrete formal means and devices by which serial narratives alert their audiences to their ongoing nature, that is, to the ways in which these narratives attempt to direct the recipient's attention toward other parts of the narrative and related opportunities for media consumption. How, in other words, do examples of serial film establish a relationship to earlier iterations of the same story in other media? How do they signal that the film at hand is merely one installment in a larger body of related works? How do films communicate that they want to be watched as part of a series? Answering these questions requires us to go beyond the easy application of seemingly clear-cut labels, and to pay close attention to the formal operations of serial film, as well as to the historically specific media environments in which they operate.

Two types of serial narration

Radio Patrol, Ace Drummond, Superman, and the comic book movies discussed later on are all doubly serial. Firstly, they are themselves serial narratives that tell their stories through segmentation into short chapters (*Ace Drummond* and *Radio Patrol*) or as installments of longer film series (*Superman, Spider-Man 2, The Incredible Hulk*) that unfold a narrative continuity across several films. As such, these productions tell ongoing stories about a core cast of central recurring characters who live through a chain of varying adventures – of which each re-iterates a basic plot schema or conflict that is usually centered around the confrontation between heroes and villains.[3] This type of serialization proceeds linearly in so far as it entails the development of one continuous story within the formats of the film serial or the blockbuster series. Secondly, since all four titles adapt ongoing comic narratives to the big screen, they are themselves mere installments of larger, cross-media series that encompass a number of parallel and separate incarnations of the same intellectual properties, central figures, and basic narrative schemata in film, comics, and elsewhere.

Ace Drummond and Radio Patrol, for example, co-exist with ongoing, eponymous series of newspaper comic strips that tell similar detective stories but exist in separate narrative continuities. Similarly, the various cinematic incarnations of *Superman, Spider-Man*, and *The Incredible Hulk* co-exist with a plethora of alternate (and, at times, markedly different) versions of their protagonists in other media, including comics, animated television cartoon series, and digital games.[4] In this respect, our examples are also products of what Shane Denson discusses as a "non-linear [...] compounding or cumulative [...] seriality" that proceeds opportunistically across formats and platforms, and which results in the creation of various separate, alternate takes on the same characters and properties (Denson 2011, 532). This second, non-linear type of serialization entails the reiteration of known narrative formulae, popular characters, and successful properties in order to translate and export them into new markets and media.[5]

Whereas linear serialization seeks to engage audiences along a singular narrative trajectory, non-linear serialization spreads multiple alternative, "loosely connected" iterations of the same narrative, which relate to each other extra-diegetically rather than diegetically, through the recurrence of iconic features that are repeated and reconfigured for the new medial contexts into which they are translated (Mayer 2014, 9). In what follows, we will demonstrate that the opening sequences of *Ace Drummond*, *Radio Patrol*, *Superman*, and more recent examples of the comic book movie negotiate both types of serialization and make this doubly serial nature explicit. More precisely, we suggest that the very first scenes of our examples position these films in relation to both linear and non-linear serial trajectories and thereby alert viewers to their embeddedness in a larger network of related narratives and media. Significantly, all of our examples do so through representations of other media, most notably the medium of comics.[6]

Film serials

In 1936, at the outset of what is considered the "golden era" of sound serials that lasted until 1944 (Higgins 2016 8, 98), Universal released the aviation serial *Ace Drummond*. Its 13 two-reel chapters appeared weekly in rural and suburban cinemas across the United States, which usually featured them in Saturday matinees and before the Friday night features. At the time, serials were tailored to a child audience, but they usually also had an adult appeal (Barefoot 2011, 180–183). Golden-era serials particularly harvested the popular action and adventure comic strips that flourished in daily newspapers at the time. Accordingly, *Ace Drummond* borrows its protagonist hero from the eponymous comic strip, which appeared in the Sunday supplements of W. R. Hearst's King Features newspaper syndicate, and thereby participates in the growing trend of comics' adaptations. While it takes up characters from the comic and its aviation theme, the serial does not adapt plotlines from the comic strip.

The serial does, however, employ the aesthetics and narrative mode of comics to introduce viewers to the ongoing plot at the beginning of each installment. From its second chapter onward, the credits of each of *Ace Drummond*'s chapters are followed by a shot of the hands of an invisible reader opening the pages of a newspapers' comic supplement. The recognizable headline "Ace Drummond – by Capt. Eddie Rickenbacker" indicates that this is the real double page spread. The following shot then shows a close-up of an individual comics' panel, which is not from the actual newspaper but shows this week's chapter title instead. A series of pans to the right arrange a number of panels in succession, which outline in drawings and narrative boxes the ongoing plot, reminding loyal patrons where last week's cliffhanger left off and enabling new viewers to enjoy the following installment. By resorting to a comic strip aesthetic, the serial's plot recap establishes a connection to the narrative off-screen, that is, to a larger referential network connected to *Ace Drummond*. This opening sequence thus comprises the two serial structures within which the weekly chapter finds itself: it places *Ace Drummond* in relation to its newspaper source in terms of a non-linear seriality, and it explains the linear seriality of the consecutive chapters.

A similar re-familiarization with plot elements of previous installments occurs at the beginning of each week in *Radio Patrol* (Universal, 1937). Again from its second week onward, each of the serial's chapters features an early sequence that adapts narrative techniques used in comic strips to recapitulate relevant plot elements: the camera zooms in on a boy on a couch who is engrossed in a comic book titled *Radio Patrol*, which has photographs of the serials' protagonists on its cover. Afterward, a close-up of an individual panel indicates the week's chapter title. The boy then turns the page from one panel to the next, each of which uses a drawing and a narrative box to explain pivotal plot points of the preceding chapter and thereby establishes a narrative continuity between the serial's installments.

In comparison to the plot recaps of *Ace Drummond*, *Radio Patrol*'s evocation of its comic strip paratext appears markedly more stylized and artificial. In *Ace Drummond*, the camera shares the perspective of the reader of the comic strip, who opens the newspaper and reads the individual panels left to right. *Radio Patrol*, by contrast, introduces a diegetic child reader with a comic book that only features a single panel on each page – which may or may not have been a result of copyright discussions between the studio and the newspaper syndicate. The layout of *Radio Patrol*'s diegetic comic book in fact resembles a Big Little Book, that is, a series of children's books that were popular and cheaply available in the 1930s. Both *Ace Drummond* and *Radio Patrol* had their own Big Little Books, which reprinted a choice of panels from the comic strip alongside sentences that explained the narrative. Through its invocation of the Big Little Book and through the mise-en-scène of its chapter introductions, the serial self-stylizes as a product marketed for a child audience. At the same time, the lacking resemblance to the actual newspaper strip underlines the fact that the serial exists apart from the narrative told daily in the newspapers.

To shortly summarize, both serials pit the narrative possibilities and affordances of comics against their own mode of storytelling in recap sequences that combine reference to a character's appearance in the coexisting medium with a strategic continuation of the more linear seriality of the installments. By addressing their own seriality as well as their relationship to media other than film, *Ace Drummond* and *Radio Patrol* articulate suggestions of what one could call an ideal mode of reception; they express a politics of audience engagement that places the film serial at the nexus of the audience address of comics and film. On the one hand, the opening sequences highlight that the place of sound serials in cinema is similar to the place of the comic strip in newspapers – they appear in the less serious kid-section, providing regularly returning entertainment that strives to be neither art nor education. On the other hand, the intro sequences of *Radio Patrol* and *Ace Drummond* point to the narrative, stylistic, or even cinematographic similarities between comics and film serials, that is, the features that distinguish the serials from contemporaneous, more prestigious films.

Film serials exist both institutionally and stylistically outside the scopes of classical Hollywood. Most sound-era serials were produced by Columbia, Republic, and Universal, and Hollywood's major studios generally avoided producing them. Serials were thus produced and released outside of the studio-era monopoly system, with its vertically integrated studios and affiliated cinema chains. However, they flourished on the independent market that provided entertainment for suburban and rural theaters throughout the country (Brasch 2018, 74–80). When Jared Gardner describes the similar modes of storytelling and cross-media relations of comics and film before American film's transition to the classical paradigms in the 1910s, he mentions the film serial as an exemption – as a form that refused to participate in Hollywood's increasing negation of modernist fragmentation and narrative gaps in favor of classical continuity (2012, 22). Indeed, film-serial narratives foreground ruptures, breaks, and fragmentation in both the silent and the sound eras, especially in their assembly of repetitions, stock characters, and plotlines but also in their mix of genre iconography and their use of recycled footage. In fact, the serials' nods toward the comics' medium transform the otherwise common editing technique of the optical wipe into a reminder of the serials' fragmentary nature.

Stylistically, the serials' main point of differentiation from Hollywood's predominant group style lies in the cliffhanger, which emerged in the 1920s.[7] Repeatedly, serials suggest the inevitable death of the protagonist in what Higgins calls "hidden ellipses"; that is, the following chapter repeats the cliffhanger scene but inserts new footage that details the hero's escape or rescue in the nick of time (Higgins 2007, 100; Brasch 2018, 102). In these instances, serials highlight what in comics' studies has been theorized as the "gutter": the space between panels that can be opened up and expanded, and that needs to be filled by the readers' imaginations (McCloud 1994, 66–67; Gardner 2012). In his introduction to comics' analysis, Scott McCloud juxtaposes the acts of closure performed by film viewers, who connect individual images involuntarily and at a rapid speed, and by readers of comics, who actively and consciously work to establish a connection between the panels (68). Film serials tell stories in between these two extremes, profiting from the closure of the moving-image medium but highlighting the interstices in their characteristic cliffhangers. Whereas recent studies criticize the equation of the visual space between comics' panels with the narrative gap of reader-response theory (Round 2014, 100),[8] the cliffhanger sequences of film serials in fact themselves perform such an equation – they literally open the gap between the film's frames, arresting the flow of images and expanding time, filling the gutter with new images and narrative information that creates a new sense of closure radically different from the previous week.

The plot recaps at the beginning of *Ace Drummond* and *Radio Patrol* each foreground the gutter – either by slowly panning over it or in the comparatively long time it takes *Radio Patrol*'s diegetic kid reader to flip a page – paradoxically in ways that remove the actual cut. These recaps thus stress the narrative particularities of comics and ask the viewers to approach the upcoming film in a similar manner – as a string of scenes that are often discontinuous, that can be opened up and expanded, and that require the participation and at times the creativity of the viewer in order to make sense.

Interlude: *Superman* (1978)

Four decades later, the opening moments of Richard Donner's 1978 *Superman* offer an engagement with the comics' medium that is strikingly similar to the ones offered by *Ace Drummond* and *Radio Patrol*. Donner's film begins with the black-and-white image of a lavish curtain that opens to reveal a darkened movie screen. Following a few quiet notes of John Williams's orchestral score, we hear the sound of a film projector starting as the screen is illuminated by an inter-title reading "June 1938," framed in a 1.37:1 aspect ratio, the old Hollywood standard. Fading to black, the letters give way to the image of an oversized comic book lying on top of an old-fashioned tablecloth, centered in the middle of the diegetic frame. Under its title (*Action Comics*) and the listing of its price (10 ¢), the comic is emblazoned with the hand-drawn depiction of two vaguely tubular starships speeding away from an outer-space explosion, but just as we are close enough to discern more detail, the book is opened by the hand of a child who flips over to the first page. With the image in the frame slowly moving in on the panels of the comic book, the child starts speaking about the "great city of Metropolis" in the "ravages of world-wide depression." Turning the page to reveal additional panels with street scenes, the child narrator tells us about the work of the journalists at the Daily Planet and their job of "informing the public," as the last panel on the lower right corner of the book's third page, which depicts the rooftop of the newspaper building, grows bigger. Moving in on the panel, the frame on the screen within our screen dissolves into an actual shot of the Daily Planet building and the sculpture of a spinning globe on its roof, with the camera panning upward into the night sky to capture nothing but black again. At this point, the film's opening titles appear in full color in the center of the image, blue-on-black in front of a field of stars moving toward the spectator and dissolving the boundaries of the screen-within-the-screen (along with its curtains) to claim the full 2.35:1 aspect ratio as the opening theme breaks into fanfare.

This opening does very little to introduce the film that follows, as it features neither Superman nor any other of the film's characters; it also does not foreshadow any of the film's central themes. The sequence does, however, draw attention to Superman's long history in comics and film – and, as Matt Yockey suggests in his reading of the scene, it uses the device of the embodied voice-over and the reference to old-fashioned comic books to evoke a sense of childlike wonder and nostalgia for bygone times (Yockey 2008, 30, see also 32–33). Upon closer inspection, the film here references two classic incarnations of the Superman figure simultaneously: the first appearance of the figure in the first issue of *Action Comics* in June 1938 and the 1948 Columbia *Superman* serial with its similar title sequence featuring black-and-white footage and a comic book.[9] Before beginning to tell its own story, Donner's film thus reminds its viewers of the long history of the protagonist in various media – and immediately afterward foregrounds its status as the latest, technologically most up-to-date version of the Superman property by having the full-color opening credits replace the old-fashioned movie screen.

In this respect, the sequence can be understood as a response to a key challenge faced by serial narratives of all types, periods, and media – the need to, as Frank Kelleter puts it, "tell the same story again, but in a new way" (2012, 27). Donner's film does so in a situation in which Superman is already firmly established within American popular culture, and at a point in time at which most Americans would have been familiar with the figure from his appearances in the comics, animated TV shows, or reruns of the 1950s *Adventures of Superman* television series.[10] Simultaneously, Donner's *Superman* also has to perform the beginning of a new series of blockbuster films and, therefore, emphasize its own innovative character – which is why it contrasts old media with the spectacle of 1970s blockbuster cinema. Like the opening moments of the serials discussed above, *Superman*'s pre-title sequence is a moment of confluence between linear and non-linear modes of serialization, in which the film tries to channel the audience's pre-existing familiarity with other incarnations of the Superman figure into an ongoing engagement with itself and its future sequels.

Since the production of *Superman II* (dir. Richard Donner/Richard Lester, 1980) was already well underway by the time Donner's film premiered in American theaters – both films were shot back-to-back to reduce production costs (see Meier 2015, 116) – *Superman* was faced with a particularly pressing need to prepare its viewers for the coming of additional installments. As a result, the scenes that follow the title sequence already lay the groundwork for events that would only play out in the sequel. After the titles, the film takes us to Superman's home world Krypton, where his father Jor-El (Marlon Brando) acts as prosecutor in a trial against fellow Kryptonians Zod, Non, and Ursa, who are eventually punished for crimes against their society and banished into the "Phantom Zone," an interdimensional prison. At this point, the three villains exit the film and are not seen again until the sequel. Although set up for future plot developments and to secure the audience's anticipation of the next installment, these early Krypton scenes create a dramaturgic problem for the film as a whole, since they set up plotlines that are left open and reprised only years later.[11]

The rest of the film's first hour features a string of episodic segments that retell Superman's origin story from his crash on planet Earth as a young child and his upbringing in Smallville, Kansas, to his hidden superhero identity in the city of Metropolis. Like the pre-credit sequence discussed above, these segments arguably do little for the narrative that follows and are hardly referenced in the second half of the film. It is only around the 54-minute mark that the film's main plot begins – namely, the hero's attempt to stop villain Lex Luthor from sinking California into the Pacific. Judged by the standards of non-serialized Hollywood cinema, Donner's *Superman* possesses a peculiarly bloated narrative structure with an overlong first act whose scenes do not advance the plot in a narratively efficient manner. Arguably, however, the film's first hour does become productive for the attempt to restart the Superman mythos from a new (yet already known) point of departure. Aside from retelling the origin story of the protagonist, the scenes featuring the young Superman provide a chance to stage his powers in a spectacular fashion and with state-of-the-art special effects. In doing so, the hero's origin story becomes worth watching, including for those already familiar with the figure. *Superman*'s unusual narrative structure can therefore be understood as a direct result of the film's serial character. Put differently, the film's narrative digressions are typical for serial narratives, which, as Kelleter notes, generally tend to forgo an adherence to classical norms of narrative closure and coherence in order to produce possibilities for further narration ("Einleitung" 25–27).

Accordingly, *Superman*'s opening sequence can be understood as a primer for the serial character of the film that follows. In this respect, the reference to comics and the evocation of the protagonist's long transmedial career remind us that the film's plot, just like the serials discussed above, might require some cognitive work and goodwill on the part of the viewer in order to make sense. The opening thus invites us to approach the film as one would a comic book or an episode of a television serial – as merely one installment in a larger body of stories about the Man of Steel that make only limited sense if consumed in total isolation from each other.

Whether viewers puzzled over the significance of the film's opening moments clearly did not detract from its box office success, which ensured the production of three sequels and laid the foundation for a first cycle of commercially successful superhero blockbuster films that lasted until the late 1990s. In the next century, the superhero blockbuster genre would rise to new heights and churn out an unprecedented number of films based on various superhero figures –of which many included similarly self-reflexive opening moments.

Convergence-era seriality: opening the 21st-century comic book movie

A quarter century after the premiere of *Superman*, allusions to the comics' medium have become a recurring motif in Hollywood blockbuster cinema. Centrally, this is due to the fact that high-profile blockbuster films based on popular graphic novels or comic book characters now constitute a major

Hollywood production trend. The subgenre of superhero blockbuster cinema alone saw a remarkable rise in the number of releases over the 1998–2008 decade, when the big Hollywood studios produced 25 big-budget films based on DC or Marvel Comics superhero titles, as well as numerous additional productions based on other comic book properties – a trend that has only intensified in the years since.[12]

Almost all recent films based on Marvel Comics properties feature an explicit reference to the medium of comics in the logo sequence that appears before any kind of opening credits have flickered across the screen. Typically accompanied by the film's soundtrack, the Marvel logo traditionally appears at the end of a quick succession of colorful comics imagery featuring the company's iconic characters as if someone was flicking through the pages of an oversized comic book.[13] Thanks to the widespread popularity and commercial success of superhero movies based on Marvel comics titles, the company's logo has become an iconic branding symbol. Whether audiences acknowledge it or not, it performs a basic gesture that echoes the operations of the opening sequences discussed above, as it references the source medium of the narrative that follows and thereby alerts us to the fact that we are watching not just any kind of film, but a comic book movie. Simultaneously, the animated Marvel logo establishes this connection in a much more abstract way than early comic book films, as it does not actually feature a visual representation of a comic book or the act of reading comics. While spectators might understand the sequence as an abstract representation of someone flipping through a comic book, no magazine page, no paper, no flipping, and no reader are actually on display. Instead we see a string of drawings in the style of classic Marvel comics flickering across the screen. The brief sequence, in other words, invokes comics as a type of visual art rather than as a narrative form bound to a specific paper-based medium.

The animated Marvel logo anticipates a more general tendency in the cinematic negotiation of comic book aesthetics that is also on display in a number of medially self-reflexive opening sequences of the period. The opening titles of Raimi's *Spider-Man 2* (2004), for example, similarly reference comics as an art form but eschew a depiction of comic books as a medium with a distinct materiality. Beginning right after the Columbia Pictures and Marvel Entertainment logos, the film's title sequence opens with a stylized, computer-rendered representation of a spider's web[14] that expands in front of a black-and-red background – an image that evokes the web motif of the *Spider-Man* title, the preceding film of the series. As the names of the film's principal players appear, the sequence combines the image of the expanding web with slow camera pans over water-color drawings depicting characters and key scenes from the first *Spider-Man*, including Peter Parker being bitten by a genetically modified spider, his beloved Mary Jane, his estranged best friend Harry, Peter's first outing as Spider-Man, and the unfortunate chain of events that lead to the death of his beloved uncle Ben. Narratively, these drawings serve to recapitulate the most important plot points of the preceding installment. Their inclusion in the title sequence thus performs a similar function as the opening sequences of *Ace Drummond* and *Radio Patrol*, which also serve to cue viewers back into the storyworld of the series.

Simultaneously, however, these reminders establish a relationship to the medium of comics, as they are painted in the recognizable style of Alex Ross, an influential comics artist with a pedigree of popular and award-winning cover artwork for both Marvel and DC Comics (see Mason 2004; "Alex Ross Bio"). However, this reference to comic books differs considerably from the scenes featured in *Ace Drummond*, *Radio Patrol*, or *Superman*. Where the earlier examples depict the practice of comics reading directly, *Spider-Man* 2 evokes superhero comics in a more abstract fashion and presents Ross's drawings floating freely against a black backdrop. In doing so, the film references comics as an aesthetic rather than as a medium – and the credits sequence as whole foregrounds a cinematic, rather than a cartoonish, quality.[15] Furthermore, the fact that part of the sequence's imagery has sprung from the hands of a well-known comics artist is hardly obvious to the average viewer. The film, in other words, here establishes a relationship to superhero comics that is legible only for spectators who possess more than a passing familiarity with superhero comics, and thus uses Ross' artwork as a form of cultural capital that legitimizes the film in the eyes of fans.

Aaron Taylor has discussed such a courting of fan audiences as a form of "cultic management," as the attempt to "acknowledge [...] and potentially colonize" fans' "influence within a more dispersed film-going community" (2014, 181). In this respect, *Spider-Man* 2's title sequence marks the film as a paradigmatic example of early 21st-century popular culture – that is, as a media object that is mass-addressed but nonetheless tailored to solicit the goodwill of particularly vocal and active niche audiences. In his *Convergence Culture*, Henry Jenkins similarly argues that the support of active, proselytizing viewers who act as "brand advocates" for their favorite media objects is increasingly central to ensure cultural visibility and commercial success within an increasingly crowded media environment (Jenkins 2006, 73; cf. 1–15, 68–74). Responding to this situation, *Spider-Man* 2 stands at the nexus of linear and non-linear types of seriality and positions itself as an object of fan(nish) appreciation. Accordingly, its evocation of the comics' medium is less literal as in our earlier examples and targeted at a particular sub-category of viewers rather than at the audience in general.

Raimi's film is not the only comic book movie from the first decade of the 21st century to appeal to the insider knowledge of dedicated fans. The first minutes of Louis Leterrier's *The Incredible Hulk* (2008), for example, re-stage the opening titles of the 1978 television drama series of the same name by recreating of some of its most iconic imagery in great detail. The credit sequence thereby references a popular earlier incarnation of the film's protagonist in a way that is legible only for spectators who are already familiar with the history of the figure.[16] Like *Spider-Man 2*'s titles, *The Incredible Hulk*'s opening also serves a constructive narrative purpose. Like in the TV show, it retells the protagonist's tragic origin story and introduces the film's central characters. At least as important, however, is the fact that the film uses a reference to a "classic" incarnation of the Hulk figure to signal its adherence to the spirit of the source material(s).

A similar double strategy is used at the beginning of Robert Rodriguez' *Sin City* (2005), which adapts stories from Frank Miller's eponymous comic series for the big screen. After the studio credits, but before the opening titles, Rodriguez's film begins with a three-minute-long episodic prologue that narrates the story of a contract killer taking out his target on a penthouse balcony overlooking the skyline of *Sin City*'s titular locale. More important than its narrative content, however, is the fact that the prologue introduces the film's trademark visual style. Like the rest of the film, the scene is presented in stark black and white with only occasional blotches of color. Framing its characters against backgrounds that are almost entirely computer-generated, the prologue sequence approximates the artwork featured in Frank Miller's *Sin City* comics – in fact, both the visual style and narrative content of the scene are patterned closely after the one-shot "The Customer Is Always Right," which is included in Miller's 1998 collection *Booze, Broads, Bullets: Eleven Sin City Yarns*. Like *Spider-Man 2*'s inclusion of Alex Ross's art or *The Incredible Hulk*'s nod to the television series of the same name, this intertextual dimension is obvious only to viewers already invested in Miller's work and the comic book origins of Rodriguez' film. Although in a more oblique fashion than the other examples discussed in this article, *Sin City, The Incredible Hulk,* and *Spider-Man 2*'s opening moments all acknowledge their status as installments in larger non-linear serial sprawls and, by doing so, reward a fannish engagement with the film.

Conclusion

All of our examples of serial films use their opening sequences to emphasize their relationship to earlier or alternate versions of the same narrative in other media, and thereby call attention to their status as mere installments in larger, non-linear series. We can understand these moments as akin to opening statements in a court proceeding or the first moves of a game of chess – they frame the events that follow and attempt to set the terms for their own reception.

By calling attention to their position in a larger serial context, the first minutes of these films make uninitiated viewers aware of the fact that what they are about to see partially necessitates broader, transmedial background knowledge and that what follows has, in a sense, already begun. These medially and serially self-reflexive opening sequences are thus endowed with remarkable narrative efficiency that runs counter to norms of narrative closure and coherence commonly associated with Hollywood cinema. By thematizing their own seriality right from the start, these films can delegate the task of filling in the gaps within their fragmentary narratives to other texts, installments, and media – or to viewers attuned to these connections.

All the examples discussed here offer comparable negotiations of their relationship to earlier and/or alternate media incarnations of the same narrative. While serials such as *Ace Drummond* and *Radio Patrol* evoke the look and feel of eponymous comic strips that co-existed and unfolded in parallel with the serials themselves, *Superman* looks back on the decades-long transmedial career of its protagonist. More recent comic book movies reference their serial pre-history to encourage and reward the interpretive and comparative practices of fan communities. This points to a central difference: where *Ace Drummond* and *Radio Patrol* alert viewers to the synchronous unfolding of related serial narratives in other media, later openings attempt a connection to earlier incarnations.

In different ways, however, all of our examples illustrate that the basic principle of popular seriality – understood as the re-iteration of success formulae through the repetition and variation of their constituent elements – continues to inform the commercial production of popular narratives today just as it did in the middle decades of the 20th century. By putting their seriality on display, all of our examples encourage a mode of reception that is mindful of the different dimensions of serial cross-reference simultaneously at work within them. As we hope to have shown, this dimension of narrative seriality is best discussed from a perspective that takes questions of audience engagement – rather than just the relationship between texts, narratives, and installments – into account. Our examples also show that some of the phenomena that are, at times, discussed as hallmarks of a 21st-century media landscape – such as comic book adaptations, formal self-reflexivity, and transmediality – are rooted in much older mass medial practices.

Notes

1 This author draws strongly on our work in the context of the German Research Foundation's research unit "Popular Seriality – Aesthetics and Practice" (2010–2016) led by Frank Kelleter. We would like to thank research unit members Nathalie Knöhr, Britta Lesniak, Julia Leyda, Bettina Soller, and Maria Sulimma for providing useful feedback on an early version of the talk on which this chapter is based. We also would like to thank the participants of the 2016 SERCIA conference on "Cinema & Seriality" at Paris Diderot University for their helpful commentary on our work.

2 Loock and Verevis list, for instance, Horten and McDougal's *Play It Again Sam: Retakes on Remakes* (1998), Mazdon's *Encore Hollywood: Remaking French Cinema* (2000), Forrest and Koos' *Dead Ringers: The Remake in Theory and Practice* (2002), Verevis' own *Film Remakes* (2006), Jess-Cooke's *Film Sequels: Theory and Practice from Hollywood to Bollywood* (2009), and Forrest's *The Legend Returns and Dies Harder Another Day: Essays on Film*

Series (2008). For recent work on adaption and media franchising as a serial practice, see Johnson (2010, 2013), and for a collection on film cycles that addresses the question of seriality, see Klein and Palmer (2016). For transmedia storytelling, see Jenkins (2006), as well as 2009, which explicitly discusses transmedia storytelling as a serial phenomenon.

3 We here follow Frank Kelleter, who defines serial narratives as "mass-addressed continuing narratives with a constant set of characters, which are produced commercially in an economically efficient and standardized fashion – i.e. by industrial means, with a specialized division of labor, and a high degree of narrative schematization" ["Es geht um Fortsetzungsgeschichten mit Figuren-konstanz, die produktionsökonomisch standardisiert, d.h. in der Regel arbeit-steilig und mit industriellen Mitteln, sowie narrativ hochgradig schematisiert für ein Massenpublikum hergestellt werden."-translation ours] (Kelleter 2012, 18). Along similar lines, Jennifer Hayward defines "serial narrative" as "an ongoing narrative released in successive parts. ... [S]erial narratives ... include refusal of closure; intertwined subplots; large casts of characters [...]; interaction with current political, social, or cultural issues; dependence on profit; and acknowledgement of audience response" (Hayward 1997, 3). Serial narratives in this sense, as Kelleter (2012) points out, have occupied a prominent place within modern commercial popular culture at least since the first three decades of the 19th century; Hagedorn similarly suggests that serial narratives have been a "dominant mode of narrative presentation in Western culture" since the 19th century (1988, 5).

4 Freeman (2015) historicizes transmedia storytelling in the United States based on the example of Superman in the 1940s and 1950s.

5 For Denson and Ruth Mayer, non-linear serialization is most obviously on display in what they term "serial figures" – that is, in immediately recognizable "cultural icon[s]" like Frankenstein's Monster, Dracula, James Bond, or the Chinese supervillain Fu Manchu, all of which have "move[d] across media and medial forms" throughout their careers (Mayer 2014, 9; see also Denson 2011, 536–539; Denson and Mayer 2012, 185–194). Superman also belongs to this group of serial figures. While Denson and Mayer connect the concept to their discussion of serial figures, non-linear seriality is not necessarily restricted to the proliferation of iconic characters.

6 In what follows, our discussion of the opening sequences of our examples follows Denson's discussion of similarly medially self-reflexive moments in various iterations of Marvel comics' Frankenstein titles (which he also connects to the notion of non-linear seriality). Like Denson, we understand medial self-reflexivity as a gesture that "directs attention towards the processes of medial construction at the same time that it serves a constructive medial purpose" (Denson 2011, 547–548; see also Denson and Mayer 2012).

7 The "group style" of classical Hollywood was defined famously by Bordwell, Staiger, and Thompson (1985). For a discussion of the number of texts arguing for particular American film cultures to exist outside the scopes of classical Hollywood, see Jenkins's introduction to *What Made Pistachio Nuts* (1992).

8 Reader-response theory, as outlined by Wolfgang Iser (2000), suggests that reading any texts, in his case literature, entails processes of gap filling, which account for each reader's individual understanding of the text.

9 Notably, the comic book featured in the opening sequence is not the historical 1938 issue of *Action Comics* that included the first printed *Superman* story, but a mock-up (with a different cover image and content) created specifically for the film. The mock-up's title and date nonetheless reference the first mass-circulated incarnation of the Superman figure, whose 40th anniversary preceded the release of Donner's film by a few months. The dissolve that connects the last shot

of the comic panel that depicts the Daily Planet building with the brief shot of the building that follows could also be taken as a reference to similar establishing shots in the first season of *The Adventures of Superman*, the first TV series featuring the figure – if only obliquely so.

10 This impression also informs the public reception of the film. In a review published on the day of the film's premiere, Roger Ebert, for example, foregrounds "the tremendous advantage that almost everyone in the audience knows the Superman saga from youth" (Ebert 1978). Much of the film's appeal, Ebert suggests, would draw on the viewers' "common memory of hundreds of comic books and radio and TV shows."

11 Ian Gordon notes that the curious absence of the three Kryptonian villains from the rest of the film was the result of last minute-changes to the plot, whose final moments were originally intended to set up the release of "Zod, Ursa, and Non [...] from their imprisonment [which occurs] at the beginning of *Superman II*" (Gordon 2015, 12). Since the final act of *Superman*'s theatrical cut – which was produced under considerable pressure and rushed to theatres before the end of 1978 to capitalize on the 40th anniversary of the Superman figure – does not refer back to the film's opening moments, the theatrical cut of the 1980 sequel first repeats the scenes that chronicle the villains' banishment from Krypton and then sets up a new chain of events that lead to their arrival on Earth (cf. Gordon 2015, 12). The *Superman* example demonstrates how external pressures like deadlines impact on the production process and narrative form of serial narratives – which are frequently made according to carefully timed schedules, and therefore more prone to be impacted by unforeseen or contingent factors than self-contained and non-serialized narrative forms.

12 For a collection that engages with the trend of comic book adaptations, see Gordon, Jancovich, and McAllister (2007); on superhero movies, see Gilmore and Stork (2014); for a discussion of comic book movies in the context of recent trends toward film franchising, see Balio (2013). See also Brinker (2016).

13 Dick Tomasovic points out that subtle differences in the coloring of the sequence and the images included serve to differentiate Marvel films and series from one another – the logo is tinted "red in *Spider-Man*, green in *The Hulk* [...], [and] black in *The Punisher*," for example (2006, 313). In recent years, the animated logo has undergone several changes and increased differentiation pertaining to studios. As a result, Marvel superhero films produced by 20th Century Fox, for example, continue to feature logos that resemble the one discussed above, while the Disney-produced Marvel movies released after 2015 feature a new sequence that has replaced the abstract comics imagery with stylized depictions of heroes like Iron Man and Captain America. The changed Disney sequence reflects an economic shift in the corporate structure of Marvel Entertainment, which has been part of the Disney conglomerate since 2011 and has become more profitably engaged in filmmaking and licensing operations than in the publication of superhero comics (which now represent a small fraction of the company's business).

14 The web motif echoes the rectangular grids of Saul Bass' opening titles for Hitchcock's *North By Northwest*.

15 Arguably, *Spider-Man 2*'s evocation of comics aesthetics and simultaneous effacing of the comics medium is related to what Lev Manovich has described as digital cinema's "new kind of realism," that is, a filmmaking practice based in digital technologies that allows for a seamless blending of computer-generated and live-action footage (cf. Manovich 2016). Twenty-first-century superhero blockbusters rely heavily on digital animation and motion capture processes to render the superhuman feats and abilities of their central figures in a photographically realistic fashion, and generally employ these technologies to

approximate the aesthetics of superhero comic books. Since recent entries of the genre have thus overcome technological constraints that limited the filmic depiction of superheroic feats during preceding decades, the spectacular action presented by films of the genre can now compete with, and perhaps outperform, equivalent scenes in superhero comics. Accordingly, superhero comic books cease to be the yardstick for what superheroes can do.

16 For a more detailed discussion of *The Incredible Hulk*'s opening titles in relation to the preceding cinematic incarnations of the figure and the film's operation in the context of Disney's 'Marvel Cinematic Universe' franchise, see Brinker (2017, 221–222).

Works cited

Allen, Rob, and Thijs van den Berg. *Serialization in Popular Culture*. New York: Routledge, 2014.

Askwith, Ivan D. "Television 2.0: Reconceptualizing TV as an Engagement Medium". Thesis, MIT. *Comparative Media Studies Writing*. 08.10.2007. https://dspace.mit.edu/handle/1721.1/41243 (accessed 01.08.2019).

Balio, Tino. *Hollywood in the New Millennium*. London: BFI, 2013.

Barefoot, Guy. "Who Watched That Masked Man? Hollywood's Serial Audiences in the 1930s". *Historical Journal of Film, Radio and Television* 31.2, 2011. 167–190.

Bordwell, David. *Narration in the Fiction Film*. London: Methuen, 1985.

Bordwell, David, Janet Staiger, and Kristin Thompson. *The Classical Hollywood Cinema: Film Style and Mode of Production to 1960*. New York: Routledge, 1985.

Brasch, Ilka. *Operational Detection: Film Serials and the American Cinema, 1910–1940*. Amsterdam: Amsterdam University Press, 2018.

Brinker, Felix. "NBC's *Hannibal* and the Politics of Audience Engagement". In Birgit Däwes, Alexandra Ganser, and Nicole Poppenhagen (eds.), *Transgressive Television. Politics and Crime in 21st-Century American TV Series*, Heidelberg: Universitätsverlag, Winter 2015. 303-–328.

Brinker, Felix. "On the Political Economy of the Contemporary (Superhero) Blockbuster Series". In Shane Denson and Julia Leyda (eds.), *Post-cinema: Theorizing 21st-Century Film*, Falmer: Reframe Books, 2016.

Brinker, Felix. "Transmedia Storytelling in the 'Marvel Cinematic Universe' and the Logics of Convergence-Era Popular Seriality". In Matt Yockey (ed.), *Make Ours Marvel: Media Convergence and a Comics Universe,* Austin: UT Press, 2017. 207–233.

Denson, Shane. "Marvel Comics' *Frankenstein*: A Case Study in the Media of Serial Figures". *Amerikastudien – American Studies* 56.4, 2011. 531–553.

Denson, Shane, and Ruth Mayer. "Grenzgänger. Serielle Figuren im Medienwechsel". In Frank Kelleter (ed.), *Populäre Serialität: Narration, Evolution, Distinktion,* Bielefeld: Transcript, 2012. 185–203.

Ebert, Roger. "Superman Movie Review & Film Summary", 12.15.1978. https://www.rogerebert.com/reviews/superman (accessed 01.21.2019).

Eco, Umberto. "Innovation & Repetition. Between Modern & Postmodern Aesthetics". *Deadalus* 134.4, 2005. 191–207.

Forrest, Jennifer, and Leonard R. Koos, eds. *Dead Ringers: The Remake in Theory and Practice*. New York: SUNY Press, 2002.

Forrest, Jennifer. "The 'Personal Touch:' The Original, the Remake, and the Dupe in Early Cinema". In Jennifer Forrest and Leonard R. Koos (eds.), *Dead Ringers*, New York: SUNY Press, 2002. 89–126.

Freeman, Matthew. "Up, Up and Across: Superman, the Second World War and the Historical Development of Transmedia Storytelling". *Historical Journal of Film, Radio and Television* 35.2, 2015. 215–239.

Gardner, Jared. *Projections: Comics and the History of Twenty-First-Century Storytelling*. Stanford, CA: Stanford University Press, 2012.

Gilmore, James N., and Matthias Stork, eds. *Superhero Synergies: Comic Book Characters Go Digital*. Lanham, MD: Rowman & Littlefield, 2014.

Gordon, Ian, Mark Jancovich, and Matthew P. McAllister, eds. *Film and Comic Books*. Oxford: UP of Mississippi, 2007.

Gordon, Ian. "Superman and America". *9a Arte* 4.1, 2015. 6–15.

Hagedorn, Roger. "Technology and Economic Exploitation: The Serial as a Form of Narrative Presentation". *Wide Angle* 10.4, 1988. 4–12.

Hayward, Jennifer, *Consuming Pleasures: Active Audiences and Serial Fictions from Dickens to Soap Opera*. Lexington: University Press of Kentucky, 1997.

Higgins, Scott. *Matinee Melodrama: Play and the Art of Formula in the Sound Serial*. New York: Rutgers, 2016.

Iser, Wolfgang. "The Reading Process: A Phenomenological Approach." In David Lodge (ed.), *Modern Criticism and Theory: A Reader*, London: Longman, 2000. 188–205.

Jenkins, Henry. *Convergence Culture. Where Old and New Media Collide*. New York: NYU Press, 2006.

Jenkins, Henry. "Revenge of the Origami Unicorn: The Remaining Four Principles of Transmedia Storytelling". *Confessions of an AcaFan. The Official Weblog of Henry Jenkins*, 12.12.2009. http://henryjenkins.org/blog/2009/12/the_revenge_of_the_origami_uni.html (accessed 01.29.2019).

Jenkins, Henry. *What Made Pistachio Nuts: Early Sound Comedy and the Vaudeville Aesthetic*. New York: Columbia University Press, 1992.

Johnson, Derek. "Learning to Share: The Relational Logics of Media Franchising". *Futures of Entertainment Conference. MIT Convergence Culture Consortium*, 07.29.2010. http://www.convergenceculture.org/weblog/spreadable_media/ (accessed 01.07.2019).

Johnson, Derek. *Media Franchising. Creative License and Collaboration in the Culture Industries*. New York: NYU Press, 2013.

Kelleter, Frank, ed. *Media of Serial Narrative*. Columbus: The Ohio State University Press, 2017.

Kelleter, Frank. "Populäre Serialität. Eine Einführung". In Frank Kelleter (ed.), *Populäre Serialität. Narration, Evolution, Distinktion*, Bielefeld: Transcript, 2012a. 11–46.

Kelleter, Frank, ed. *Populäre Serialität: Narration, Evolution, Distinktion*. Bielefeld: Transcript, 2012b.

Kelleter, Frank, and Kathleen Loock. "Hollywood Remaking as Second-order Serialization". In Frank Kelleter (ed.), *Media of Serial Narrative*, Columbus: Ohio State University Press, 2017. 125–147.

Klein, Amanda Ann, and R. Barton Palmer. *Cycles, Sequels, Spin-offs, Remakes, and Reboots. Multiplicities in Film and Television*. Austin: University of Texas Press, 2016.

Lambert, Josh. "'Wait for the Next Pictures': Intertextuality and Cliffhanger Continuity in Early Cinema and Comic Strips". *Cinema Journal* 48.2, 2009. 3–25.

Loock, Kathleen. "The Sequel Paradox: Repetition, Innovation, and Hollywood's Hit Film Formula". *Film Studies*, 17.1, 2017. 92–110.

Loock, Kathleen, and Constantine Verevis. "Introduction: Remake | Remodel". In Kathleen Loock and Constantine Verevis (eds.), *Film Remakes, Adaptations, and Fan Productions: Remake | Remodel*, London: Palgrave Macmillan, 2012. 1–15.

Manovich, Lev. "What Is Digital Cinema?" In Shane Denson and Julia Leyda (eds.), *Post-cinema: Theorizing 21st-Century Film*, Falmer: Reframe, 2016.

Mason, Chris. "EXCLUSIVE – Alex Ross Spider-Man 2 Art." *SuperHeroHype*, 07.01.2004. www.superherohype.com (accessed 11.10.2018).

Mayer, Ruth. *Serial Fu Manchu. The Chinese Supervillain and the Spread of Yellow Peril Ideology*. Philadelphia, PA: Temple University Press, 2014.

McCloud, Scott. *Understanding Comics. The Invisible Art*. New York: Harper Perennial, 1994.

Meier, Stefan. *Superman Transmedial. Eine Pop-Ikone im Spannungsfeld von Medienwandel und Serialität*. Blielefeld: Transcript, 2015.

Miller, Frank. "The Customer Is Always Right". In *Booze, Broads, Bullets: Eleven Sin City Yarns,* Milwaukie: Dark Horse Comics, 1998. 29–33.

Ross, Alex. "Alex Ross Bio". *Alex Ross Official Online Store – Prints, Posters and Hard Covers For Sale,* n.d. www.alexrossart.com (accessed 01.10.2019).

Round, Julia. *Gothic in Comics and Graphic Novels: A Critical Approach*. Jefferson: McFarland, 2014.

Taylor, Aaron. "Avengers Dissemble! Transmedia Superhero Franchises and Cultic Management". *Journal of Adaptation in Film & Performance* 7.2, 2014. 181–194.

Tomasovic, Dick. "The Hollywood Cobweb: New Laws of Attraction". In Wanda Strauven (ed.), *The Cinema of Attractions Reloaded*, Amsterdam: Amsterdam University Press, 2006. 309–320.

Yockey, Matt. "Somewhere in Time: Utopia and the Return of Superman". *The Velvet Light Trap* 61.1, 2008. 26–37.

Ziegenhagen, Sandra. *Zuschauer-Engagement. Die neue Währung der Fernsehindustrie am Beispiel der Serie Lost*. Konstanz: UVK, 2009.

Films cited

Ace Drummond. Ford Beebe and Clifford Smith, Universal, 1936.

The Incredible Hulk. Louis Leterrier, Universal, Marvel Enterprises, 2008.

Radio Patrol. Ford Beebe and Clifford Smith, Universal, 1937.

Sin City. Robert Rodriguez, Dimension Films, 2005.

Spider-Man. Sam Raimi, Marvel Enterprises, 2002.

Spider-Man 2. Sam Raimi, Marvel Enterprises, 2004.

Superman. Richard Donner, Warner Bros., 1978.

1.2 Ensemble storytelling

Dramatic television seriality, the melodramatic mode, and emotions

E. Deidre Pribram

> There should be more than one word for love.
> I've seen love that kills and I've seen love that
> redeems. I've seen love that believes in the
> guilty, and love that saves the bereaved.

The above epigraph reflects the words of fictional Detective Inspector John River (Stellan Skarsgard), from Episode 1 of the 2015 BBC series *River*. DI River is struggling with the very recent murder of his female police partner, Detective Sergeant Jackie "Stevie" Stevenson (Nicola Walker). River explains his views on the term "love" to the police psychologist he has been assigned to see, following his partner's shooting.

River's declaration that the single word, love, stands as insufficient because it fails to capture the myriad of experiences we refer to, when we use the term, merits greater consideration. A single word is never adequate to account for any emotion. Further, compensating for the limitations of rational, linguistic explanation remains one of the reasons we occupy narrative worlds, with their emotionally resonant images, sounds, characters, and stories.

Narratives provide us with emotional pleasures, sometimes uplifting, for example, when we laugh or feel hope. At other times the emotions experienced are more somber, but pleasurable nonetheless, as in the case of police and detective series. In many ways, film and television studies are ideally suited for detailed analyses of emotions, and scholars are starting to turn their attention to the processes, meanings, and purposes of emotionality in mediated narrative forms. Yet emotionality has always been central to how popular culture "works," to the ways it creates its impact. Popular culture's complex, intricate narrative deployments rely on widespread emotional appeals and resonances. Mediated texts remain fertile sources for exploring the diverse, always changing, and contested meanings of emotions.

I pursue a cultural approach to the study of emotions in popular film and television. Cultural emotion studies consider emotions as socially shared and historically developed. However, this approach moves beyond social construction perspectives that assume the pre-existing, autonomous presence of emotions that are then shaped, adapted, and made to conform to social norms through mechanisms such as socioemotional scripts, rules, or roles. Rather, cultural emotion studies regards the circulation of emotionality as a primary means of bringing social relations into existence to begin with. It attempts to account for the ways certain emotional configurations become possible at various points in place and time, why they might take shape as they do, and what purposes and functions they serve (Pribram 2016).

A cultural approach works to understand how emotions are experienced – which is to say, felt, practiced, and expressed – in continually varying conditions and in complex, nuanced ways. From this perspective, emotions are never solely individual or "inner" phenomena but also, necessarily, some form of collective, communal event. To these ends, I borrow the delineation of emotionality used in recent affect theory, which regards emotions as acculturated affect (Massumi 2002; Gould 2010). In this perspective, emotions account for the quality or content of experiences, because they are caught up in processes of meaning making. Although intended as critique, affect theory's outline of emotionality proves productive because it circumvents radically biological, psychological, or individualistic accounts of emotions, precisely by locating the latter as thoroughly entangled with sociocultural existence.[1]

The boundless plurality and variability of emotions render a vast array of social relations and cultural meanings possible. They exist as unceasing continua of change, moving us, as their etymology suggests, from one encounter to the next. In narrative forms, emotions serve as a fundamental means by which we make sense of characters, stories, and other aesthetic elements. Certain characters, actors, and narratives take on emotional significance, shared by groups of people, which allow them to express aspects of what they feel and, therefore, who they are. Or conversely, narratives may be used to constrain or refuse various ways of feeling.

In media studies, melodrama exists as the most notable exception to scarce close analysis of narrative deployments of emotionality. However, too often the opposite has been the problem: emotionality has been closely associated with melodrama's operations, only to then be dismissed as exercises in "excess." Instead of regarding its use of emotions as excessive, I consider a number of ways emotionality endures as essential to melodrama's aesthetic structure and cultural value.

The melodramatic mode

Considerable attention is currently being devoted to melodrama as a narrative and aesthetic *mode*, most notably in film/television studies through the work of Christine Gledhill and Linda Williams (2018). Melodramatic modality refers to a trans-genre – and, indeed, a genre producing – storytelling system that pervaded 19th-century theatre and sentimental literature and, subsequently, has shaped large swathes of 20th- and 21st-century popular film and television.[2] And it is the aesthetic form that underlies and enables most contemporary Anglo-American television serials.

Prominent among melodrama's determining features stands the struggle for justice in a recurringly unjust world, a world in which we encounter "forbidden or deeply disturbing materials" (Thorburn 1976, 80). Importantly, characters usually incur the depicted injustices as a result of oppressive social, economic, political, or ideological forces that, for its victims, exist "beyond their control and understanding" (Gledhill 2002, 30). Melodrama's wronged parties confront "avoidable fates" that could be ameliorated if the modern world were a different, more caring and equitable place (Williams 2014, 89). The contestation for a sometimes won, but often lost, sense of justice provides melodrama with much of its emotional poignancy.

For the study of emotionality, melodrama offers two significant benefits. First, melodrama as mode has long and deeply been associated with emotions, in both critical and popular reception. Second, more scholarly work has taken place around the centrality of emotions to melodrama studies than for other cultural forms, although it seems evident that emotionality (or its absence) plays a pivotal role in other aesthetic modes, such as tragedy, comedy, or realism.

Dramatically, melodramatic justice occurs as moral legibility: a recognition that "ethical forces can be discovered and made legible" (Brooks 1995, 20). Melodramatic morality demands awareness of the flawed ways things stand in the contemporaneous world and works toward identification of how they might exist otherwise. As Gledhill and Williams note, moral legibility is made evident as a "felt sense of justice" (2018, 5), a *felt recognition* among audience members that, in part, accounts for the centrality of emotions to melodrama. Audiences are meant to feel the events portrayed through their immediate emotional engagement, instead of having "the moral of the story" relayed solely in cognitive or rational terms. That is, moral legibility is equally a matter of emotional legibility in melodrama. Indeed, Peter Brooks describes melodramatic morality and emotionality as so intimately linked that they are "indistinguishable," referring to their combined effect as "moral sentiments" (1995, 42). As a phrase, "moral sentiments" better elucidates the pivotal role emotions play in melodrama than Brooks' more frequently borrowed term, moral legibility.

Speaking of the daytime serial dramas known as soaps, Louise Spence points out that social and ideological issues may well be "experienced in emotional terms," in such a fashion that "emotional spectacle [...] makes the moment intelligible" (2005, 81, 93). Emotional spectacle emphasizes the meanings and impacts, the repercussions and costs, of social, economic, political, or ideological issues. Thus, melodrama functions on the basis of a dramatic emotionality lodged in sociocultural circumstances, in contrast to psychological realism that is more individualized and inward turning.[3]

Significantly, moments of emotional intelligibility require a tiered structure, involving at least two levels or aspects in order to arrive at felt recognition. Gledhill outlines melodrama's use of pathos as a complex emotional structuration in which audience members feel for a character's suffering and, simultaneously, are led to critique the causes of that suffering (Gledhill 1991, 226). She describes a double movement in the emotional positioning of audience members so that pity or empathy for the victim's tribulations might co-mingle with anger or sadness for the social or other factors causing the wronged person's pain.

Indeed, the enactment of moral sentiments or emotional spectacle may well concern a tripartite structure of felt recognition on the part of viewers. First, we are brought to recognize a character's feelings, for instance, terror, grief, or a deep sense of isolation as a result of the circumstances in which they find themselves. Second, we engage with a felt response to that character's emotions, such as pity or empathy, as noted above. Finally, in recognizing the unjust source of a character's suffering, other emotions, like anger or frustration, may be evoked.

Through moral sentiments, then, melodrama holds the capacity to put into play a myriad of emotions. In addition to empathy and anger, we may feel shame or guilt at the induced pain, or experience admiration and affection for those who survive, and occasionally thrive, in hapless social circumstances. Here, I've outlined a potential network of emotions aroused by a single character type, she or he who is made to suffer. Clearly other characters, such as villains or wrongdoers, have the ability to prompt quite different webs of felt recognition. For example, the process of creating wronged characters may well be dependent upon cruelty on the part of wrongdoers. Historically, melodrama's impulse for social justice has been played out through binary relations of good and evil, as embodied in the tripartite character formulation of heroes, villains, and victims. While still motivated by concerns for social justice, contemporary, revamped melodrama is more likely to blur clear distinctions between good and evil, making us question who or what exactly qualifies as heroic, villainous, or victimized (*The Wire, Breaking Bad*).

One of the strengths of melodrama's deployments of emotionality can be found in the mode's capacity, through moral sentiments, to tie individuals to larger institutional frameworks. Addressing the depiction of historical events in recent Chinese melodramas, Kenneth Chan argues the "personal is always political, just as the political ruptures, transforms, and sometimes disfigures the personal," in melodrama's use of emotionality (2014, 143). Melodrama's particular use of an aesthetics of emotions enables the placement of individual characters within social contexts, in order to trace how we might be disfigured or otherwise transformed through the life-worlds we occupy. In the next section, I consider three specific strategies taken up in melodrama's narrative engagement with emotionality, applied to *River* as a serial television drama.

Dramatic televisual seriality

As a connected web of genres, crime or detective dramas exist as generic variants of the melodramatic mode, for example, cohering around their role "in civic society as a fantasy of morality and justice" (Shepherd 1994, 25).[4] Williams traces the development of contemporary televisual serial melodramas "from 19th-century serial fiction, radio and television soap operas, family saga miniseries" (*Roots; Rich Man, Poor Man*) through prime-time serials like *Dallas* and *Dynasty* (2014, 47). Of course, specific genres also build upon other traditions. In the case of serial crime dramas, they emerge from a lineage linked to detective fiction, gangster, noir, and police films, as well as mystery and police procedural TV programs, all of which, as 19th-, 20th-, and 21st-century genres, are themselves influenced by melodrama.

In the generic network of crime dramas, the central injustice most often deals with the loss of human life through murder: death as avoidable fate. In the instance of DI River, the primary mystery concerns the unsolved shooting death of his partner and closest, perhaps only, friend, Stevie. Following the traditional generic pattern, the principal plot arc for the six-episode series turns upon the enigma of who has killed her and why. The accompanying main character arc, as a central and complexly delineated narrative enigma, revolves around how her death affects River, and why it so deeply debilitates him.

In what follows, I explore three specific strategies found in serial melodrama's engagement with emotionality. I invoke the particular example of *River* to elucidate how melodrama mobilizes emotionality toward its aesthetic goals. The first strategy considers emotions as a narrative structuring device. The second concerns melodramatic performative techniques as forms of emotional expressionism. And the third recognizes serial melodrama's capacity to put into play multiple meanings and practices attached to any seemingly singular emotion.

Emotion and narrative structure

The first strategy allied with melodrama is the activation of emotions as narrative structuring devices. An expanded form of storytelling is a signature feature of television serialization, in which plot developments are ongoing, concluding only when the program ends its run. This model is often differentiated from an episodic format that follows a more circular pattern in order to return to the position of balance, at the end of the episode, from which it began. In simplified terms, episodic television commences from an established equilibrium that weekly events throw out of kilter. Characters then work to restore stasis by episode's end, in preparation for the same circular movement in subsequent weeks. Serialization, in contrast, pushes ever ahead, over time and evolving circumstances. It cannot establish an equilibrium but must pursue constant change, preferably unanticipated in order to provide the audience with such pleasures as surprise and shock.

Speaking of early theatrical melodrama, Matthew Buckley describes its core aesthetic structure as based on movement from emotion to emotion, quite intentionally swinging among opposing or contrasting emotional effects. Through this process, we are engaged by conflicting "scenes of fracture and reconciliation, flight and refuge, horror and comedic relief, and exilic loss and restorative justice" (2009, 182). Critical work on daytime serials has described a similar pattern of continual emotional shifts. For example, Jennifer Hayward notes that soap operas offer:

> several ongoing storylines, carefully balanced to satisfy very different levels of interest – romance, humor, intrigue, suspense – and to unfold at different rates so that the crisis of one subplot is juxtaposed with the exposition or complication or another.
>
> (2009, 149)

Like Buckley, Hayward outlines swings among contrasting emotional effects, from romance or humor, to intrigue and suspense. Additionally, she points out that serials are structured so that the beats, or scene segments, for each subplot do not align emotionally with the other storylines in motion. That is, every subplot in an episode occurs at varying stages (crisis, exposition, complication) in its emotional progression so that, for instance, tension and suspense recur routinely in one of the subplots. Similarly, happiness or sorrow at the resolution of specific subplots remains an ongoing affair. Spence argues further that resolutions in daytime serials are purposefully structured in a temporary fashion, in which any resolution contains within it the kernels generating "the potential for new tensions and new suffering" (91). Resolutions are designed to be fleeting, serving as momentary answers that, in themselves, generate a renewed set of conflicts, problems, and dilemmas. Emotional structuration, therefore, may be present in manifold ways.

The character ensembles and multiplicity of plots pursued by recent television serialization prove conducive to such emotional fluctuations, so that we often career among a dizzying array of events and felt responses. The juggling of concurrent and sequential events that render the multiple parallel actions of a film like *Inception* intriguingly complex and difficult to follow has been taken up as the seemingly effortless, narrative norm in TV serials.

One way to think about serialized narrative structure, then, is by tracking its emotional trajectories, in particular pinpointing its nodes of emotional transition. Following Buckley's and others' arguments, the emotional trajectory of melodramatic serials ought to be constituted by abrupt shifts, composed through frequent, disruptive contrasts in tenor. Although Buckley speaks of conflicting scenes as the building blocks of emotional structuration, such tonal switches also occur as specific moments located *within* scenes. We can find such junctures that trigger movement in alternative emotional directions in the case of *River*. Established as a pattern early in the series, "feeling switches" embedded in the internal operations of scenes become a running motif, recurring throughout *River*'s narrative.

The series opens with River and his partner, Stevie, in the drive-through lane of a fast-food restaurant. As they wait in the car to get and then eat their food, the two hold a lively conversation, during which Stevie expresses her opinion that River needs to take a holiday. Established immediately as antisocial and curmudgeonly (he doesn't "get" fast food), River replies that he hates holidays. Undeterred, Stevie tells him that his holiday should include sun and karaoke. She then turns up the radio and sings along to Tina Charles' 1970s disco hit, "I Love to Love (But My Baby Loves to Dance)." River refuses to join in with her, but he smiles and laughs throughout their time together, establishing their relationship as one of fun, camaraderie, and deep connection.

Only later, when River and Stevie find themselves at a crime scene at which other police colleagues are present, do we see a shot of the back of her head hollowed out and surrounded by bloody, matted hair from the bullet that has killed her. It is fully nine and a half minutes into the 58-minute episode before the audience realizes Stevie is already dead. This is certainly a moment of shock, and a transition in narrative and emotional trajectory, positioning viewers to reevaluate everything that has come before and to journey through what follows in an entirely different manner. However, the signature emotional switch, serving as motif running throughout the series, comes immediately after we realize Stevie is a dead figment, rather than a "living" character. River and Stevie walk along the exterior corridor of the apartment complex that constitutes the crime scene, talking animatedly. The camera cuts to a wide shot of the same scenario, in which we see that Stevie is absent and River is talking to himself.

Cutting to the wide shot occurs as movement to an "objective" view, positioned from the perspective of his colleagues or the public, to indicate River's mental health troubles. It is utilized in a recurring manner, as brief punctuation at the end of sequences in which River has been interacting with Stevie or other dead characters. The single, wide shot clearly is intended as a reminder of what is physically or materially "real" in this narrative world, thereby fulfilling a plot function. But the wide shot also serves as a recurring emotional switch that throws the audience, in this instance, from the felt intimacy we have shared with River and Stevie to an objective, externalized reality in which River's behavior, due to the depth of his loss of his partner, is both poignant and troubling. The wide shot functions as a visual *and* emotional transition in which the audience is abruptly ejected from sharing whatever felt experience immediately precedes it for River, whether happiness as in the instance with Stevie, or sadness or anger in other scenes, to an external position from which we observe and are invited to judge.

Here, we have the multitiered movement Gledhill describes as central to melodramatic pathos. The audience joins in the energy and upbeat mood of the opening exchange between River and Stevie, only to be thrust from the intimacy of their interaction into recognition of something much more disturbing. The abrupt switch to an external position provides a *felt* recognition of River's twofold tribulation of mental illness and his partner's murder. Audience realization registers as shock, certainly, but also disturbs in the awareness that, akin to River, what we have previously witnessed is our misprision of the circumstances.

As narrative structure, we have been lulled into one emotional mood based on our perception of the camaraderie that underpins River and Stevie's relationship, only to be confronted with an emotional reversal, resulting in a startlingly different comprehension of the pair's connection. Thus, the series signals the multiple structuration of pathos quite literally, by means of the externalizing wide shot. The dual positioning of audience members is made apparent through camera framing, relocating us from sharing in their intimacy to occupying the diagnostic view of the lone, and lonely, River.

The emotional tone of camaraderie that precedes the audience's sudden removal to an objective reality is crucial to the narrative's workings. Although dead, Stevie remains a living, breathing, palpable presence for River. And through the upbeat, easy intimacy in which her relationship with River is presented, she remains narratively "alive" for the audience. We spend more time in the company of River and Stevie than with any other relationship depicted in the series. River genuinely smiles and laughs only when in her presence, seeming most himself when they are together. She exhibits a vitality and energy that draws us to her, that makes her feel like a more tangible force than other characters, particularly living ones. And River, in response, is never more "alive" than when he is with her.

At the end of the first episode, a dispirited, near-broken River goes to a karaoke club, following Stevie's suggestion from the beginning of the episode that this is what he needs. When he hands the cashier his ticket, she notes that it is a two-for-one voucher, although he is there alone. Once inside, when he turns on Stevie's song from the show's opening, "I Love to Love," we see that he is not alone after all. In a series of medium close and medium shots, Stevie urges River to sing, and joins in with him, both laughing and enjoying themselves as they let loose. Then, from a medium wide shot of River singing alone, the camera dollies back so that we are positioned on the exterior of the karaoke space. The wide shot punctuating this sequence, and making our observational distance clear, is captured through the porthole-like window of the door, secluding River in an isolated room as we watch him singing by himself, his visually and emotionally confirmed loneliness, painfully poignant.

As in the case of *River,* serial melodrama may well be constituted by abrupt swings in emotive tone, rather than following a linear, cause-and-effect emotional track. Additionally, a roiling, non-linear emotional path can be carved out even when situated within the bounds of causally determined plot trajectories. Considering emotionality as a structuring mechanism holds the possibility of productive, alternative ways to think about narrative configurations in television seriality, particularly for programs built around expanded storytelling practices, through ensemble casts of characters and multiple plot lines. Further, conceptualizing *emotional* structuration offers a means of augmenting the traditional dominance, in narrative theory, of plot analysis as linear causality and teleological unity of purpose.

Emotional expressionism

The second strategy found in melodrama to mobilize emotionality concerns its aesthetics of emotional expressionism. This is an aesthetics based in performance, focused on externalizing feelings rather than on private, psychological introspection (Pribram 2018 [2016], 49–53, 2018). Historical melodrama has long been associated with lack of character depth, when the latter is understood as interiorized, psychological development (Brooks 1995, 35). Traditionally, "dramatic conflict is not enacted *within* such characters, but *between* them and other external forces," whether those forces take the shape of other people, social institutions, or natural events (Gledhill 1991, 210; italics in original). Current melodrama is much more likely to incorporate aspects of psychological characterization, an example of how the melodramatic mode is constantly updated in order to reflect the contemporaneous culture in which it exists, in this case by adjusting to criteria of psychological realism. We find the introduction of psychology in *River*, in the significant subplot concerning the DI's interactions with his police psychologist, Rosa (Georgina Rich). Additionally, we are offered an explanation for River's susceptibility to envisioning dead people through the familiar, psychological trope of personal childhood trauma. Yet, although psychological motifs are engaged in *River*'s narrative world, they neither convince nor succeed, as discussed below. Instead, melodrama's brand of performative emotional expressionism prevails.

Melodramatic expressionism insists on externalizing and socializing feelings, rather than focusing on internalized, individual psychologies. Its aesthetics of performance employs extroverted, expressive behaviors that *enact* emotional states, in order to provide audiences with moments of felt recognition. Melodrama's dynamic is not primarily self-reflective, but an impulse to communicate, to make sense of a world of social relations. Gledhill notes that glances, gestures, and body movement become "major channels of communication when verbal exchanges fail to express" or actually obscure the import of events and felt experiences (1992, 119). Alternative forms are called upon to extract the linguistically inexpressible, in which category emotions feature prominently. Gesture, facial expression, physical action, and other categories of nonverbal communication (spatial relations, paralanguage, silence), as well as formal elements such as music, mise-en-scène, and editing, are invoked to reveal what words alone cannot. Melodrama relies on numerous techniques to make apparent experiences that would not otherwise be adequately recognized or acknowledged.

We can turn, again, to *River* to illustrate how melodrama's aesthetics of emotional expressionism plays out. River has seen, heard, and existed in the company of the dead since childhood. When meeting with his psychologist, Rosa, River adamantly denies that the dead who engage with him are ghosts. Instead, he describes them as "manifests." It is a small leap to assume he describes them as such because they manifest or externalize his feelings. But I do not believe they operate solely or simply as reflections of his internal feelings, with which he must come to terms. On the contrary, these manifests help constitute a portrayal of River's social relations.

The series emphasizes the abysmal way River interacts with other people, whether they are living or dead. Much is made of his social ineptitude, involving relationships that are effectively nonexistent or awkward disasters. Most of his manifests are, or were, "real," just as Stevie was: once living characters in this narrative world, in the sense of deriving from a material, social plane. They are not figments of his imagination but the remnants of his disastrous social relations. However, River interacts differently with the deceased than with the living. To a significant degree, he displays greater honesty about his feelings with manifests, as if he finds more safety in their company than with the living. With the dead, he seems able to express himself, to communicate with them, whether to convey his joy, sorrow, or fury.

The series works to depict something about emotional life in the context of our existence as social beings. The emotions displayed by River in his encounters with manifests, as well as the emotions expressed by them, exist only by virtue of relationships with others. River's troubles occur when he interacts with other social beings. If Stevie and Rosa pose different solutions to River's problems – the first toward a relational world, the second in the direction of a private self – it is Stevie who wins out. Rosa is presented as a sympathetic figure who wants to aid River by helping him make his manifests disappear. Yet River seems strangely unconcerned about this. Instead, what he most wants is to make sense of his relationship with Stevie. At one point, Stevie wryly comments on the appropriately named Rosa for a psychologist, referencing her optimistically tinted worldview. In this, Stevie suggests that the psychologist's proffered solution to River's difficulties is somehow inadequate or unrealistic. No one can make emotional relations disappear, as troubling as they often may be. They exist because we are social beings who always live in the complicated company of others.

None of this is to minimize the program's treatment of mental illness. Quite the contrary, emotions are central to those categories of existence we understand as mental disorders (Pribram 2018 [2016]). But I do believe the series tries to get at the complexity of our emotional experiences in broad terms, as part of our individual, felt existence and as part of the social worlds we occupy. Here, we can return to the recurring wide shot that punctuates River's encounters with the deceased from an observational, public view. Earlier, I described this shot as an emotional switch, repositioning the audience from sharing in River's emotions of the moment to a more distant, poignant position of assessment. Expanding on this, the repeated cuts to wide shots also transpose us between the worlds of felt experience and material existence.

At one point in episode three, River rides an elevated commuter train. Stevie appears seated across from him, as he tries to figure out the unknown four-digit user code for a cell phone that belonged to her. Stevie tells him to try 4496, the day they first met. He does; it fails. She next suggests 4458. He looks at her quizzically. She explains it's their combined ages. He shouts in response, "59; I'm 59," annoyed that she has forgotten his correct age. We see two people seated behind him, staring at River as he yells out loud. An immediately following, second shot reveals others passengers dismayed at River's outburst, whom we now see is seated alone.[5] He is the "crazy" person we encounter in public places talking to himself and whom, out of fear, we do our best to avoid. At the same time, in narrative terms he also depicts an externalized, performed version of human emotional life. People sitting quietly, in apparent silence, on subways, buses, or trains, may well be engaging in arguments with non-present family, friends, and colleagues, or exchanging stories and laughter with them. The life of his mind and emotions are more real to River than the material world that surrounds him, as is true for all of us, on occasion.

In its visual and audio presentation, River's behavior constantly transports us between our experiences of a physical world and the life of our feelings. In Spence's terms, River's public outbursts function as moments of emotional spectacle that make intelligible the felt effects of social issues, in this case both mental disorder and grief over the death of others. Such moments of emotional legibility are not rendered moral sentiments solely because we feel sorry for River, registering pity or empathy for him. The transposition *from* narratively sharing his perspective *to* the observational wide shot pushes us to recognize how we, as the public, understand persons "suffering" – in melodrama's terms – from mental illness.

The dual perspective, originating within the visual and aural expressions of River's emotional state and then abruptly shifting to an external position, creates the pathos demanded by moral sentiment. Transition from one spectatorial position to another accomplishes a moment of felt recognition, in which we more fully realize how River hears and speaks with manifests but, also, by switching to the perspective of other people on the train, carries us to an uneasy awareness of the depths of River's isolation. Moral sentiments require an audience's felt recognition toward the emotional harm confronted by individuals, in conjunction with some degree of social complicity or neglect, which results in the experienced, and expressed, emotional situations witnessed in narratives.

Narratives about emotion

Third and finally, the mobilization of emotionality in serialized melodrama enables an exploration of the compound meanings attached to and conveyed by specific emotions. Any singular word or idea that stands for an entire network of emotional meanings and relations can never be straightforward, transparent, or self-evident. Rather, every emotion involves countless variations, dependent upon the cultural, contextual circumstances of its use. This is true in the social worlds we occupy and applies also to the narrative worlds we visit. Serialization's expanded form of storytelling and prolonged time spent with characters who evolve enable the creation of narratives *about* emotions. Similarly, melodrama's long-standing alliance with emotionality offers complex depictions of particular emotions, ranging from their expansiveness to their most minute intricacies. Here, we can recall River's caution concerning the failure of singular words to describe complex systems of feeling. As he tells us: "I've seen love that kills and I've seen love that redeems. I've seen love that believes in the guilty, and love that saves the bereaved." More than anything else, *River* is a series about love. But only in its most complicated sense.

Television serialization has become closely associated with ensemble casts of characters whose stories are told through an alternating pattern of numerous plots and subplots. However, *River* does not follow such a model, in that there are only two principal characters – River and Stevie – and we stay with River, as protagonist, throughout the series. Yet, *River*'s narrative structure coheres by means of another sense to "ensemble storytelling," in Michael Newman's phrase (2006, 18). In addition to serialization's complex development due to ensemble plots and characters, Newman points to "thematic parallelism" in which multiple, diverse stories interrelate so that they "inflect and play off each other, revealing contrasts and similarities" (21). *River*'s serialized charge relies less on an extensive range of plots or a community of revolving characters; instead, it unfurls as variations on the emotional theme of love.

The main plot arc driving the series concerns solving Stevie's murder, which River helplessly witnessed without being able to intercede. As discussed earlier, in the generic terms of the detective series, "solving" refers to finding out who killed her. However, for the show's meditation on love, "solving" her murder means coming face to face with losing her. The first episode of the series also involves a self-contained murder case – self-contained in the sense of being resolved within the episode's 58 minutes. This second case focuses on the death, two and a half months previously, of a young woman, Erin Fielding (Shannon Rivers), who functions as another of River's manifests. Her boyfriend, Aten (Fady Elsayed), confessed to her murder and sits in prison awaiting trial. However, he refuses to divulge to River how he murdered Erin or where he left her body.

Although technically solved with the arrest of the culprit, the case remains open due to Erin's mother, Marlena (Cathy Murphy). Marlena remains steadfast that the case cannot be considered closed until her daughter's body has been retrieved so that the grieving mother can bury her. A soft-spoken woman, Marlena nevertheless manages to make her presence felt through the action of delivering to River's police station, on a weekly basis, items that once belonged to Erin: a teddy bear, her journal, a videotape of Erin as a child. In doing so, Marlena's intent is to remind River that he, and Stevie, promised they would find Erin's remains. When River meets again with Marlena, her pain is raw.

> Seventy-two days and still no body ... She's mine. I made her. And I will bury her. I have to bury her, so I know where she is.

Marlena cannot rest until she has put her daughter to rest. She has made it her mission to take care of her daughter in death, just as she did in life. Marlena and her determination to bury her child is "love that saves the bereaved."

River visits Erin's boyfriend, Aten, in prison in order to pressure him, once again, to reveal how he killed Erin and where he left her remains. Breaking down into sobs, all Aten will say is, "I killed her." Ultimately, River discovers Erin's body, concealed within the tree from which she has hung herself. When he finds her, Erin – as manifest – explains to River that the couple had a suicide pact, with which Aten could not go through at the last moment, although she did, leaving him tortured with shame. Returning to the prison, when River tells Aten he will be released and not charged because Erin's death was not murder, Aten attempts suicide. His feelings of shame are "love that kills."

For its part, River's despair over his relationship with his murdered partner, Stevie, becomes "love that redeems." But he must journey through numerous other kinds of love, over the course of the series, including bereaved love, ashamed love, joyful love, angry love, and so on, in order to reach a form of love for Stevie that feels redemptive. His relationship with Stevie proves more of a saving grace than anything or anyone else in the series, including the interactions with his psychologist. *River* focuses most centrally on River and Stevie's relationship, rather than on his internal psyche, because the series is a story *about* love. Brooks reminds us that melodrama renders "the world we inhabit, one charged with meaning, one in which interpersonal relations are not merely contacts of the flesh but encounters that must be carefully nurtured, judged, handled as if they mattered" (1995, 22).

For River, Stevie's case is not "solved" until he acknowledges the depth of his love for her. In the end, that love is redemptive precisely due to his capacity to feel so intensely about her, despite his social ineptitude and the circumstances of his social isolation. The series emphasizes River and Stevie's relationship because it unfolds as an extended foray into one emotion:

love as a complex, sometimes joyful, oftentimes painful state of experience that can *only* exist in a social world comprised of other beings. Notable in the series are the multitude of ways that love is depicted, the host of different stories told about love: the narratives surrounding this one emotion.

River stands as an illustration of ensemble storytelling because its emotional arc provides us with multiple variations on a theme, instead of driving toward one universal, singular determination on what love must be. Melodramatic serialization holds the capacity to circle carefully around its emotional themes, progressively unveiling layer upon layer of complex circumstances, along with their assorted implications and outcomes. The extended, ensemble mode of television seriality does not strive toward stasis but, rather, builds complex variations on a theme, accruing contradictions, continuities, and relentless change. Much of contemporary television's narrative configurations rely on the intricate patterning of parallel action *and* parallel emotion. Another way of making sense of televisual seriality, then, is to explore how its narratives engage not only with plot and character arcs but, also, with emotional arcs.

Conclusion

Emotions are central to most forms of popular narrative. Because of the scholarly attention that has been devoted to it, the melodramatic mode's mobilization of emotionality is particularly useful in understanding television seriality's distinctive dynamism, intensity, and power to make us care. The melodramatic mode sheds light on an array of ways that emotions contribute to the multifaceted narrative processes of contemporary television seriality. Here I have traced three potential strategies by which the presence of emotionality helps shape serialized narrative: as structuring device, performatively as emotional expressionism, and in the form of intricate thematic content.

However, my discussion is far from an exhaustive account of emotionality's role in narrative processes. Emotions are too vast, complex, and pervasive a form of both life and storytelling experience to be that neatly, concisely accounted for in seriality or in narratives beyond. Yet the endeavor to do so remains worthwhile. The effort to make sense of emotionally resonant images, sounds, characters, and stories offers up alternative ways to journey through the narrative worlds we often care about so passionately.

Notes

1 For a more detailed explanation of these arguments, see Pribram (2019).
2 The idea of melodrama as a trans-generic *mode* dovetails with Steve Neale's research into the Hollywood trade press (*Variety, Hollywood Reporter*) between 1938 and 1960 (1993). He found the term "melodrama" was used consistently to describe adventure films, thrillers, horror films, westerns, and other genres. Similarly, Daniel Gerould outlines how, in 1926–1927, Russian theorists like

Sergei Balukhatyi and Adrian Piotrovsky referred to "judicial, criminal, adventure and detective variants" of theatrical melodrama, as well as the "American adventure melodrama" in cinema, with its detectives, policemen, "break-neck chases and racing trains" (qtd. in Gerould 1978, 162, 167).
3 It is important to note that Gledhill takes pains to argue that the melodramatic mode works *with*, not in opposition to, various forms of realism, in part as a means for melodrama to continually update itself in changing historical circumstances and, therefore, evolving notions of realism (2002).
4 For more on crime, detective, and other related genres as a complex generic network, organized around concepts of justice and injustice, see Pribram (2013, chapter 3).
5 In fact, River is so caught up in his preoccupation with Stevie that he can only imagine her choosing a phone code that has something to do with him and their relationship: the day they first met, their combined ages.

Works cited

Brooks, Peter. *The Melodramatic Imagination: Balzac, Henry James, Melodrama, and the Mode of Excess*. New Haven, CT: Yale University Press, 1995 [1976].
Buckley, Matthew. "Refugee Theatre: Melodrama and Modernity's Loss". *Theatre Journal* 61.2, May 2009. 175–190.
Chan, Kenneth. "Melodrama as History and Nostalgia: Reading Hong Kong Director Yonfan's *Prince of Tears*". In Michael Stewart (ed.), *Melodrama in Contemporary Film and Television*, Basingstoke: Palgrave Macmillan. 2014. 135–152.
Gerould, Daniel. "Russian Formalist Theories of Melodrama". *Journal of American Culture* 1.1, Spring 1978. 152–168.
Gledhill, Christine. "Signs of Melodrama". In Christine Gledhill (ed.), *Stardom: Industry of Desire*, London: Routledge. 1991. 210–234.
Gledhill, Christine. "Speculations on the Relationship between Soap Opera and Melodrama". *Quarterly Review of Film and Video* 14.1–2, 1992. 103–124.
Gledhill, Christine. "The Melodramatic Field: An Investigation." In Christine Gledhill (ed.), *Home Is Where the Heart Is: Studies in Melodrama and the Woman's Film*, London: BFI. 2002 [1987]. 5–39.
Gledhill, Christine, and Linda Williams. "Introduction." In Christine Gledhill and Linda Williams (eds.), *Melodrama Unbound: Across History, Media, and National Cultures*, New York: Columbia University Press. 2018. 1–12.
Gould, Deborah. "On Affect and Protest." In Janet Staiger, Ann Cvetkovich, and Ann Reynolds (eds.), *Political Emotions*, New York: Routledge. 2010. 18–44.
Hayward, Jennifer. *Consuming Pleasures: Active Audiences and Serial Fictions from Dickens to Soap Opera*. Lexington: University Press of Kentucky, 2009.
Massumi, Brian. *Parables for the Virtual: Movement, Affect, Sensation*. Durham, NC: Duke University Press, 2002.
Neale, Steve. "On the Meaning and Use of the Term 'Melodrama' in the American Trade Press". *The Velvet Light Trap* 32, Fall 1993. 66–89.
Newman, Michael Z. "From Beats to Arcs: Toward a Poetics of Television Narrative". *The Velvet Light Trap* 58, Fall 2006. 16–28.
Pribram, E. Deidre. *Emotions, Genre, Justice in Film and Television: Detecting Feeling*. New York: Routledge, 2013 [2011].
Pribram, E. Deidre. *A Cultural Approach to Emotional Disorders: Psychological and Aesthetic Interpretations*. New York: Routledge, 2018 [2016].

Pribram, E. Deidre. "Melodrama and the Aesthetics of Emotion". In Christine Gledhill and Linda Williams (eds.), *Melodrama Unbound: Across History, Media, and National Cultures*. New York: Columbia University Press. 2018. 237–251.

Pribram, E. Deidre. "Storied Feelings: Emotions, Culture, Media". In Roger Patulny, Alberto Bellocchi, Rebecca Olson, Sukhmani Khorana, Jordan McKenzie, and Michelle Peterie (eds.), *Emotions in Late Modernity,* Milton Park: Routledge, 2019. 223–236.

Shepherd, Simon. "Pauses of Mutual Agitation". In Jacky Bratton, Jim Cook, and Christine Gledhill (eds.), *Melodrama: Stage Picture Screen,* London: BFI. 1994. 25–37.

Spence, Louise. *Watching Daytime Soap Operas: The Power of Pleasure*. Middletown, CT: Wesleyan University Press, 2005.

Thorburn, David. "Television Melodrama". In Douglass Cater (eds.), *Television as a Cultural Force,* New York: Praeger. 1976. 77–94.

Williams, Linda. *On The Wire*. Durham, NC: Duke University Press, 2014.

Films and series cited

Breaking Bad. AMC, 2008–2013.
Dallas. CBS, 1978–1991.
Dynasty. CBS, 1981–1989.
Inception. Christopher Nolan, Warner Bros., 2010.
Rich Man, Poor Man. ABC, 1976.
River. BBC1, 2015.
Roots. ABC, 1977.
Wire, The. HBO, 2002–2008.

1.3 The cinematic-televisual

Rethinking medium specificity in television's new Golden Age

C.E. Harris

Over the course of the last decade, there has been a surge in writings on what is canonically being recognized as a new Golden Age of Television (ca. 2000 to present). The interesting common feature of the majority of these contributions, however, has less to do with the explicit arguments that they proffer, and more to do with the implicit disclaimer that seems to accompany all of them: that the television shows in question can be listed but not always easily described, that they can be grouped together but nonetheless still manage to escape typology and classification. As a result, what unites this new corpus of writings on television is the seeming indiscernibility of its own object, despite the fact that we have nonetheless developed an intuition for what is being referred to.

The golden ages of television?

The first point of contention among these writings results from the difficult problem of historicizing the present. Many writings on television, in both academic and popular spheres, have used periodization as a means of focusing the corpus of television shows and modes of production or distribution being addressed. Especially in more recent instances, we see references not only to the Golden Age of Television, but to *several* golden ages, often numbered, ranked, or otherwise qualified in terms of technological evolution, aesthetics, or content. This has resulted in a confusing and redundant means of classification, which has the tendency to recourse to evaluative claims that are difficult to systematize and often problematic in their own right.

The first Golden Age refers to the period of the late 1940s to the late 1950s and is typically associated with the emergence and popularization of live television dramas. This is the case not only in reference texts on television (such as Slide 1991; Newcomb 1997; Stephens 2000) and in studies on television and the history of popular culture in the post–Golden Age through 1990s (including Wilk 1977; Kerbel 1979; Baughman 1981; Marshall 1987; Sturcken 1990; Caughie 1991; Ritchie 1995; Spigel 1995; Krampner 1997), but also in contemporary texts written since the claim to a second and even third golden age has been made. The term "Golden Age" (unless otherwise qualified) still tends to refer to this period in television history (see for example Everitt 2001; Hawes 2001, 2002; Deming 2005; Kellison 2006; Press 2009; Angelini 2010). Outside of academic works, film- and television-oriented organizations likewise continue to apply the designation of "Golden Age" to refer to the 1940s–1960s (Newcomb 1997). Despite some variation in the specific milestones and dates of this category, it is the most widely accepted referent for those referring to television's "Golden Age."

However, a search in journalistic and popular forms of writing turns up a wholly different point of reference for the "Golden Age of Television" moniker. In recent writings, the high acclaim received by US and British series beginning in the early 2000s has prompted this period to be widely regarded as a (or the) "Golden Age" or "New Golden Age" of television (Patterson and McLean 2006; Lawson 2013; Thompson 2013; Ryan 2016; Smith 2017; Suskind 2017; Brennan 2018; Bunch 2018). This is particularly with reference to shows made and distributed by premium channels such as HBO, Showtime, or AMC, or platforms such as Netflix and Hulu. Even a search on Wikipedia notes the possibility to refer to either period as a Golden Age, returning two disambiguated entries: "Golden Age of Television," referring to the 1940s–1960s, and "Golden Age of Television (2000s–present)," with reference to the contemporary period or periods, respectively. Still further distinctions within this framework have been made in order to account for groupings of works cited in other periods; both the 1980s and the 1990s have each on occasion been referred to as a "Second Golden Age" (R. Thompson 1997 notably;[1] Lawson 2013; Vorel 2014), while the post-2000 landscape of television series has been called a "Second," "Third," "New," or even "New, New" Golden Age (Cowan 2013; Leopold 2013; Weisenthal and Robinson 2013; Carr 2014).

Certainly, there have been attempts to move beyond the "Golden Age" designation, whose shortcomings have long been noted. The AV Club's Todd Van Der Werff points out in his 2013 piece "The Golden Age of TV is dead; Long Live the Golden Age of TV" that "[t]he dirty little secret here is that essentially every decade except the 1960s has been proclaimed the 'golden age of TV' at one time or another," as television continuously explores and expands its potential, resulting in more and more "good TV." Further critiques of Golden Age discourse and of existing classifications for television have been steadily emerging in the landscape of recent Television Studies publications (Jacobs 2001; Spigel and Olsson 2004; Wheatley 2007; Brunsdon 2008; Dasgupta 2012; Newman and Levine 2012; Logan 2016, among others), but the impulse to return to these taxonomies persists nonetheless, up to and including in recent pieces that already announce the decline and/or death of this golden age (Van Der Werff 2013; Brennan 2018).

While some, in both academic and popular contexts, have preferred other qualifiers to refer to periods of, for lack of a better term, "good

TV" – terms like Peak TV and Quality TV have found widespread usage, each with its own merits and flaws – perhaps the most sustained alternative has been the TVI, TVII, TVIII (and occasionally TVIV) classification system first proposed by Steve Behrens (1986) and developed further by Reeves, Rogers, and Epstein throughout their work (1996, 2002, and 2007 notably). These classifications focus not on the ambiguous notion of "good TV" but rather on industrial structures, modes of production, and availability. TVI refers to the network era (1948–1975), TVII to the post-network era (1975–1995), and TVIII to the era of digital content (post-1995); TVIV has been proposed as a means of signaling the age of streaming and television on demand facilitated by platforms such as Netflix (Reeves et al., in and qtd. in Creeber and Hills 2007; McCabe and Akass 2007; Jenner 2014). While a productive model in many respects, it is employed almost exclusively in work looking at television from its industrial point of view, and also seems to have not yet established a foothold in the often high-quality popular work being done in Television and Media Studies outside of the academe proper.[2] Furthermore, it does not explicitly account for the aesthetic concerns particular to certain moments in television evolution that seem to be, for audiences, a primary point of legibility in navigating types and subtypes of content in their emerging contexts and in relation to each other.

In light of this history of complex – and often problematic – systems of classification, it is unsurprising that we lack a unified discourse with which to address contemporary television content and production today. In lieu, a series of descriptive formulae have emerged in many recent academic and popular works in order to clarify the object of analysis when referring to certain subsets of contemporary television series, as a placeholder system of classification. Among the most common:

1   They open by establishing a historical context (referring to a corpus of television shows that have emerged since the late 1990s or since the early 2000s, in the context of platforms like premium cable channels or else in the context of an auteurist renaissance);

2   They make reference to a standard of evaluation (describing the international acclaim of the shows in terms of critical response, or using designations such as "peak," "quality," "ambitious," or even "good" television);

3   They book-end the series in question within a set of milestones (at times, naming specific shows as cultural or temporal reference points, such as *The Sopranos*, *Twin Peaks*, *Buffy the Vampire Slayer*, and *The Wire*, and leading up to the current popularity of Netflix Originals); and/or;

4   They list out examples of the series in question (shows like *Breaking Bad*, *Game of Thrones*, *House of Cards*, *True Detective*, *Mad Men*, etc.).

While we are able to find some legibility from these formulae, it is none-theless telling that it is still so difficult to locate an adequate discursive apparatus for discussing groupings of television series in relation to each other and the categorical parameters describe them. Therefore, a central question that organizes this chapter is that of why our language for talking about television seems to still be so inadequate, despite the proliferation of high-quality scholarship in the field of Television Studies in recent years.

What we lack in concise, unified ways of classifying these shows, we make up for in their well-established foundational narrative. Synthesizing from elements repeated in a large number of recent academic and popular accounts of these productions: there is a certain type of Anglo-American series of high-quality and high production value popularized in the mid-2000s–2010s that we can draw together through a common genealogy and through their shared vision in rethinking the treatment of narrative and of aesthetic practices of popular television programming. This genealogy is said to have begun in the 1990s, on the one hand with HBO original pro-grams and the rise of cable specialty channels, effectively establishing a sort of studio system for big budget television shows which offer exclusive, high-quality content; on the other hand, it also begins with specific milestone shows, like David Lynch's *Twin Peaks*, which bring cinematic auteurism to television, ushering in a vision of television as a site for artistic and aes-thetic experimentation. Typically, these shows are characterized by: their innovative storytelling structures and non-traditional treatment of plot; a large, ensemble cast granted a perhaps unprecedented psychological depth; the creative recombination of genre categories; a pronounced attention to formalism and a poetic use of filming techniques; a drive toward realism and cultural critique; and a high level of self-consciousness and even cine-matic reflexivity. These shows have been referred to as "high-brow televi-sion"; they have been called "Quality TV" (McCabe and Akass 2007) or "complex TV" (Mittell 2009, 2015); they have been treated as something *other* than television (reminiscent of the "It's not television … it's HBO" motto); and they have largely been debated with regard to their relation to the cinema, in light of a corpus of (mostly) popular writings that have put forth the possibility of something cohesive that could be called "cinematic television."

"Cinematic television"?

"Cinematic television" emerged as a possible designation for the geneal-ogy of series described above beginning roughly around 2010. It was, first, largely used in popular and journalistic writings on shows of high acclaim from the beginning of the age of Netflix Original productions (Wagner and Maclean 2008; Thorpe 2011; Sachs 2013; Epstein 2014a, 2014b; Seitz and Wade 2015; Titoria 2018), and then debated extensively in film and television scholarship, where this notion was the object of understandable critique. Among the most noteworthy critiques of the idea of cinematic television are certainly Brett Mills' "What Does It Mean to Call Television 'Cinematic'?" and Deborah L. Jaramillo's "Rescuing Television from 'The Cinematic': The Perils of Dismissing Television Style," in both *Television Aesthetics and Style* (Jacobs and Peacock 2013) and Jason Mittell's work, for example, on narrative complexity in television (2006, 2015). The primary axis of criticism in these accounts of the problems with the designation of "cinematic television" is that they seem to situate television as conceptually subordinate to cinema. Brett Mills also notes that it implies defining a medium through its technological platforms or through binaries (such as the analog versus the digital) that are already being undone in the evolving contemporary media landscape.

> The discourses that surround cinematic television are ones reliant on knowledge of the kinds of equipment used to make it, and the growth of high-definition television equates technology with expense and quality. But, of course, at the same time as this has been occurring much cinema production has moved towards abandoning celluloid and instead adopting digital technologies, thereby bringing the kinds of technologies used by film and television much closer together.
>
> (Mills, in Jacobs and Peacock, eds. 2013, 60)

Even more importantly, he draws attention to the already problematic question of "what it is about *cinema* that we can call cinematic" (60), invoking not only the already ambiguous nature of the concept but also the perennial problem of essentialism inherent in such designations. Finally, he diagnoses the consequences of such a model: "that the 'cinematic' might be seen as a positive term when applied to (some) television can only be seen as a reassertion of a hierarchy that sees television as film's poor relation" (64), stunting potential conversations about television on its own terms and in terms of its own style. Deborah L. Jaramillo's position is very much in line with Mills's on many points – the problematic subordination of television to cinema, the essentialist and ultimately evaluative nature inherent in the idea of cinematic television, and certainly the notion that it "does not advance our understanding of where the look and sound of television are going in any meaningful way" (67). Yet despite her urgency to "rescu[e] television from 'the cinematic'," she notes that even now "we still do not have one coherent language" for treating television (73), and that "[p]recisely what makes a television aesthetic so important is the web of relations behind it" (74).

These are all valid points that are not being contested here. However, what stands out in each of these critiques of cinematic television is that they echo arguments that have also been made regarding the question of "cinematicity" in cinema since the 1970s.

That the term "cinematic" is problematic, in referring to both films and other forms of media, is not new. We can find arguments both for and against the use of this designation throughout film history, with particular intensity in the shaping of medium specificity–related arguments (in the 1920s and in the 1950s), and again with a series of publications in the 1970s on the topic of film art. The most prominent arguments against the term "cinematic" have to do with its inadequacies in terms of coverage rather than any inherent wrongness per se: Gerald Mast makes this point in 1974 in a piece called "What Isn't Cinema?" for example, in which he points out certain lacunae such as how we might classify animation with reference to cinema.[3] This line of thinking reveals historical anxieties about the purity of the filmic medium and its abilities to distinguish itself among the arts.

Then, "cinematic" also suffers from the same ambiguity as its analogues – painterly, literary, or theatrical, for example – referring to some inherent, defining quality of the medium that is recognizable, although difficult to pin down discursively. But already, we can see that this is a bit of a false innocence: "cinematic" is rarely, if ever, used to simply mean "of the cinema." Instead, these terms are charged with a surplus meaning that is already evaluative. This reveals the third problem with the term "cinematic" – it doesn't refer to *all* cinema, but, instead, is most often inflected with an approving sense of high-art grandeur or a quality of epicness. In short, it is used as a statement of virtue.[4] (This is the case for television, and when we hear the term "cinematic television," it is common shorthand for a more artistic, aesthetically oriented, higher-quality mode of television.) Such a line of thinking can in many ways be traced back to Bazin's aesthetics in *What Is Cinema?* and entails the implicit argument that some sorts of films have the *virtue* of being more cinematic than others, and that this is a question of technique, art, and genius, or, in other words, a marker of prestige.

And for all the struggle that it took to elevate the status of the cinema to that of a "true" art, this is troublesome because, necessarily, it implies that there must also be such a thing as "uncinematic" cinema. In fact, this designation has been thrown around before as a means of expressing low regard for certain forms of aesthetic or narrative treatment in specific films or film movements, for example, in the case of British social realism in the 1960s, or, famously, even in reference to some of Eric Rohmer's films, with regard to their theatrical nature (Smuts 2013, 78). We should, of course, be somewhat troubled, as well as perplexed, by this: attempting to define the "cinematic" through the notion of the "uncinematic," as understood only through the "cinematic" does little more than reveal the tautological impasse at which we have arrived. Both notions – of "cinematic cinema" and "uncinematic cinema" – are rendered further incomprehensible through these internal contradictions.

Finally, and as a result of this vision of virtue and aesthetics, the notion of "cinematic" forecloses on the value of the popular by reserving the attribution of status and prestige only to that which is considered "high-brow" (in this sense, the "high-brow" and the "popular" are understood to be diametrical opposites). When the term "cinematic" is used as a statement of virtue, it implies that anything outside of this high-brow, fine arts vision of the cinema is less worthy of being considered a part of the medium. For television, this is even further compounded by the fact that, for most (if not all) of its history, it has been considered an exclusively popular (and decidedly not high-brow) form. In short, it undoes the work of medium specificity all the while insisting on medium specificity in order to do so.

Still, despite the overwhelming critiques against the notion of the cinematic, it has served as a productive discursive tool in Film Studies and perhaps in some areas of Television Studies as well. Some recent works, written during and after the cinematicity debates, attempt to reformulate and recuperate the concept in potentially useful ways. Mittell refers to David Bordwell's treatment of cinematic modes as strategies, distinct yet relating to one another, of storytelling, which Kristin Thompson relates to television, "suggesting that programs like *Twin Peaks* and *The Singing Detective* might be usefully thought of as 'art television,' " as an analog to art cinema (2006, 29). While Mittell critiques this practice of importing analogs from cinema, a notion such as art television seems to be formulated in the spirit of addressing – even serving as a potential corrective to? – the more problematic versions of cinematicity described above; it seems to confirm the "web of relations" among visual art forms that Jaramillo calls for without imposing hierarchies or falling prey to essentialism. The underlying premise of these recent works that still (or again) invoke cinematicity – often explicitly outlined in their introductory chapters – is that, despite past misuses and lingering flaws, cinematicity as a conceptual field might afford us a vocabulary for addressing media practices that may have emerged in or been theorized through the cinema but certainly extend beyond it.

In the introduction to their 2015 work *Cinematicity in Media History*, Jeffrey Geiger and Karin Littau attempt to recuperate the concept of cinematicity, staging it not as a measure of value, or as a hierarchizing term, but "conceiv[ing] of it as an instance of intermediality" (2). They quote André Gaudreault's formulation that "cinema was so intermedial that it was *not even* cinema" (Gaudreault 2009, qtd in Geiger and Littau 2015) to this end, preferring to retain the term "cinematicity" as a means of affirming context and historical relevance. They ask:

> How does cinema, itself once a new medium, relate to what we now refer to as the New Media, or conversely, how did cinema as an emergent medium relate to its predecessors and contemporaries – eclipsing, challenging and transforming them it its wake?
>
> (1)

Indeed their focus on using cinematicity as a means of theorizing *the emergent* seems to fill a theoretical gap that has relevance for technological art forms at large. In their "Medium Specificity Re-visited" (2000), Steven Maras and David Sutton discuss at length Noël Carroll's observation that these art forms "undergo an initial phase in which each attempts to legitimize itself as art" in order to "highligh[t] the need for a theory of 'established' and 'emergent' forms [negotiated] by media theory in a variety of ways" (103). Studying how media have emerged in the past can inform how we understand media in the process of emerging or media yet to emerge. Perhaps we can do so in more productive ways than in earlier periods, for example, avoiding the essentialism that plagued decades of early film theory. Geiger and Littau dispel concerns that cinematicity might be associated with the outmoded medium specificity thesis's reliance on the concept of purity with the observation that this purity is a myth. Cinema itself could never lay claim to purity, and, instead, what characterizes cinematicity is not its nature or identity, but rather its "creation and perception: a mode of mind, method or experience that will surely endure beyond the life or death of celluloid" (4); they take up an extended discussion of how cinematicity pre-dates cinema (part 1 of their monograph is entitled "Cinematicity before Cinema" and treats a history of visuality and views in literature, optical toys, phantasmagoria, and then-emergent forms of experimentation with moving pictures) and is often outside of cinema (as treated in part 2 of their work), as a practice of seeing and creating means of seeing.

In a similar vein, Jane Stokes's *On Screen Rivals* (2000), which addresses the productive but also often contentious relationship between cinema and television, "begins from the premise that each cultural technology defines itself through its relationship with other cultural technologies," insisting that, rather than staging the two media in opposition, they should instead be seen as "fecund sources of information about one another" (3). She cites Bourdieu's notion of "fields" to elucidate this relationality, in which "the products of each cultural technology exercise forces of attraction and repulsion to one another," and in which "[t]elevision and film comprise two of the many technologies in this complex constellation of cultural technologies struggling to define one another" (4). Her work grounds media emergences on a mutual cultural biography, and though she focuses largely on cinematic representations of television, she nonetheless conceives of the two media as cooperative rather than competitive or hierarchical, especially in light of the fact that many of cinema's hostilities – perceived or real – can be traced back to questions of studio politics. Jon Nelson Wagner and Tracy Biga MacLean operate from a similar methodology, privileging a vision of cinematicity qua intermediality in their 2008 work *Television at the Movies: Cinematic and Critical Responses to American Broadcasting*, in order to develop a "close and critical reading of how an established medium engages with a newer but related one" (1).

In light of these recent reformulations of the category of the cinematic in works on media history, there has been a number of publications that reclaim this terminology as a mechanism of intermediality in the aftermath of the Television Studies debates. For example, Gary R. Edgerton's works on series such as *Mad Men* (2011) and *The Sopranos* (2013) include discussions of what cinematicity means to these shows. First, he notes the potential discomfort in using the term:

> I realize some television scholars chafe at the use of cinematic television as a metaphor – as if it detracts in some way from the value and integrity of TV as a medium – but series such as *The Sopranos*, *Mad Men*, and many other contemporary small screen dramas owe a great deal of their technical and production design to the movies.
>
> (Edgerton 2016)

He then offers examples attesting that the impetus to continue (or return to) referring to these series as "cinematic television" is now being used as shorthand for the relationality between cinema and television, and that it often comes from those responsible for creating the series themselves, not as a means of evaluation but rather as a means of contextualization. In his 2011 work *Mad Men: Dream Come True TV*, Edgerton describes Charles Collier (executive supervisor and general manager at AMC) as being "committed to combining the network's great movie library with high-end originals" (Becker qtd. in Edgerton 2013, 8). He cites an interview with Collier affirming this further: "We're trying to do cinematic-television shows, series that stand side-by-side with the best movies on TV" (Brodesser-Akner qtd. in Edgerton 2013, 8). This hyphenated concept of "cinematic-television" seems to elucidate particularly well the idea of cooperation between these media in the contemporary landscape.

In *The Sopranos* (2013), Edgerton's chapter entitled "Cinematic Television" delves at length into the biography of *The Sopranos*'s head writer, director, and producer David Chase, in order to demonstrate how Chase himself conceived of the series as being in a direct lineage with the films that were most foundational for him – in particular the works of Martin Scorsese, Francis Ford Coppola, and, later, David Lynch, as well as films like William Wellman's *The Public Enemy* and Jean-Luc Godard's *Pierrot le Fou* (35–61). Chase insists that, rather than aping cinematic devices on television, he saw what he was doing as a form of filmmaking and of film-intertextual quotation. In this vein, Edgerton considers that *The Sopranos* and similar such series qualify as "cinematic-television" not as a means of praising their big-budget productions or stylistic concerns, but because they can in fact be situated within film history as direct descendants of films like the ones mentioned above.

Further works reformulating cinematicity include Roberta Piazza et al.'s *Telecinematic Discourse* (2011), which provides a linguistic point of view to argue that contemporary television and film share in a complex discourse that "offers a re-presentation of our world,"[5] and Angelo Restivo's *Breaking*

Bad and Cinematic Television (2019), which conceives of the cinematic as "tethered to affect rather than to medium or prestige."[6]

What all these recent works have in common is that they shift the concept of cinematicity and cinematic television toward a vision privileging not what cinema might provide for insights into television, but rather how they mutually inform each other within a greater discourse on mediality. While there are certainly valid critiques regarding the theorization of media as "established" or "emerging"/"emergent" forms,[7] it is true that media such as cinema and television have had, each in turn, to pass through similar phases in terms of how they are addressed critically and academically. Both have had to fight for legibility and legitimacy as academic objects, both have had to answer to ontological demands for self-definition and identity, and both have undergone technological and aesthetic evolutions that have provoked media scholars to rethink mediality. In short, both have at times relied on, and at times been plagued by, the ongoing conversation surrounding medium specificity. But what if we could shift the discursive framework for thinking about terms like "cinematicity" beyond medium specificity, and instead consider their contemporary implications within a greater landscape of intermediality?

Medium specificity in the age of intermediality

By way of summary, medium specificity has historically entailed two things for the cinema: (1) insisting on the purity or, in other words, the singularity of the medium (that cinema is more than simply a hybrid of the other recognized arts, such as theatre, music, photography, etc.), and (2) arguing that there is a special capacity that the cinema alone has among the other arts that makes its expression unique. These two provisions, despite their obvious flaws, have served to elevate the status of the cinema to an art form, establish its prestige, and justify its pursuit as academic and intellectual objects. This is not unique to the cinema; we can see with other arts as well the important role that *singularity* and *specialness* have played historically in the attribution of prestige and recognition as legitimate objects of inquiry, at least in their emergent stages.

Though some recent works offer theorizations of "televisuality" as a potential analogue category (see Caldwell 1995 and Deming 2005 for sustained discussion of this concept), it suffers from a similar lack of discernibility as "cinematicity" does, on the one hand, and it does little to help us escape from this model of taxonomy and evaluation, on the other. As has already been argued at length (Dunne 2007; Johnson 2007; Van Der Werff 2013), the question of asking what it is that television does best does little to provide for television's medium specificity, and instead further is mired in questions of essentialism. In light of this, we must consider whether the burden for this lies with television, or, rather, whether it is *symptomatic* of a larger problem – that of medium specificity itself.

Indeed the question of medium specificity seems to be a key factor responsible for keeping television within its discursive holding pattern. The most obvious failing of medium specificity, as has been argued already at great length, is its essentialism. It is a model that is largely focused on the detection of inherent traits and characteristics that come from or else make up the very essence of an art or a medium. This kind of thinking winds up being more prescriptive than descriptive and is difficult, if not impossible, to reconcile with the inherent mutability of artistic experimentation and the ever-evolving media landscape. In short, there is an internal contradiction in our preoccupation with defining television's most innate and universal traits while simultaneously recognizing that today's television – particularly, what has been called cinematic television – is in many ways radically different from any of its previous incarnations. Nevertheless, rather than abandon medium specificity, we can use the so-called cinematic television of the contemporary age to rethink it, as a means of working through the discursive difficulties detailed above, in particular by focusing not on what television *is* but instead on what television *does* – and as an extension, what it does that other media also do.

In their article "Medium Specificity Re-Visited" (2000), Steven Maras and David Sutton provide a comprehensive survey of the critiques of the medium specificity thesis and other medium specificity arguments throughout the history of film theory, from questions of purity to essentialism to problems of medium fixity and finality. In doing so, they point out that, while these are old debates in the discipline of Film Studies, many of the same conversations resurface in discussions of New Media and emergent media. Rather than repeat the same conversations and critiques in the context of each new technological apparatus or aesthetic style, oriented toward questions of what a medium like cinema or television does best, Maras and Sutton propose a discussion of medium specificity that would "den[y] any finality or fixity to media forms, but nonetheless, and at the same time, allow us to identify the ways in which they coalesce around particular formations, apparatuses, and assemblages" (109).

If the notion of "cinematic television" has at times implied that television is relegated to the shadows of the cinema, perhaps we can rescue both media from their competitive holding pattern by taking them as an assemblage. By restaging their common specificity as that of a programmatic treatment of moving images in time – a common denominator that can almost certainly be agreed upon by both film scholars and television scholars alike – we might begin to theorize a cooperative, intermedial apparatus that undoes the harm of previous incarnations of the Medium Specificity Thesis, all the while paying heed to any potential shared lineage or common "cultural biography" (Stokes 2000). If we seek to associate cinema and television as cooperative media within a larger "web of relations" (Jaramillo), it seems that their treatment of time would be the crucial starting point.

Time and seriality as an intermedial common ground

Certainly, the category of time has been one of the most widely theorized aspects of film, ranging from its status as a primary material (along light and movement) of the cinema to its role in constructing narratives. For film, and especially for Hollywood cinema as the mainstream, dominant ideological mode of production, the perception of time conforms to the classicism of continuity, performing as economically as possible in service of narrative. Deviations from economical treatments of time – in other words, that time be felt only when pertinent to the furthering of the narrative – are treated as niche modes of production or artistic experimentation, for example, in what is often called "contemplative cinema," "slow cinema," or, even more generally, "art cinema." Particularly in recent years, the category of drama has been a site for types of cinema that take their time: as drama moves away from designating action-oriented productions and toward productions focused on the development of characters and their relationships to each other and to their circumstances, the elapsing of time and its registered perception becomes a greater preoccupation. Because today's dramas are about characters, their relationships to each other and to their environments, and the circumstances in which they find themselves, they require time, they thematize and problematize time, and they make the spectator *feel* time first hand. This is reminiscent of Jean-Louis Schefer's dictum: that "cinema is the only experience where time is given to me as a perception," or else, that poetic cinema "comes from another time; its movements are made of time, and its grain or flake is perceptible time" (Schefer 1980, 13). It is interesting to note that perhaps the most important work in drama, in the giving of time as a perception, is increasingly happening on television rather than on the big screen; where the exploration of time might be considered an experimental element for the cinema, it is the primary currency of contemporary television.

In most theorizations of time in drama, the notion of seriality is central. While we must certainly pay heed to the manifold roles that seriality plays in cinema – as we can see in the diversity of work presented in this volume – it is the very condition of possibility and organizing principle for the type of television that we are concerned with here. At the most basic level, we think of the serialization of narratives – a means of storytelling that has a shared intermedial legacy in its own right – in the history of novels, in film history, in radio, and certainly in television. However, before addressing the means by which cinema and television serialize narratives, we might first turn to some perhaps unconventional ways of understanding how television serializes – or operates *in series* – particularly in the recent era of what we might best refer to as cinematic-televisual aesthetics.

External seriality

First of all, this mode of television converts many of cinema's conceptual (at times, problematic) binaries into terms *in series*. If we understand "series" here in its polyvalence – as a group of coordinated elements that are *linked* rather than differentiated, then it gives us a space for rethinking some of our prior assumptions and theoretical hierarchies with reference to both cinema and television.

1   Where we might have considered extreme visual or formal stylization as being at odds with realism, the cinematic-televisual stylizes aesthetics *in service* of realism (what has been called affective realism or psychological realism, but also the broader category of poetic realism that we know from cinematic movements like Expressionism or Impressionism, which depict, for example, the realism of mental or emotional states by trading photographic or naturalistic realism for expressive style).

In this light, artistic stylization and the drive toward realism are not binary, but rather complementary, functioning in series.

2   In terms of modes of production throughout film history, the Studio System has often been considered to be in theoretical opposition to alternate modes such as auteurism. Where the studio system is an industrial model focusing typically on large-scale commercial entertainment projects, auteurism is an art-oriented model, focusing on smaller-scale, often experimental, projects and invested most primarily in the expression of the filmmaker's personal creative vision. We might even consider genre-oriented projects as a possible third term here, as narrative-driven productions that are achieved through the expression of narrative formulae and their corresponding visual codes. The cinematic-televisual bridges these three modes of production: large-scale, big-budget productions are often organized by studio equivalents (channels like HBO or AMC, or platforms like Netflix), and simultaneously express the unique artistic project of their creators (themselves often auteurs from cinema, in the case of David Fincher's work on *House of Cards* or dating back to *Twin Peaks* with David Lynch, literary auteurs like *Game of Thrones*' George R. R. Martin, or the emerging category of television auteurs, like *Breaking Bad*'s Vince Gilligan or Ryan Murphy and Brad Falchuk from *American Horror Story*, to name just a few examples). Furthermore, they present innovative new reconfigurations of genre (*House of Cards*, in addition to being a political thriller, can also be seen as a revisiting of the film noir genre; *Breaking Bad* is a family drama but also a gangster thriller and even a western; *American Horror Story* is itself an in-depth examination of and commentary on the horror genre and its related subgenres, and, in its sixth season, has even taken up an interrogation into the typical codes of the documentary "talking heads" genre, for example).

In short, contemporary television engages in modes of production that foster cooperation rather than hard lines between traditional notions of studio system, auteurism, and genre, likewise staging these as serial modes.

3   The cinematic-televisual bridges the highbrow and the popular. On some level, these shows seem to share a lineage with the blockbuster films of the so-called auteurist renaissance in the 1970s and 1980s, made by filmmakers extremely aware of and dedicated to the history of cinema who, in addition to being deeply invested in entertainment, were just as invested in sophisticated formal techniques, high-concept stories, looser narrative constructions, and an overarching artfulness. Likewise, the cinematic-televisual maintains a careful dedication to sophisticated aesthetic projects, all the while reshaping spectatorship through the extreme popularity of the series in this category and new modes of engaging audiences. They have high production value; they display an unprecedented level of self-awareness and cinematic reflexivity; they treat genre in new and innovative ways through a creative revisitation of classical codes; they use innovative, non-traditional treatments of narrative and continuity; they demonstrate a newfound attention to formalism and poetics; they drive toward realism and even toward cultural critique. But they also fulfill the promise of novelty and entertainment, as evidenced by the binge-watching practice that was born with them. They create engaged spectators and provoke the creation of fandoms, allowing for a variety of access points, interpretative levels, and apertures for interactivity that we might ultimately consider as something like serial modes of engagement.

4   These series also bridge, as we have seen in some of the above examples, the classical and the experimental. They rely on the well-established codes of their forms – whether it be genre-based, as in the codes of fantasy or the narrative structures of the family drama, or in terms of aesthetics, all the while working to innovate and experiment. This ranges from experimental narrative structures to the inventive revisiting of genres, from providing unprecedented intimacy with and development of characters to television formats rarely seen in contemporary programming, such as the anthology series, representing a renaissance of narrative modalities rarely used after the first Golden Age of Television. In this case, we could say that there has been an increasing drive to deploy commercial forms of entertainment in series with formal experimentation and innovation.

Certainly there are still further terms that the cinematic-televisual bridges, but these examples help illustrate the cinematic-televisual's unique project of articulating, linking, and setting in series terms that have traditionally been considered in opposition to each other. Furthermore, these forms of seriality seem to be specific to the contemporary mode with which we are concerned.

Another form of external seriality in the cinematic-televisual has to do with the relationship *between* and *across* individual television shows and streaming platforms. These shows seem to drive and mobilize one another, also functioning serially. We can see this with the exponential rise in the sheer number of these shows – if we look at Netflix Original Productions alone, the first example (*House of Cards*) dates back to only 2013 and was one of three original productions that year; today there are hundreds of Netflix original series across several genre categories, including region-specific international content. This model has been so successful that it has even pushed other streaming platforms (Amazon, Canal+) to follow in step in the move from hosting content to creating and marketing their own original production. We have reached a point where these series share so much of their mode of production, aesthetic program, spectatorship practices, and even philosophies with one another that we could almost speak of them as a cohesive "genre" in some light: they establish and perpetuate their own codes and formulae among themselves. Furthermore, they do not seem to overtly compete with each other; instead, they seem to operate in series, provoking a momentum among audiences who can now specifically seek out further content of the same category and caliber simply by choosing a platform to subscribe to.

Internal seriality

Returning to a more conventional understanding of seriality, in other words seriality as a diegetic or interdiegetic temporality in film and television, typically there are two primary categories cited: the episodic drama and the serial drama. Episodic dramas are generally procedurals, highly codified and formulaic shows in which every episode has more or less the same shape (e.g., the solving of a new crime or medical mystery), and they can be watched out of order without being unintelligible to a spectator familiar with the show's codes. Serial dramas, on the other hand, are cumulative; each episode serves as a chapter that progresses the action forward in an ongoing story. Each of these two modes employs a series of formal features that organize the structure and guide the spectator (codes of repeatability for the episodic drama; devices like the recap, the cliffhanger, and the tune-in-next-time montage for the serial drama, for example). In reality, it is quite rare for a show to be entirely situated within only one of these modes, and most television shows are generally a hybrid of both of these to some extent, making use of both micro- and macro-continuity devices within an individual episode, across episodes, and across seasons. However, if most shows are somewhat hybrid, perhaps we can argue that the series in the cinematic-televisual category seem to be, in some ways, neither. As discussed above, they can often be classified as a return to drama in a more classical sense, operating within an entirely different economy of time and continuity in order to find new ways of rendering time as a perception. The cinematic-televisual is often invested in tracing the micro-transformations of a character or situation over the course of several seasons (or years, effectively); and still, the rendering of time as a perception is more than a mere by-product of seriality. Indeed, we might argue that their treatment of time is transformed by giving a primary role not to the elapsing time of continuity but instead to what we could call *surplus* or *extemporaneous* time, or aestheticized time.

Time as an aesthetic category

Surplus or extemporaneous time involves a treatment of time beyond the furthering of narrative action. The cinematic-televisual series we are considering all seem to deploy devices for the treatment of time that not only are *not* directly in service of furthering diegetic time, but that specifically serve to undermine it in service of something else altogether. These can be as simple as poetic sequences of contemplation that take us out of the narrative for a moment to give us an introspective look at a character or a landscape (which we often see in classical cinematic dramas), or they can be as complex as building an entire episode that does nothing to further the narrative other than show a more profound vision of a character's psyche or conditions. It can be the repeated use of figurative motifs that do more to imbue a sense of mystery and mystique than to give the spectator information, or perhaps it might even serve as an interlude that reorganizes the pace and rhythm of the show. And almost universally, this is given through devices that serve to demonstrate the range and repertoire of a show's aesthetic palette and style. This emphasis on style or stylization is often, paradoxically, what is most responsible for giving the sensation of affective realism.

One such case in which the use of stylized extemporaneous time works toward the perception of affective realism is the critically acclaimed "Fly" episode of *Breaking Bad*. The tenth episode of Season 3 of the show halts the progression of the plot and inserts a sort of 47-minute poem into the season's overarching structural trajectory. In this episode, we see the two main characters, Walter White and Jesse Pinkman, attempt to chase down a fly that has supposedly contaminated their laboratory. There are some profound and philosophical conversations that take place between the two characters, and there is a startlingly beautiful use of poetic cinematographic devices (stark, unusual camera angles, lighting that is atypical for the rest of the show, jarring close-ups, a circular structure that has the episode end almost exactly as it had begun), but truly it is an entire episode of the show in which nothing *happens* in terms of action. Character development and treatment of mise-en-scène take a primary role over the progression of plot. There is an element of surrealism in the episode that takes the form of a dream-like state; and there is an expressionist impulse, as the mise-en-scène of the laboratory appears more and more distorted as if mirroring or focalizing the questionable mental state and motivations of Walter White as an anti-hero. So certainly, while no action furthers the plot in this episode, it still, nonetheless, makes a contribution to the show if we understand it as a sort of time-lapse study of characters in their environment and circumstances. But the episode is an extemporaneous contemplation packaged in the autonomous unit of a single, stand-alone episode.

Also from *Breaking Bad*, we can cite the infamous "pink teddy bear" sequences. Four discrete episodes begin with the same three-and-a-half-minute cold opening sequence that features a surreal and ethereal mysterious scene with a burnt pink teddy bear floating in a swimming pool. Only much later is this mysterious sequence given contextual meaning to the spectator – we later learn that this scene was a sort of cunning flash-forward meant to mislead the audience and influence their expectations about an upcoming cliff-hanger – but at the time of airing, it seems entirely unrelated to the diegesis other than for the fact that we see small Easter-egg-like tokens of this sequence hidden in the background of other episodes (a poster on a wall, a music video, etc., which use the same symbolism and motifs as this sequence). So mysterious and powerful is this repeated motif of the pink teddy bear that it even has its own website in the *Breaking Bad* wikis[8] in which fans have attempted to collect every related reference littered throughout the show. Even when we can finally make sense of it, it is hard to ignore the pure amount of time dedicated to little more than the creation of a complex aesthetic motif; it works not in service of plot advancement (in fact, it mostly tends to undermine the forward progression of action, as a sort of McGuffin), but instead its primary function is the fleshing out of the stylistic palette and aesthetic experimentalism of the show.

Another such case is the seventh episode of Season 3 of *House of Cards*, which arrests the show's otherwise cutthroat suspense and inserts a sense of quiet and pause. In this episode, the audience is mesmerized by repeated sequences in which we observe a group of Tibetan monks constructing a mandala in the White House. At four different points in the episode, the progression of the story is interrupted and we are brought back time and time again to a series of long, slow sequences in which we watch the monks at work. There is a barely veiled symbolic function to these sequences that mirror the contemplative transition of the show's protagonists, but this works in a fascinating way: it seems to be a substitute for the typical Hollywood montage-of-transition sequence. Unlike the famous *Rocky IV*-style montage sequence in which we get a condensed-for-time vision of a character's deep and toilsome transition, here, it is as if the character in question (Claire Underwood) – and the episode itself – has instead gone into state of suspended animation. These mandala sequences *substitute* our gaze – instead of seeing the actual transformation of Claire Underwood (who in this episode decides to use her marriage for her own political gain), we see only the figuration of a transformation. As if waiting for a butterfly to emerge from its cocoon, we know that something is happening but we do not see *what* happens inside; instead, we simply are made to feel the passage of time until it happens.

We could compare this with the six-minute-long take of a fight sequence in *True Detective*, so striking that the *Guardian* wrote an entire article on this shot the day after the episode aired, calling it the "most incredible TV moment for years" (Fukunaga). In Season 1, episode four, we're given pure action, presented as a meticulously choreographed fight sequence showing a police raid. But despite this indisputable action sequence, little actually *happens* to necessitate a six-minute passage of real time: the succession of micro-actions depicted do not seem to matter in detail. Instead, the lack of cutting forces us to feel the pure duration, immediacy, and disorientation of the raid. The fight sequence itself is little more than a ruse to give the spectator the sensation of implication in the passage of time.

This aestheticization of time has important effects beyond the narrative construction of these shows, namely, in terms of spectatorship. Because of the already expanded economy of time that television series enjoy due to their already serial nature, they simply *have the time* to experiment with time. This, in turn, requires a significant investment of time on the part of the spectator. Through new platforms for watching these shows, the spectator is more in control than ever before of the organization of this time, and this has become a determining facet of the spectatorship experience. The cinematic-televisual offers an *experience* that, in some ways, we ourselves curate and dictate. Within an increasingly intermedial landscape in which we can engage with these series in various ways and on a variety of platforms, the immersive experience and engagement with content in new (and serial) ways are expanding: through new spectatorship practices such as binge-watching, through the creation of communities and fandoms organized around them; through direct access to various online off-shoots, such as discussion forums or innovative marketing campaigns; through types of merchandizing that were once reserved for the cinema and perhaps video games; through media adaptations (from television to cinema or other forms; from cinema and other forms to television; the creation of related games or video games, etc.); and through the increasingly more flexible and customizable relationship that we have to the content that we consume. The cinematic-televisual has aestheticized time as an internal mechanism of narrative but also as an experiential relationship to spectatorship and reception.

As with any reflection on a medium that occurs in its prime, perhaps some of the discursive and methodological difficulties that we encounter in classifying contemporary television series will resolve themselves in retrospect as subsequent forms begin to emerge in their wake. Nonetheless, even despite our current discursive limitations, it is clear that this intermedial mode of television is doing important work (re)shaping not only television but also a wider web of media at large. The high profile accorded to these series, in both academic and popular realms, furthermore contributes to our theoretical and philosophical conversations about issues such as medium specificity, theories of spectatorship, and questions of media, mediality, and intermediality for the contemporary moment. Even if we cannot (and perhaps even need not) create a clean taxonomy with which we can precisely categorize what this mode of television *is*, we are nonetheless beginning to see what it *does*: like other experimental forms, if nothing else, we can affirm the cinematic-televisual to be, at the very least, a reflexive critical enterprise in of itself.

Notes

1 Thompson argues that the 1970s and the 1980s could each be considered a "Second Golden Age" in his 1997 *Television's Second Golden Age*.
2 This is true namely in *revue* culture and journalistic writings on contemporary media, in circles of cinephilia, which, though often outside of academia, organize important conversations on contemporary media online or in popular publications, in the area of Fan Studies, or in works aimed primarily at film and television "buffs" who play an important role in the reception of and debate surrounding the works in question.
3 He says:

> To prove this failure at definition is so simple that it requires a simple sentence for all nine of these theorists [...] These theorists clearly imply that animation is an exception—a special kind of cinema. To which implication, one can simply reply, a special kind of *what*?

4 For a detailed discussion of this, see Aaron Smuts's article, "Cinematic," in *The Nordic Journal of Aesthetics*, 46, 2013. 78–95.
5 https://benjamins.com/catalog/pbns.211
6 https://www.dukeupress.edu/breaking-bad-and-cinematic-television
7 For an in-depth discussion of these critiques, as well as how we might get past them, see also Maras, Steven, and David Sutton. "Medium Specificity Revisited". *Convergence: The International Journal of Research into New Media Technologies* 6.2, June 2000. 98–113.
8 For a detailed description of this, see also: "Pink Teddy Bear". *Breaking Bad Wiki*, 07.10.2016, http://breakingbad.wikia.com/wiki/Pink_Teddy_Bear. Accessed 02.03.2020.

Works cited

Angelini, Sergio. "The Golden Age of Television". *Sight and Sound* 20.4, April 2010. 90.

Baughman, James L. "*See It Now* and Television's Golden Age, 1951–58", *The Journal of Popular Culture* 15.2.1981. 106–115.

Bazin, André. *What Is Cinema?* Berkeley: University of California Press, 2005.

Becker, Anne. "GM Charlie Collier Raises AMC's Profile." *Broadcasting & Cable*, 01.19.2008. http://web.archive.org/web/20130419060943/broadcastingcable.com/article/99734-GM_Charlie_Collier_Raises_AMC_s_Profile.php (accessed 06.24.2020).

Behrens, Steve. "Technological Convergence: Toward a United State of Media". *Channels of Communication*, Field Guide, 1986. 8–10.

Brennan, Matt. "The Golden Age of Television Is Officially Over". *Paste Magazine*, 05.31.2018. www.pastemagazine.com/articles/2018/05/the-golden-age-of-television-is-officially-over.html (accessed 01.15.2020).

Brodesser-Akner, Claude. "*Mad Men* Gives Wide Berth to Madison Avenue". *Advertising Age*, 10.08.2001. https://adage.com/article/special-report-mad-men/mad-men-wide-berth-madison-ave/120987 (accessed 06.20.2020)

Brunsdon, Charlotte. "Is Television Studies History?" *Cinema Journal* 47.3, 2008. 127–137.

Bunch, Sonny. "Overload: Will Any Shows from the Golden Age of TV Endure?" *The Weekly Standard*, 03.16.2018. www.weeklystandard.com/sonny-bunch/overload-will-any-shows-from-the-golden-age-of-tv-endure   (accessed 01.15.2020).

Caldwell, John Thornton. *Televisuality: Style, Crisis, and Authority in American Television*. New Brunswick, NJ: Rutgers, 1995.

Carr, David. "Barely Keeping Up in TV's New Golden Age". *The New York Times,* 03.09.2014. www.nytimes.com/2014/03/10/business/media/fenced-in-by-televisions-excess-of-excellence.html (accessed 01.15.2020).

Carroll, Noël. *Theorizing the Moving Image*. Cambridge, MA: Cambridge University Press, 1996.

Caughie, John. "Before the Golden Age: Early Television Drama". In John Corner (ed.), *Popular Television in Britain: Studies in Cultural History*, London: BFI, 1991. 22–41.

Cowan, Lee. "Welcome to TV's Second 'Golden Age'". *CBSnews.com*, 10.01.2013. www.cbsnews.com/news/welcome-to-tvs-second-golden-age/   (accessed 01.15.2020).

Creeber, Glen, and Matt Hills. "Editorial—TVIII". *New Review of Film and Television Studies* 5.1, 2007. 1–4.

The Criterion Collection. *The Golden Age of Television*, 2009. www.criterion.com/films/3560-the-golden-age-of-television (accessed 02.01.2020).

Dasgupta, Sudeep. "Policing the People: Television Studies and the Problem of 'Quality'". *NECSUS European Journal of Media Studies*. 1.1, Spring 2012. 35–53.

Deming, Caren J. "Locating the Televisual in Golden Age Television". In Janet Wasko (ed.), *A Companion to Television*, Oxford: Blackwell Publishing, 2005. 126–141.

Dunne, Peter. "Inside American Television Drama: Quality Is Not What Is Produced, But What it Produces". In Janet McCabe and Kim Akass (eds.), *Quality TV: Contemporary American Television and Beyond*, London: IB Tauris, 2007. 98–110.

Edgerton, Gary R, ed. *Mad Men: Dream Come True TV*. London: I.B. Tauris, 2011.

Edgerton, Gary R. *The Sopranos*. Detroit, MI: Wayne State University Press, 2013.

Edgerton, Gary R. "A *Mad Men* Potpourri". *CST Online,* 03.17.2016. cstonline.net/a-mad-men-potpourri-by-gary-edgerton/ (accessed 01.15.2020).

Epstein, Adam. "'*Game of Thrones*' Is the Most Cinematic TV Show Ever Made". *Quartz*, 06.21.2014a. qz.com/712430/game-of-thrones-is-the-most-cinematic-tv-show-ever-made (accessed 01.15.2020).

Epstein, Adam. "The Directors Who Make Television Cinematic". *The Atlantic*, 08.22.2014b. www.theatlantic.com/entertainment/archive/2014/08/not-just-a-writers-medium/378990/ (accessed 01.15.2020).

Everitt, David. *King of the Half Hour: Nat Hiken and the Golden Age of TV Comedy*. Syracuse, NY: Syracuse University Press, 2001.

Fukunaga, Cary. "How We Got the Shot: Cary Fukunaga on *True Detective*'s Tracking Shot". *The Guardian*, 03.17.2014. www.theguardian.com/tv-and-radio/tvandradioblog/2014/mar/17/true-detective-cary-fukunaga-tracking-shot (accessed 01.15.2020).

Geiger, Jeffrey, and Karin Littau, eds. *Cinematicity in Media History*. Edinburgh: Edinburgh University Press, 2015.

"Golden Age of Television". *Wikipedia.* en.wikipedia.org/wiki/Golden_Age_ of_Television and en.wikipedia.org/wiki/Golden_Age_of_Television_(2000s-present) (accessed 01.15.2020).

Hawes, William. *Live Television Drama, 1946–1951.* Jefferson, NC: McFarland & Co., 2001.

Hawes, William. *The American Television Drama: The Experimental Years.* Jefferson, NC: McFarland & Co., 2002.

Jacobs, Jason. "Issues of Judgement and Value in Television Studies". *International Journal of Cultural Studies* 4.4, December 2001. 427–447.

Jacobs, Jason, and Steven Peacock, eds. *Television Aesthetics and Style.* New York: Bloomsbury, 2013.

Jaramillo, Deborah L. "Rescuing Television from 'The Cinematic': The Perils of Dismissing Television Style". In Jason Jacobs and Steven Peacock (eds.), *Television Aesthetics and Style*, New York: Bloomsbury, 2013. 67–76.

Jenner, Mareike. "Is This TVIV? on Netflix, TVIII, and Binge-Watching". *New Media & Society* 18.2, July 2014. 257–273.

Johnson, Catherine. "Negotiating Value and Quality in Television Historiography". In Helen Wheatley (ed.), *Re-viewing Television History: Critical Issues in Television Historiography*, London: I.B. Tauris & Co., 2007. 55–66.

Kellison, Catherine. *Producing for TV and Video: A Real-world Approach.* Amsterdam; Boston: Elsevier, 2006.

Kerbel, M. "The Golden Age of TV Drama". *Film Comment* 15.4, July–August 1979. 12–19.

Krampner, Jon. *The Man in the Shadows: Fred Coe and the Golden Age of Television.* New Brunswick, NJ: Rutgers, 1997.

Lawson, Mark. "Are We Really in a 'Second Golden Age for Television'?" *The Guardian*, 05.23.2013. www.theguardian.com/tv-and-radio/tvandradioblog/2013/may/23/second-golden-age-television-soderbergh (accessed 01.15.2020).

Leopold, Todd. "The New, New TV Golden Age". *CNN Entertainment*, 05.06.2013. edition.cnn.com/2013/05/06/showbiz/golden-age-of-tv/index.html (accessed 01.15.2020).

Logan, Elliott. "'Quality Television' as a Critical Obstacle: Explanation and Aesthetics in Television Studies". *Screen* 57.2, June 2016. 144–162.

Maras, Steven, and David Sutton. "Medium Specificity Re-visited". *Convergence: The International Journal of Research into New Media Technologies* 6.2, June 2000. 98–113.

Mast, Gerald. "What Isn't Cinema?" *Critical Inquiry* 1.2, December 1974. 373–393.

Marshall, Rick. *The Golden Age of Television.* Twickenham: Hamlyn, 1987.

McCabe, Janet, and Kim Akass, eds. *Quality TV: Contemporary American Television and Beyond.* London: I.B. Tauris & Co, 2007.

Mills, Brett, "What Does It Mean to Call Television Cinematic?" In Jason Jacobs and Steven Peacock (eds), *Television Aesthetics and Style*, New York: Bloomsbury, 2013. 57–66.

Mittell, Jason. "Narrative Complexity in Contemporary American Television". *The Velvet Light Trap* 58, Fall 2006. 29–40.

Mittell, Jason. *Television and American Culture.* Oxford: Oxford University Press, 2009.

Mittell, Jason. *Complex TV: the Poetics of Contemporary Television Storytelling.* NYU Press, 2015.

Newcomb, Horace, Cary O'Dell, and Noelle Watson, eds. *Encyclopedia of Television*. Chicago, IL: Fitzroy Dearborn Publishers, 1997.

Newman, Michael Z., and Elana Levine, eds. *Legitimating Television: Media Convergence and Cultural Status*. New York: Routledge, 2012.

Patterson, John, and Gareth McLean. "Move Over, Hollywood". *The Guardian*, 05.20.2006. www.theguardian.com/film/2006/may/20/features.weekend (accessed 01.15.2020).

Piazza, Roberta, Monika Bednarek, and Fabio Rossi, eds. *Telecinematic Discourse: Approaches to the Language of Films and Television Series*. Philadelphia, PA: John Benjamins Publishing, 2011.

"Pink Teddy Bear". *Breaking Bad Wiki*. 07.10.2016. breakingbad.wikia.com/wiki/Pink_Teddy_Bear (accessed 01.15.2020).

Press, Andrea. "Gender and Family in Television's Golden Age and Beyond". *The Annals of the American Academy of Political and Social Science* 625.1, September 2009. 139–150.

Reeves, Jimmie L., Mark C. Rogers, and Michael M. Epstein. "Rewriting Popularity: The Cult *Files*". In D. Lavery, A. Hague, and M. Cartwright (eds.), *Deny All Knowledge: Reading the X Files*, London: Faber& Faber, 1996. 22–35.

Reeves, Jimmie L., Mark C. Rogers, and Michael M. Epstein. "*The Sopranos* as HBO Brand Equity: The Art of Commerce in the Age of Digital Representation". In D. Lavery (ed.), *This Thing of Ours: Investigating The Sopranos*, New York: Columbia University Press, 2002. 42–59.

Reeves, Jimmie L., Mark C. Rogers, and Michael M. Epstein. "Quality Control: The Daily Show, The Peabody, and Brand Discipline". In Janet McCabe and Kim Akass (eds.), *Quality TV: Contemporary American Television and* Beyond, London: IB Tauris, 2007. 79–97.

Restivo, Angelo. *Breaking Bad and Cinematic Television*. Durham, NC: Duke University Press, 2019.

Ritchie, Michael. *Please Stand By: A Prehistory of Television*. Woodstock, NY: The Overlook Press, 1995.

Ryan, Maureen. "Will Nostalgia Overkill Smother the Golden Age of Television?" *Variety* 330, 01.26.2016. 28.

Sachs, Ben. "Can Television Be 'Cinematic'?" *Chicago Reader*, 11.04.2013. www.chicagoreader.com/Bleader/archives/2013/11/04/can-television-be-cinematic (accessed on 01.25.2020).

Schefer, Jean-Louis. *L'Homme ordinaire du cinéma*. Cahiers du cinéma/Gallimard, 1980.

Seitz, Matt Zoller, and Chris Wade. "What Does 'Cinematic TV' Really Mean?" *Vulture*, 10.21.2015. www.vulture.com/2015/10/cinematic-tv-what-does-it-really-mean.html (accessed 01.28.2020).

Slide, Anthony, ed. *The Television Industry: A Historical Dictionary*. New York: Greenwood Press, 1991.

Smith, Gerry. "Golden Age of TV Shows Signs of Cracks as Some Channels Give Up". *Bloomberg*, 05.24.2017. www.bloomberg.com/news/articles/2017-05-24/golden-age-of-tv-shows-signs-of-cracks-as-some-channels-give-up (accessed 02.01.2020).

Smuts, Aaron. "Cinematic". *The Nordic Journal of Aesthetics* 46, 2013. 78–95.

Spigel, Lynn. "From the Dark Ages to the Golden Age: Women's Memories and TV Reruns". *Screen* 36.1, April 1995. 16.

Spigel, Lynn, and Jan Olsson. *Television after TV: Essays on a Medium in Transition*. Durham, NC: Duke University Press, 2004.

Stephens, Mitchell. "The History of Television". *Grolier Multimedia Encyclopedia*, 2000. www.nyu.edu/classes/stephens/History%20of%20Television%20page.htm (accessed 02.01.2020).

Stokes, Jane. *On-screen Rivals: Cinema and Television in the United States and Britain*. New York: St. Martin's Press, 2000.

Sturcken, Frank. *Live Television: The Golden Age of 1946–1958 in New York*. Jefferson, NC: McFarland & Co., 1990.

Suskind, Alex. "It's the Golden Age of TV. And Writers Are Reaping the Rewards and Paying the Toll". *The New York Times*, 08.18.2017. www.nytimes.com/2017/08/18/arts/television/its-the-golden-age-of-tv-and-writers-are-paying-the-toll.html (accessed 01.21.2020).

Thompson, Derek. "It's the Golden Age of TV—But Why, Exactly?" *The Atlantic*, 03.19.2013. www.theatlantic.com/business/archive/2013/03/its-the-golden-age-of-tv-but-why-exactly/274165/ (accessed 02.03.2020).

Thompson, Kristin. *Storytelling in Film and Television*. Cambridge, MA: Harvard University Press, 2003.

Thompson, Robert J. *Television's Second Golden Age: From Hill Street Blues to ER*. Syracuse, NY: Syracuse University Press, 1997.

Thorpe, Vanessa. "Cinematic TV Dramas Spark a Revolution in Online Viewing". *The Guardian*, 10.23.2011. www.theguardian.com/media/2011/oct/23/cinematic-tv-dramas-online-viewing (accessed 01.25.2020).

Titoria, Anmol. "The 20 Most Cinematic Television Episodes of All Time". *Taste of Cinema*, 06.16.2018, www.tasteofcinema.com/2018/the-20-most-cinematic-television-episodes-of-all-time/ (accessed 01.27.2020).

Van Der Werff, Todd. "The Golden Age of TV Is Dead; Long Live the Golden Age of TV". *The AV Club*, 09.20.2013. tv.avclub.com/the-golden-age-of-tv-is-dead-long-live-the-golden-age-1798240704 (accessed 02.01.2020).

Vorel, Jim. "The 90 Best TV Shows of the 1990s". *Paste Magazine*, 09.25.2014. www.pastemagazine.com/blogs/lists/2014/08/the-90-best-tv-shows-of-the-1990s.html (accessed 01.27.2020).

Wagner, Jon Nelson, and Tracy Biga Maclean. *Television at the Movies: Cinematic and Critical Responses to American Broadcasting*. New York: Continuum, 2008.

Wheatley, Helen, ed. *Re-viewing Television History: Critical Issues in Television Historiography*. London: I.B. Tauris & Co., 2007.

Wilk, Max. *The Golden Age of Television: Notes from the Survivors*. New York: Dell, 1977.

Films, series, and episodes cited

American Horror Story. FW, 2011–.

Breaking Bad. AMC, 2008–2013.

"Fly". *Breaking Bad*, S03E10. AMC, 03.23.2010.

Buffy the Vampire Slayer. The WB, 1997–2001, UPN, 2001–2003.

Game of Thrones. HBO, 2011–2019.

House of Cards. Netflix, 2013–2018.

"Chapter 33". *House of Cards*, S03E07. Netflix, 02.27.2015.

Mad Men. AMC, 2007–2015.
Pierrot le Fou. Jean-Luc Godard, SNC, 1965.
The Public Enemy. William Wellman, Warner Bros., 1931.
Rocky IV. Sylvester Stallone, MGM/UA, 1985.
The Singing Detective. BBC1, 1986.
The Sopranos. HBO, 1999–2007.
True Detective. HBO, 2014-.
Twin Peaks. ABC, 1990–1991.
 "Who Goes There". *True Detective*, S01E04. HBO, 02.09.2014.
The Wire. HBO, 2002–2008.

Part II
Marketing seriality

2.1 A forgotten episode in the history of Hollywood cinema, television, and seriality

The case of the Mirisch Company

Paul Kerr

The Mirisch Company provides, one might even say it helped build, a bridge between classical studio era Hollywood – which ended in about 1960 – and the birth of the so-called New Hollywood, often identified with the Movie Brats – who emerged approximately a decade later. As such, it is a kind of transitional company, producing films that are hybrids between the generic output associated with classical Hollywood and the blockbuster franchises that have been seen as characteristic of much post-1970s American cinema. And one of the many ways in which their work, and the way in which they worked, epitomizes such a transition is their role in the development of series and sequels. As a company making both films and TV series and as executives who worked in the industry before and after the Paramount Decision put an end to vertical integration, the Mirisches saw the financial benefits and risk reductions inherent in a business strategy that included an impetus to repetition.

As Stuart Henderson points out, "the boundaries of any definition between the sequel, the series, the serial and the saga will always be highly porous" (Henderson 2014, 5). Having been a producer[1] in British television before becoming a scholar, I know that first and foremost, in British TV, a series is a program scheduled over a period of weeks (or days, or at other regular intervals), usually in the same slot, with the same subject and star(s), the same characters and situation if it is a sitcom or a drama. Each episode is, conventionally, a self-contained, complete narrative. A serial, on the other hand, carries its storylines as well as its dramatis personae and situation over from one episode to the next. One crucial distinction between a sequel and a series film, meanwhile, seems to be that the latter, while featuring recurring characters, almost never acknowledges the events of previous films in the series. I will return to the question of memory at the end of this chapter. Of course, the boundaries between these forms remain porous, but the essential distinctions remain useful.

In the film industry, as *Variety*'s usage confirms, the terms are equally blurred. For instance, in 1959, *Variety* reported that the Mirisch Company was one of four production companies developing "60-minute film stanzas for the 1960–1961 TV season" for NBC (*Variety* 2.9.59: 33). A stanza, in *Variety*'s lexicon, is a series episode. Two years later, *Variety* reported that the Mirisch Company was developing another series, with another partner, this time for the cinema. Under the headline, "Shepherd's Mirisch Series" it noted that producer Richard Shepherd "has set a deal with Mirisches for series of pix, first of which will be *Seven Men At Daybreak*" (*Variety* 2.8.61: 3).

Industry usage of the term "series" at the time often referred to a contracted number of otherwise unrelated projects rather than a cycle of similar ones. In the absence of the Mirisch Company papers (unavailable until the death of the surviving brother, Walter), this chapter relies heavily on *Variety*'s reports on Mirisch activities.

The regularity with which the terms "serial," "series," "sequel," "spin-off" and "franchise" are sometimes assumed to be virtually interchangeable certainly makes it difficult to speak with any precision. For the purposes of this chapter I will use the words "series" and "serial" as above, while a sequel is an irregular and perhaps singular further episode about a character or characters without a continuing storyline (and indeed often without coherent causal or chronological continuities with its predecessor and progenitor). Sequels seem to me, by definition, to be generated one at a time, as individual one-offs, while serials and franchises are preplanned to contain multiple episodes. Following Henderson, I use the term "spin-off" to refer strictly to films, TV programs, and other audiovisual material featuring what were secondary characters from the initial episode. I acknowledge that these definitions are themselves relative but hope that they provide some fire-proofing against confusion and conflation. Henderson suggests that "the defining characteristic of the sequel is its acknowledgment of a chronological narrative relationship with a prior instalment [...]. The dividing line between the sequel and the series film is this: while both forms revisit characters from an earlier episode, the latter can be identified primarily by its general lack of commitment to maintaining narrative continuity from one installment to the next" (Henderson 2014, 3–4). He also distinguishes usefully between sequels that were what he calls "preconceived" and those which were "ad hoc" (Henderson 2014, 4).

Recent scholarship on the history of Hollywood series, serials, and sequels (e.g., by Henderson, Jess-Cooke, and Jess-Cooke and Verevis) suggests a critical consensus that they were a commonplace of the early silent period, that in the sound era they were largely, though not exclusively, relegated to second feature status, and that they only re-emerged into respectability (even, occasionally, increasing, rather than decreasing, box office receipts for subsequent episodes) in the era of the Movie Brats with *Jaws*, *The Godfather*, and *Star Wars* in the mid-1970s. It is the contention of this chapter, on the other hand, that sequels and series (and some aspects of seriality) were reintroduced into mainstream Hollywood cinema in the 1960s by the new independent production companies created in the wake of the Paramount Decision, one of which was the Mirisch Company. I also argue that the Mirisch Company and its successors contributed disproportionately to the production of such films.

In 1957 the majors released 268 movies, 58% of which were produced by independent production companies. One such independent, the Mirisch Company, was formed by three brothers in August 1957, with a distribution deal and finance from United Artists (UA), and over the next 18 years the company and its offshoots became both the most critically respected (an unprecedented three Best Picture Academy Awards in eight years) and one of the most commercially successful independents in Hollywood. *The Apartment* won Best Picture, Best Director and Best Original Screenplay Oscar in 1960. *West Side Story* won Best Picture and Best Director in 1961 and was the second highest grossing film of the year. In 1963 *Irma La Douce* was the fifth highest grossing film of the year. In 1966 *Hawaii* was the top grossing film of the year and *The Russians Are Coming. The Russians Are Coming* was nominated for Best Picture that year. In 1967 *In the Heat of the Night* won Best Picture and Best Adapted Screenplay Oscars. In 1971 *Fiddler on the Roof* was the highest grossing film in the United States. The company also produced *Some Like It Hot, The Magnificent Seven, The Great Escape, The Pink Panther, The Thomas Crown Affair,* and many more.[2]

Among the films produced by the Mirisch Company and its corporate successors (the Mirisch Corporation, Mirisch Productions, Mirisch Films, and Mirisch Pictures) for UA between 1957 and the end of their corporate relationship in 1974, several spawned sequels or series. Mirisch titles with returning characters include *The Magnificent Seven* quartet – *The Magnificent Seven* (1960), *The Return of the Seven* (1966), *Guns of the Magnificent Seven* (1969), and *The Magnificent Seven Ride* (1972); *The Pink Panther* (1963) and two sequels, *A Shot in the Dark* (1964) and *Inspector Clouseau* (1968) as well as *The Pink Panther Show* (TV 1969); *In The Heat of the Night* (1967) and its two follow-up films *They Call Me MISTER Tibbs* (1970) and *The Organization* (1971); and *Hawaii* (1966) and its semi-sequel (both films were adapted from different sections of the same novel) *The Hawaiians* (1970).

There were fewer than 130 Hollywood sequels and series films between 1955 and 1974 (Henderson 2014, 55). The Mirisch Company and its successor corporations produced 12 such films in this period – almost 10% of Hollywood's output in the categories over those years. Considering how many majors and independents were then producing features, the proportion of such films made by the Mirisch brothers is striking. More specifically, Hollywood produced 70 sequels and series films between 1965 and 1974. Mirisch companies between them were responsible for nine of these, so over 12.8% of Hollywood's sequels and series films in that ten-year period were Mirisch productions. A total of 62 sequels and series films were among the hundreds of films made in Hollywood during the 1960s. Of those 62, six were produced by Mirisch companies. Given that the major studios and numerous independent production companies were then making features, this too is impressive at almost 10% of the total. Sequels were clearly a crucial part of the Mirisch production strategy throughout this period, initiated soon after the company came into existence and only abandoned shortly before the end of their output deal with UA in 1974.

For all their obvious success as a sequel factory, however, the Mirisches are rarely given the credit they deserve. Indeed, production companies are rarely considered "authors" in film or TV studies, as one look at the conventions for academic citations reveals – directors and distribution companies are named for films, networks for TV programs. The name Mirisch is conspicuously absent from academic citation lists for their films. This has consequences on assumptions about corporate authorship. Thus Henderson himself writes that "United Artists was also behind two other series in this period producing multiple follow-ups to *The Pink Panther* (1964) and *The Magnificent Seven* (1960)" (Henderson 2014, 70). Actually, of course, it was Mirisch, rather than UA, which produced them – UA financed and distributed them. Equally inaccurately, he notes that "*The Magnificent Seven* inspired two sequels" (Henderson 2014, 187). In fact there were three.

Industrial determinants

What explanatory frameworks have been provided for the re-emergence of "cinematic seriality" in post–studio era Hollywood? Three overlapping industrial imperatives – horizontal integration, television series production, and the package-unit system – can be mentioned here, and the Mirisch Company and its corporate successors were pioneering in each of these spheres. Firstly, in the form of media conglomeration and convergence; secondly, the advent of production not only for film but also for TV and, crucially, of TV as a destination for film (as well as other media spin-offs, including soundtrack albums, novelizations, and so on) and including industrial synergies across and between media; and thirdly, the package-unit system of production, by which the film, rather than the firm, became the organizing principle of the movie business. Perhaps paradoxically, it was the very atomization of the industry that, in the case of independents like the Mirisch Company, propelled them toward the idea of film series and sequels. Furthermore these imperatives proved mutually reinforcing.

For Kristin Thompson, film franchises "came about largely because the Hollywood studios were in the process of being bought up by large corporations and then by multinational conglomerates. The process began in 1962, when MCA (Music Corporation of America) bought Universal" (Thompson 2008, 4). The Mirisch Company was wholly owned by the three brothers from its founding in 1957 to 1963, when it was acquired by UA.[3] The brothers responded by setting up several new production companies for each new contractual period, including Mirisch Films, Mirisch Productions, and the

Mirisch Corporation. Nevertheless, the Mirisch brothers did acquire some personal stakes both in exhibition (*Variety* 13.6.62: 3) and in distribution, through stock in UA, which they received in exchange for their back catalogue (*Variety* 20.2.63: 3) and, when UA was taken over by Transamerica, in Transamerica itself (*Variety* 29.5.68: 3).

When, in 1967, UA was bought by the Transamerica Corporation, a multimedia conglomerate, sequels and spin-offs may, as Thompson suggests, have been one possible method for increasing revenue from film properties beyond their original theatrical box office takings:

> [T]he film industry had gone through a crisis in the late 1960s and was trying new strategies to regain its audience. Capitalizing on the success of certain titles would be one such strategy. Another reason might be that the old Hollywood production firms were in the process of being bought up by big conglomerates during that decade, and new business practices may have dictated an "efficient" use of narrative material. (Thompson 2008, 98–100)

Such synergies across the now horizontally, rather than vertically, integrated industry might begin to explain this shift as the new multimedia conglomerates emerged. The Mirisch Company was never part of such a conglomerate, but its relationship to UA – and UA's to Transamerica (from 1967) – may well have influenced them. Nevertheless, the impetus toward sequels and series was clearly with the company from the start.

Another indirect imperative on sequel production was "the insatiable demand of network television for feature films. As the number of movie nights increased and as rental prices skyrocketed, Hollywood became complacent. The thinking became that if a picture didn't make it in the theatrical market, it would break even or earn a profit from the network television sale" (Balio 1990, 260). And sequels or film series were attractive acquisitions as they provided a more efficient solution to scheduling holes than individual films.[4] By the mid-1950s, television production had shifted from being largely live and New York–based to being largely Hollywood-based and made on film (Mann 2007, 93–94). Subsequently – and not surprisingly – syndication rights for TV series reruns became extremely valuable economically for the Hollywood studios but also hugely influential aesthetically. Ageing film stars and filmmakers could be conveniently redeployed to television, while new talent could be "screen-tested" on the small screen.

In 1965, under the headline, "Sequel Trend May Bring Return To 'Series Films' of 1940 Vogue," *Variety* reported that "United Artists seems to be staging a one-company campaign to revive the concept of the 'series film,' so popular in the 1930s and 1940s with such then-continuing characters as 'The Hardy Family,' 'Tarzan,' 'Charlie Chan,' etc. Although the series concept has since become the backbone of TV programming, UA has presently got the makings of several in the works" (*Variety* 24.2.65: 7). The article went on to identify the Bond series and the second Beatles film before discussing the three nascent franchises then being produced by the Mirisch Company. If series were proving the "backbone" of network TV, they could also provide a risk avoidance strategy for feature film independents, wrestling with the insecurities of the one-offness inherent in the package unit system. Even Wilder's *The Private Life of Sherlock Holmes* prompted similar trade press conjecture: "could this be the start of a new 'Bond' series for UA?" (*Variety* 22.12.69: 2).

The Mirisch Company was quick to recognize TV both as a marketing medium for its films (*The Magnificent Seven* received a $260,000 TV and radio campaign of five thousand 10- to 60-second spot advertisements, prior to its initial release – *Daily Variety* 30.9.60: 24) and as a possible final destination for them. The Mirisch Company had a perspective on films that foregrounded their potential as "episodes" because the company producing them was also simultaneously producing TV series. And because of its comparatively small size, the Mirisch Company was producing series episodes and films from within the same building, and deploying many of the same personnel across those productions.[5] Christopher George, one of the stars of the Mirisch-Rich TV series *Rat Patrol*, played the lead in the company's *The One Thousand Plane Raid* (1969). When it signed deals with bi-media stars like Janet Leigh or Robert Fuller, it was able to offer both big and small screen possibilities.

In 1963 the Mirisches had produced *The Great Escape*, which proved hugely successful and the opportunity to make further war films, or even a "cycle" of "British" Second World War movies was extremely attractive. Mirisch employed John C. Champion to develop just such a cycle of such films. As *Variety* reported it, "writer-producer John C. Champion's entire six-pix program with Mirisch-United Artists will be devoted to that war, and firm start dates and some key assignments already have been made on his first two" (*Variety* 12.4.67: 4). But not only did they produce a "six-pix" British war movie cycle, mostly released as double bills, but one of them was even described as a sequel. Their first war film made primarily for the British market, *633 Squadron* (1964), provided not only the blueprint for the subsequent *Mosquito Squadron* but also footage for many of its aerial and air raid sequences. According to *Variety*, "Next on producer Lew Rachmil's B slate for Mirisch-UA will be 'Mosquito Squadron', to be filmed in England. Boris Sagal will direct pic, sequel to '633 Squadron' " (*Daily Variety*, March 26.3.68: 1). In fact, the former film is not a sequel, sharing neither characters nor squadron with the latter production. But it was clearly inspired by the latter film; indeed the entire cycle of Mirisch Second World War films shared narrative similarities and, in several cases, stock footage.

Cinematic sequels

This new industrial strategy saw films as, among other things, potential pilots – not unlike television pilots – of cinema series. More specifically, certain films could be seen as performing the function that pilots performed in television – as blueprints for characters, situations, and story arcs – that could be reprised by sequels. And, reversing that process, a film could also be deployed as the source material for a television pilot and, ideally, a TV series spin-off of its own. What Mann refers to as synergies between film and television thus include not only the possibility of spinning off films from TV series and TV series from films but also of interchanging the narrative grammars of those respective media, so that a film package could lead to cinematic sequels in just the same way that a small screen pilot could spawn a TV series. The simultaneous production of films and TV programs at the Mirisch Company, and an inevitable awareness that the small screen was an increasingly important destination for feature films, must also have had an impact on the impetus for properties with potential for series.

During the so-called studio era, the majors had both on screen and behind the camera talent on long-term contracts, even renting them out on occasion to their rivals. Stars, screenwriters, directors, and so on were seen as studio assets, the properties of the big five vertically integrated film businesses. In the post-studio world of independent production companies, talent was freelance but the films themselves became crucial properties – each company building up its own back catalogue (vitally valuable for sale to syndication on the new medium of television). The Mirisch brothers, with their previous experience on Poverty Row, had already learned how to operate at much lower budgets than many of their rivals. Their years at Monogram and subsequently Allied Artists accustomed them not only to tight budgets and schedules but also to cinematic series production, through the *Bomba* series of films that Walter had initiated and overseen. In 1955 Harold Mirisch's perspective on series films was already clear. "While 'big' pictures are being stressed under AA's production policy, Mirisch said that the company's 'series' pictures such as The Bowery Boys would be continued for 'unquestionably there's a definite distributor desire and need for these films'" (*Variety* 13.7.55: 4). Furthermore, AA's corporate parent, Monogram, had been one of the first companies to sell its features to TV, in 1951, several years before the majors began making deals with the networks.

Before becoming a producer, Walter Mirisch had attended Harvard Business School – one of the first, if not the first, Hollywood producer to do so. At Harvard he learned "accounting and finance and merchandising and marketing and economics" (Mirisch 2008, 20–21). In 1943, Mirisch received an Industrial Administrator qualification from Harvard, and this paved the way for his subsequent career as a producer. His first job, though, was at the Lockheed Aircraft Corporation where he was "assigned to a project involving the simplification of assembly-line procedures" (Mirisch 2008, 20–21). He went on to take the idea of maximizing output on minimum outlay, rationalizing assembly line processes, minimizing staff, and outsourcing facilities into the film industry, first at Monogram/Allied Artists and later at the Mirisch brothers' own company.

At Monogram, Mirisch was asked: "How do we make this place work better? Do we have too many guards at the gate? Can we operate the editorial department differently? Should we move it off the lot? … We were constantly attempting to determine whether we were operating in the most cost-effective way possible." Mirisch applied the scientific management skills he had learned at Harvard to film production and, subsequently, at Mirisch. A decade before co-founding the Mirisch Company, Walter Mirisch went from being a salaried staffer at Monogram to a freelance producer, paid a fee for each production. "I soon realized that I could quickly starve to death while waiting for subsequent films to be approved. Now I understood the value of the series pictures to their producers. They provided a minimum subsistence income to producers who were trying to survive in a most unstable profession" (Mirisch 2008, 27). Nevertheless, Hollywood in the late 1940s was far more stable than it was in the early 1960s, and the Mirisch Company quickly learned to benefit from the "minimum subsistence income" which series production – for TV and the cinema – could generate.

Henderson also notes the impact of independent production itself on serialization. He cites Janet Staiger's work on the package-unit system of production by which long-term contracts were replaced by one-off, film-by-film contracts. The end of the mass production of films by the majors, each of which had had their own distribution arms and cinema chains, resulted in the package unit system of production (Bordwell et al. 1985, 330). This was based on the idea that an independent production company organized each film project, from finance to hiring cast and crew as well as equipment, facilities, locations, and studios. "The major differences between this system of production and the prior one, the producer-unit system, were the transitory nature of the combination and the disappearance of the self-contained studio" (Bordwell et al. 1985, 330). This institutionalization of short-termism seems to have helped seed a desire for securing the future, which in turn favored sequels (Henderson 2014, 46). The Mirisch Company was one of the independent production companies to emerge in the wake of the 1948 Paramount Decision and the divorcement of what had been the vertically integrated production and distribution arms of the film industry.

Staiger describes "the industrial shift away from mass production and toward film-by-film financing and planning" (Bordwell et al. 1985, 332). If an impetus toward film-by-film rather than firm-by-firm production was characteristic of the independent package producers, including Mirisch, then one way of resisting this intrinsic "one-off-ness" was to think in terms of series of films – whether cycles, star vehicles, or sequels. In such cases, while each individual film might require a unique contract with cast and crew, it would also be replicable for future films in the cycle, future vehicles with the same star, and future sequels that were the equivalent of filmic episodes in a cinematic series. Another characteristic of the package-unit system Staiger notes is profit-sharing, whereby major stars received a per-centage of the profits in addition to their fee (Bordwell et al. 1985, 334). One perhaps unforeseen side effect of the "star-replacement strategy" op-erated by the Mirisches is exemplified by the casting changes in the three *Magnificent Seven* sequels and the replacement of Sellers with Arkin as the titular *Inspector Clouseau,* which neatly side-stepped such profit-sharing, whether or not this was a conscious strategy of replacing a recalcitrant or reluctant star.

Sequels were a way of squeezing cinematic assets dry – by recycling not only characters, but also plots, and even occasionally dialogue. Thus the title of *They Call Me MISTER Tibbs* is actually a line of dialogue from *In the Heat of the Night* and was used as such in the trailer. Poitier's contract also paved the way for further films in the series. "In the deal we had made with Sidney (Poitier) for *In the Heat of the Night,* he agreed to give us an option for two more pictures if we chose to make Virgil Tibbs movies" (Mirisch 2008, 293). Furthermore, as *Variety* reported, well before the first film was made, "Mirisch also has acquired TV rights to the Tibbs character for potential use in a tv series" (*Variety* 16.6.65: 18).

The original *Magnificent Seven* was released in November 1960. It was re-released in 1961 and again, on double bills, in 1962. Meanwhile, in 1961, Mirisch had proposed a 90-minute TV Movie and a subsequent series to NBC, Sam Peckinpah was to be the executive producer, and Sturges agreed to direct five episodes. UA refused to sign up to the deal, however, and instead *The Magnificent Seven* set a record for the fastest post-theatrical feature film to appear on TV when it premiered on Sunday February 3, 1963, and was a huge small screen hit. In January 1964 a first cinematic sequel, *Return of the Seven,* was announced. Eventually, three sequels were made – *Return of the Seven* (1966), *Guns of the Magnificent Seven* (1969), and *The Magnificent Seven Ride* (1972).

In 1970 the Hollywood trade press reported "Upcoming triple feature – *The Magnificent Seven* and its sequels *Return of the etc* and *Guns of-* by the Mirii, being readied for UA theatre package billing, despite the fact that two 'Sevens' will have been seen on TV by release time" (*Daily Variety* 17.11.70: 2) Two years later, *Variety* noted that the fourth film about *The Magnificent Seven, The Magnificent Seven Ride,* was to be shot in South-ern California while the first had been filmed in Mexico and the other two in Spain (*Variety* 23.2.72: 3). Walter Mirisch revealed that the final film's budget of "around $1000,000" (ibid.) on a short, 30-day, schedule was less than that of any of the three previous pictures and that the film required fewer horses and riders than its predecessors too. If the first film had exem-plified "runaway production" characteristic of cost-cutting indies, *Variety* wondered whether *The Magnificent Seven Ride* was "the vanguard of a ride into a 'runback' era" (*Variety* 23.2.72: 3). Three years later, in 1975, Walter Mirisch signed a deal with Universal TV and CBS-TV for an hour-long pilot for *The Magnificent Seven.* In fact the long awaited *Magnificent*

Seven TV series did not appear until 1998 and ran on CBS until 2000. It is credited to Trilogy Entertainment, MGM Television, and The Mirisch Corporation. Walter Mirisch even got an Executive Producer credit on the recent remake of the film, but there was no corporate Mirisch credit.

Diminishing returns?

Both aesthetically and financially, a law of diminishing returns tends to operate on sequels, including the Mirisch's, but the company proved adept at averting major losses by reducing the budgets and maximizing the long tail of their series films. That all three proved iconic enough to eventually spin off successful TV series – only the first of which was produced by Mirisch – is one thing. That two of the three film series were largely filmed outside America and found a huge audience beyond the US box office is even more striking. According to *Variety*, by 1975 the four *"Seven"* films had generated world rentals theatrically of about $25,000,000 and, strikingly, "foreign rentals always outran domestic performance" (*Variety* 24.12.75: 1). *The Magnificent Seven* itself is reported as having taken about $2,400,000 in the United States and Canada and "a whopping $11,300,000 in the foreign market" (ibid.). *Return of the Seven* in 1966 cost $1.78 million to produce. The film took about $1.6 million profit of $3.2 million gross domestically and another $3.4 million internationally and came in 70th in the annual rankings by box office takings (Hannan 2015, 218). In 1967 Mirisch announced *Quest of the Magnificent Seven*, which was finally produced two years later, on a budget of 1.36 million, and released as *Guns of the Magnificent Seven*. It took $1.5 million in rentals in the United States but an additional $2.5 million abroad (Hannan 2015, 218–219 – *Variety* reports foreign rentals as $2,200,000). *The Magnificent Seven Ride* had earned only $700,00 domestically and international box office figures were unavailable at the time of *Variety*'s report.

These sequels succeeded in re-promoting the original, which was regularly re-released and re-exhibited on double and treble bills with the new entries.[6] Accounts show that *The Magnificent Seven* generated US rentals of 2.25 million and overseas rentals of 6.27 million amounting to an overall profit of 321,600 on first release. Of the three *Seven* sequels only *Return of the Seven* made a slight domestic profit, just $37,000 on its initial release. *Guns of the Magnificent Seven* lost $605,000 and *The Magnificent Seven Ride* $21,000. However, network television and subsequent syndication netted *Return of the Seven* an extra $2.23 million, *Guns of the Magnificent Seven* $1.16 million, and *The Magnificent Seven Ride* $1.05 million. According to Hannan, taking theatrical release and television sales together, the first sequel was sitting on a profit of $588,000, the second $595,000, and the third $236,000. (Hannan 2015, 228). Domestic profits were transformed by TV sales, just as the international theatrical market increasingly rivaled and sometimes outweighed domestic takings.

"The average price of a theatrical movie rose from $100,000 for two net-work runs in 1961 to around $800,000 by the end of 1967" (Litman 316 in Kindem 1982). *Hawaii* cost over $14 million but only grossed $19 million, while *In the Heat of the Night* cost $2 million and initially grossed $16 million (Balio 1987, 181 and 187).

Of course, not all box office hits lent themselves to sequelization – "because the conclusion of the original largely precluded future continuation, as with the tragedies *West Side Story* (1961) and *Doctor Zhivago* (1965)" (Henderson 2014, 62). Similarly the protagonists of *The Great Escape* are almost all dead at the end. (According to *Variety*, "The rough cut of the World War II Film [...] runs five and a half hours, and this will eventually be sliced to 240 minutes" – *Variety*, 31.10.62: 24 – and, thus might conceivably have been released as a two-parter.) This is also, of course, true of *The Magnificent Seven* but did not prevent Mirisch from recruiting replacements for the fallen gunmen after each of the films in the series. There are, after all, only three survivors of the original seven in the first film and only one of the original actors opted to reprise his role. Indeed, the mortality of a high proportion of each seven facilitated, rather than frustrated, the production of sequels, as it allowed new, cheaper contracts with talent than might have been possible with veterans of previous outings. Thus the disposability of the actors in the series, rather than their irreplaceability in new offerings, was one characteristic of the *Seven* films. Other blockbuster projects with a previous existence in the theatre or, indeed, real life, like *Fiddler on the Roof* or *Cast a Giant Shadow*, respectively, did not lend themselves to sequels, but clearly the Mirisches were quick to detect and exploit opportunities where they existed (Henderson 2014, 62).

There was a recession in Hollywood in 1969 and in response "the majors learned to offset the risks of production by adopting defensive production and marketing tactics. During the seventies, the majors themselves increasingly relied on sequels and series. Sequels solved a major promotion problem for the studios – how to make known to an audience what a film is about" (Balio 1990, 261). By the end of the first twenty-picture deal with UA, only five Mirisch productions had earned a profit – including *The Magnificent Seven* (Balio 1987, 177). Among the second twenty, *The Pink Panther* seemed such a surefire hit that the Mirisches had a sequel in the works before the original was released, but that sequel, a repurposed stage play transformed into an episode in the Clouseau series, lost money (Balio 1987, 184). The last, 28-film deal included more sequels. "Exploiting the blackpix trend and the Academy Award honors won by *In the Heat of the Night*, the Mirisches had produced two sequels starring Sidney Poitier ... At best, the two pictures just about broke even" (Balio 1987, 192). Of the final 14 films owed to UA, all lost money except for *Fiddler on the Roof* and *The Magnificent Seven* sequels (Balio 1987, 194).

While *The Magnificent Seven* had been the first Mirisch production to eventually spawn a sequel, the first Mirisch sequel was actually *A Shot in the Dark* – the follow-up to *The Pink Panther*. The script of the original initially centered on the jewel thief, played by David Niven, but according to Walter Mirisch, "the Clouseau character really took over and it became the centre of the film" (Mirisch, quoted in Balio 1987, 176). By 1964 the average weekly cinema attendance in the United States was half that of what it had been in 1957 and, consequently, companies that had seen their box office figures falling seized on anything that might maximize their revenues (Maltby 2003: 570). One such strategy was, of course, revisiting past successes and *The Pink Panther* was swiftly followed by a sequel as Blake Edwards and William Peter Blatty repurposed a screenplay they were already working on, based on a Leland Hayward stage production, to incorporate the Clouseau character, played again by Peter Sellers. According to Henderson's definition, *A Shot in the Dark* is a spin-off rather than a sequel, as "the spin-off tends to follow characters which were either previously subsidiary or parts of an ensemble" (Henderson 2014, 5). (The film fails to fully meet Henderson's criteria, however, as it is not a follow-up in another medium.) *The Pink Panther* took its title from the name given to the jewel that the Niven character was attempting to steal. In the sequel, Sellers's detective character took center stage, but the pink panther remained in the audience's memory. There followed a four-year gap before *Inspector Clouseau* (1968) re-appeared, this time starring Alan Arkin as the bumbling detective. *Life* magazine, in 1966, wrote of this second sequel, that "*Inspector Clouseau* is, in its little way, a historic film, proving not only that the title character is now so well established that his name alone can lure us into the theatre, but that his spirit can survive delightfully unscathed the migration from Peter Sellers, in whom it resided so comfortably in *The Pink Panther* and *A Shot in the Dark*, to Alan Arkin" (cited in Mirisch 2008, 169). By the time of Sellers's return to the role, Mirisch had lost their copyright on the character, which had reverted to UA.

Although contract staff numbers had fallen dramatically, sequels reduced not only the risk but also the pre-production budgets and schedules necessary for hiring freelance crews, finding locations, casting, hiring costumes, and so on. The theme music of *The Magnificent Seven* finally won an Oscar nomination – second time around. The imperative to minimize risk (with a propensity toward pre-sold properties – literary, theatrical but primarily cinematic) encouraged a reliance on remakes, sequels, series, and spin-offs. Thus not only is *The Magnificent Seven* a remake of *Seven Samurai* but it spawned three cinematic sequels and, eventually, a TV series. Similarly *The Pink Panther* functioned as a live action film and an animated TV series but also inaugurated a series. The first sequel, *A Shot in the Dark* (an adaptation of a play initially acquired as a vehicle for Marilyn Monroe), actually began life as an entirely distinct property from the *Pink Panther* series, before it was adopted and adapted for the Clouseau character. As *Variety* reported, "Mirisch Corp. prexy Harold Mirisch said the company is 'determined to do a third picture to continue the Inspector Jacques Clouseau series.' " Mirisch, noting the enormous success of the James Bond character series, said this has "inspired us to pursue the idea of our own series," also revealing the imminent production of *Return of the 7*, a sequel to its earlier successful *The Magnificent Seven* (*Variety* 24.2.65: 7). Mirisch pointed out that "*A Shot in the Dark* reversed the usual ratio of sequel grosses by taking more at the domestic box office than the original film" (*Variety* Jan 20 1965: 4 and 20). Clearly, the Mirisches calculated the predicted grosses of sequels and cycles extremely carefully.

The Mirisch Company had been founded on September 1, 1957, and in 1958 the William Morris Agency submitted the manuscript of James Michener's novel *Hawaii* prior to publication, to a number of possible purchasers, including the Mirisch Company with Fred Zinnemann attached to direct an adaptation (Mirisch 2008, 134). "Fred became convinced that the script had to be done as two films [...]. He wanted to shoot both films continuously [...]. In a sense it would have been a theatrical miniseries" (Mirisch 2008, 218–219). This was 40 years before the first *Matrix* film and more than 50 before the first of *The Lord of the Rings* trilogy! But the era of the TV mini-series was much closer and the bi-media approach of the Mirisches seems to have eclipsed their rivals. Mirisch acquired the movie rights to the book before publication, for "$600,000 against 10% of the gross after break-even" (Balio 1987, 181). According to *Variety*, this set an industry record. Once the 1000-page novel was published by Random House, it was on the bestseller lists for over a year – and was read by an estimated 100 million people, making it one of the most widely read novels of the period (Balio 1987, 181). Zinnemann and screenwriter Daniel Taradash (who had collaborated with the director on *From Here to Eternity*) started work on a screenplay in 1960 but after a year, still struggling with the structure of the novel and its huge chronology (from colonization to independence) and ensemble cast of characters, Taradash was replaced by Dalton Trumbo. Two years later still, the pair proposed a four-hour feature to be shown in two parts. When UA vetoed this idea, Zinnemann left the project and was replaced by George Roy Hill, who had just directed *Toys in the Attic* for Mirisch.

The Mirisch Company resolved to focus the (first) film on the first half of the book, which dramatizes the period between 1820 and 1841. Shot on location not only in Hawaii itself but also in Tahiti, Norway, and New England, the film was budgeted at $10 million but cost another $4 million. It grossed almost $19 million, however, the highest box office for any of the films in the Mirisch Company's second twenty-picture deal with UA (Balio 1987, 181). But the second half of the novel remained to be exploited. "I had always felt that if *Hawaii* was successful, we should make a follow-up film utilizing the excised material" (Mirisch 2008, 291). The subsequent film, *The Hawaiians*, starring Charlton Heston, picked up the story from the second half of Michener's book, with the development of the islands in the 20th century. *Variety* variously referred to it as "the Mirisch *freres'* sequel, 'The Hawaiians' " (4.11.68: 2) and "sequel to the earlier *Hawaii*" (21.5.69: 28) but also as "not strictly a sequel to company's 1966 *Hawaii*" (*Variety* 4.10.68:19). This belated follow-up was finally released in 1970 but had little of the first film's success at the box office or with the critics. At a Christmas 1969 party in Hollywood, Charlton Heston was reportedly "[t]alking the third *Hawaii* pic" (*Daily Variety* 22.12.69: 2), but this joke only reaffirms the role sequels played in the Mirisch strategy.

Television series

While the company was developing *Hawaii*, it was already in production on the first of its TV series. Having been founded on September 1st 1957, by January 1958 the Mirisch Company was already announcing TV projects. As *Variety* reported, "Yul Brynner and Walter Mirisch, in inking multi-motion picture deals with UA, stated they would also join UA in TV projects. It's considered likely that both Brynner and Mirisch will do episodes for UA TV's projected anthology series, tentatively titled *UA Playhouse*" (*Daily Variety* 1.1.58: 23). But anthology series, by definition, have neither returning characters nor reusable sets – the economies of scale of conventional series production. By early the following year, the Mirisch Company had signed two new production deals, this time with NBC, for a series, *Wichita Town*, and another western, though this time only a pilot, *The Iron Horseman* (*Daily Variety* 11.3.59: 32). Indeed, as well as the feature films for which it is most remembered, the Mirisch Company also (co-) produced a number of TV series: *Wichita Town* (NBC 1959–60), *Peter Loves Mary* (NBC 1960–61), *Hey Landlord* (NBC 1966–67), *Rat Patrol* (ABC 1966–68), and *The Pink Panther Show* (NBC 1969).

Thus the first Mirisch "series" was not for the cinema but for the small screen – *Wichita Town* – though, significantly, this too was a kind of cinematic spin-off. Walter Mirisch had produced the B Western, *Wichita* (1955) about Wyatt Earp and Bat Masterson, for Allied Artists starring Joel McCrea as Earp. In 1959 the Mirisch Company produced *The Gunfight at Dodge City* in which McCrea played Masterson. The series, *Wichita Town*, starred McCrea and his son Jody. Though the names of the characters they played were fictional, they were loosely based on Masterson and Earp. (Jody's character's name was even "Ben Masters," allowing for a hint at the actual historical figures they couldn't name, because Hugh O'Brian and Alan Dinehart were already starring in a dramatization of the story of the Earp/Masterson friendship on ABC with *The Life and Legend of Wyatt Earp*.) In 1967 Mirisch produced *Hour of the Gun*, directed by John Sturges, which was a return to the story of Wyatt Earp – after the gunfight at the OK Corral (Sturges had directed a film about the legendary gunfight for Paramount in 1957 – *Gunfight at the OK Corral*). Balio refers to *Hour of the Gun* as "a follow-up" (Balio 1987, 185) rather than a strict sequel for Sturges, since the entire cast, if not the characters they played, was new.

Wichita Town was swiftly followed by the production of a pilot for a series, spun off from the company's first major hit, 1959's *Some Like It Hot*.[7] The unsold pilot episode was produced by the Mirisch Company in 1961 and starred Vic Damone and Tina Louise. Jack Lemmon and Tony Curtis made brief cameo appearances as Daphne and Josephine in a hospital scene at the beginning of the pilot, with Lemmon being treated for an impacted tooth and the pair deciding to have plastic surgery to escape the mob forever. The pilot got close enough to commission as an NBC series for Mirisch to clear copyright in the title for TV (*Variety* 19.4.61: 3). A second TV series, *Peter Loves Mary*, was also produced, in co-production with Four Star. Another western pilot, *The Iron Horsemen*, was also made, but wasn't commissioned as a series. "Wichita Town [...] was dropped after 26 weeks and the Mirisches dropped out of television" (*Daily Variety* 31.3.65: 10).

The year 1965 witnessed the Mirisches' dramatic re-entry into TV. As *Variety* noted, the Mirisch Company, in partnership with Lee Rich, "marked the end of one full year in TV [...] with a record unmatched by any producing company in TV. Three shows, its entire output for the year, sold and on network schedule next fall [...]. His shows for next season are well baited with sponsorship. Proctor & Gamble bought all of 'Hey Landlord', Reynolds Tobacco took half of 'Rat Patrol' and NBC is having no difficulty selling its third sale, 'The Super Bwoing Show', an animated cartoon for Saturday afternoon" (*Variety* 30.3.65: 36). *Rat Patrol* was to prove the most successful of these, though it had been developed as *The Trojan Horse*, an "hour-long adventure series which takes place behind German lines in World War II" (*Daily Variety* 20.5.65: 1).

Despite the lack of success of the *Some Like It Hot* pilot, there continued to be synergies between Mirisch films and TV series. The company's sitcom, *Hey Landlord*, may have only run for a single season but seems to have helped inspire (or been inspired by the source material for) their feature, *The Landlord*, which had the same premise – and premises – a run-down New York brownstone owned by a wealthy young white man. While this was far from unique as a cinematic spin-off, it is indicative of the Mirisch Company's eye for seriality and its ability to market television seriality in/as cinema, as well as seeing one-off feature films as reproducible on both small and big screens. In the summer of 1965, under the headline "TV Rights Along With Feature Deals, Mirisch Thought for Future," *Variety* reported that the Mirisch Company was thinking about series, for both media, in tandem with their new production partner.

"The Mirisch Co. plans to acquire TV rights in addition to theatrical film rights, whenever possible, in acquisition of properties for its production slate for the future. This was revealed by Lee Rich, prexy of Mirisch-Rich Television Productions [...] Rich said he thought most theatrical film properties could be converted into series, and that the Mirisch brothers agreed with him" (*Variety* June 30th 1965: 29). One of these projects became *Rat Patrol* – which, indeed, ended up both as a TV series and, by combining three consecutive episodes, a feature film, released theatrically outside America as *Massacre Harbor* (Variety 17.8.68). The three episodes were originally transmitted as *The Last Harbor Raid* (ABC-TV 19.12.67, 26.12.67, and 2.1.68).

In October 1966 *Variety* reported that they had completed production on the first *Rat Patrol* series. Filming had run from July 5th to October 8th and "the total output came to 14 half-hour segments, a trio of episodes for a three-parter, and a feature film assembled from those three episodes." Indeed, *Variety* was explicit about the synergies between the two media. "*Rat Patrol* will significantly influence television and filmmaking" *Variety* reported, adding that "[t]he program, to begin with, tested and proved that TV series can be made in Spain at a production rhythm comparable to Hollywood [...]. The fact remains that 17 segments and three-parter film called *The Rat Patrol* were produced in three months [...]. Of significance is the close creative span between telefilming and motion picture, once the organization is moving in high gear" (*Variety* 19.10.66: 43). The synergies between TV series production and cinematic sequels (and assemblies) were clearly apparent to the company.

The downside of the discovery of such textual synergies between the two media, however, was the revelation of their contextual differences in terms of finance. The series was deficit financed, which meant that Mirisch-Rich suffered "substantial losses" on it and, once renewed for a second season on ABC, the company had to continue to deficit finance production, as the budget advanced by UA never met its costs (*Variety* 31.6.67: 26). The previous week, Marvin Mirisch, the company's executive vice president, acknowledged that Mirisch was undergoing an "agonizing reappraisal" regarding the viability of a future in TV, while denying exiting the medium altogether. However, Rich, who had spearheaded the company's small screen ventures, left Mirisch-Rich Productions to take up a position as VP at the Leo Burnett Agency (25.5.67: 1). Walter Mirisch claimed that the company wanted to continue in series production but preferred to prioritize one-off specials or three-camera sitcoms, which were cheaper and where there would not be substantial losses. Although their sitcom, *Hey Landlord*, had been axed, there had not been heavy costs involved. "But no profit was racked up, either, and the future of 32 segs in syndication is a question mark" (*Daily Variety* 25.5.67: 10). As for *Rat Patrol*, Mirisch admitted the company had "substantial losses" on the series that had been renewed for another season on ABC, "If the series is on three or four years and eventually gets a good distribution setup, the series may come out okay, he said" (*Variety* 31.5.67: 26).

Animation

When *The Pink Panther* was released in 1963, one of its most celebrated aspects was the title sequence. The producers had commissioned an animated sequence from Fritz Freleng and the result proved so popular that an animated short film, 1964's *The Pink Phink*, was produced. In 1964, a full-page advertisement in *Variety* announced:

> YOU HAVEN'T SEEN THE LAST OF THE PINK PANTHER! That egocentric, rubicund critter who made such a sensational film debut in the main titles of Blake Edwards' *The Pink Panther* returns to the screen as the hero (?) of a new one-reel color cartoon series presented by the Mirisch Organization, Geoffrey Productions and DePatie Freleng Enterprises. (*Variety* 12.8.64)

The following year, another full-page advertisement in *Variety* announced:

> First I was a movie title then I became a movie star now I'm an academy award nominee. *The Pink Phink*, the very first subject in the new Pink Panther color cartoon series. (*Variety* 25.3.65)

The Pink Phink duly won the Academy Award for Animated Short Film. The animated titles were reused in subsequent features. In 1969 *The Pink Panther* made his first appearance on television in his own show. Each 30-minute episode comprised two animated shorts, shown on Saturday mornings for a decade until the series ended in 1979. In 1968 DePatie Freleng were reportedly making a new theatrical cartoon series for Mirisch-UA, *The Ant and the Aardvark*, to be released monthly (*Variety* 8.5.68:10).

Memory

Eventually, three sequels to *The Magnificent Seven* were made – *Return of the Seven* (1966), *Guns of the Magnificent Seven* (1969), and *The Magnificent Seven Ride* (1972) – but Sturges, McQueen, and Wallach (who was invited back to play the uncle of the Calvera character) all turned down the idea of revisiting their roles in the initial production. Brynner alone agreed to take part again – and he signed up for only the first sequel; Robert Fuller was cast as Vin. The role of Chico (played by Horst Buchholz in the original) was taken by Julian Mateos and that of Petra (Rosenda Monteros in the first film) was played by Elisa Montes. George Kennedy replaced Brynner as Chris in the second sequel; the third and final sequel recast the role again, this time with Lee Van Cleef.

Henderson notes that road-show era hits, like *The Magnificent Seven*, often used large ensemble casts. For any sequel to a multiple star film, "Given that the majority of these stars were no longer under long-term contract, reassembling all or even some of them presented a major logistical headache" (Henderson 2014, 62). For *The Magnificent Seven*'s sequels, the death of the majority of the ensemble in each episode facilitated, rather than frustrated, such a reassembly, as new "sevens" were easily recruited.

Meanwhile the gap between episodes perhaps erased or at least blurred the memories of audiences about the identities of the survivors. But advertising was able to refresh viewer memories. The trailer for *Return of the Seven* begins with the words, "They rode into screen history with *The Magnificent Seven*. Now they ride on to greater adventure in *Return of the Magnificent Seven*."

In the first sequel, *Return of The Seven*, Chico is wounded trying to defend his village against (another) bandit attack. His wife Petra goes in search of Chris and finds him at a bullfight where, fortuitously, he has just bumped into Vin. Chris and Vin team up and recruit another five men. Of this seven, the eventual survivors are Chris, Vin, Chico, and Colby (Warren Oates). *Guns of The Magnificent Seven* followed with another Mexican, Max, seeking Chris out to help rescue an imprisoned rebel leader. "All I know is he's a friend and his name is Chris." When Chris saves the life of a horse thief about to be hung, a gunman shouts, "I know you Chris. A lot of people know you. Mostly sheriffs!" So Chris is by now famous, even infamous, but on the wrong side of the law. When Max approaches them after a shootout in town, he says, "Hello Chris. You were magnificent. Both of you." Not only is Chris famous, therefore, he is also already "magnificent." Chris decides to accept the challenge. "I need help. More men. Six men. Not enough to cause suspicion. Just enough to do the job." Max replies, "My cousin says seven is a lucky number for you." Audiences are always already aware of the film's place in a series in which magnificent seven gunmen will triumph, against the odds. Of the assembled seven only Chris, Max, and another gunman, Levy, survive the final gunfight.

In *The Magnificent Seven Ride*, Chris is a newly married Marshall. When approached by an old friend, Jim, to help yet another Mexican village, he says, "I've crossed that border three times to fight bandits. I ain't going down there again." During the three previous films Chris has indeed already crossed that river three times (in both directions). However, when Jim reminds him of their exploits together ("Remember that first time? Seven of us got 350 dollars. Fifty bucks apiece"), we recall that there was no Jim in the first Seven adventure – or indeed any other – or any previous mention of another Mexican skirmish in the series. Furthermore, if such an escapade with Jim had taken place, then Chris would already have crossed that border four times. When Chris initially refuses his request for help, Jim prompts, "Maybe some of the others?" But none of the names Chris mentions refer to anyone we have previously encountered in the series. These sequels seem to suffer from a filmic false memory syndrome – a kind of "cinemamnesia."

By this time, the collective memory of the series has become so blurred that there is virtually no reliable shared narrative of the seven left to exploit – or repeat. In future, such series would be far more rigorously and rigidly enforced, with a combination of blockbuster budgets and auteur authority (most successfully in *The Godfather* trilogy and the *Star Wars* franchise). Trilogies like *The Matrix* or *Lord of the Rings* as well as the *Star Wars* films have been beneficiaries of a pre-production plan incorporating multiple episodes. This doesn't ever seem to have been the case with any of the Mirisch sequels. Each film was a one-off, exploiting a familiar title or character or situation, but never as part of a self-conscious strategy, within which several spin-offs had been simultaneously conceived. Instead, the *Panther*, *Seven*, and *Tibbs* sequels were all spawned individually. Poitier had an option for sequels films in his contract, but neither the writers nor the directors nor even fellow cast members were reunited in them. This was part of what was to change as franchises subsequently became more imbricated in the economic logic of production.

In Mirisch sequels, characters (and actors) change inexplicably from one film to the next. Ironically, in the unsold pilot to *Some Like It Hot*, Mirisch had prematurely played with this idea, by using the plot device of plastic surgery to transform the leads from Jack Lemmon and Tony Curtis into Vic Damone and Tina Louise.[8] In the company's subsequent cinematic sequels, on the other hand, in which one actor is casually replaced with another, no such deus ex machina is summoned to post-rationalize the changed cast or character. *The Magnificent Seven*'s Chris was played by Yul Brynner, George Kennedy, and Lee Van Cleef. Chico is played by Horst Bucholz in *The Magnificent Seven* but by another actor in *Return of the Seven*. Vin, McQueen in the original, is played by Robert Fuller in *Return*. Colby is one of the three survivors in *Return*, but in *Guns of the Magnificent Seven* that name is given to a villain, played by an entirely different actor – though no mention is made of Chris's former comrade with the same surname. Similarly, the Clouseau character was married in *The Pink Panther* but is living in a bachelor apartment in the sequel, *A Shot in the Dark*, with no mention of his marital status. At the end of *The Pink Panther*, Clouseau was sentenced to jail, but in *A Shot in the Dark* that jail sentence seems to have been forgotten.

In the Heat of the Night was released in 1967 and by the following year Sidney Poitier was, albeit briefly, America's top box office star, and the film made ripples for its depiction of racism and for Tibbs's refusal to turn the other cheek in the face of racial violence. By comparison, however, *They Call Me MISTER Tibbs* (1970) and *The Organization* must have seemed anachronistic in their essentially color-blind focus and framing narratives. But these sequels aren't merely bleached in comparison with their predecessor and progenitor; they are virtually brainwiped. The discontinuities identified above in the *Seven* and *Pink Panther* films become biographical in the Tibbs trilogy. *In the Heat of the Night* (1967) tells us that its protagonist, police detective Virgil Tibbs (Sidney Poitier), works for the Philadelphia force and that he is unmarried. In the sequel *They Call Me MISTER Tibbs!*, however, Tibbs is working for the San Francisco force ("We've got 12 good years invested in you," notes his police chief boss) and is married with two children, one of whom, his son Andy, appears close to adolescence (Henderson 2014, 4).

Writing about more recent films, the late Mark Fisher notes that "it is not surprising that memory disorders should have become the focus of cultural anxiety" (Fisher 2009, 58) and cites *Memento*, *Eternal Sunshine of the Spotless Mind*, and the *Bourne* films. "Bereft of personal history, Bourne lacks *narrative* memory, but retains what we might call *formal* memory: a memory – of techniques, practices, actions – that is literally embodied in a series of physical reflexes and tics" (Fisher 2009, 58). This sheds unexpected light on the Mirisch sequels – which seem to suffer from a similar amnesia. Fisher sees this as symptomatic of a postmodern, post-Fordist culture – "a culture that is excessively nostalgic, given over to retrospection, incapable of generating any authentic novelty" (Fisher 2009, 59). This is both true and untrue of the Mirisch films – it is not (just) their fictional characters but their actual makers – indeed, the films themselves, which seem oblivious or ignorant of prior outings in their respective series. The Mirisch moment was on the crest of post-Fordism in Hollywood, as vertical integration was being replaced by horizontal integration and studio staff positions were being transformed into freelance ones. And while a film culture – and audience – content with sequels may or may not be "excessively nostalgic," what is pertinent is Fisher's phrase about "a memory – of techniques, practices, actions – that is literally embodied in a series of physical reflexes and tics." Thus, in *The Magnificent Seven*, the seven heroes are identified almost exclusively in terms of their techniques and tics – their professional specialisms. The six men Chris recruits in each of the sequels also all have their particular, individuating prowess and specific skillset. The series re-echoes, each time rather more faintly, the initial assembly of the heavily outnumbered team, the journey, a first skirmish with, preparation for, and then final battle with the antagonists.

Another commentator has noted that since the mid-1970s the reception of American films can be characterized by a "disrupted and interrupted viewing that, to put it simply, remembers moments and images but not motivations" (Corrigan 1991: 169). And this in turn has impacted, he argues, on the textures of the films themselves. Perhaps the detectable decline in causality and increasing reliance on narrative recycling, exemplified by Mirisch productions from the mid-1960s on, is an early symptom of this condition. Alternatively, this textual tic may be no more than a characteristic of the television series with its episodic amnesia, by which each new adventure erases the past, being absorbed by the features which were often produced, as with Mirisch, by the same companies, on the same sound stages and increasingly by the same personnel. If the series is the gift that keeps on giving, then part of that productivity seems to have necessitated forgetting the previous production.

Henderson notes that from the mid-1950s to the mid-1970s "the role of the Hollywood sequel was in flux [...] neither what it had been in the years of vertical integration, nor what it would go on to become in the late 1970s, as horizontal integration became a fact of Hollywood life" (Henderson 2014, 56). This perhaps explains the less than assembly-line smoothness with which sequels, specifically those produced by the Mirisch brothers, whose deal with UA precisely corresponds with this period, were characterized. Their sequels were, in general, afterthoughts, rather than preconceived series. Nevertheless, the Mirisch companies were experimenting with serial, series, and sequel forms throughout the 1960s and into the 1970s in that transitional period before the Movie Brats. It was among those companies that re-invented the sequel, well over a decade before *Jaws, The Godfather*, and *Star Wars* made them famous as a long tail strategy for the studios in the 1970s. And it showed the way in which film franchises and cinematic series (or sequels) could provide synergies between film and television, with productions like *The Pink Panther* and *The Magnificent Seven* (and *In the Heat of the Night*, which spawned a successful TV series of its own, but only after the rights to the original had reverted to UA) – not to mention *Wichita Town, Rat Patrol*, and even an unlikely pilot for a *Some Like It Hot* series. The Mirisch companies helped pioneer the monetization of their films as potential prequels or pilots for series (both in the cinema, as sequels and on television as spin-off series). They were thus among the first of the post–Paramount Decision independents to see the long tail, bi-media potential of sequels.

As an independent set up in 1957, the Mirisch Company came into existence less than two years after the first deals were done between the major Hollywood studios and TV networks in 1955. This in turn meant that Mirisch was structured to be able to produce both feature films and television series from the outset. It did not have to adapt or transform itself in order to turn from one audiovisual medium to another or one form of storytelling to another. It was always already prepared to produce for both media either single films or series "episodes." Furthermore, the capacity to produce TV series meant that the Mirisch Company and its successors had in their DNA, or institutional infrastructure, the ability to produce episodic narratives on an assembly line. This may have begun as a capacity to make episodic television, with recurring characters and situations, but cannot but have raised the possibility of applying the same "repetition with difference" framework to cinematic storytelling. The industrial infrastructure for full-fledged film franchises may only have arrived in the 1970s and 1980s, and perhaps needed the authorial imprimatur and box office impetus provided by major filmmakers like Coppola, Lucas, and Spielberg to gather momentum – and respectability. However it was in the late 1950s and 1960s that the seeds for that new Hollywood were sown and a new imperative toward synergy emerged from the ashes of the studio era, ushering in new forms of serial and series production for the big screen. The Mirisches were on the crest of that wave.

Notes

1 Before becoming an academic I spent 20 years as a producer making arts and history programs for the BBC and Channel 4 in the UK, working on one-off documentaries, series, and three-parters (documentary series that are effectively actually "serials").
2 For more information about the Mirisch Company, see Balio (1987), Mirisch (2008), and Kerr (2010).
3 UA had an output deal with the Mirisch companies from 1957 to 1974 and financed them to the extent of paying their overheads and core staff salaries. But UA had no ownership in any of the firms while they were producing entities, only acquiring them as libraries at the end of each contractual period.
4 This continues to be the case. In 2000 I was commissioned to produce a documentary for Channel 4 in the UK about *The Magnificent Seven* to complement a screening of the film and its sequels. Subsequently the documentary was included as part of a DVD Box Set alongside all four films.
5 Walter Mirisch describes appointing the editor Richard Heermance to run the TV operation for him. Heermance had edited Mirisch's *Man in the Net* and had been supervising editor on their films *Fort Massacre*, *Man of the West*, *Gunfight at Dodge City*, and *Cast a Long Shadow*, and went on to supervise production on their series *Peter Loves Mary* and *Wichita Town* and *The Iron Horseman* pilot and thus provided continuity and corporate identity for their output across both media.
6 *Guns for Hire: The Making of The Magnificent Seven* was transmitted on Channel 4 on 13.5.00 as part of a Magnificent Seven season. Such groups of productions with shared copyright ownership continue to circulate on new media platforms, proof of the long tail the Mirisch Company somehow sensed.
7 I produced and directed a BBC2 documentary about the making of the film, entitled *Nobody's Perfect* and transmitted on 04.16.01. I interviewed surviving cast and crew members, including Walter Mirisch himself.
8 Plastic surgery is also a key dramatic device in another Mirisch production, *Return from the Ashes*.

Works cited

Balio, Tino. *United Artists: The Company That Changed the Film Industry*. Madison: University of Wisconsin Press, 1987.
Balio, Tino, ed. *Hollywood in the Age of Television*. New York: Routledge, 1990.
Bordwell, David, Janet Staiger and Kristin Thompson. *The Classical Hollywood Cinema: Film Style and Mode of Production to 1960*. New York: Routledge, 1985.
Fisher, Mark. *Capitalist Realism – Is There No Alternative*. Hants: Zero Books, 2009.
Hannan, Brian. *The Making of The Magnificent Seven: Behind the Scenes of the Pivotal Western*. Jefferson, NC: McFarland and Co, 2015.
Henderson, Stuart. *The Hollywood Sequel: History & Form, 1911–2010*. London: Palgrave Macmillan, 2014.
Jess-Cooke, Caroline. *Film Sequels*. Edinburgh: Edinburgh University Press, 2009.
Jess-Cooke, Caroline and Verevis. *Second Takes: Critical Approaches to the Film Sequel*. Albany: State University of New York Press. 2010.
Kerr, Paul. "A Small, Effective Organization: The Mirisch Company, the Package-unit System and the Production of 'Some Like It Hot'". In Karen McNally (ed.),

Billy Wilder, Movie-maker: Critical Essays on the Films, Jefferson, NC: McFarland & Co, 2010. 117–131.

Maltby, Richard. Hollywood Cinema (2nd Edition). Malden; Oxford: Blackwell Publishing, 2003.

Mann, Denise. *Hollywood Independents: The Postwar Talent Takeover.* Minneapolis, MN: University of Minnesota Press, 2008.

Mirisch, Walter. *I Thought We Were Making Movies, Not History.* Madison: Wisconsin University Press, 2008.

Thompson, Kristin. *The Frodo Franchise: The Lord of the Rings and Modern Hollywood* Berkeley: University of California Press, 2008.

Films and series cited

Ant and the Aardvark, The. NBC, 1969.
The Apartment. Billy Wilder, UA, 1960.
Bomba the Jungle Boy. Ford Beebe, Monogram Pictures, 1949.
Bowery Boys, The. George Nichols, Keystone Film Company, 1914.
Cast a Giant Shadow. Melville Shavelson, UA, 1966.
Doctor Zhivago. David Lean, MGM, 1965.
Eternal Sunshine of the Spotless Mind. Michel Gondry, Universal, 2004.
Fiddler on the Roof. Norman Jewison, UA, 1971.
From Here to Eternity. Fred Zinnemann, Columbia, 1953.
The Godfather. Francis Ford Coppola, Paramount, 1972.
The Great Escape. John Sturges, UA, 1963.
The Gunfight at Dodge City. Joseph M Newman, UA, 1958.
Gunfight at the OK Corral. John Sturges, Paramount, 1957.
Guns for Hire: The Making of the Magnificent Seven. Channel Four, 13.5.00.
Guns of the Magnificent Seven. Paul Wendkos, 1969, UA.
Hawaii. George Roy Hill, UA, 1966.
The Hawaiians. Tom Gries, UA, 1970.
Hey Landlord. NBC, 11.9.66–14.5.67.
Hour of the Gun. John Sturges, UA, 1967.
In the Heat of the Night. Norman Jewison, UA, 1967.
Inspector Clouseau. Bud Yorkin, UA, 1968.
Irma La Douce. Billy Wilder, UA, 1963.
The Iron Horseman. NBC, TV Pilot, 1959.
Jaws. Steven Spielberg, Universal, 1975.
The Landlord. Hal Ashby, UA, 1971.
The Life and Legend of Wyatt Earp. ABC, 1955–1961.
The Lord of the Rings: The Fellowship of the Ring. Peter Jackson, New Line Cinema, 2001.
The Magnificent Seven. John Sturges, UA, 1960.
The Magnificent Seven. CBS, 1998–2000.
The Magnificent Seven Ride. George McCowan, UA, 1972.
Massacre Harbor. John Peyser, UA, 1968.
The Matrix. The Wachowskis, Warner Bros, 1999.
Memento. Christopher Nolan, Newmarket, 2000.
Nobody's Perfect. BBC2, 16.4.01.
The Organization. Don Medford, UA, 1971.

Peter Loves Mary. NBC, 12.10.60-31.5.61.
The Pink Panther. Blake Edwards, UA, 1963.
The Pink Panther Show. NBC, 1969.
The Pink Phink. Fritz Freleng and Hawley Pratt, UA, 1964.
Rat Patrol. ABC, 1966–68.
The Return of the Seven. Burt Kennedy, UA, 1966.
The Russians Are Coming, The Russians Are Coming. Norman Jewison, UA, 1966.
Seven Samurai. Akira Kurosawa, Toho Company, 1954.
A Shot in the Dark. Blake Edwards, UA, 1964.
Some Like It Hot. Billy Wilder, UA, 1959.
Some Like it Hot. NBC, un-transmitted TV pilot, 1961.
Star Wars. George Lucas, TCF, 1977.
The Super Six. NBC, 1966–1969.
They Call Me MISTER Tibbs. James. R. Webb, UA, 1970.
The Thomas Crown Affair. Norman Jewison, UA, 1968.
Toys in the Attic. George Roy Hill, UA, 1963.
West Side Story. Robert Wise and Jerome Robbins, UA, 1961.
Wichita. Jacques Tourneur, AA, 1955.
Wichita Town. NBC, 30.9.1959-6.4.60.

Chronology of Mirisch cinematic sequels (films inaugurating series are in bold)
The Magnificent Seven. John Sturges, UA, 1960.
Some Like It Hot. NBC, un-transmitted TV pilot, 1961.
The Pink Panther. Blake Edwards, UA, 1963.
A Shot in the Dark. Blake Edwards, UA, 1964
The Return of the Seven. Burt Kennedy, UA, 1966.
Hawaii. George Roy Hill, UA, 1966.
Rat Patrol. ABC, "The Last Harbor Raid", 19.12.66, 26.12.66 and 2.1.67. The three-parter was then re-edited and released as a feature film entitled *Massacre Harbor* in 1968.
In the Heat of the Night. Norman Jewison, UA, 1967.
Inspector Clouseau. Bud Yorkin, UA, 1968.
Guns of the Magnificent Seven. Paul Wendkos, 1969, UA.
They Call Me MISTER Tibbs. James. R. Webb, UA, 1970.
The Hawaiians. Tom Gries, UA, 1970.
The Organization. Don Medford, UA, 1971.
The Magnificent Seven Ride. George McCowan, UA, 1972.

2.2 Diversions in the *Hunger Games* film series

The fragmented narrative of hijacked images

Chloé Monasterolo

The Hunger Games is a series of four films adapted from Suzanne Collins's book trilogy for young adults. It tells the story of young Katniss who becomes a "tribute" in yearly heavily mediated gladiator-like games. As the story progresses, Katniss's role within the country's political dynamics evolves as the games she is drafted in mutate into civil war. The "games" reveal themselves to be a mirror of the country's inner turmoil and internal politics, transposed into a deadly diversion that enables the totalitarian government of Panem to keep the masses either entertained or subjugated in fear. The games' disturbance by Katniss's subversive actions leads to repercussions on the whole nation as the televised warfare bleeds into a full-blown revolution, but when it does, it continues to assume the same patterns and structure as the games, maintaining the media conflicts at the heart of the narrative. Seriality in the narrative structure of the *Hunger Games* films is thus apparent in its repeated pattern of using diverting and diverted propaganda images and mediating warfare. At stake in *The Hunger Games* are the many uses of images as diversions to manipulate and channel its viewers to various ends.

In what follows, I mean to exploit more than one of the meanings of the term "diversion," which denotes either an entertaining activity or, as the online *Longman Dictionary* defines it, "a change in the direction or use of something, or the act of changing it," or finally "something that stops you from paying attention to what you are doing or what is happening" ("Diversion," Longman). I will expand on the use and manipulation of images in the *Hunger Games* films and transmedia marketing both in and outside the diegesis. Indeed, the Lionsgate franchise and transmedia marketing present a number of paradoxes, among which we find the deployment of blockbuster films and exploitative marketing instalments to relay a narrative critical of a society of spectacle and image consumerism. I will therefore deal with the film adaptations and the expansion of the storyworld[1] through the transmedia marketing deployed by Lionsgate. Marketing is not always accepted as an element of transmedia storytelling.[2] However, I will posit that, in the case of a story like *The Hunger Games* that sustains a social critique on the commodification of individuals by the mass media, and considering the ambiguous nature of the marketing employed, the marketing instalments need to be viewed as expansion of the storyworld. This will lead me to build on the findings of Nicola Balkind and Mélanie Bourdaa, who have detailed the fan activity surrounding the first films. I will extend my study to the marketing for the last instalments. That said, the chapter is primarily concerned with narrative strategy and aesthetics, so while some attention will be paid to transmedia elements, actual fan responses will be explored but briefly and only insofar as to reflect on the ambivalent viewer commodification and resistance in and around Lionsgate's self-reflexive narrative strategy. Like Marie-Laure Ryan and Jan-Noël Thon who expanded on current research on narrative circulation to rethink the place of the storyworld, I will consider the storyworld as an important narrative element, made more so because of its important place in the comprehension of a contemporary teen series.

In an article about seriality that predates the 21st century's digital media explosion, T. Oltean argued that the perspective on series is based on the idea "that all narratives form and expose a unity in diversity" (1993, 8), that "the media use as entertainment the serial patterns that involve and fictionalize the audience" (6), and that "the purpose of serial transformation is to bind the audience to a narrative sequential process [...] attempting to seduce it as a co-author of the whole" (11). What is striking in this vision of seriality is that it announces points recently raised by scholars about transmedia storytelling. Henry Jenkins, for example, tends to emphasize coherence by considering each story fragment as "text making a distinctive and valuable contribution to the whole" (95–96), and places fans' active participation as an important source of change in new media landscape. *The Hunger Games* adaptations have attracted interest specifically because of the use they make of the time between each film to deploy a transmedia marketing that relied on contemporary media to interact closely with fans' everyday personal spheres, made possible by the media connectedness of young Americans. This furthered the narrative by having the viewers implicate themselves through this culture of propagating iconography. Hence the intimate inclusion of fans as simulated co-author of world-building processes within the marketing should not be dismissed in the narrative expansion comment; rather, *The Hunger Games* has given us the opportunity to witness how a contemporary film series makes the time in between each film relevant, employing it to affect the conditions of how the story is apprehended and, ultimately, remembered.

Regarding Jenkins's principles of transmedia storytelling, Mélanie Bourdaa writes, "the phenomenon of seriality attests to the coherence of this fragmented universe and reinforces the idea of an augmented narration"[3] (2013, 47, my translation). Continuity and multiplicity reinforce seriality, she, and Jenkins, tell us. Colin B. Harvey also notes, "Central to transmedia storytelling is consistency – perhaps of scenario, of plot, of character – expressed through narrative and iconography" (279). A franchise like *The*

Hunger Games relies on transmedia to expand its serial narrative, and the serial form to expand its transmedia, and so there is an organic relationship that is being established between the serial pattern and the transmedia explosion of the 21st century. Both are fragmented forms that rely on balancing repetition and transformation to immerse spectators, and, in cases like *The Hunger Games*, involve them in the dispersion of clear iconography to ensure its development as source mythology for the story. I will therefore analyze the dissemination and self-conscious process within the *Hunger Games* franchise, consistently in films and marketing, of constructing images and endowing them with meaning. There is a clear internal critique of mass media in each platform, made clear by the irony that each element directs at its own form and purpose within the diegesis. Paradoxically, it manages to be both exploitative and critical of exploitation, and deserves to be considered as encouraging media-literacy even as it aims for profit. The transmedia platforms, ensuring consumers' continued entertainment during the wait for each new installment, were also another complicated media game that utilized the non-diegetic reality as an element to expand the storyworld. It drew an ambiguous parallel between diegetic propaganda and artistic entertainment, which, in echoing the story's own interrogations on media, allows a better understanding of the films' own self-reflexivity. I will therefore study how the serial's use of images as diversions and the process of diverting images to channel their viewers, both inside and outside the *Hunger Games* diegesis, helps construct a better understanding of the questions regarding media at stake in the narrative. The serialization of images as political entrapment, exploitation, and repetition preventing change will be considered first, as I focus my analysis on the franchise's use of images as entertainment and the political depth behind this in *The Hunger Games*. I will then expand on the re-appropriation of images as a territory of resistance and show how seriality is also exploited as a transformative device.

Images as entertainment

Image consumption

The story of *The Hunger Games* begins with a first opus about the annual televised "games." Twenty-four children compete to the death in a deadly arena operated by "Gamemakers" in which the very landscape contains hidden cameras. In a manner that places it in the continuation of the Orwellian tradition, the structure of Jeremy Bentham's panopticon pervades the aesthetics,[4] flooding the décor with circular stages even as each new addition is developed parallel to themes of subjugation, repeatedly teaching the audience the power of the look.

Once children become "tributes," they are instantly deprived of any rights over their own bodies and image. More specifically, the moment the

Capitol camera's circular lenses focus on them, they become imprisoned within the nation's eyes. The reaping ceremony in the first film insists on this point by first filming the arrival of a maze of innocent people (reminiscent of the labyrinth in which the Theseus-Katniss will be cast[5]) around which cameras navigate, their images appearing live on giant screens in the center of the public square [9:42–10:30]. The cameras do not isolate Katniss from the crowd until she speaks up in defense of her sister and volunteers as tribute, following which she is escorted toward the stage and sees herself reproduced on the screen [15:47]. Turning individuals into images enables the director Gary Ross to define cameras as the central entrapping devices within the films. Deprived of rights over their physical appearance and, to a certain degree, their physical continuation outside the television show, the select sacrifices are led away to be groomed into aesthetically pleasing forms. They are fashioned into stars and thrust into the public eye, becoming a form of copyright property of the government-owned show. The more the producers profit from the tributes' popularity (getting sponsors to pay enormous sums of money to send help packages inside the arena), the greater the characters' chances of survival. This means that the tributes' survival hinges on their ability to project an entertaining and memorable image, to fashion themselves into noticeable diversions to appeal to their viewers' hunger for the sensational. From the start, Katniss is encouraged to play this game and to understand that her star-quality trumps her combat abilities. Her and the other District 12 tribute Peeta's first victory is their grand entrance in flaming clothing [31:32]: they enter the radar as possible winners because they make a great picture considered ideal for serialized imagery[6] and stardom. The characters are reduced to the legal status of images and, as such, are transformed into public objects of consumption. The heroine's very name, Katniss, an edible plant, evokes a society whose own starving population can become consumable. The tributes' survival depends on their palatability to the Capitol. Our discovery (in *Catching Fire*) that Capitol citizens use emetics at social gatherings to continue gorging themselves on food foreshadows President Snow's plot twist maneuvering of that year's "Quarter Quell" (a special Hunger Game season organized every 25 years) to flush out the cumbersome Katniss by dragging old victors back to the arena.

This consumer culture is, in the films, partly expressed through a strategy of repetition and serialization of tribute images that are constantly framed in on-screen screens, posters, and surveillance equipment. The self-reflexivity of this process within the films is mirrored in some of the marketing's images. For example, one of the early posters ("Hunger Game" *IMDB*), which combines images from the film, functions as a *mise en abyme*, with Katniss's back to us while her face and Peeta's are multiplied along the path bordered with Capitol citizens. All eyes within the poster are drawn to the burning mockingjay pin, Katniss's symbol, which towers above engulfed in bright flames that stand out against the duller tones of the other elements. Attention to the pin is further encouraged by the composition, as the use of a vanishing point entices the gaze to travel upward, and the lit semi-circle at the end of the road acts like a stage for the burning icon. The poster seems to allude to the othering of tributes into highly visible images and icons of themselves, showing how the threat that Katniss faces is mostly the system of viewership itself.

This pattern of multiplying images is just as present in the transmedia marketing as the majority of it was oriented toward the propagation of elements of visual consumption. Among the first platforms created was an official website (*The Capitol,* thecapitol.pn), on which fans would acquire Panem citizenship. Its main menu resembled the control and viewing panels of the Gamemakers, implying it was a place to look. It led through links to many social media platforms, encouraging the circulation of images between fans. Other main attractions included the creation of a faux Capitol fashion blog, Capitol Couture (capitolcouture.pn), in which real fashion personalities and fictitious ones published articles and photoshoots, spreading examples of the recognizable eccentric fashions of the Capitol, as well as angling toward the selling of fashion articles and cosmetic products. The pattern of repetition continues in some of the publications, revealing a conscious wish to echo the film's images.

The parallels between marketing and propaganda

The parallel developed between marketing and propaganda is another element of continuity between the *Hunger Games* films and online platforms. Both images and content produced by Lionsgate and the logic of organization of some of the platforms coherently echoed the Capitol's use of images to entertain as well as manipulate information.

Nicola Balkind dedicates a whole chapter to documenting the transmedia marketing for the first two films, paying special attention to "the conflict between the marketing and Suzanne Collins's message" (2014, 51). She addresses the discomfort of fans faced with a Lionsgate-produced marketing content that consciously adopted a Capitol-generated tone. Balkind quotes Tim Palen, Lionsgate's chief marketing officer, who, detailing the creation of the trailers, reportedly claimed, "We made a rule that we would never say '23 kids get killed.' We say 'only one wins'" (Barnes 2012, qtd. in Balkind 2014, 24). Such a strategy of removing all images of the games from the trailers was partly imagined as a solution to the problem Lionsgate faced when trying to appropriately market a story featuring child-on-child violence to a teen audience, a "potential perception problem in marketing," Palen explains (Barnes 2012). The issue was thus resolved by censoring the violent reality of the games in the vein of the mandatory propaganda film that Panem citizens have to watch before the reaping ceremony in the first film, one that focuses solely on the victors

[12:20–13:30]. The character Gale's lip sync [12:22] exposes it as a serial viewing, a suggestion of the long unchanged propaganda of Panem. Ironically, the Capitol Couture articles routinely presented tributes like fashion icons, censoring the dark nature of their presence in the public eye. An etiquette guide by the *Hunger Games* character Effie Trinket begins with introductory words telling readers that her years as District 12 Escort has provided her with the opportunities to "observe culture both in the Capitol and the less sophisticated areas of Panem" (capitolcouturev1). This cartoon guide of dos and don'ts (with the dos representing the Capitol's ideas of polite behavior) teaches in an infantilizing tone that it is impolite not to provide enough food for a guest. This echoes the deeply ignorant view of the country's rich population who, in the films, are shown gorging themselves on feasts, not realizing or caring that other districts are starving. Furthermore, images of past victors released online combine aesthetics drawn from high fashion magazines and celebrity front-page pictures, such as luxurious clothing, sophisticated makeup, elaborate poses, and the filtered quality of the images (@TheCapitolPN). Ironically, the at-times-painful-looking eccentricities of high fashion are what is most reminiscent of the violence of the games. This is clearly the case in a 2015 fashion shoot (@TheCapitolPN 9 November 2015), with a past victor displaying an elaborate head and neck brace that resembles a torture contraption and is a testament of the violence the tributes are subjected to in the games, only for it to be rendered glamorous. Suffering, in the transmedia images, is only made visible enough to be eclipsed by sensational aesthetics, much in the manner that the Gamemakers veil the dark nature of the bloody Hunger Games by turning its images and meaning into a sensational narrative. The Capitol TV platform offered, among other things, short documentaries about other districts, always in a very patriotic tone, revealing no poverty and celebrating their hard work as cultural.

Furthermore, as I have said before, the platforms were structured to suggest Lionsgate hegemony over fan activity. As in the games, where tribute popularity always profits the producers, the website organized fan participation into districts and hierarchies, creating a credit system so that the more fans participated, the more credits they would acquire. The most participative fans would gain invitations, prizes for best fan creations, or even positions as district mayors or recruiters on the social network accounts. This system echoed the diegetic world's structure of privilege and expanded the franchise's representation of it, as the films hint toward the uneven wealth distribution but do not develop the full extent of the hierarchy system that the novels described in detail.

The *Hunger Games* online marketing instalments were, therefore, much like the films, media-conscious, as they ironically developed a convincing extension of the Capitol online that made the viewers self-conscious of their role as consumers and implicated them in the hierarchy of viewership in *The Hunger Games*.

Political diversions

Inspired by ancient history, Collins named the country Panem, from the Latin "Panem et circenses," bread and games. In ancient Rome, this was imagined as the political tactic of using entertainment to divert the citizens' gaze away from political matters. The diegetic Hunger Games have a similar design. As a representation of reality television they serve to draw a parallel between societies of televised consumption and ancient Rome, suggesting the potential of such forms of popular entertainment to be manipulative and to alienate from social and political reality. When, in *Catching Fire*, Haymitch (Katniss's mentor) tells her that her "job" is "to be a distraction" [19:52], it further denotes the role imposed on victors whose tabloid images continue to be used as further forms of patriotic propaganda. This pattern was echoed in the marketing, as shortly before the last film the CapitolPN twitter account released posters of past tributes, again underlining only tribute-persona attributes rather than any real personality (@TheCapitolPN).

The heroes themselves become engaged in a pattern of viewing and reviewing images to better mediate their own public narrative. In the first film, their public appearances enable them to gauge each other's confidence, potential for crowd popularity, and thereby the degree of threat they pose to each other. In *Catching Fire*, Haymitch has Katniss and Peeta review footage of other tribute reapings, as he lists their abilities and friendly potentials [49:58–51:10]. These short soundless clips are seen on a diegetic screen in their living quarters in a sequence that oscillates between shots that encompass Haymitch zapping and commenting on the images, reverse shots of the couch from which Katniss and Peeta are watching, and longer shots from behind the couch. These low-angle shots ensure the screen's ominous visibility as it towers over them, highlighted by the brighter colors of the footage that distracts our gaze as it contrasts with the dull grey room and clothing of the protagonists. This constitutes the non-diegetic audience's own introduction to some new important protagonists. Making the diegetic screen so conspicuous has multiple effects. First, it is indicative of the threat they pose, as well as the importance of their inclusion in the narrative. Secondly, the fact that they are first presented on television is a clear reminder of how tributes' on-screen time dominates their narrative. And thirdly, the way the narration (notably through composition) draws our attention to the diegetic screen in the room is itself a reflexive comment on how Capitol media are employed to keep the attention on certain glamourous images. This brings to mind the message of the second film repeated to Katniss by several characters: "Remember who the real enemy is." Indeed, the films' strategy of showing screens and cameras on-screen, and of integrating Capitol-made footage within the film narration, ensures its conspicuously self-conscious attitude on the matter of image manipulation and mediation. In a dystopia where political control and societal hierarchy are partly defined by viewer status, political conflicts are fought with media. Katniss's extreme visibility initially places her at the bottom of this panoptic hierarchy, but it also grants her the public gaze, which she learns to take advantage of by developing her own images of resistance and turning the system around.

Images of resistance

Claiming, reclaiming, icon making

The Hunger Games tells the story of a woman struggling with the various roles she is cast into. As a tribute, she has to play the game of entertainment, while personally attempting to retain her humanity and identity. Later, she has to play the role of the heroine, while personally attempting to retain her sanity. What is striking is that resistance is repeatedly shown as an action that requires the subversion of the means of entrapment into means of empowerment. In a system that appropriates individuals by claiming them as objects of visual consumption, defiance is possible through a subversive use of visibility. Katniss's victory, in the first installment, is gained by turning the game against itself. She engages her viewers, drawing on their Hollywood-like addiction to romantic developments, so that even the Gamemakers are carried away by her performance. She finds empowerment in reclaiming her own image and narrative. This becomes a pattern as, like any politician or celebrity, she is both routinely empowered and threatened by the images made of her and by her. In his research about Hollywood stardom, Richard Dyer analyzes the manufacture of stars after defining them as "a phenomenon of production." He writes, "Stars are images in media texts, and as such are products of Hollywood (or wherever). [... S]tars are to be seen in terms of their function in the economy of Hollywood, including, crucially, their role in the manipulation of Hollywood's market, the audience" (Dyer 1979, 10). Katniss's visibility is also a product marketed to manipulate the consumers of her images, but that same visibility gives her a modicum of assertion, as it holds sway over thousands of fans. Dyer also speaks of some stars' efforts to manage and use their public image, writing that "[t]he 'subversiveness' of these stars can be seen in terms of 'radical intervention' (not necessarily conscious) on the part of themselves or others who have used the potential meanings of their image" (1979, 34) As stars are first and foremost images, subversion (by themselves or others) comes from the subversion of their image. Just as she can be threatened by a single image of her kissing Gale instead of Peeta in *Catching Fire* [8:36], Katniss can provoke an uprising with a single image of defiance, precisely because it is not singular but multiplied on all the country's screens to become an icon shared, propagated, and imbued with the force to rally an army.

The Hunger Games seems to be a lesson in iconography, as we witness the process of meaning-making of symbolic images in the films, the paratext, and the online marketing images. Katniss is seen as evolving separately throughout the films both as character and as living icon. In the world of *The Hunger Games*, in which the panopticon-like arenas are a mirror of the very country they are designed to subdue, imposed visibility equates glamorous imprisonment. However, it also becomes the means of resistance, as Katniss learns to manipulate her mediation to her advantage by revealing forbidden images or reappropriating signs to change their meaning. From the beginning she stands out at the first volunteer of District 12 in her sacrifice to save her sister, initially marking herself as a character of agency in the very act that costs her freedom. Thus, as the serial progresses, she comes to embody a chain-breaker as well as a figure of change, as her initial act is combined with her following actions, thus growing and accumulating meaning. She initially gains a respectful farewell salute from her district (the three-finger salute). When she covers little Rue's body with flowers to impose a martyr image to the Capitol viewers she salutes the camera [1:39:43], an act that is immediately seen multiplied on the many screens viewed in District 11 (Rue's district). In the second film, the brutal repression of people making that salute reveals it has become an anti-Capitol symbol. In the marketing of *The Mockingjay Part 2*, giant posters of this salute appeared in public spaces throughout the world (Billington), leading to the revolution websites but not displaying the title, relying solely on this iconographic element of Katniss to carry meaning. She is associated with the mockingjay pin she wears (a bird holding an arrow, framed within a circle), initially just a gift for her sister. That token, too, becomes part of her persona, an icon that people brandish from the second film onward, as well as in the images published on the revolution online platforms and hashtags. It evolves in its representation in short film segments that precede or follow the end credits of the films (and appears in the menus of the DVDs). The films end with the final appearance of a flaming mockingjay icon, which spreads its wings and, after the second film, breaks the circle, thus echoing Katniss's destruction of the circular panopticon-arena of *Catching Fire*. Her dress of false fire, initially designed by her friend and stylist Cinna to symbolize their coal-mining origins, becomes her trademark, and as such it too makes her "the spark" that lights a fire. Consequently, in *Catching Fire*, Cinna creates a wedding dress for her that publicly transforms into a black mockingjay dress [1:11:00], a rebellious act that costs Cinna his life but further marks Katniss as a figure of resistance and warfare.

In the novels, the mockingjay is defined as derived from a species of mutated talking birds called jabberjays created by the Capitol as spying devices, as they would memorize and repeat rebel talks. The jabberjays ended up being used by the dissidents to relay false information to the Capitol, who stopped relying on them, but the birds somehow managed to reproduce with wild mockingbirds, thereby creating the mockingjays. In Katniss's own words, "[a] mockingjay is a creature the Capitol never intended to exist. They hadn't counted on the highly controlled jabberjay having the brains to adapt to the wild, to pass on its genetic code, to thrive in a new form" (Collins 2009, 112). The symbol comes to represent Katniss herself, something the Capitol failed to control, and can also be interpreted as a metonymy of an icon – or a metaphor for a media – diverted from its use.

It may seem that Katniss's own personality is only developed in the films and novels, while her images in the transmedia platforms are exclusively iconographic, as she is represented either as tribute or as revolutionary icon. But she is, in effect, also developed in her trademark pose, one where she is looking straight at the camera, defying her status as object of the gaze while also paradoxically becoming an image of herself, serialized by others. The proliferation of this iconic pose contributes to foregrounding a motif present throughout the films: that of Katniss looking at the camera. In the first film, these looks to the camera occur typically to signal to diegetic audiences (and real audiences) that Katniss is aware of their subjecting presence. In her gazing back, she thus stands out as an accusatory figure. She disturbs the hierarchy of viewership of the panoptic society by symbolically reclaiming her own status as one also capable of vision. Looks to the camera in film have a history of being considered as linking diegetic space and non-diegetic space in narration, making viewers self-conscious. Marc Vernet writes that one of the effects of the look at the camera is "to reveal the spectator's voyeurism, brutally creating a link between the space of the film's production and that of its reception" (1988, 9, my translation).[7] While these looks remain ambiguous when mediated by the presence of diegetic cameras, they are more clearly addressing real audiences each time they occur in the absence of such cameras. They thus participate in the filmmakers' strategy of expanding the meaning of the motif beyond diegetic signification.

The marketing of Katniss the icon, with its insistence on the activist potential of fashion and engagement with consumer culture as a means of empowerment, may appear to draw from or cater to postfeminist discourses and the prospect of female empowerment found in "more individualistic assertions of (consumer) choice and self-rule" (Genz and Bradon 2009, 24). However, this publicity contradicts the diegetic characterization of Katniss as reluctant icon. While the instrumentalization of the heroine's body and image is simultaneously a site of oppression and her biggest source of power, the fact remains that she seldom has the luxury to refuse being mediated. She must therefore assert herself in the wriggle room of the roles she is made to play (e.g., tribute, victor, rebel), which denotes a resistance to iconicity itself as she strives not to be erased by the glamorous or patriotic representations of her, or let her narrative and discourse be written by others. The character's struggle recalls Judith Butler's idea of the paradoxical place of repetition in matters of discursive resistance through resignification. Butler uses the example of hate speech to reveal the subject's "vulnerability to language" (1997, 26), and a dependence on "the address of the Other" (26). But while the repetition of such speech effects an "ongoing subjugation," Butler posits that there is "no way to ameliorate its effects except through its recirculation, even if that circulation takes place in the context of a public discourse that calls for the censorship of such speech." Thus, subjugation by another's discourse may be resisted through resignification, which involves repetition. In Butler's words, "it is precisely the *expropriability* of the dominant, "authorized" discourse that constitutes one potential site of its subversive resignification" (157, original italics). Transposing this to audiovisual discourse, it could be argued that Katniss's struggle with iconicity and her empowerment through it then stage the necessary contradictions of her resistance, further underscored by the ambiguity of the online serialization of her iconic images to be acquired and shared by fans. As the dichotomy between the message and the publicity developed by Balkind (2014, 51) resurfaces yet again, the look to the camera initially inscribed as a challenge may then be offered as the grounds to a more challenging problem: that of the possibility of insurrectional resistance by means of conscious objectification. The relationship between these problems and the place of feminism in *The Hunger Games* and Lionsgate's productions would merit a full article of its own. But clearly, the insistence on showing the processes of Katniss's iconification throughout the narrative is an invitation to reflect on the significance of iconicity itself, and in what manner it may engage and challenge viewers within and without the diegesis.

Hijacking images

The third film, *Mockingjay Part 1*, is particularly relevant in this struggle of dominance through images. This particular episode focuses on initiating an open civil war narrative, and yet physical conflicts are almost secondary throughout, and often become objects in the main conflict under focus: the war of propagandas between the Capitol and District 13. Indeed, battle for dominance is patent in the battle for image assertion, as the two factions attempt to control narrative by controlling media supremacy and subverting the Capitol's monopoly over images.

The plot of *Mockingjay Part 1* mostly revolves around Katniss and a small film team, part of the District 13 resistance, who make strongly symbolic propaganda pieces ("propos") to exploit Katniss as the figure of the Mockingjay and use her to inflame resistance and pose an opposing voice to the Capitol's own propaganda. The repetitive serial structure of the first two novels may be reminiscent of the entertainment industry's creative process. Both times, half of the novel focuses on the selection of tributes and their mediated preparations, such as makeovers, presentations, and interviews. The actual filmed event of the games only constitute a second portion of the novels, and a very short one in the case of *Catching Fire*. In the third novel, this narrative dynamic is surprisingly similar, cumulating in Katniss's time in the Capitol that turns out to be the final arena of the "Seventy-sixth

Hunger Games" (Collins 2010, 293). However, as is now the fashion in franchises, the last book was divided into two films, making the third film an extended version of the paratext-like first part of each diegetic Hunger Games, highlighting what Jessica R. Wells explicated in an article (2014): that from the first film onward *The Hunger Games* can be analyzed as a war film. An echo of the first films, we see her getting prepared by her old Hunger Games mentors and watch the process of scripting, directing, filming, and editing these pieces. Significantly, Katniss is yet again coerced into selling her image to protect her loved ones and is not always aware of being filmed. Each clandestine broadcasting of "propos" in the film is accompanied by a significant attack scene, formally binding the propaganda images to the concrete consequences they inspire. The most consequential attack led against the Capitol follows a "propo" made of Katniss edited with a voiceover from a recording [1:07:03] (she is once again recorded unknowingly) of her singing to a responsive flock of mockingjays to entertain her "avox" friend Pollux.[8] Soon after we hear her voice rising up for the benefit of the voiceless [1:05:40–1:06:41], the attack sequence begins with a mass of people humming that very tune [1:07:40–1:08:12], binding their actions to Katniss's political figure. This is followed by a sequence where District 13 hacks a live broadcast of Peeta [1:10:42–1:12:26]. In order to distract their enemies, the Capitol strategically films him reading a scripted speech against the attacks. His emaciated and fearful countenance makes the live footage resemble a hostage video, an impression reinforced by his off-screen gazes at the people behind the camera putting the words in his mouth. The broadcast becomes hijacked by District 13, which manages to replace these intimidating images with their "propo" (the same as above). We then witness the two sequences blurring, struggling to overlap each other and impose itself on the national screen. Glitches are used in the diegetic footage to suggest the hacking, endowing the images with a retro cyber underground texture that adds to the resistance symbolism of the scene. Yet, once again both sequences battling to overlap each other and dominate viewership portray distorted and exploitative images of the characters. Even though they are friends, their images are featured as opposed forces in this struggle, while the ubiquitous presence of footage-Katniss and character-Katniss on-screen, and Peeta's alternate looks offscreen (at footage-Katniss) and at the camera while calling her name, tragically build up this idea of a schizophrenic othering of their iconic selves. While the sequences at times overlap, their real selves fail to connect. Peeta can only assume he will be heard when he uses the live broadcast to warn Katniss of the impending attack.

Hence, this hijacking motif is also visible in the way characters become objects of dispute in this film, symbols to be claimed and reclaimed in the propaganda conflict. The term "hijacked" is often used in the last film to describe the mental state of Peeta, who, in the third film, is held captive by the Capitol and submitted to conditioning torture that modifies his memory and trains him to see Katniss as an enemy to kill. "Hijacking" is described as a form of mental conditioning that renders him unable to tell falsehood and reality apart. The Capitol diverts Peeta's mind and his calm nature in an attempt to use him against Katniss, a reverse image of the mockingjay metaphor as a Capitol mutation turned against them.

Mutation is a recurrent theme in *The Hunger Games*. Like the Minotaur in Theseus's labyrinth or the beasts in Roman circuses, the Capitol arenas have their fair share of monsters flung at the tributes. But in the last two films, the threat of mutations reappears as what threatens the protagonists: the Capitol's power to change them. Just as diverted media are vectors of resistance and change, "mutts," as they are called in *The Hunger Games*, are creatures distorted from their natural state by the Capitol to be used as weapons against their opponents. Both Katniss and Peeta are "hijacked" in a way, as Katniss's rescue in *Catching Fire* was a political move on District 13's part to acquire the Mockingjay. Both are used as opposed icons in the various broadcasts in the third film to try to change the course of each faction's narrative. Their bodies are territories of conflict as media warfare inscribes itself with and on them.

This hijacking of icons and viewership reappeared in the "presidential addresses" released by Capitol TV online as teasers for *Mockingjay Part 2*, in which Peeta dressed in white stood by Snow until at some point the segment was interrupted by a District 13 hacking. Warfare in *The Hunger Games* is displayed in battles over images and icons to be claimed and reclaimed as territory, even at the expense of individuals. This also implicated the fans in media disputes of sorts, as it was mirrored on the online marketing platforms following the third film. The transmedia completed and extended the media conflict by having it bleed into fans' media territory and enrolling them as rebels in anticipation of the last film.

Images and media as territory

Before the third film, there had been "disruptions" in the Lionsgate-Capitol-operated online platforms. Temporary "hacks" in social media feeds and "hacked" Capitol TV announcements appeared around the same date as the theatrical release, reproducing in real time on fan territory the very hacking aesthetics and rebel propaganda leaks the film exhibited. Capitol TV mentioned "technical difficulties" and released countering messages of unity and loyalty, either sound recordings or videos, termed "mandatory viewings," a phrase and written presentation echoed in the last film as similar "mandatory viewings" invade Capitol citizens' homes in hologram screens that switch themselves on [54:43; 1:22:00].

After months of silence, a major change occurred on the online platforms. As if all Capitol channels had been hijacked, all the official accounts became flooded with countless rallying messages, images of Katniss to enroll young fans into the resistance. The Capitol.pn website was overthrown like a coup, all links replaced. All of them now led to the revolution websites. Like the people of Panem, whose homes had become battle grounds uniting them against one enemy, the fans' adoptive districts and media platforms had become a site of territorial media overthrow, and the fans were drafted into the revolutionary narrative, reflecting on the questions of involvement raised in the diegesis. Their own reality became drafted further into the civil war narrative, as the shifting forces of image producers in the films led to a change of performing producers of transmedia images.

The new links encouraged fans to log on to their websites from their smartphones, provided with access codes to unlock sites, or links would lead to a countdown-like site where fans would enroll in the revolution by clicking, thousands flooding the web platforms, visually echoing the countdown-like sequence in the third film during a mission to seize back the stolen tributes. Some videos used a mixture of hacking aesthetics (glitches) and fanvideo aesthetics, recycling film images while involving the fans more personally. So the *Hunger Games* franchise used the potential provided by both the serial form and contemporary teen-used media to enroll the fans in the performance of a territory reclaiming narrative, channeling them in a process of changing roles within said narrative. Indeed, they went from being citizens of a Capitol-run Panem to being swept up by the resistance as fellow dissidents. The fans themselves had, then, become characters reclaimed from the first Capitol-run installments to be on the same side as their heroine.

Coherently with the story's conclusion that reveals Alma Coin, District 13's leader, to be as power-driven as the Capitol, this second phase of marketing retained a propaganda and exploitative tone, with some ambiguity regarding the roles given to fans. It consistently maintained a media-conscious tone that questioned the legitimacy of appropriating images and symbols, something that reflected on the very fan activity it triggered. Much like the objectification of tributes as images in the Capitol-run Panem, the dispute of tributes as symbols and media territory in the civil conflict is very much in keeping with yet another reflexive point raised by the diegesis: the question of legitimate image ownership in a culture of image appropriation. The very integration of some degree of fan activity as narrative fragments of transmedia in *The Hunger Games* is itself a reflection of the problem of how to consider fan participation in the narration, as they are only here integrated as co-authors insofar as they play a role devised by the legal authors, while being simultaneously faced with a story that encourages them to feel rebellious against media exploitation.

This ambiguity accounts, to a certain extent, for the groups of "fan resistance" who produced their own *Hunger Games*-diverted icons for social change, viewing Lionsgate as betraying the narrative and ideals. Both Balkind (2014) and Bourdaa (2015) study the phenomenon of fan activism specific to *The Hunger Games*. The activist band Bourdaa documents is partly motivated by the financial exploitation of the story of *The Hunger*

Games by Lionsgate, which they reacted to. Following a first legal intim-idation by the production company to the fans over an Oxfam campaign and intellectual property matters, the activists' flame was revived around the release of the second film. Ironically, while Oddsinourfavour.org (the activists' web group) was multiplying its actions, angered by the market-ing of the second film which rang too close to the diegetic Capitol's own marketing of their tributes, they were ambiguously in disagreement with Collins, the author of the very novels motivating their actions. Indeed, as Balkind notes (2014, 56), Collins had applauded the ambiguous market-ing, allegedly telling *Variety* in an email: "It's appropriately disturbing and thought-provoking how the campaign promotes '*Catching Fire*' while si-multaneously promoting the Capitol's punitive forms of entertainment. [...] That dualistic approach is very much in keeping with the books" (Graser 2013).

Lionsgate's strategy would appear, then, to exploit what fan studies scholar Matt Hills analyses as "the curious coexistence within fan culture of both anti-commercial ideologies and commodity-completist practices" (2002, 28). Analyzing target marketing in television, Hills posits that fans' resistive consumption practices "are rapidly recuperated within discourses and practices of marketing. Fandom has begun to furnish a model of ded-icated and loyal consumption" (36). Hills underscores how fans appearing to "get what they want" (36) is a way of disempowering them but later also points out that cult fans' anti-commercial ideologies can counteract producers' "too obviously manufactured" cult texts or icons (143).[9] What becomes apparent, then, in the *Hunger Games* marketing is the territorial negotiation between the producers' attempt to simultaneously exploit both fans' consumeristic activity and their propensity for resistance in a manner that mirrors the very methods the text criticizes, and how it clashes with the fans' own fidelity to that text. Lionsgate's continuous attempts to diffuse fan resistance by writing them roles in transmedia games that promoted the illusion of activism are perhaps one of the most ambivalent examples of the story's topicality when it comes to contemporary media usage and exploitation. By providing viewers with all the keys to apprehend its own diversions, be it by its own producers, fans, and any other appropriation its very text anticipates, this self-reflexive franchise becomes both a business strategy and a cautionary tale. The media territory negotiations at play in the films and transmedia dramatically reflect on contemporary issues and problems regarding the contemporary mediascape and the fragmented na-ture of transmedia itself.

Conclusion

The *Hunger Games* franchise offers much in terms of research on contem-porary film series, though the possibility to experience its online platforms was short-lived (several no longer exist since the online revolution of the fourth film). The different media platforms' use of serial repetitions of images allows the series as a whole to raise questions about image consumption in entertainment. Moreover, the process of transformation allowed by the serial pattern displays how images can evolve into icons. At stake in this series that includes the films and the transmedia extensions is an undercurrent question that permeates the entire narrative: the possibility and conditions of resistance and change. Seriality appears in *The Hunger Games* as combining repetition and evolution of form. It echoes the threat within the narrative of the failure to bring about social change and to break repeated patterns as characters struggle to change history for the better. In a dystopia where images are used as diversions to avoid that change, the diversion of these very images from their initial use into new forms is a meta-filmic comment on both the creative possibility and dangers of serial transformation through appropriation. And the use of diverting transmedia images to channel and keep the attention of the fans while implicating them in a relationship of fragmented authorship with the dynamic storyworld binds transmedia to the films' serial narration. Like a serial, a transmedia storyworld is a constantly renegotiated space in an ongoing process of transformation. Considering as storyworld extensions, and thereby elements of storytelling, the ambiguous transmedia marketing is justified for this particular franchise because the themes of the story itself are a reflection on the commodification of characters as marketed images. And because this work is partly defined by the teen audience that views it, it required the fashioning of extensions that would best reach them, which meant employing the contemporary media they best (co)responded to. This strategy aimed to efficiently draft them into the type of co-authorship that is structural to the serial form, thereby ensuring their better immersion. This also resulted in topical conflicts between the fans responsive to the story's lessons and the producers profiting from these very responses, echoing the dystopian representation of modernity in which spectatorship has become a primary currency. Part of the interest of the *Hunger Games* franchise's adaptation strategy is that it experiments with, and evaluates potential changes in, narrative form and spectatorial demands in transmedia series. As an object of scientific study, it may also serve to better apprehend the extent to which such narrative forms script fan activity within their serial structure.

Notes

1 This chapter invokes the notion of *storyworld* as it is defined by Marie-Laure Ryan (2013), who posits that "to inspire the mental representation of a world [...] is the primary condition for a text to be considered a narrative" (363) and goes on to specify that she defines *storyworlds* "through a static component that precedes the story and a dynamic component that captures the unfolding of the events" (364).

2 In her dissertation, Christy Dena differentiates works that have been initially imagined as transmedia storytelling from a tendency of "identifying all franchises,

marketing campaigns, indeed almost any intercompositional phenomena with this structurally additive trait throughout time as transmedia storytelling," remarking that "works with an additive structural relationship can be (and have been) articulated by anyone – by fans, by practitioners in different departments, different companies, without any creative impetus or oversight – and can be completely inconsequential to the meaning of the work" (106–107).

3 "[A]ugmented narration" ("narration augmentée") is Bourdaa's own term, which she applies to the example of the *Hunger Games* franchise, among others. The original French passage goes: "Le phénomène de sérialité atteste de la cohérence de cet univers éclaté et renforce l'idée d'une narration augmentée."

4 Kelley Wezner analyses in great detail how the "physical structure of Bentham's panopticon appears throughout Collins's trilogy" (2012, 149), allowing us to reflect on the film's visual rendering of the literary aesthetics of imprisonment and control.

5 Suzanne Collins's inspirations for the novels included Greek mythology and history of Ancient Rome. She mentioned this early on in an interview with Scholastic (Collins 2016, "A Conversation").

6 This is highlighted by the giant flag-like screens that line the streets and crowd and in which Katniss sees herself framed as she gazes about. To captivate the attention of the commentators and the cameras and to be thus made visible, more so once she and Peeta hold up their clasped hands, can be understood as an indication of what power they can have. They become real competition to the other tributes because they are approved as image.

7 Here is the original French passage: "de dénoncer le voyeurisme du spectateur, mettant brutalement en communication l'espace de production du film avec l'espace de réception."

8 One of the Capitol's means of punishment is the enslavement of individuals and their symbolic subjugation by rendering them mute. The victims of this are called "avox."

9 Hills's analyses primarily concern cult texts and cult fandom. Regardless of whether or not *The Hunger Games* falls under such categories, Hills offers us a perspective into phenomena and strategies that are, I believe, relevant in the study of the franchise.

Works cited

@TheCapitolPN. "#CapitolCouture Reviews the Unearthed Poster of D4 Darling Mags, Winner of the 11th Games. CapitolCouture.pn". *Twitter*, 11.11.2015, 11:09am. twitter.com/thecapitolpn/status/664520277603172352 (accessed 30.11.2016).

@TheCapitolPN. "Straight from the Archives, Augustus Braun! #CapitolCouture Reviews Styles of the D1 Victor: CapitolCouture.pn". *Twitter*, 11.13.2015, 9:20am.   twitter.com/thecapitolpn/status/665217781789384704   (accessed 11.30.2016).

@TheCapitolPN. "The Capitol Salutes Past Victors. #CapitolCouture Looks to the Styles behind the Icons: CapitolCouture.pn". *Twitter*, 11.9.2015, 11:56am. twitter.com/thecapitolpn/status/663807460767981568 (accessed 11.30.2016).

Balkind, Nicola. *Fan Phenomena: The Hunger Games*. Bristol, Chicago, IL: Intellect, 2014.

Barnes, Brooks. "How 'Hunger Games' Built Up Must-see Fever". *The New York Times*, 03.18.2012. https://www.nytimes.com/2012/03/19/business/media/how-hunger-games-built-up-must-see-fever.html (accessed 11.30.2016).

Billington, Alex. "#Unite – Salute Marketing for '*The Hunger Games*' Launches Globally." *FirstShowing.net,* 06.19.2015. https://www.firstshowing.net/2015/unite-salute-marketing-for-the-hunger-games-launches-globally/ (accessed 11.30.2016).

Bourdaa, Mélanie. "La construction d'un univers de marque à travers des stratégies transmédia : le cas de *The Hunger Games*". In Hélène Laurichesse (ed.), *La Stratégie de marque dans l'audiovisuel,* Paris: Armand Colin, 2013. 43–56.

Bourdaa, Mélanie. "Les fans de *Hunger Games*, de la fiction à l'engagement". *Ina Global,* 03.27.2015. https://larevuedesmedias.ina.fr/les-fans-de-hunger-games-de-la-fiction-lengagement (accessed 11.30.2016).

Butler, Judith. *Excitable Speech: A Politics of the Performative.* New York; London: Routledge, 1997.

The Capitol - The Official Government of Panem – The Hunger Games. www.thecapitol.pn/ (accessed 09.15.2016).

Capitol Couture. capitolcouture.pn/ (accessed 09.15.2016).

Capitolcouturev1. "Effie's Enlightening Etiquette Guide". *74ᵗʰ Capitol Couture.* Tumblr. 02.14.2012. 74th.capitolcouture.pn/post/44106872328/effies-enlightening-etiquette-guide (accessed 11.30.2016).

Collins, Suzanne. *Catching Fire.* London: Scholastic, 2009.

Collins, Suzanne. "A Conversation", *Scholastic.com,* 11.18.2013. https://fr.scribd.com/document/91293035/A-Conversation-With-Suzanne-Collins (accessed 11.30.2016).

Collins, Suzanne. *The Hunger Games.* London: Scholastic, 2008.

Collins, Suzanne. *Mockingjay.* London: Scholastic, 2010.

Dena, Christy. *Transmedia Practice: Theorising the Practice of Expressing a Fictional World across Distinct Media and Environments.* University of Sydney, PhD dissertation, 2009.

"Diversion." *The Longman Dictionary of Contemporary English Online.* https://www.ldoceonline.com/dictionary/diversion (accessed 11.30.2016).

Dyer, Richard, and Paul McDonald. *Stars.* 1979. London: BFI Pub., 1998.

Genz, Stéphanie, and Benjamin A. Bradon. *Postfeminism: Cultural Texts and Theories.* Edinburgh: Edinburgh University Press, 2009.

Graser, Marc. "Lionsgate's Tim Palen Crafts Stylish Universe for 'Hunger Games: Catching Fire'". *Variety,* 10.29.2013. https://variety.com/2013/biz/news/lionsgates-tim-palen-crafts-stylish-universe-for-hunger-games-catching-fire-1200772931/ (accessed 11.30.2016).

Harvey, Colin B. "A Taxonomy of Transmedia Storytelling". In Marie-Laure Ryan and Jan-Noël Thon (eds.), *Storyworlds across Media: Toward a Media-Conscious Narratology*, Lincoln: University of Nebraska Press, 2014.

Hills, Matt. *Fan Cultures.* London: Routledge, 2002.

Jenkins, Henry. *Convergence Culture: Where Old and New Media Collide.* New York: NYU Press, 2006.

Oddsinourfavour.org (accessed 09.15.2016).

Oltean, T. "Series and Seriality in Media Culture", *European Journal of Communication* 8.1, 1993. 5–31.

Ryan, Marie-Laure. "Transmedial Storytelling and Transfictionality". *Poetics Today* 13.3, 2013. 361–388.

Ryan, Marie-Laure, and Jan-Noël Thon. "Introduction". In Ryan, Marie-Laure, and Jean-Noël Thon (eds.), *Storyworlds across Media: Toward a Media-conscious Narratology.* Lincoln: University of Nebraska Press, 2014. 1–24.

Vernet, Marc. *Figures de l'absence: De l'invisible au cinéma*. Paris: Editions de l'Etoile, 1988.

Wells, Jessica R. "Rebel Tributes and Tyrannical Regimes: Myth and Spectacle in *The Hunger Games* (2012)". In Karen A. Ritzenhoff and Jakub Kazecki (eds.), *Heroism and Gender in War Films*, New York: Palgrave Macmillan, 2014. 173–186.

Wezner, Kelley. "'Perhaps I Am Watching You Now': Panem's Panopticons". In Mary F. Pharr and Leisa A. Clark (eds.), *Of Bread, Blood and The Hunger Games: Critical Essays on the Suzanne Collins Trilogy*, Jefferson, NC: McFarland, 2012. 148–157.

Hunger Games films

The Hunger Games. Gary Ross, Lionsgate, 2012.

The Hunger Games: Catching Fire. Francis Lawrence, Lionsgate, 2013.

The Hunger Games: Mockingjay – Part 1. Francis Lawrence, Lionsgate, 2014.

The Hunger Games: Mockingjay – Part 2. Francis Lawrence, Lionsgate, 2015.

2.3 Raising Caine

Hollywood remakes of Michael Caine's Cockney cycle

Agnieszka Rasmus

Whereas certain directors' works have often been remade (e.g., Alfred Hitchcock's), it is less common to observe consistent and repeated engagement with the output of one single actor from a specific period in their career. Michael Caine's acting persona has been the subject of (mis)quotations, appropriations, and impersonations since he became an international star following his appearance as a working-class hero in *The Ipcress File* (1965) and *Alfie* (1966). For instance, the British TV program *Harry Enfield & Chums* from the 1990s features a sketch called "My name is Michael Paine and I'm a nosy neighbour," whose character sounds like Caine's Charlie Croker from *The Italian Job* (1969) and Jack Carter from *Get Carter* (1971) and looks like Harry Palmer – a spy Caine played in *The Ipcress File* (1965). The most recent impersonations include a duel between two British comedians in *The Trip* (2010) and its sequel *The Trip to Italy* (2014), in which Steve Coogan and Rob Brydon try to outperform each other doing Caine's accent and famous one-liners from *The Italian Job* and *Get Carter.*

Caine's is thus one of the most quoted and impersonated voices in the film business. However, looking at the above examples also shows that there is a preference for revisiting some of his works over others. I wish to focus on four titles: *Alfie* (1966), *The Italian Job* (1969), *Get Carter* (1971), and *Sleuth* (1972) for two reasons. First of all, they form a coherent cycle that will be referred to as Caine's Cockney cycle for reasons explained below. Secondly, all of them were selected for Hollywood remaking purposes. This chapter shows that a proliferation of the remakes of the actor's iconic works in the years 2000–2007 is more than just a coincidence; on the contrary, it is a phenomenon worth investigating as it may help us understand the nature of remakes in the digital era where both films co-exist side by side. Since in this particular case the British originals and their Hollywood remakes are in English, there is a greater opportunity for the original and its remake to "connect, circulate, and interact with each other" (Rasmus 2014, 98), facilitating the process of recall and cross-referencing. As both have identical titles, a sense of seriality and continuity becomes even more firmly established, which is often seen in the choice of actors replacing Caine in the remakes as well as in Michael Caine's own personal endorsement of such projects. The films analyzed below seem to prove Loock and Kelleter's observation about remaking as "a more implicit practice of serialization" where "a source text that is initially marked as a stand-alone story is re-activated, repeated, changed and indeed *continued* (as we argue) in the act of remaking" (2017, 115). In the case of the remakes of Caine's output, the process of retrospective serialization is achieved, among other things, through casting, paratextual materials, reviewing practice, and audience response.

When looking for reasons why these particular titles starring Michael Caine were chosen for remaking over others, one has to discuss a complex web of elements that set them apart and yet allow them to form a coherent group. The first noticeable element they all share is their dates of release, within a short period from 1966 to 1972, thus at the time of Hollywood's most active financial and creative involvement in the British film production that Alexander Walker refers to as *Hollywood England* (1974) in the appropriately titled book about the British domestic film industry in the 1960s. Even though Britain's and America's cultural exchange and film industries' cooperation have always been referred to as "special," cultural mobility between them was especially close during the 1960s when London was seen as the global capital of the cultural revolution. As Sarah Street points out, "By the end of the 1960s as much as 90% of films made in Britain had US backing" (2002, 169–170). Some of these British films from the golden era in the British film production are now often revisited by Hollywood studios without copyright battles. Both *Alfie* (1966) and *The Italian Job* (1969) were produced by Paramount Pictures, *Get Carter* (1971) by MGM British Studios, and *Sleuth*[1] by Palomar Pictures International, a subsidiary of American Broadcasting Companies, Inc. Thanks to several publications, for example, Chibnall's *Get Carter* (2003), Michael Deeley's *Blade Runners, Deer Hunters, and Blowing the Bloody Doors off My Life in Cult Movies* (2008), or Mathew Field's *The Making of The Italian Job* (2001), lots of production, distribution, and promotion details are now available, revealing the extent of Hollywood's involvement in the original films' creation from start to finish.

The four films discussed here seem to form a coherent cycle for a few reasons. The iconicity and appeal of Caine's early roles lie in their repetitive nature. They are all engaged in a serial exploration of the same central motif and conflict. In fact, all of Caine's characters seem to be variations on the same theme. Despite differences in scale and tone, they represent different sides of the same coin: the avenger (*Get Carter, Sleuth*), the lover (*Alfie, The Italian Job, Get Carter, Sleuth*) and the thief (*Sleuth, The Italian Job*). They have a common denominator even though they belong to different genres from comedies to crime dramas. In all of them, Caine comes across as a "cool lover" (the advertising gimmick for his starring role in *Get Carter*) and in each and every film he breaks the rules by, for example, seducing another man's partner (*Alfie, Get Carter, Sleuth*), "working a fiddle" on the job (*Alfie*) or being a member of a criminal underworld (*The Italian Job, Get Carter*).

Another important element that distinguishes these roles from Caine's output in the 1960s and 1970s is class consciousness. From the beginning of his career, Caine insisted on speaking with his own Cockney accent. As Shail explains, he is unique in "never having made any attempt to disguise his origins as a [...] working-class Londoner who had come up the hard way. In fact, he has created a screen persona which deliberately plays upon the qualities associated with his background" (Shail 2004, 68). All of his four roles display a strong class awareness and a rebel-like attitude. They also embody a desire to escape one's circumstances and to better oneself. In *Get Carter*, Jack leaves his hometown of Newcastle for a more financially rewarding and exciting career as an enforcer in the capital. In Swinging 1960s London, Alfie (*Alfie*) lives in the illusory world of guilt-free sex and Carnaby street fashion and tries to rise up in life by settling down with an older rich American lady. In *The Italian Job*, he is a leader of a gang stealing money from under the noses of the Italian Mafia.

Yet, it is in *Sleuth* above all other titles from the Cockney cycle that his character's class awareness becomes most pronounced. Whereas in Anthony Shaffer's stage play the conflict between the protagonists revolves around sexual jealousy, the motif of class difference dominates the adapted screenplay. Caine plays Milo Tindle, a young second-generation Italian immigrant hairdresser, who seduces the wife of Andrew Wyke, an eccentric upper-class crime fiction author played by Sir Laurence Olivier. Unlike in the play, Andrew continuously corrects Milo's "foul" English and the two often mock each other's accents. Milo comments on their class difference using the following words, "We are from different worlds, you and me, Andrew. In mine, there was no time for bright fancies and happy inventions, no stopping for tea. The only game we played was to survive, or go to war. If you didn't win, you just didn't finish. Loser, lose all. You probably don't understand that," which recalls many of the remarks Caine has made throughout his career about his own humble origins and early struggle in the acting profession:

> The screen was always where I wanted to be, but there were no screen acting schools. There was theater, but no one ever dreamed of becoming a film actor. It was very difficult for me because I had the wrong voice and the wrong accent. I refused to change my accent because so many people had said to me, "Who do you think you are?" I thought to myself, "If I can become a success, it will be an inspiration to other boys. You don't have to have a posh accent to succeed." It's very hard to explain class boundaries to an American. But the mistake they made

in England was equating accent with intelligence – not to mention skill, determination, and ability. (qtd. in Porton 2004, 5)

Such statements not only equate actor with character (exemplified earlier on in Caine's career through advertising campaigns such as "Michael Caine IS Alfie" and "Caine is Carter") but also show a tight link between the on-screen class wars in *Sleuth* and their off-screen reality. Aside from the two different acting schools that both actors represent, the real-life class difference creeps onto the set of *Sleuth* with Olivier's upper-middle-class background and Caine's (not a "Sir" yet) working-class belonging as a son of a charlady and a fish-market porter. Caine often mentions a letter he received from Olivier before the shoot, "Larry Olivier was Lord Olivier, we'd never met and yet we were going to do this very intimate movie together. He wrote to me saying: 'It occurred to me that you might be wondering how to address me when we meet. Well, you must address me as Larry at all times'." As he recalls, "So there's this incredible snobbery that goes on and that did impart itself to the original movie in the script. Out of the script it did because everybody, the papers said Michael Caine working-class Alfie, he's going to have to work with Lord Olivier. Boy is he gonna get showed a lesson, this little scum-bag" (qtd. in Weintraub 2017).[2]

There are of course other films in which Caine seduces other men's girl-friends or wives, steals, breaks someone's neck, and even speaks with a Cockney accent. What separates these four films from other seemingly similar roles is their iconic status. Robert Shail observes that even though Caine has often returned and reused some of the elements of his working-class screen image in many of his later works, such as *Mona Lisa*, *Dirty Rotten Scoundrels*, or *Little Voice*, it is during the 1960s in Britain that it had most cultural resonance (Shail 2004, 68). Amanda Klein defines film cycles as "useful social documents" that occur at "one specific moment in time, accurately revealing the state of contemporary politics, prevalent social ideologies, aesthetic trends, and popular desires and anxieties" (2012, 9). According to her, they offer "a time capsule of the cultural moment" and, most importantly, they give "the audiences exactly what they want" (9). Caine's rise to stardom in the 1960s is visible proof of the social transformations that had occurred in Britain. Shail believes that the actor "remains an iconographic figure of the period, embodying both the strengths and limitations of a historic moment when the credentials required to be the all-conquering hero were essentially to be male, young and working-class" (Shail 2004, 75). *Alfie*, *The Italian Job*, *Get Carter*, and *Sleuth* are therefore part of a coherent cycle of films that consistently and consciously revisited working-class themes that appealed to audiences by tapping into the then-prevalent sense of cultural shift while reflecting a desire for further changes.

Undeniably, these parts also tread in the footsteps of Caine's first break-through role as Harry Palmer, the suave Cockney spy from *The Ipcress File*, which introduced the world to Michael Caine's Cockney vowels for the first time. Released the same year as the more famous *Thunderball* (1965), which features her majesty's spy with a license to kill whose Scottish accent precludes any class identification, Palmer's Cockney accent pins him down quite clearly to one specific class and location. Analyzing the importance of Caine's accent and working-class identity, Bray notices:

> [b]efore Caine, the typical British movie hero was either a nob or wannabe nob. After Caine, local accents became more and more acceptable – so much so that even public-school-educated journalists and television presenters would take to speaking the ersatz London dialect of mockney. Where would the likes of, say, Johnny Vaughan or Jamie Oliver be without Caine's example – perhaps most crucially his example in *Alfie*? (Bray 2006, 81)

Harry Palmer blends the ordinary qualities exemplified by his NHS prescription glasses with extraordinary mental perseverance and a penchant for insubordination of his superiors – the qualities that help him survive in a highly bureaucratic, authoritarian, and hierarchical system and at a critical moment even save his life. Shail explains the phenomenon of his appeal further:

> His combination of an astute sense of urban style and a streetwise canniness made him an immediate icon of the fashionable male pro-letarian ascendancy. Even his "National Health specs" became part of the downbeat image. Caine's persona brought together a sense of ordinariness, which made it easy for audiences to identify with him, with a feeling that his rough-edged, quick-wittedness was the essential ingredient in his success, a quality that any working-class lad might equally possess. (Shail 2004, 69–70)

While at first sight the features of Caine's 1960s and 1970s iconic Cockney roles mentioned above may not necessarily lend themselves easily to Holly-wood make-overs, the fact remains that he was responsible for creating a new type of English screen masculinity that was seemingly more similar to Hollywood leading men. Starting with his first role in *The Ipcress File* that depicted him as a sophisticated working-class Londoner, his next four roles from the Cockney cycle further established Caine as an icon of contemporary style and fashion. As Shail observes, Caine with his carefully orches-trated image on- and off-screen dictated how to dress, where to shop, and what to eat to many young males of his generation (2004, 69). His char-acters are also highly sexualized, physical, streetwise, smart, and tough in contrast to the then more prevalent image of the English man on screen as articulate, physically awkward, and sexually ambivalent. Caine explains it best in an interview with *The Times*: "if you look at English males in our films, they're either homosexual, bisexual, cold, repressed, fucked up, no

good with women, bad lovers, kinky or insane ... The Englishman in films
has always been weird with women. Here you have an actor who in *Alfie*
went out and screwed them all, in *The Italian Job* he stole the gold and
screwed them all, and in *Get Carter* he killed all the bad guys and screwed
all the girls. So there you have three icons ... which is me" (qtd. in Field
2001, 110). Jonathan Stubbs sets the scene further: "Three years after the
release of *Dr. No* (1962), Michael Caine rose to stardom through his role
in *The Ipcress File* (1965). Like Connery, Caine was distinguished from
his contemporaries by his working-class, non-theatre school background,
this time in London's East End and the British Army. Later British films,
notably *Alfie* (1966) and *The Italian Job* (1969), established Caine as a la-
conic, cockney variant on Connery's suave, hedonistic tough-guy" (1999,
89). Thus, together with Connery, Stamp, and Finney, Caine seems to have
paved the way for an alternative British screen hero more along the lines of
Hollywood stars than the famous English stage actors of his time. Stubbs
discusses the impact Connery and Caine have had on the generation of
British actors to come in the following words:

> In the last twenty years, Caine and Connery have been joined by a range
> of British actors who have also eschewed the cultural trappings of the
> British thespian tradition on their way to Hollywood. Most prominent
> are Tim Roth, Jude Law, Ewan McGregor, Gary Oldman, Clive Owen,
> Christian Bale and Pierce Brosnan. Collectively, these actors might be
> said to embody a different kind of British masculinity. In almost dia-
> metric contrast to the traditional British stage actor, these actors are
> defined by their heavily physical performance styles, which enable them
> to take on more action-based and often more explicitly heterosexual
> roles [...] In this way, the masculinity of the non-thespian British actors
> may be understood to occupy a middle ground between the British
> stage actor and the American star actor. By rejecting the high-culture,
> socially elite associations of the British stage, two generations of British
> actors, from Sean Connery to Jude Law, have forged a set of identities
> for British actors that adhere more closely to Hollywood's dominant
> representation of masculinity. (Stubbs 1999, 90–91)

This also explains why two of Caine's roles, Jack Carter and Charlie Croker, were given to icons of Hollywood tough guy masculinity, Sylvester
Stallone and the actor-remaker par excellence Mark Wahlberg when they
were remade in America in the new millennium.

Another reason why Hollywood may have become interested in revisiting Caine's 1960s and 1970s Cockney cycle can be observed in its critical
importance and cultural return toward the end of the 1990s. Examining
the list of the Best 100 British Films published by the BFI in 1999 reveals
the iconic status of his roles and reflects on their continued cultural relevance. The ranking mentions three titles from the cycle.[3] *Get Carter*, a film
largely forgotten by the establishment, takes the 16th place, showing its

newly found status. The film was remade[4] in 2000 as *Get Carter*, featuring Sylvester Stallone. The time of the publication also coincided with Warner Bros.' decision to re-release the original *Get Carter* in UK theatres before the remake hit the screens. *Alfie*, number 33 in the ranking, was then re-made in 2004 with Jude Law reappraising Caine's role as a London wom-anizer with the DVD release of the original *Alfie* occurring even earlier, two years after the BFI poll, and confirming its cultural importance and status. *The Italian Job*, which occupies the 36th place in the ranking, was remade in 2003, but the idea was already forged in 1999 when Paramount announced their interest in remaking the original film.

Toward the end of the 1990s Caine returned not only to the charts but also on a larger cultural scene. His characters seemed to speak to a new generation of young men who similarly liked lager and violence, and treated the opposite sex instrumentally, apparently finding solace in Caine's cool machismo. *Get Carter* was adopted as a symbol of the new Lad movement, while Guy Ritchie in his *Lock, Stock and Two Smoking Barrels* (1998) paid tribute to *The Italian Job* in its cliff-hanger ending and to *Get Carter* by fetishizing the rifle that features in the 1971 film.

What also turns these four films into a separate category, although ret-rospectively, is of course the fact that they were all singled out for Hol-lywood remaking purposes. The timing of the remakes could not have occurred at a better moment as they seem to have continued and solidified the process of the many "returns" of Michael Caine already underway. The remakes were made in the period from 2000 onward that was marked by a growing awareness of film history, the rise of the "movie-geek" phe-nomenon, and the arrival of DVDs in the late 1990s, which, as Barbara Klinger observes, inspired "cinema's contemporary cultural omnipres-ence" (2006, 58), not only encouraging film collecting but also helping revive forgotten cult and classic films of the past as Tryon notices in his work on DVD culture (2009). Its importance in the continued revival of Michael Caine's iconic roles cannot be underestimated. Table 2.3.1 shows

Table 2.3.1 Theatrical and DVD release dates of Michael Caine's British originals and their Hollywood remakes

Original films	Theatrical release	US DVD release	UK DVD Release	Hollywood remakes	Theatrical release	US DVD release	UK DVD release
Alfie	1966	2001	2001	Alfie	2004	2005	2005
The Italian Job	1969	2003	2002	The Italian Job	2003	2003	2003
Get Carter	1971	2000	2000	Get Carter	2000	2001	2002
Sleuth	1972	1998	2002	Sleuth	2007	2008	2008

that each of the remakes of his works also resulted in the release of the originals on DVD. By finding titles that have a cult or classic status and a built-in audience, Hollywood not only ensures financial profits but also plays an active part in the originals' preservation and longevity. Looking at the significance of the remakes in assisting the revival of the original British pictures confirms Barbara Klinger's words: "Like museums and memorials, Hollywood acts as a custodian of the past, orchestrating meaningful and influential confrontations with its archive for viewers" (2006, 92–93).

All of the remakes show close ties to the originals in several ways. *Get Carter*'s link to the original is established by casting Caine as the villain he kills in the "first installment," evoking the earlier version by "celebrity intertextuality" that Verevis refers to (2006, 20). Caine's decision to act opposite Stallone is challenging to read, especially as following the remake's bad reputation, he has dismissed his participation as a joke. It seems, however, that he was initially keen to show his support for the project.[5] Moreover, the fact that in the remake of *Get Carter*, located in Seattle, Caine speaks with his London accent clearly alludes to the original British classic.

"But how often do remakes (as opposed to sequels) really succeed commercially and/or creatively? The 1960s and 1970s are now seen as something of a golden age in cinema, but retooling the iconic pictures of the era had rarely yielded dividends. For example, nobody seemed to profit from the Sylvester Stallone remake of Mike Hodges's *Get Carter* in which Michael Caine had made a riveting anti-hero," wonders Michael Deeley, the producer of the 1969 *Italian Job* (2008, 271). However, even if the remake failed financially and critically, it seems to have solidified the original's status and helped its revival process that was already in full swing in Britain but needed prompting in the United States. Through its association with Sylvester Stallone and thanks to the studio's efforts to promote the original on DVD, the 1971 *Get Carter* has achieved an almost equal measure of success on both sides of the Atlantic. As Steve Chibnall explains:

> In October 2000 [...], Warner Bros. released a digitally remastered *Get Carter* for the first time on DVD and in widescreen video. The movie was accompanied by its American trailer, footage of Roy Budd playing the theme tune, and Caine's filmed introduction for the Newcastle première, with additional commentary by Hodges, Caine and Suschitzky. Warner's marketeers pulled out all the stops, offering a limited-edition run in "luxury film cases" with a copy of the screenplay and four collectors' images, and bally'hooing the release with full-page advertising in the film monthlies and point-of-sale displays in retail outlets. (Chibnall 2003, 110)

That the original film profited through its association with the remake is evident when one examines a sudden surge of interest in the film online, which, as Chibnall notices, is "astonishing for a thirty-year-old film, and a revealing measure of *Carter*'s new stature" (2003, 103) and a tell-tale sign that Caine's decision to act in the remake was not a joke but possibly a shrewd move that allowed the actor to have the last laugh. On the 1971 *Get Carter* DVD commentary Caine discusses the original ending in which Jack Carter gets shot by an unknown assassin: "I would have loved him to have walked away but we used to kill people in pictures those days. They were no sequels [laughs]. Maybe it's better that there's just *Carter* instead of *Carter* 1, 2, 3 and 4. I've already done a series, which is Harry Palmer. Played the same character three times." Still, the remake has not only "resurrected" Carter but also seems to have allowed Caine to act in a version of *Carter* 2.

Even though Caine expressed his interest in taking the part of Mr. Bridger in the remake of *The Italian Job* to show his support for the project in the same way he did with Stallone's *Carter*, the role went to Donald Sutherland instead as Caine was committed to another film at the time. However, the remake does feature a small cameo appearance by Caine when the villain of the film played by Edward Norton watches the 1969 *Italian Job* on his new plasma TV. With or without Caine's acting part in the film, the remake's success, together with the DVD release of the original as a collector's item with numerous supplemental features, has sealed the earlier film's status and given it a new lease of life, proving Verevis's point about contemporary remakes that tend to enjoy a more "symbiotic relationship with their originals, with publicity and reviews often drawing attention to earlier versions" (2006, 16) as the two co-exist "in the contemporary media marketplace" (2006, 138).

The reason why Paramount decided to revisit *The Italian Job* definitely lies in its strong cult status and success in Britain, which offered a ready-made audience. Whereas in the original, Caine is a lover and thief, in the remake, Wahlberg's character is a lover, a thief, and an avenger, which shows that the new version revisits all the central motifs from Caine's entire Cockney cycle. While the original could be screened in British high schools as a Christmas film (G rating), the remake has a PG13 (parents strongly cautioned) rating and thus would not qualify. Unlike its progenitor, it contains less humor, is much darker, includes the death of Mr. Bridger, the gang leader played by Donald Sutherland, and has a strong revenge and family theme. Introducing the motif of revenge romanticizes the thieves and makes them more likable since they appear to be on the side of justice and honor. The film thus blends numerous genre elements: heist, revenge, and also romance by focusing on Croker's relationship with Bridge's daughter, which was not the case in the original film.

In the 1969 version, the majority of the famous one-liners belong to Michael Caine's Charlie, a womanizer and a veritable rogue, whose charismatic persona overshadows everybody else in the picture. These features are purged from a much nobler version of Wahlberg's hero and moved instead to the background. A member of supporting cast, Jason Statham's Handsome Rob, a Brit and a new movie icon of London underworld and Lad culture, is the true successor to the original Croker. His talent is fast driving and the ease with which he can charm the opposite sex. For many viewers, Statham's cool and charming gangster persona is also a playful re-minder of *Lock, Stock and Two Smoking Barrels*, which treads in the foot-steps of the original *Italian Job* and contributed to the revival of Caine's Cockney cycle in Britain at the time.

In contrast to the first two remakes updated to suit the star image of their leading American men, the next two remakes star a British actor, Jude Law. It is debatable to what degree Law is able, however, to adhere to a Holly-wood's dominant representation of masculinity as many of his roles appear to question gender stereotypes. If one remembers, however, that Caine's first Cockney character in *The Ipcress File* also challenged heteronormative paradigms by preparing a meal for a woman and doing his own shopping, then Law seems to be a very interesting casting choice that continues and develops some of the elements of Caine's own acting persona. Law plays not just in one but two remakes from Caine's cycle, *Alfie* and *Sleuth*, which establishes him as Caine's British successor and also links the two remakes together, turning them in effect into an ongoing series with two install-ments and possibly more to come in the future.

To start with, it is worth citing one of the user comments on IMDb about the *Alfie* remake that seems to hit the mark: "If you see the original first and then watch the remake you'll feel like you've seen the same movie, which as a great director once said, 'that's what everyone wants from a se-quel'. Not that this is a sequel, but it could have been, it would have worked almost as well as Alfie 2: son of Alfie" (pling-3 2017). Although not to be taken literally, this idea is quite interesting to explore. In the 1966 version, Alfie fathers a cute blond boy whom he quickly abandons, unwilling to commit. Although Jude Law was born seven years later in 1973, many have commented on a physical resemblance between the two actors especially following the remake of *Alfie*. In a sense, Caine might be seen as a surrogate father figure to Law, especially since he has often expressed his admiration for the young actor.

Despite Caine's personal endorsement, the remake did not perform very well financially or critically. One of the reasons could be the type of mas-culinity that Law inhabited for the role. Law substituted Caine's machismo with metrosexuality – a term coined in 2002 by Mark Simpson. His Al-fie's unhindered interest in fashion, appearance, and accessories, previously coded homosexual, was supposed to reflect society's supposed gradual ac-ceptance of the new man into the mainstream. At the beginning of the film, speaking of his wardrobe, he proudly asserts, "If you ooze masculinity, like some of us do, you have no reason to fear pink." Law's new millennium Al-fie is not entirely at odds with Caine's own on- and off-screen 1960s image considering that Caine was a fashion icon photographed by David Baily for

"Box of Pin-ups" and that the actor's long eyelashes almost cost him his career as he was found to be too pretty to be the leading man by Joseph E. Levine, the producer of his screen debut *Zulu* (1964). With hindsight, however, perhaps the new version of *Alfie* arrived a few of years prematurely when Lad culture was still active in the UK with Caine's 1960s and 1970s cool machismo serving as its key model.

The battle between two types of masculinity continues in *Sleuth*, where Jude Law plays Milo, the character Caine personified in the 1972 version, and Caine takes on the part of Andrew, previously played by Laurence Olivier. Whereas class animosity was the main driving force behind the original's conflict, the remake is more concerned with two opposite images of gender, one represented by Caine and glorified by Lad culture, the other personified by Law and defined as camp and narcissistic through associations with Law's earlier roles including Alfie. Whereas *Sleuth* 1972 addressed the issue of a performative nature of class, the update dwells on a performative nature of gender as both Milo and Andrew adapt their roles throughout the film to outwit, surprise, and humiliate their opponent. Considering that the adapted screenplay was authored by Harold Pinter, it is no surprise that crossing the borders of sexual/gender normativity becomes the subtext of *Sleuth* 2007. The protagonists at first threaten, then flirt with, each other, and in the end, they openly challenge each other's sexual orientation and gender identity.[6] The film failed at the box office and produced very mixed critical response when it came out but seems to have found favor with viewers who give it a relatively high score of 6.5 on IMDB.com, where it keeps provoking vibrant discussion.

Finally, it is worth mentioning one more film starring Michael Caine as a Cockney lover and gangster – *Gambit* (1966), which was remade in 2012 with Colin Firth reappraising Caine's part. Even though the original was a US production, unlike the other four titles discussed here, which are more distinctly identifiable as British due to their location and themes, allowing them to be treated as a coherent cycle, the remake of *Gambit* nonetheless shows the trend of returning to Michael Caine's Cockney roles. There are two elements in the remake written by the Coen brothers that seem to pay respect to Caine's Cockney cycle in general. First of all, the action from the original comedy caper that takes place in Hong Kong is moved to London, paying tribute to Caine's birthplace and returning to the roots. Secondly, Firth's character (significantly called Harry just like in the original but also in reference to Michael Caine's first starring Cockney role) wears think-rimmed glasses that Harry Palmer of *The Ipcress File* made famous. Caine's character in *Gambit* does not wear them at all. What is more, Caine wore such glasses in real life and helped define male fashion in the 1960s Swinging London. He brought them to the set of Harry Palmer spy series, reinventing the look of a typical spy. Despite numerous assertions from Firth that *Gambit* (2012) is only a loose adaptation of the original, its London location and his character's retro "Ipcress File" spectacles are imbued with nostalgia for Caine's 1960s London films and the actor's style and look that made him an icon of the period

As seen above, Michael Caine has been uniquely supportive of the re-making of his films, realizing, it seems, that they all promote "Michael Caine" as a brand. He has endorsed these projects irrelevant of their financial or critical success, aware that, as far as show business is concerned, all publicity is good publicity. With or without Caine's acting part in the films, the remakes, together with the DVD releases of the originals often as collector's items with numerous supplemental features, have sealed the earlier films' status and given them a new lease of life.

Caine's reputation as one of Hollywood's best storytellers may have also added extra value and incentive for DVD releases of his earlier works. Known for his humor, charm, wit, and a great memory, Caine seems exceptionally attuned to the medium with over 30 years of practice on numerous talk shows, finding in the DVD format a perfect outlet for the information he wishes to impress upon his viewers and preserve for posterity. Ready to impart production details, acting tips, and numerous anecdotes about film industry insiders, he functions as a well of information for any movie buff and collector. The DVDs of 1971 *Get Carter*, 1969 *The Italian Job,* 2004 *Alfie*, and 2007 *Sleuth* stand out for the depth and wealth of information in their bonus materials. The actor's entertaining and highly informative comments have also found their way into academic publications, for instance, Chibnall's *Get Carter* (2003) or *The Man Who Got Carter* (2013), showing the new value of trivia that Klinger (2006) or Jenkins address (1992). Klinger observes that "while film trivia may lack respect as a form of knowledge in certain circles, it is not genuinely marginalized or unsanctioned; it is a major form of currency that helps to build relationships not simply among fans but also between fans and media producers and promoters" (87). Looking at the impact the remaking process has had on the preservation and dissemination of Caine's early films, one can see how they have benefited by being repackaged and rebranded for new audiences and sold as part of an essential viewing canon.

"If to narrate is to triumph over death" (2006, 9) as Anat Zanger puts it, then Caine, with his ability to retell the same stories over and over again, is the perfect embodiment of the actions of Hollywood itself – a self-preservation society or a snake that eats its tail, re-inventing its products while archiving originals. In the digital era marked by a growing awareness of film history, the long tail now remains enjoyed and in the memory of many causing Hollywood remakes to not obliterate the originals but often contribute to their second life, be it through theatrical re-releases or DVD reissues. Caine's 1960s and 1970s Cockney cycle has not suffered from its associations with the remakes but has, on the contrary, gained in popularity on an even larger scale. American funding was thus not only essential at the moment of the original films' inception but also played a crucial role in their reinstatement in the new millennium.

Notes

1 *Sleuth* was also the last film directed by a Hollywood veteran – Joseph L. Mankiewicz.
2 The opposite happened when Olivier paid Caine the greatest compliment of his career by saying that he thought he just had an assistant but in fact he had a partner. Olivier's appreciation of Caine was manifested again posthumously during his funeral service in Westminster Abbey. Caine was selected to carry Olivier's Oscar for Lifetime Achievements, which shows the measure of respect the late actor bestowed on his onetime co-star.
3 Caine features in the total of seven films on the BFI Top 100.
4 There is one more film that rewrites the original *Get Carter: The Limey*, made in 1999 and starring Terence Stamp, which is a remake/sequel/homage to the original work.
5 For a more detailed discussion see Rasmus (2013).
6 For a more detailed discussion see Rasmus (2012).

Works cited

Bray, Christopher. *Michael Caine: A Class Act*. London: Faber and Faber, 2006.
Caine, Michael. "*Sleuth*–Sir Michael Caine Interview". *IndieLondon*, n.d. www. indielondon.co.uk/Film-Review/sleuth-sir-michael-caine-interview (accessed 01.15.2017).
Chibnall, Steve. *Get Carter: A British Film Guide 6*. London: I.B. Tauris, 2003.
Davies, Hugh. "America Will Fall for Jude Law's Alfie, Predicts Michael Caine". *The Telegraph*, 10.08.2007. www.telegraph.co.uk/news/uknews/1469976/America-will-fall-for-Jude-Laws-Alfie-predicts-Michael-Caine.html (accessed 01.15.2017).
Deeley, Michael. *Blade Runners, Deer Hunters, and Blowing the Bloody Doors off: My Life in Cult Movies*. London: Faber and Faber, 2008.
Field, Matthew. *The Making of The Italian Job*. London: B. T. Batsford, 2001.
Jenkins, Henry. *Textual Poachers: Television Fans and Participatory Culture*. New York: Routledge, 1992.
Kelleter, Frank, and Kathleen Loock. "Hollywood Remaking as Second-order Serialization". In Frank Kelleter (ed.), *Media of Serial Narrative*, Columbus: Ohio State University Press, 2017. 112–133.
Klein, Amanda. *American Film Cycles: Reframing Genres, Screening Social Problems, and Defining Subcultures*. Austin: UT Press, 2012.
Klinger, Barbara. *Beyond the Multiplex Cinema, New Technologies, and the Home*. Berkeley: University of California Press, 2006.
pling-3 from Maidstone, Kent. "The Point Isn't That It's a Remake." *IMDb*, 10.25.2004, https://www.imdb.com/review/rw0951804/?ref_=tt_urv (accessed 01.15.2017).
Porton, Richard. "The Character Actor as Movie Star: An Interview with Michael Caine". *Cineaste* 29.2, 2004. 4–7.
Rasmus, Agnieszka. "'I Know Where I've Seen You Before!': Hollywood Remakes of British Films, from DVD Box Sets to the Online Debate". In Kathleen Loock (ed.), *Serial Narratives*, *LWU* 47.1–2, 2014. 97–110.
Rasmus, Agnieszka. "Crossing Frontiers, Staking Out New Territories: Hollywood Remaking British Crime Locations in *Get Carter*". In Jacek Fabiszak, Ewa

Urbaniak-Rybicka and Bartosz Wolski (eds.), *Crossroads in Literature and Culture*, Berlin, Heidelberg: Springer, 2013. 493–503.

Rasmus, Agnieszka. "Same but Different: Comparing Transgression in *Sleuth*". In Miroslawa Buchholtz and Grzegorz Koneczniak (eds.), *The Visual and the Verbal in Film, Drama, Literature and Biography*, Frankfurt: Peter Lang, 2012. 29–42.

Shail, Robert. "Masculinity and Class: Michael Caine as 'Working-Class Hero'". In Phil Powrie, Ann Davies, and Bruce Babington (eds.), *The Trouble With Men. Masculinities in European and Hollywood Cinema*, London: Wallflower Press, 2004. 66–76.

Street, Sarah. *Transatlantic Crossings: British Feature Films in the USA*. New York; London: Continuum, 2002.

Stubbs, Jonathan, "Sleeping with the Hegemony: British Cinema and Hollywood in the 1990s". Master's thesis, University of Warwick, 1999.

Tryon, Chuck. *Reinventing Cinema Movies in the Age of Media Convergence*. New Brunswick, NJ: Rutgers University Press, 2009.

Verevis, Constantine. *Film Remakes*. Edinburgh: Edinburgh University Press, 2006.

Weintraub, Steve 'Frosty'. "Michael Caine and Kenneth Branagh Interview–*SLEUTH*". *Collider*, 10.7.2007. https://collider.com/michael-caine-and-kenneth-branagh-interview-sleuth/(accessed 03.15.2020).

Zanger, Anat. *Film Remakes as Ritual and Disguise: from Carmen to Ripley*. Amsterdam: Amsterdam University Press, 2006.

Films cited

Alfie. Lewis Gilbert, Lewis Gilbert Productions, 1966.
Alfie. Charles Shyer, Paramount, 2004.
Gambit. Ronald Neame, Universal, 1996.
Gambit. Michael Hoffman, Crimes Scene Pictures, 2012.
Get Carter. Mike Hodges, MGM GB, 1971.
Get Carter. Stephen Kay, Morgan Creek Entertainment, 2000.
Ipcress File. Sidney J. Furie, The Rank Organisation, 1965.
The Italian Job. 1969. Peter Collinson, Paramount, 2009.
The Italian Job. F. Gary Gray, Paramount. 2003.
Sleuth. Joseph L. Mankiewicz. Palomar Pictures International, 1972.
Sleuth. Kenneth Branagh. Sony Pictures, 2007.

Part III
Seriality and the cinematic/ televisual convergence

3.1 The (re)making of a serial killer

Replaying, "preplaying," and rewriting Hitchcock's *Psycho* in the series *Bates Motel*

Dennis Tredy

Undertaking a new remake of or sequel to the vast and complex *Psycho* book and movie franchise would be a mammoth task for any writer or filmmaker, and this is not only due to the original film's iconic status, its recognition by all and its adulation by many. One would also have to deal with the massive weight of the well-established mythology and seriality that grew out of the initial novel and film adaptation through a wide range of sequels and re-makes in book and movie form, of both official and unofficial entries in the franchise, along with lookalikes and scores of stories of Bates-like slashers.

In the public consciousness, this vast Bates mythology began with Hitch-cock's unforgettable 1960 masterpiece – though technically it began with the Robert Bloch's 1959 novel, which Hitchcock and his screenwriter Joseph Stefano had very closely transcribed. Much like Stanley Kubrick's adapta-tion of Anthony Burgess's *A Clockwork Orange* a decade later, Hitchcock's *Psycho* was remarkably faithful to but far outshined the original novel, briefly bringing the book out of obscurity before totally eclipsing it in the minds of the public at large. There are indeed only a few very slight differ-ences between Bloch's and Hitchcock's storyline (the shower-scene victim is beheaded and named Mary in the novel, stabbed and named Marion in the film, for example). The more striking differences stem from those inherent in the two media, such as how we are led to believe that Nor-man's mother is still alive throughout the novel because we often see things through the protagonist's demented point of view, whereas in the film the same shocking reveal is pulled off through Hitchcock's narrative and visual trickery.[1] Another key change would involve making the Norman Bates character younger and far more sympathetic to movie-goers than he had been to readers, for Bloch had closely modeled his gruff and off-putting Norman after one of America's first-known serial killers, Ed Gein, a Wis-consin farmer who was so infatuated with his dead mother that he used the skin and hair of his victims to dress up as her.[2] It would appear that those two main changes – Hitchcock's twist-inducing narrative trickery and the disturbingly endearing persona created for Norman – could go a long way to explaining why the film so outshined the novel.

The film would indeed make such an indelible mark on cinema and on the general public that it would take nearly 22 years before either Bloch or the film industry would dare to pick up the storyline again, and each of them would advance the serial narrative in starkly different directions. In Bloch's sequels, there would be no attempt to stoke sympathy for Norman Bates or to keep him alive too long, for at the outset of *Psycho II* (1982) Norman is killed off while escaping a mental institution, just after he murders two nuns, raping one's dead body (though his early death is revealed later in the novel). The novels then focus on new murderers who seem to have somehow "caught" Norman's psychosis and whose victims are people who are somehow trying to benefit from the notoriety of Norman's initial crimes at the motel – thus, in the sequel, the madman killing participants in a new film (*"Lady Killer"*) about the famous Bates murders is revealed to be Norman's longtime psychiatrist, Dr. Claiborne, while Bloch's follow-up, *Psycho House* (1990), stages serial murders by a deranged and obsessed journalist staying at the Bates Motel, now a sleazy tourist attraction glorifying long-dead Norman's exploits 30 years earlier.

However, the serial timeline created by Universal Studios and Showtime's film sequels – rather than following the Norman-less "contagion storyline" of the novels – sought to keep Norman Bates alive and on-screen for the duration, realizing that for film audiences the presence of Anthony Perkins *as* Norman Bates was as iconic and ineluctable to the film franchise as the gloomy house on the hill or the shower in Room One.[3] In this parallel continuity created for the film *Psycho II* (1983), Norman is released from the asylum, rather than escaping, and returns to the motel, where he falls victim both to false accusations of murders that are actually committed by a long-lost relative and to an elaborate charade, designed to make him doubt his sanity, perpetrated by Marion Crane's descendants. Thus our sympathy for Norman greatly increases (he is not the heartless slasher and necrophiliac of the book sequel), even if he does snap at the end of the sequel and begins to kill again. In *Psycho III* (1986), directed by Perkins himself, unstable Norman falls for a young woman who is the spitting image of his mother, finally "curing" himself by stabbing the corpse of his mother (or rather his aunt, who claimed to be his mother), while in *Psycho IV - The Beginning* (Showtime, 1990), the timeline forges ahead with Norman being again released from an institution and this time founding a family, while having him call in to a radio show on "matricide" so as to frame a series of flashbacks to Norman's childhood and adolescence with his mother (thereby strongly reinforcing their backstory as outlined in the first novel and previous films). In this timeline, Norman has a chance for a happy ending, having once again "cured" himself – this time by burning down his childhood home.

And though these three novels and the four successive films, in spite of their diverging plotlines, would provide the bulk of the enormous backstory and mythology on the Bates characters that a new filmmaker would have to deal with, there were additional remakes that brought no new backstory but might influence new narrative elements or the aesthetics of a new film or series. What, if anything, should be kept of the failed 1987 TV-pilot, *Bates Motel*, which was a contrived ghost story dealing not with Norman but with a longtime roommate of his at the asylum who inherits the motel at Norman's death? Similarly, though no backstory was added through Gus Van Sant's much-maligned "nearly identical" remake of *Psycho* (1998) – an experiment in filmmaking in which a new filmmaker in the late 1990s shot from the same script that was used by Hitchcock – one might still find some inspiration in the film's unusual mixture of modern and early 1960s aesthetics in terms of costume, set design, and use of color. Also, by showing how two different directors in two different eras shot the same script, and by creating a remake in which the slightest differences in filming stand out all the more, the second film stresses the director's role over the screenwriter's in terms of *authorship* and the inherent modernizing and *reaccentuation* of the story that come from shooting it nearly 40 years later. These issues would be of paramount importance to anyone taking on an adaptation, remake, or sequel of such a landmark film today.[4]

In addition, should one even consider the vast array of low-budget, unofficial sequels, and lookalikes, such as Robert Vincent O'Neill's *Psycho Lover* (1970), Pete Jacelone's *Psycho Sisters* (1998), or Alex Downs's *Motor Psycho* (1992)? And if, as many critics have pointed out, the original *Psycho* film can be seen as the template for Brian De Palma's neo-Hitchcockian thrillers such as *Dressed to Kill* (1980), or popular horror franchises like *Friday the 13th* or *Halloween*, or perhaps even the entire slasher film sub-genre (Verevis 2006, 72–74, Zanger 2006, 22), would a new showrunner or filmmaker be at all tempted to make those films part of the intertextual makeup of his new project? Finally, should a new addition to the *Psycho* legacy go as far as to take into consideration the extradiegetic, *non-fiction* backstory that was the basis of Bloch's first novel: the story of Minnesota madman Ed Gein, for was this horrid news event not the *real* making of Norman Bates?

Deciding how to deal with such a vast legacy and firmly established mythology – and the high expectations that go with them – undoubtedly made for a daunting challenge when writer/producer Carlton Cuse (*Lost*, ABC, 2004–2010) agreed to be lead showrunner, along with the authors of the initial teleplay, Kerry Ehrin (*Friday Night Lights*, NBC, 2006–2011), and Antonio Cipriano (director of the film *12 & Holding*, 2005), for *Bates Motel* (*A&E*, 2013–2017). The 50-episode series, produced by Universal Television, was devised as a five-season "contemporary prequel" to and eventual remake of Hitchcock's *Psycho*. Cuse and his team thus decided to take on the added challenge of using the iconic 1960 film as an endpoint rather than a starting point, even though the series would take place in today's world. The first four seasons would then be a 40-episode prequel to the original film, the making of a serial killer or a Bates-*Bildungsroman*, if you will, focusing on the troubled life of Norman and his mother Norma long *before* Marion Crane ever rings the front-desk bell at the Bates Motel. The ten-episode fifth season, which will be occasionally referred to but will not be the focus of this study, would then technically be a remake rather than a prequel, for the series' continuity will have caught up to that of the original film by then and will run parallel to it.

The myriad challenges inherent to Cuse, Ehrin, and Cipriano's prequel endeavor are all somehow related to notions of established seriality and viewers' expectations, and each part of the following study will explore a different way in which the showrunners re-authored that legacy and dealt with those issues.[5] The first focus will be to explore the creation of a modified plotline and revamped character development *vis-à-vis* the well-established Bates mythology outlined above. What, if anything, was kept from the original continuity and backstory for Norma and Norman Bates, and how did the new serialized storyline retro-engineer the icon that is Norman Bates? What changes were made to increase our sympathy for Norman and Norma, and to ensure intense and suspenseful seriality when, paradoxically, we all know exactly where it is all going, what will become of the main characters, and how it will all end? The second part of this analysis sets aside such character- and plot-related concerns to focus on more theory-based dimensions stemming from the choice of making the series a "contemporary prequel" – that is, a story set in 2013–2017 that somehow looks *ahead* to the 1960 film by Hitchcock. What games do Cuse and his team play with visual aesthetics and cultural references to somehow bridge that non-linear time gap? How can viewers look forward and backward at the same time? Finally, this dialectic of past and future will lead to another level of non-linear continuity between the contemporary series and the classic film, for Cuse attempted to satisfy both new audiences and tried-and-true *Psycho* film-buffs through a complex network of cross-referencing between the film and the series, one that involves serial repetition and replay – or what Andrew Scahill has dubbed "preplay" (2016, 327) – of allusions, motifs, or references that repeatedly look ahead to (i.e., look back to) Hitchcock's masterpiece, and that keep the anticipation strong though well outside more linear and conventional forms of seriality.

Rewriting the Bates legacy – enhanced suspense, seriality, and sympathy

Carlton Cuse and his team thus had a dizzyingly vast legacy of backstory and a set Bates mythology with which to work when rebooting the storyline. Though Bloch's trilogy, with its "Bates-contagion" timeline, and the successive "official" film sequels, with what could be called the "perpetual-Perkins" timeline, occasionally provided contradictory elements of backstory regarding Norman's pre-Marion Crane existence, there are a few core tenets of the mythology that all of these previous works shared and respected:

1 Norman's father was killed when he was about six years old (by his real mother in the second film, by his aunt pretending to be his mother in the third film).
2 Norma and Norman lived in seclusion and in a state of total co-dependence for years, though she was cruel and overbearing, repressed her son's sexual development with violent, Puritanical zeal, and suffered from either schizophrenia and/or borderline personality disorder.
3 Jealous of her mother's taking a lover, Norman poisoned both of them and forged a murder-suicide note from his mother.
4 The horror and guilt of matricide *created* Norman's split personality as a coping mechanism, pushing him to dress as his mother and kill women when they sexually aroused him. His psychosis thus did not exist before he killed his mother.

The showrunners seem to have decided from the start that nearly all of this mythology would have to go, particularly in terms of Norman's relationship with his mother, and before the series pilot aired Cuse warned viewers of this change: "The mythology that you think is what dictates the relationship between Norma and Norman is not what it's going to turn out to be" (Goldberg 2016). Indeed, nearly all the main tenets listed above will be broken. The series begins with Norma (Vera Farmiga) and Norman (Freddy Highmore) starting over in a new town just after the death of the boy's father (though we soon learn that it was Norman, as a teenager and not a child, who killed him during one of his blackouts, while defending his mother). Secondly, and more importantly, Norman's descent into total madness would have to happen gradually over the first four seasons – thus *long before* he kills his mother – so that we truly have a "becoming" story for Norman Bates, the *making of* a serial killer as it were, in 40 episodes or so. Thirdly, though Norma and Norman are indeed deeply co-dependent, they are not completely cut off from the rest of society, at least not at first, and Norma Bates is drastically rewritten. Though she may fit the psychiatrist's description of her as a "clinging, demanding woman" in the original film (1:39), she is by no means a cruel and sadistic oppressor but instead a flawed but warm and endearing working mother whose love for her son and desire to protect him prevent her from seeing the growing menace he represents. This allows for deeper sympathy for and identification with both Norma and Norman from the onset of the show, thereby making the tragedy of what everyone knows is to come in the final season even more striking and poignant.

The progressive decline of Norman also allows for stronger seriality and suspense, as viewers will eagerly await the next sign that the nervous and kind-hearted schoolboy from the early episodes is getting one step closer to the adult Norman Bates they know from Hitchcock's film. This gradual development was one of several key devices devised by Cuse to ensure gripping seriality and forward-driving suspense – on par with that of *Breaking Bad* or *Homeland*, he claimed (Goldman 2016) – again for a tale for which everyone knows the ending. Other devices included creating additional main characters, like Dylan (Max Thieriot), Norman's foil and rugged, well-adjusted half-brother, Emma (Olivia Cooke), a quirky and attractive love interest to both Norman and Dylan who suffers from cystic fibrosis, and Sheriff Romero (Nestor Carbonell), a crooked but righteous cop who will later be Norma's love interest and who opens the door, along with Dylan, to many unsavory characters who crawl out of White Pine Bay's seedy underworld of drugs, crime, and intrigue. The multiplicity of criminal activities and unwholesome or ill-fated relationships, in addition to those directly involving Norman and Norma, allows the showrunners to provide intense seriality throughout its entire 40-episode "prequel" story arc, with each episode ending on a twist, cliffhanger, climax, or reveal – regarding either Norman's development or one of the myriad other storylines – that will drive each episode forward. Cuse, however, would admittedly reserve the greatest climaxes regarding Norman's overall transformation for the end of each season, considering each of the four prequel seasons a ten-hour film on the next big stage in the "becoming" of Norman Bates (Goldman 2016). Thus Season 1 ends with Norman's first murder of an innocent during one of his blackouts, Season 2 when Norman's mind clearly splits into his own and that of the persona of "Mother," Season 3 when he kills Bradley's mother, the first time we see him killing *as* "Mother," and Season 4, which ends with him killing the last person who needs to die to set the stage for the film remake that is Season 5.

As if this matrix were not enough to ensure suspense-driven seriality, Cuse and his team, perhaps in silent tribute to Hitchcock, frequently used what the master had called "MacGuffins." or some desired object or other pursuit that drives the characters (and thus the plot) forward. For example, in the first season there was the quest to get back the belt of the rapist that Norma had killed in self-defense in episode one, as well as a search for an imprisoned Asian sex slave and, later in the season, a missing stash of $150,000 – each such pursuit covering several episodes. In the second season, it is the missing pearl necklace that Norman had kept as a keepsake of his murdered teacher, and later it is a mad search for Norman himself, who has been kidnapped and lies dying in a "hot box" somewhere in the forest. In Season 3 it is a compromising flash drive that could either save or doom Norma Bates, and in Season 4 yet another bag of ill-gotten cash and a mysterious safe deposit key. Together, these many devices and rival plotlines do indeed allow for remarkably dense, suspense-driven seriality.

Of all of these lines of development, however, those involving Norman's relationship with his mother and his steadily declining mental state are of course the main driving force of the series. One of the clever devices devised for the show would be creating rival developmental trajectories between Norman and those closest to him, with Norman ever in decline and other characters ever on the rise. For example, this is particularly evident when comparing Norman's "love life" with that of his mother. In the beginning, Norman is the one with a healthy sex life, particularly for a shy teen, dating the popular Bradley (Season 1), endearing Emma (late Season 1 and early Season 3), and bad-girl Cody (Season 2), though these relationships are hindered by his frequent blackouts and doomed by his growing psychosis and incestuous attraction to his mother. On her end, Norma's sex life begins in shambles (her wife-beating husband has just died and she is raped in the first episode), only to move on to a perverted relationship with Officer Shelby, who blackmails her into becoming her lover. By Season 2 she misses a chance at happiness with a decent man, George, while in Season 3, after a misguided fling with a psychology professor, James, she finally finds true love and a chance for happiness in Sheriff Romero, whom she later marries while Norman is institutionalized. It is Norman's growing jealousy of the men his mother dates that quickly becomes a key source of conflict between the two of them, with Norma systematically choosing her son over her lover when the chips are down. Similarly, the trajectories of other characters are also steadily on the rise over four seasons. This would include Romero, who goes from two-dimensional corrupt cop to protector of the Bates family, to Norma's husband and one chance at happiness. Even more importantly, Dylan is also always on the rise, as the drug-dealing "bad son" and painful reminder of Norma's rape by her brother soon becomes the show's voice of reason and integrity and the "good son" Norman could have been. As both protector of and foil to Norman, our sympathies soon shift – as do those of Emma – from the younger to the older brother. In fact, all three upward trajectories (that of Norma, Dylan, and Romero) allow us to shift our sympathies away from Norman as he descends into madness, and just as importantly they give the coming tragedy even more impact, for we know Norma will not survive and doubt that Dylan and Romero will fare much better.

However, that does not mean that viewers are made to feel no sympathy for Norman; it is just that a strong feeling of empathy and identification is established early on and grows more nuanced as Norman eventually becomes the main antagonist. Indeed, one of the show's biggest challenges was surely to generate such intense sympathy for a boy who will become a serial killer. To pull this off, Cuse made certain that, in the first seasons at least, Norman was more often a victim than a predator, not only of bullying at school but of kidnapping and even torture by drug smugglers. To further stress his status as a victim, Norman is occasionally accused of crimes he committed in self-defense (e.g., Cody's father in Season 2) or that he did *not* commit at all (e.g., the murdered call-girl Annika in Season 3). If Norman is also seen as brave throughout the first season (defending his mother from a rapist, rescuing a sex-slave, standing up to bullies, etc.), it is indeed the fact that he is initially *not* the deadliest presence in White Pine Bay that gives him a relative air of innocence. Each of the first three seasons has at least one brutal villain to draw our ire away from Norman: in Season 1 there is the rapist Keith Summers (S01E01), the blackmailing deputy Shelby (S01E02–S01E06), and murderous sex-trafficker Abernathy (S01E07–S01E10); in Season 2 there are two vicious drug-lords that dominate the entire season, Nick Ford and Zane Morgan, while in Season 3 Romero and Norma fight against Bob Paris, the head of the town's secret Arcanum Club and its criminal underworld. Not only do these antagonists constantly place Norma and Norman in the role of victims, but in the early seasons their body count far outweighs Norman's. For example, during the first nine episodes of the first season, viewers learn of Norman's killing of his father in self-defense through a flashback but do not see him kill anyone along the main storyline; they do, however, witness four separate murders committed by the town's various villains, an additional murder by Romero, two killings by Dylan (only one in self-defense), and a killing by Norma (also in self-defense). Norman comes across initially as a troubled teen, certainly, but he seems far less lethal than those around him, and thus far more likely to draw our sympathy. And even when the tables later turn in the third and fourth seasons and Norman becomes the only deadly menace in White Pines Bay, we maintain a good deal of that early sympathy, in part from the simple fact that, as he commits crimes during his blackouts and has no memory of them, Norman is "sick" and is in fact ignorant of his condition, and thus "innocent" to a certain degree, until he finally realizes his true nature when he escapes from Pineview in Season 4 (S04E04). Anthony Perkins, remarking on how intrigued the public was with his character in the film series, noted people's strange need to somehow sympathize with Norman: "They want to know him, [to] understand why they feel sympathetic toward him" ("Production Notes"). If Perkins had helped the film series to move in the direction of a more sympathetic portrayal of Norman Bates, it seems Cuse and his writers came up with scores of structural and narrative devices to increase that sympathy tenfold, just as Freddy Highmore's ambiguous and carefully balanced portrayal of young Bates allows for such sympathy to be generated.[6]

The choice of a contemporary prequel:
a dialectic of past and present

As demonstrated above, the showrunners played with viewers' expectations in terms of the mythology, continuity, and character development they would carry with them from the original book and film series, all the while working steadily to an endpoint that viewers know all too well, the fifth-season remake of Hitchcock's film. If this in itself is a means of playing with our notions of past and future (we are looking ahead to a 1960 film storyline), the game is taken to an even more astonishing level in terms of visual aesthetics, most notably in the very choice of doing a "contemporary prequel." Cuse himself announced that they would not be doing a "period piece" or an "homage" to the film (Goldman 2016), but instead would set it in today's world of smartphones and iTunes, even though it looks ahead to 1960 film sequences embedded in our minds in black and white.

As Paul Sutton has argued, prequels are, by definition, also sequels, as they require us to think back to the previous film even if the narrative happens to be situated earlier. Being a new film, it always maintains a certain "afterwardsness" and a "peculiar dual temporality that enables it to both precede and follow the film or films of which it is a prequel" (Sutton 2010, 141–142). By setting the series in the time of its production (2013–2017) with numerous visual references calling back to the 1960 film and a timeline and trajectory that look forward and backward at the same time, Cuse creates an even stronger dialectic of then and now, of old and new. Andrew Scahill, in his comparative study of A&E's *Bates Motel* and NBC's *Hannibal* series, goes so far as to coin a new term that would apply to such a dialectic when it is most intense, that of *preboot* (Scahill 2016, 328), an extensive game of "familiarity and revision" that "makes the familiar narrative legible as modern" (317–318).

One of the ways this is given visual impact in *Bates Motel* is through the vintage clothing, possessions, and home furnishings of Norma and Norman Bates. For their clothing, the goal was to make them look as if they had driven into the first episode from another time, circa 1960, rather than simply another town, with costume designer Monique Prudhomme providing Norma with sundresses and outfits for the entire series inspired by those worn in various films from the 1930s to the 1960s, while scouring thrift

Figure 3.1.1 Starting Over: The idyllic shot of Norma Bates (Vera Farmiga) that bookends the entire *Bates Motel* series (S01E01, S05E10).

shops for vintage clothing that would make Norman look like a boy whose mother "dresses him funny" (Snead 2013). Norma also drives a vintage car, a 1972 Mercedes-Benz 280 SEL to be exact, a vehicle that constantly brings to mind Marion Crane's 1957 Ford Sedan in Hitchcock's film (see Figure 3.1.1). And completing this vintage setting is the Bates house, an exact replica of the decrepit Victorian monstrosity from the film that was recreated in British Columbia and that houses a veritable time capsule of amenities straight from the 1950s, from the vintage stove in the kitchen and old furnace in the basement to the outdated furniture and rickety lamps and tables in the living room. Even the television set is a throwback, as demonstrated when Norma comes home late to find Norman has fallen asleep in front of the television (S01E03), which is broadcasting snow – a reminder of a pre-digital age. (In Season 4, Romero will replace this set with a modern widescreen television, but the device is as strikingly out of place in the Bates home as Romero is and is almost immediately thrown out by Norman.)

Along with their clothes and their décor, Norma and Norma's preference for vintage films and music help cement their status as nostalgic "old souls" in a decadent modern world. This is in fact stressed from the very first image we have of Norman in the pilot episode, as he lies catatonic on a bed while a scene from Howard Hawks's *His Girl Friday* (1940) with Cary Grant plays in the background (we later learn that this bedroom scene is a flashback set in Arizona just after he had killed his father). This film will again be referenced as one of the many films Norma and Norman pick out for "movie night" at home, later dubbed "mother-son date night" by the pair (S04E02; S02E08), the incestuous undertones of which are coyly disturbing. Other "date night" features include Billy Wilder's *Double Indemnity* (1944), John Huston's *Key Largo* (1948), and an unspecified selection of Bob Hope and Bing Crosby *Road to…* comedies from the 1940s and early 1950s (S02E08, S04E02).Thus the mother–son couple has a taste for old films we viewers have come to see as "good wholesome entertainment" when compared with modern movie fare –in spite of the growing unwholesomeness of their relationship. Even when Romero tries to settle in this hermetically sealed time capsule that is the Bates home, he hopes that the DVDs he has picked up for his own movie night with Norma will be his ticket into their nostalgic world: *A Fistful of Dollars* (1964) and the aptly named *Third Man* (1949) given the triangle formed by his presence in their lives. Their love of these old films also implies both an innocence compared to today's decadence and an attachment to certain values of goodness and integrity that were touted by more populist fare from the golden age of cinema, and this is stressed for example while Norman is being held captive in a "hot box" in the woods, dying of thirst and only semi-conscious, but repeatedly reciting Gary Cooper's inspiring everyman's speech from Frank Capra's *Meet John Doe* (1941) to get himself through the ordeal.

Further cementing the pair's difference from the rest of the fictional world and their ironic connection to simpler times is their choice in music.

Family singalongs, duets with Norma at the piano, include such ditties as "Mr. Sandman" by The Chordettes from 1954 (S02E02, S04E09) – a song that has often been used ironically in horror films, including the *Halloween* franchise – along with Judy Garland's 1934 "Zing! Went the Strings of My Heart" or Bobby Darin's 1959 "Dream Lover," to which the pair slow dance (S02E10). Perhaps even more than the film titles referenced, the song titles themselves appear more telling, nearly all pointing to Norman's fantasy love-affair with his "dream lover" Norma. Even in the last scene in which we see his mother alive, Norman lulls her to sleep by singing Don Ho's 1964 "Pearly Shells" (a reference to their recent plan to run away to Hawaii together), and then "Dream Lover" once again plays as Norman calmly attempts murder-suicide (S04E09). In addition to these musical choices symbolically reminding us of their incestuous attraction and of the pair's nostalgia and love of a sugar-coated past, one is also reminded of how, much like Alex's love of classical music in Burgess and Kubrick's *A Clockwork Orange*, in this case as well music will not fulfill Congreve's infamous claim that it can "soothe a savage breast" – quite the contrary, as it will instead drive Norman forward on his path to incestuous infatuation, murder, and self-destruction.

The "vintage" veneer that touches everything related to Norma and Norman's private world thus serves myriad purposes. In terms of narrative, it reinforces our impression that Norma and especially Norman have a certain innocence and wholesomeness about them, that they are shut off from the corrupt and dangerous modern world and thus ill-equipped to deal with the rampant corruption and modern criminal enterprises that pervade White Pine Bay. We thus more easily sympathize with them throughout the early seasons and see them as potential and then actual victims, reinforcing other devices used for that same purpose that were outlined in previous sections of this study. In terms of aesthetics, it provides what Scahill has dubbed "a post-modern temporal pastiche," a disturbingly offset aesthetic and setting that is quite close to that of David Lynch's *Twin Peaks* (ABC 1990–1991), as both do indeed present us with a "bucolic community in the northwestern United States hiding a seedy underworld" and that somehow constantly seems to stress that time is out of joint (324–325). As Scahill also notes, this temporal mash-up also points to the series being a striking example of what Andrew Tudor called "elsewhen narratives" (Tudor 1989, 12; Scahill 2016, 325), for stories like this one that, rather than occupying two contrasting places ("else*where*"), seem instead to co-exist in two contrasting time periods simultaneously ("else*when*"). *Bates Motel* clearly fits the bill, and Cuse and his team ingeniously use these nostalgic narrative and aesthetic tricks to constantly draw parallels in the viewers' mind between their modern era and the era of Hitchcock's landmark film, both the show's starting point and endpoint – a connection that is frequently reinforced when the series goes so far as to *directly* reference the film itself.

Serial repetition, "preplay," and "operational aesthetics"

As demonstrated above, the series plays with viewers' expectations on a great many levels – including aesthetics, backdrop and setting, soundtrack, cultural referencing, backstory from the novels and films, and so on. Taking it even one step further, Cuse and his team have added yet another layer to this game of anticipation, one particularly aimed at those who know the original film inside and out and are hungry for visual and narrative references that look back to (and thus ahead to) Hitchcock's landmark film. More than just providing "Easter eggs" for film buffs or throwing an occasional bone to impatient fans, the showrunners create yet another network of what Scahill cleverly calls "preplay" (2016, 327), or the repetition of an iconic film scene *before* the narrative actually gets to it. Such interplay constantly refuels the viewers' desire for the new work to catch up with the old work through repetition, pastiche, foreshadowing, and false leads. One example of this, from outside the narrative itself, can clearly be seen in certain promotional clips and teasers that recreate iconic scenes from the original film more faithfully than they will actually be rendered when the series reaches that point in the storyline. For example, many promotional posters for the series had Freddy Highmore recreating promotional photos that had been used for Perkins back in 1960, particularly in the run-up to the fourth season. Teasers for coming seasons similarly tried to prod viewers into thinking the series would soon meet up with the film, even though the convergence was still far off and would be a far less "literal" recreation of the scene in question when it does occur. Take for example the 2015 teaser for Season 3, which had Highmore's Norman Bates remove a painting from the wall of his back office to peep on an alluring young woman in Room One undressing for a shower. Though the woman, seen in vignette through the peephole, is more in line with today's notions of beauty and sensuality and is dressed in modern clothing, the framed paintings of birds on the wall behind her are identical to those on the same wall in the original film, which Perkins as Bates disturbs upon seeing Marion's dead body. The painting that Norman removes to expose the peephole is also a rendition of the same painting Bates removes in the original film, *Susanna and Her Elders*, the iconic representation of voyeurism that Hitchcock had pointed out himself when giving a tour of the Bates Motel set in his own 1960 teaser. The viewer, however, will have to wait nearly a year and half before this scene is recreated, at the end of Season 4 when Norman removes a banal hotel-style seascape from that same wall, drills his infamous peephole, and instead watches his mother and Romero have sex (the scene will also be recreated twice during the fifth season, once the series has passed from prequel to remake – and in both cases the differences with the original are more striking than the similarities). These networks of forward- and backward-looking anticipation and referencing do indeed keep viewers tuned in throughout the four-year march to the remake (the above-mentioned "voyeur" trailer's tagline was unabashedly "He's watching – so should you!"), but they also create one of the more pleasurable systems of replay involved in the showrunner–viewer engagement.

And it is indeed the notion of pleasure that is evoked, for the success of the series with any fan of the original film has much to do with what Jason Mittell refers to as "operational aesthetics," a mode of pleasurable engagement that is concerned with the formal construction of the program and that requires more active and engaged spectatorship (Mittell 2006, 38; Scahill 2016, 319). Here the pleasure is derived from a mechanics of repetition and anticipation, of repeated foreshadowing and occasional false leads. Anat Zanger, in her 2006 study of remakes in general as an interplay of recognition and disguise, stresses the pleasure principle in the engagement as well: "The remakes, the sequels, even the trailers all participate in a pleasurable game of repetition, which has contributed to turning the [original] film into a fetish" (16). In the case of *Bates Motel*, this "fetishist" dimension of the engagement with the active viewer is amplified by the very nature of what we know is coming when the program catches up to the film: a tale of breaking taboos, of cross-dressing and voyeurism, of incest, matricide, and serial murders.

The series thus constantly finds ways to tease that fetishist pleasure of repetition and recognition of references to the original *Psycho* film, as much within the show itself as in the ad campaign. The pilot episode itself involved a good deal of this "preplay": besides the visual references such as Norma's vintage car or the replica of the Bates home, numerous plot elements already called ahead to the film, for the episode involves Norma killing a man, Norman using a shower curtain to hide the body in the bathroom of one of the motel rooms, and the two of them dumping the body in the lake behind the motel – all a rather blatant early staging of events viewers know from Hitchcock's film. Other references in this same pilot are far less obvious. When we see Norman waiting for the school bus he is listening to music through dangling earpods (the first touch of modernity added to his already well-established "vintage" appearance). However, he is listening to classical music, which lessens that air of modernity, and the piece he is listening to is Beethoven's *Symphony n° 3, the Eroica*, which film buffs will recognize as the record that Lila Crane found on Norman's turntable as she rummaged through his child-like bedroom near the end of the original film. Doubling down on this effect, in that original scene Lila also discovered a mysterious black book, which inexplicably shocks her when she opens it. The series pilot ends with Norman finding a similar black book hidden under the carpeting in one of the motel rooms, though it is some kind of diary filled with manga-style drawings of women being tortured and treated as sex slaves. More than an Easter egg, this little book will soon become one of the key MacGuffins of the first season and first signs of Norman's deviant sexuality. Cuse will carefully insert many such discreet references throughout the four-season prequel, including details such as the choice of a periwinkle blue dress for Norma's funeral (mentioned by the sheriff's wife in the original film) or the license plate of Bradley's car (the car which Norman, as "Mother," pushes into the lake to dispose of her dead body), which reads "NFB 418" – the same number as that of Marion Crane's car in the original film.

If the "operational aesthetics" of such uncovered references may very well send avid Hitchcock fans into a frenzy, there are others that depend more squarely on the dramatic irony inherent in the show's very premise, as we all know, or think we know, what is coming. Double-entendres related to Norman's future abound, notably when Norma says things like "Everybody's mother lives inside them" or "We're like the same person, Norman" (S03E09, S03E10), which are far less innocent out of context. Other lines of dialogue with a second level of meaning may more easily go unnoticed, as, for example, when Norman and Dylan are disposing of the mattress from Norma's bed, because Abernathy had put Shelby's autopsied corpse in it as a macabre warning. Dylan cannot understand why they are throwing away a perfectly good mattress, to which Norman replies, "Come on, would *you* want to sleep on a mattress a dead body had been on?" (S01E09) – which of course brings to viewers' minds the image of Norma's mattress in the original film, deformed by the indentation her corpse had made over the years. Similarly, when Norma tells Romero to be careful on the stairs of her home, as someone could break their neck (S04E07), viewers remember another investigator, Arbogast (Martin Balsam), theatrically falling down those same stairs to his death in the original film.

Of all of these elements of "preplay," however, the most complex network of repetition, and the one with the biggest payoff, would have to be those that slowly build up over time and stage the slow but steady decline of Norman Bates in 2013 to Norman Bates in 1960/2017. In Cuse's philosophy of composition, as in Poe's, Norman's decline would have to be achieved steadily, "by degrees," each step of which will take Norman's character one step closer to his final and much anticipated persona. For example, Norman's penchant for taxidermy is a recurring motif throughout all four seasons, with Norman learning the trade from Emma's father at the end of Season 1, sparked by the death of his dog Juno and his desire to have it stuffed (S01E02, S01E07–S01E09) – something he will repeat when institutionalized and making another replica of Juno out of papier-mâché (S04E07). At the end of Season 2, he completes the stuffed owl viewers know will eventually be displayed in the back office (S02E08, S02E10), but by the end of Season 3, we begin to see his stuffed dog Juno the way Norman actually sees it, as alive and well (S03E06, S03E08, S03E10), thus demonstrating his growing inability to distinguish fantasy from reality.

This technique of progressive and repetitive preplay is even more striking when considering how Cuse and his writers carefully staged Norman's psychological decline throughout the four prequel seasons, spacing out the arrival and subsequent repetition of at least five troubling symptoms that will culminate in a film-worthy Norman Bates by Season 5. A penchant for voyeurism is hinted at from the start, when he accidentally glimpses his mother undressing in the pilot episode, though he will reiterate his peeping-tom antics with his English teacher (S01E10) and with a showering guest seen through her window (S03E01) before his climactic act of peeping on his mother and Romero from the back office (S04E08) and the three subsequent voyeurism scenes regarding Sam Loomis and Marion Crane in the Season 5 remake. However, Cuse would wait until the end of Season 1 to start showing Norman and Norma, innocently enough at first, sleeping in the same bed (S01E09), though it grows more and more disturbing with its repetitions in each passing season. The third stage would involve Norman kissing his mother too passionately on the lips, an act initiated by a desperate Norma looking for a way to get her suicidal son to put down the gun in the Season 2 finale, and an overstep that she will repeat after a later blackout and that will be initiated by Norman in the dreadful finale to Season 4 (S04E02, S04E10). The last two "symptoms" start almost simultaneously in the middle of Season 3: his overt sexual attraction for his mother begins to manifest itself when he can no longer perform sexually with other women and when James, one of Norma's lovers, mortifies him by suggesting that deep down he wants to have sex with Norma (S03E04, S03E07–S03E09), later followed by his visceral jealousy and vomiting when he learns that Norma and Romero are married (S04E07, S04E08). At nearly the same time, Norman begins cross-dressing as "Mother," first stealing her dresses and greeting Dylan "as" his mother and making him breakfast (S03E05–S03E07), then later cross-dressing before killing Emma's mother (S04E01, S04E09), before openly and regularly cross-dressing as the "Mother" he has lost in the early episodes of Season 5. If one charts out this steady and incremental decline, the careful staging of these developmental "preplays" of the adult Norman Bates is quite striking, and one might even imagine similar charts on the walls of Cuse's writing room (see Figure 3.1.2). It also shows how Cuse's use of repetition and "preplay" were part and parcel with the many crisscrossing developmental trajectories discussed earlier in this study and yet another means of moving Norman from sympathetic protagonist to more repulsive antagonist over four seasons.

One of the reasons for *Bates Motel*'s popular and critical success most certainly stems from it being part of a remarkably widespread general trend for rebooting landmark horror films and film franchises as contemporary television series, yet Cuse's project has been the only one thus far to complete its entire intended run. Only a fortnight after *Bates Motel* first aired, NBC broke the stale network mold with Bryan Fuller's series *Hannibal* (2013–2015), a groundbreaking work in both storytelling and gore aesthetics that similarly was to provide a prequel to and subsequent remakes of the horror film franchise based on Thomas Harris's book series. However, rather than create an origin story as Cuse did, the first season works to quickly rewrite the power struggle between the two main characters before the series starts

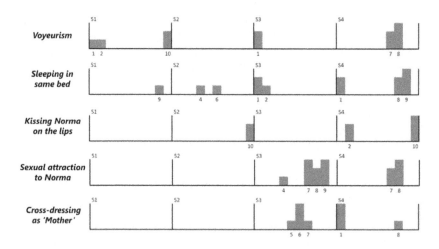

Figure 3.1.2 The Gradual Decline of Norman Bates: this chart indicates episodes
over all four "prequel" seasons which stage the progressive symptoms
of Norman's descent into madness. Higher bars indicate episodes that
give more intense focus on that trait.

catching up with the novels in Season 2, bringing in well-known plotlines
from film adaptations of *Red Dragon* (1981) and *Hannibal* (1999) – before
being so untimely and inexplicably canceled (budget problems? too much
gore for network TV? rights or piracy issues?), just when the new continuity was about to join that of the most popular novel/film of the franchise,
The Silence of the Lambs (1988/1991). As groundbreaking as the program
was, it did not create as nearly a dense or complex network of "preplay"
and cross-referencing as *Bates Motel* did, and it definitely sought "operational esthetics" more through the creation of striking *new* images rather
than a calling to mind of old ones. Even more short-lived was A&E's 2016
attempt to double down on the success of *Bates Motel* by launching the
series *Damien* immediately after it on Monday nights. In this case, writer/
producer Glen Mazzara (*The Shield*, *The Walking Dead*) was given the task
of rebooting the horror film franchise that began with Richard Donner and
David Seltzer's film *The Omen* (1976). Much like *Bates Motel*, the series
set out to dump nearly all of the mythology derived from the film and book
sequels and use the original film as sole reference. Although making a new
sequel to the original storyline, Mazzara found his own clever way to make
it feel like a prequel and thus set up a network of "preplay" for engaged
viewers, as the 30-year-old Damien Thorne (Bradley James) has no idea he
is the anti-Christ and no memory of his violent childhood, until events in
the series start bringing them back. Cleverly, these snippets and flashbacks
in the new series are in fact actual grainy clips from the 1976 film – of his
nurse's suicide, of his murdering his own mother, of his father's attempt

to kill him, and so on. He even discovers a shrine full of items from his childhood (actually props from the original film), a collection that surely brings as much "fetishist" pleasure to his Satanic followers as it does to fans of the original film. In spite of these clever means of making us look both forward and backward to the landmark film, all surely inspired by those used in *Bates Motel* on the same channel, the series was canceled after a single season, perhaps because though it greatly pleased "engaged viewers," there simply were not enough of them. Slightly more successful was the recent modern series reboot of *The Exorcist* (Fox, 2016–2017), which was canceled after its second season and instead maintained and followed the long seriality launched by the 1971 film by Friedkin, but added occasional visual references to key scenes from that first film and as well as surprise tie-ins to Friedkin's masterpiece, thereby generating that coveted "operational aesthetic."

Bates Motel thus seems to serve as a model for this new sub-genre of classic horror film rebooted as television series, having most thoroughly and most effectively created a dialectic of old and new, of past and present, and of familiar and unexpected. The continuity of the original film is at once preserved and reinvented, and the new seriality and myriad storylines that result keep suspense and anticipation high both *in spite of* and *because of* the fact that all viewers know how it will all end. Character development, myriad plotlines, visual aesthetics, cultural references, serial repetition, and preplay of cult images and events from the original film – the 40-episode prequel that formed the first four seasons of *Bates Motel* coordinated all of these devices to set up the much anticipated fifth-season remake. As one might expect, such games continue as the fifth season meets up with Bloch and Hitchcock's initial storyline, once again playing with the viewers' expectations through unexpected casting choices (e.g., pop star Rihanna as Marion Crane) and Hitchcock-like cameos (e.g., Cuse himself appears as the police officer who pulls over a fleeing Marion), rewritten characters (e.g., Sam Loomis as a despicable philanderer), ideas borrowed from other films in the *Psycho* series (e.g., Norman falls for a young woman who is the spitting image of his deceased mother, just as he did in *Psycho III*), clever film angles to showcase Norman's double persona and the continued presence of Vera Farmiga on screen (though as the "Mother" persona rather than Norma), as well as a rewriting of the shower-scene that will leave viewers shocked for completely unexpected reasons. It seems that Bates Motel, under new management, is the ideal venue for the remaking of a murderer.

Notes

1 For a detailed discussion of the differences between Bloch's initial novel and Hitchcock's film, see Stephen Rebello, 1998.

2 One should note that when Ed Gein was arrested at his farm in Plainfield, Wisconsin, in 1957, Robert Bloch was living only 35 miles away and thus

fictionalized a horrific local news story (Zanger 2006, 20). In addition to the entire *Psycho* franchise, Gein could be seen as a template for many of popular culture's most heinous serial killers, including Leatherface from Tobe Hooper's original *Texas Chainsaw Massacre* film (1974) and its many sequels and remakes; Buffalo Bill from Richard Harris's novel *Red Dragon* (1981) and its film and TV adaptations (Michael Mann's *Manhunter* in 1986, Brett Ratner's 2006 *Red Dragon*, Season 3 of NBC's series *Hannibal* (2013–15), and so on; the character of Dr. Thredson from the second season of *American Horror Story* (*Asylum*, 2012–13); and the list goes on).

3   For more detailed analysis of these film sequels, see Loock 2014, 81–98; Kutner 2006; Thomas Leitch 2003, 248–59, and Verevis 2006 "For Ever Hitchcock", 15–29.

4   Among those slight changes that stand out in Van Sant's work, there is more explicit sexuality and nudity (e.g., a clear indication that Norman is masturbating while he peeps on Marion, or full dorsal nudity of Marion in the shower) and slightly more gore (e.g., Arbogast's bloody slashing at the top of the stairs and added intercuts from the shower scene) that would not have been possible in 1960, yet Van Sant resists the urge to take things "too far" in terms of sex and violence, even though he could, perhaps out of respect for the original film and for Hitchcock's own intentions, thus stressing the dilemma that comes with doing a "modern" remake of such a seminal work. Van Sant's other changes (including increased roving camera work, disturbing and discordant background music and echo effects, and his own visual references, such as the discovery of the mother's corpse in an aviary – a possible nod to Hitchcock's *The Birds*), along with the decidedly different portrayal of the main characters, point to matters or re-authorship inherent to projects like *Bates Motel*.

5   It is important to note that there is a lively debate today on the subject of *authorship* in television series, one questioning whether the showrunner and screenwriters should be considered the authors of a given series or – as series now often have narrative and filming methods, production values, and aesthetic quality on a par with those traditionally associated with cinema – whether the director should reign as "auteur." It is true that in many cases concerning contemporary television series, particularly those that use a single director for most, if not all, of the episodes, the authorship of the final product would tend to lean more toward that director. This would be the case with, for example, Cinemax's 2014–15 series *The Knick*, all 20 episodes of which were directed by Steven Soderbergh, thereby seemingly displacing authorship of the series away from screenwriters Jack Amiel and Michael Beglier and toward the well-established filmmaker at the helm. The same could be said of the first season of the critically acclaimed *True Detective* (HBO, 2014–present), with all eight episodes directed by Cary Fukunaga, though in the second season the series had six different directors and may have lost some of the coherence that had made the first season so successful. In the case of *Bates Motel*, authorship seems to be firmly placed in the hands of its showrunner Carlton Cuse and his fellow-writers Kerry Ehrin and Antonio Cipriano. The 50 episodes of the series saw 20 different directors film the series, most doing only one or two episodes – including guest directors like Freddie Highmore himself, the young actor playing Norman, testing his directing chops for an episode (S05E08). Though certain aesthetic aspects of the series may be clearly attributed to Tucker Gates, who directed half of the first season and often the opening and closing episodes of later seasons, there is no doubt that authority and authorship of the series in this case rest firmly in the hands of Carlton Cuse. In this study, it will thus be Cuse's reauthoring and reaccentuating of the Bates universe that will be focused on.

6 One should note that Freddy Highmore's much acclaimed performance as young Norman Bates and his ability to draw sympathy in spite of his character's complex psychological issues may have resulted in his being typecast for such complex roles, as after the series *Bates Motel* he immediately went on to star as Dr. Shaun Murphy, a severely autistic surgical intern with savant syndrome, in the ABC medical drama series *The Good Doctor* (2017–).

Works cited

Bloch, Robert. *Psycho*. New York: Tom Doherty Associates, 1959.

Bloch, Robert. *Psycho II*. New York: Whispers Press, 1982.

Bloch, Robert. *Psycho House*. New York: Tor Books, 1990.

Goldberg, Lesley. "*Bates Motel* Using *Psycho* as 'Inspiration' Rather Than an Homage". *The Hollywood Reporter*, 01.04.2013. http://www.hollywoodreporter.com/live-feed/bates-motel-psycho-carlton-cuse-408631 (accessed 08.11.2016).

Goldman, Eric. "*Bates Motel*: Why the *Psycho*-based Series Is Set in the Present Day". *IGN (Imagine Games Network–US)* 01.04.2013. http://www.ign.com/articles/2013/01/05/bates-motel-why-the-psycho-based-series-is-set-in-the-present-day (accessed 08.11.2016).

Kutner, Jerry C. "Who Owns Norman Bates? On *Psycho IV, III, II, I* and More". *Bright Lights Film Journal* 54, November 2006.

Leitch, Thomas. "Hitchcock without Hitchcock". *Literature Film Quarterly* 31.4, 2003. 248–259.

Loock, Kathleen. "'The Past Is Never Really Past': Serial Storytelling from *Psycho* to *Bates Motel*". In Kathleen Loock (ed.), Serial Narratives Special Issue of *LWU: Literatur in Wissenschaft und Unterricht* 47.1/2, 2014. 81–98.

Mittell, Jason. "Narrative Complexity and Contemporary Narrative Television". *Velvet Light Trap* 58, Fall 2006. 29–40.

Production Notes on *Psycho III*. Universal Studios, 1986. 1–10.

Rebello, Stephen. *Alfred Hitchcock and the Making of* Psycho. New York: St. Martin's Press, 1998.

Scahill, Andrew. "Serialized Killers: Prebooting Horror in *Bates Motel* and *Hannibal*". In Amanda Ann Klein and R. Barton Palmer (eds.), *Multiplicities: Cycles, Sequels, Remakes and Reboots in Film & Television*, Austin: University of Texas Press, 2016.

Snead, Elizabeth. "Bates Motel Costume Designer Monique Prudhomme Opens Norman's Mother's Closet". *Hollywood Reporter*, 03.19.2013. http://www.hollywoodreporter.com/fash-track/bates-motel-costume-designer-monique-429488 (accessed 08.11.2016).

Sutton, Paul. "Prequel: The Afterwardsness of the Sequel". In Carolyn Jess-Cooke and Constantine Verevis (eds.), *Second Takes: Critical Approaches to the Film Sequel*, Albany: SUNY Press, 2010.

Tudor, Andrew. *Monsters and Mad Scientists: A Cultural History of the Horror Movie*. Oxford: Basil Blackwell, 1989.

Verevis, Constantine. *Film Remakes*. Edinburgh: Edinburgh University Press, 2006.

Verevis, Constantine. "For Ever Hitchcock: *Psycho* and Its Remakes". In David Boyd and R. Barton Palmer (eds.), *After Hitchcock: Influence, Imitation, and Intertextuality*, Austin: University of Texas Press, 2006. 15–29.

Zanger, Anat. *Film Remakes as Ritual and Disguise*. Amsterdam: Amsterdam University Press, 2006.

Series and films cited

12 & Holding. Antonio Cipriano, Serenade Films, 2005.
Bates Motel. A&E, 2013–2017.
Bates Motel. Richard Rothstein, NBC, 1987.
Breaking Bad. AMC, 2008–2013.
A Clockwork Orange. Stanley Kubrick, Warner Bros., 1971.
Damien. A&E, 2016.
Double Indemnity. Billy Wilder, Paramount, 1944.
Dressed to Kill. Brian De Palma, Filmways Pictures, 1980.
The Exorcist. Fox, 2016–.
A Fistful of Dollars. Sergio Leone, Constantin Films, 1964.
Friday Night Lights. NBC, 2006–2011.
Friday the 13th. Sean S. Cunningham, Paramount, 1980.
Halloween. John Carpenter. Compass Intl Pictures, 1978.
Hannibal. NBC, 2013–2015.
His Girl Friday. Howard Hawks, Columbia, 1940.
Homeland. Showtime, 2011–.
Key Largo. John Huston, Warner Bros., 1948.
The Knick. Cinemax, 2014–2015.
Lost. ABC, 2004–2010
Meet John Doe. Frank Capra, Warner Bros., 1941.
Motor Psycho. Alex Downs 1992.
Psycho II. Richard Franklin, Universal, 1983.
Psycho III. Anthony Perkins, Universal, 1986.
Psycho IV – The Beginning. Mick Garris, Showtime, 1990.
The Psycho Lover. Robert Vincent O'Neill, Taos-Libra Productions, 1970.
Psycho Sisters. Pete Jacelone, E.I., 1998.
Psycho. Alfred Hitchcock, Paramount, 1960.
Psycho. Gus Van Sant, Universal, 1998.
Road to Bali. Hal Walker, Paramount, 1952.
The Road to Hong Kong. Norman Panama, United Artists, 1962.
Road to Morocco. David Butler, Paramount, 1942.
Road to Rio. Norman McLeod, Paramount, 1947.
Road to Singapore. Victor Schertzinger, Paramount, 1940.
Road to Utopia. Hal Walker, Paramount, 1946.
Road to Zanzibar. Victor Schertzinger, Paramount, 1941.
The Shield. FX, 2002–2008.
The Silence of the Lambs. Jonathan Demme, Orion Pictures, 1991.
The Texas Chainsaw Massacre. Tobe Hooper, Vortex, 1974.
Third Man. Carol Reed, London Films, 1949.
True Detective. HBO, 2014–.
Twin Peaks. ABC, 1990–1991, 2017.
Walking Dead, The. AMC, 2002–.

3.2 *Fargo* (FX, 2014–) and cinema

"Just like in the movie"?

Sylvaine Bataille

Like other recent television series, such as *True Detective* (HBO, 2014–) or *American Horror Story* (FX, 2011–), *Fargo,* created by Noah Hawley, produced by Joel and Ethan Coen,[1] and broadcast since 2014 on FX, has explored the anthology format, with each season telling a new story around a new set of characters. Like *Bates Motel* (A&E, 2013–2017) vis-à-vis *Psycho*, it has also engaged with the ways in which a television series can relate to a cult film.[2] Hawley has offered frequent comments on the show and its artistic ambitions: "I had a fascinating challenge before me: create a series that gave you the same feeling you got from watching the movie *Fargo* but wasn't the movie" (Hawley 2014); "in my case, I could say, 'Well, I'm making a Coen brothers movie'"(Couch 2014). Hawley, then, approached the television show as a pastiche,[3] an imitation of the Coens' style in *Fargo* (1996) but also in other films, as appears from the numerous accounts of echoes and resemblances between Hawley's *Fargo* and various productions by the Coen brothers.[4] Such a project implied identifying the characteristics of the Coens' films in terms of tone, situations, and narrative choices (Hawley 2014; Arnold 2014) but also comparing cinema and television as far as narrative possibilities, traditions, and conventions were concerned. Each of the existing three seasons was conceived as a ten-episode movie (Arnold 2014). Hawley's artistic motto was: "You're making a movie, not a television show" (Boren 2015). Hawley, who has also published several thrillers and crime novels since 1998, stressed his work on the end of each season and his effort to provide a sense of closure, which he contrasts with the openness that characterizes serialized television narratives according to him: "The most critical part is that you're telling a story with an end [...]. It's not just about killing people off. It's that characters serve their function, they play their part and move on. That's not how a TV show is designed, it's more of a perpetual motion machine" (Boren 2015). Of course such a view of serial storytelling lacks nuance, since a lot of heavily serialized dramas, especially in the context of the "New Golden Age" of television, actually do end. Making such a clear-cut distinction allows Hawley to appropriate HBO's famous "It's not TV" slogan and thus locate his own show in the televisual landscape, while using the legitimacy of cinema as an art form, as well as the Coens' renown as celebrated auteurs, to promote his work. Moreover Hawley has to admit that assimilating the show to a film is not quite right either: "A movie is only two hours and as a result it becomes a plot device. By the third act of a movie all you can do is really resolve all the stuff you established in the first two hours. When you have 10 hours you can take these digressions and focus on characters or parts of the story or create these turns that you can set up in ways that make the story unexpected" (Boren 2015). Hawley's uncertainties reflect the uncertain nature of the show, a hybrid importing cinematic features while also exploiting the possibilities given by serial storytelling. Hawley's declarations point both to an attraction for the narrative opportunities offered by a format that is much longer than a two-hour film, even if it is shorter than the 22- or 24-episode season typical of network series, and a form of resistance against the proliferating aspect of serialized narration.

The series *Fargo* was also constructed against other possible forms of serialization of the Coen brothers' film. The remake, presumably a version of the original fleshed out with subplots, would have been a simple "carbon copy" of lesser quality than the film, according to Hawley (Kizu 2016; Couch 2014). The sequel or the prequel would have reopened the narrative that had been closed in the film to apply to it, for instance, the traditional model of the detective television series and tell the story of another investigation by Police Chief Marge Gunderson (portrayed by Frances McDormand in the film), giving the character an afterlife *à la* Sherlock Holmes. This option was eliminated by Hawley on the grounds that it clashed with the "Coenesque" quality he sought to achieve in the series: "It seemed like the wrong idea to make a *Picket Fences*[5] idea show where something cooky happens every day. That's not a Coen model. She's not going to be same person after seeing so much dark stuff" (Goldberg 2014). Another reason he invoked was the famous disclaimer opening the film *Fargo* (announcing that "[t]his is a true story"), which was kept in a slightly adapted form at the beginning of each episode of the series: Hawley considered that this precluded showing Marge having to deal with another "crazy Coen brothers case" (Egner 2015).

The creation of transfictionality – the relationship between two texts whereby diegetic data, such as characters, "migrate" from one text to another[6] – was thus impacted by the constraints of the pastiche. However it was not discarded entirely. Even though it does not tell what happens to Marge after the end of the Coens' *Fargo* – or to any other character still alive at the end of the film – the series does share the same "fictional universe" (*univers fictionnel*, Saint-Gelais 2011, 7) as the film. This is signaled in the pre-credits sequence at the beginning of the fourth episode, in the discreet, allusive way that is the hallmark of "Easter Eggs" intended for the spectators who are familiar with the film (Ray 2014), since its identification as such has no incidence on how the series' plot is understood or even appreciated.[7] The fourth episode starts with a flashback about Stavros Milos, a secondary character and one of Lorne Malvo's victims: in this scene depicting a crucial event in his life, Stavros is stranded in the middle of a snowy road with his wife and child after his car ran out of petrol. By sheer chance, he finds a briefcase full of money buried in the snow, after his eye was caught by a red scraper planted near one of the poles of a fence stretching endlessly along the road. Viewers who know the film will recognize this attaché case as the very briefcase hidden in the snow by Carl Showalter (portrayed by Steve Buscemi), one of the kidnappers in the Coens' *Fargo*. Not only is the sequence very Coen-esque and *Fargo*-esque, thanks to the accompanying musical theme, the car on the snowy road, the coincidence that is so extraordinary that it is absurd, but it is also the moment when the universe of the film and that of the series meet to form one and the same diegesis. The discovery of the case thus serves as a "diegetic bridge" (*passerelle diégétique*, Saint-Gelais 2011, 23). The circulation of the briefcase between the two fictions, which frees the object from the filmic environment that had accommodated it so far, has the effect of strengthening the illusion of a reality supposed to exist outside the film and the series, a reality that the two works simply record (see Saint-Gelais 2011, 14), as the fake disclaimers placed at the beginning both of the film and of each episode of the show would have it, for instance in Season 1: "This is a true story. The events depicted took place in Minnesota in 2006. At the request of the survivors, the names have been changed. Out of respect for the dead, the rest has been told exactly as it occurred."

While the first season (2014) brilliantly carried out the series' intertextual and transfictional ambitions, the second season (2015) not only further widened the scope of the pastiche (Assouly 2016) but also presented several striking instances of reflexivity, whereby in the diegesis or in the margins of the narrative, the show itself made explicit its cinematographic, narrative, and transfictional aspirations, drew attention to them, or formulated a comment – often of an ironic or absurd nature – on them. This, as it turned out when the third season was aired in 2017, was part of the uniqueness of the anthology's second opus.[8]

Situated at the threshold of each episode, the fake disclaimer starting with "This is a true story" works as a reminder of the Coens' *Fargo* in a paradoxical way: this explicit and eminently recognizable borrowing from the 1996 opening actually deprives the film of its role as the matrix of the series to attribute this function to "reality." The device is developed in the introduction of the penultimate episode of the second season, which reconstructs the series as the adaptation, not of a film but of a (fictitious) book, entitled *The History of True Crime in the Midwest* and authored by a certain "Brixby" – who (as is revealed in the DVD bonus feature about the book) turns out to be another writer named "Barton," in a hidden homage to the Coens' filmography (*Barton Fink*, 1991).[9] This opening, which is reminiscent of the traditional "storybook opening" in Disney films,[10] starts with a shot of a book on a library shelf, before it is opened by an invisible reader. The disclaimer, in a slightly adapted form, can be read on the first page of the book instead of appearing superimposed on the filmed image as it usually does in each episode of the series. The pages of the book are then flipped over until the unseen peruser reaches Chapter Fourteen: "Luverne, Minnesota -1979, The Waffle Hut Massacre." An extract from the chapter is then read in voice-over (by Martin Freeman, who also played Lester Nygaard, one of the main characters of Season 1) while the pages of the chapter are being turned. The voice-over will return later in the episode for occasional remarks, but for now it is heard reading the beginning of the chapter. Brief shots of the illustrated pages prepare the transition from the literary mode to the moving image, from "telling" to "showing," and from the "world in which one tells" to "the world of which one tells" (Genette 1980, 236). The color etchings also reproduce images seen in earlier episodes, thus serving the function of a "previously on" sequence and posing as the original pictures that inspired a number of shots in the show. The action of the series resumes when one of the color illustrations turns into a filmic picture while the page that frames it gradually disappears from the screen. The animation of the static book illustration figures the transformational process of book-to-film adaptation in a way that is too good to be true – so obviously stressed and quaint that it reveals the fraud.

As is explained in the DVD bonus material, the book was the materialization of a conception of the series that was refined over time. "I like the idea that somewhere out there is a big, leather-bound book that's the history of true crime in the Midwest, and the movie was Chapter 4, Season 1 was Chapter 9 and this is Chapter 2 [...]. You can turn the pages of this book, and you just find this collection of stories. [...B]ut I like the idea that these things are connected somehow, whether it's linearly or literally or thematically," Hawley explained in an interview about the second season in July 2014, a month after the Season 1 finale aired on FX (Porter 2014). The show fictionalizes and dramatizes considerations about its own nature as an anthology, offering a version of its origin and genesis that contradicts the mention closing the end credits, "Based on the film *FARGO*," situated at the other end of the episode, in a far more marginal and unobtrusive position. The written medium plays a part in the film-to-TV adaptation as a fictitious intertext used by the TV show to bypass the film as a primary text – the book and, ultimately, the (pseudo) historical events it relates become the source for both the film and the series. The alternative narrative of the series' origin levels the implicit cultural hierarchies that place the classic above the derivative, and cinema above television as an art form, as both the film and the television show appear as secondary works, inspired not only by a book, a medium traditionally more prestigious than the audio-visual mode, but also by "History" and "Truth." However, the Disney intertext, in which the storybook typically tells a fairy tale, suggests a parodic reading of this redistribution of cultural values.

By reconfiguring its relation with the Coens' *Fargo*, the show also incorporates the film into a serialized whole. As early as January 2014, a few months before the first season debuted (in April), Hawley had explained that "[a]fter a season or two of the show, people who see the movie might say that was a great episode of *Fargo*. Each season is a separate true crime story from that region. The movie now fits into the series as another true crime story from the region" (Goldberg 2014). Whether the film is assimilated to a "chapter" of the book created by the show or to an "episode" of the television series itself, its cultural status as an autonomous, discrete work authored by the Coen brothers undergoes a thorough revision. In this view, the series itself becomes the matrix of the film, because it generates the fictitious "reality," or the pseudo extradiegetic level, of the 1996 *Fargo*. In a dynamic that runs counter to the series' actual expansion of the *Fargo* diegesis *from* the film, the show builds the world that supposedly gave birth *to* the film.

When it also expands the famous disclaimer from the Coens' film, providing it with a backstory (a specific source, an author), the series goes beyond transfiction and practices what could be termed "meta-transfiction." The series' transfictional relations with the film are not only with the film's diegesis (the events told in the series and in the film belong to the same universe, the "*Fargo*verse"[11]), but also with the film's liminal "metanarrative comments" (Neumann & Nünning 2014), for example, the fictional claim that "[a]t the request of the survivors, the names have been changed." The introduction to S02E09 even provides a narrative about the transfictional nature of the show itself, offering a fictional explanation (the book) of the links between the series and the film.

"Storybook openings," as their name indicates, are usually situated at the beginning of a film. In the case of the second season of *Fargo*, the multiscalar dimension of the series was exploited to subvert this filmic convention: on the scale of the episode, it is situated at the beginning, as is to be expected; however, on the scale of the season (which Hawley assimilated to "a ten-hour long movie," Arnold 2014), the "storybook opening" is situated near the end and is unique. This particular episode infringes one of the series' "intrinsic norms" (Mittell 2007, 166), since it differs from the other episode openings to an extent that exceeds mere variation on a common model. The narration of the story, which had henceforth been accomplished by an impersonal, unambiguously extra-diegetic narrative instance, is now taken over by the narrator of Brixby's chapter (whose voice is heard now and again in the course of the episode). At this point in the show, the introduction of an additional narrative instance has troubling effects that call attention to the very act of narrating the series and can cast doubt and suspicion on it. Does this episode reveal who has been telling us the story all along, in the previous 18 episodes of Season 1 and 2 – and in the film? – or does it present an alternative narrative act, an experience of what the narration could have been, but was not? At the very least, this unexpected opening blurs the definition of the diegetic and the extradiegetic. What is disquiet-ing is not so much the embedding device as the possible revelation that there was another narrative level all along, because it shatters our assumptions as to where we stand as viewers. It suggests that the extradiegetic world of the moving image narrative is actually intradiegetic, and it seems to support "this unacceptable and insistent hypothesis that the extradiegetic is perhaps always diegetic and that the narrator and his narrates – you and I – perhaps belong to some narrative" (Genette 1980, 236). In the end, then, the story-book opening of S02E09 both presents more developed evidence that "this is a true story" and undermines this evidence, paradoxically contradicting what it insists so much on saying.

The relation between the film and the series can then be read both ways, like the "palindrome" that gives its title to the last episode. This eminently liminal title, since it actually never appears in the episode *per se*, offers a comment on the way the series works as transfiction, allowing the viewers to watch the two seasons of the show and the film in an order that differs from the chronological order of their release dates: the "diegetic bridges" between Season 1 and Season 2 (and more recently Season 3), between Sea-son 1 and the film, can be crossed both ways.

Barton Brixby's book can also be interpreted as a materialization and a representation, inside the show itself, of the series' "Bible," the document containing all the necessary information about the characters, the places, and all the other components of the series' storyworld. The viewers' cu-riosity is both aroused and frustrated by the shots of the book they are given to see, as they can catch a furtive glance of a paragraph telling Peggy Blumquist's past but are unable to read it. The narrator wonders about Hanzee's biography and motivations in a number of voice-over interven-tions in the course of the episode, but he stresses the unknowability of the character rather than giving the answers to the questions he asked ("Not much is known about Ohanzee Dent," "Historians of the region have long debated [...]," "Who knows?"). The series thus draws our attention to pos-sible narrative ramifications that will never come into being, to stories that it refuses to tell on Peggy (Kirsten Dunst) and Hanzee (Zahn McClarnon), two particularly intriguing characters. The totalizing potentialities of serial narration, or what Matt Hills refers to as the "endlessly deferred narrative" associated with "hyperdiegesis"[12] (Hills 2002, 101), are thus both fore-grounded and left blatantly fallow.

Interestingly, the third season does not use Brixby's book again but rather presents its own version of its artistic origins and nature, thereby resisting the unifying, all-encompassing aspirations of the second season's reflexive narrative. Episode S03E04 also starts with a prologue narrated in voice-over by an actor from the first season, this time by Billy Bob Thornton (who played devilish killer Lorne Malvo) rather than by Martin Freeman. This introduction is taken from Prokofiev's musical composition *Peter and the Wolf* (1936) and accompanies sequences successively showing each of the main characters going about their business. For instance, Emmit Stussy is presented as "the bird," the bulimic villain Varga as "the wolf," and Gloria Burgle, the police officer, as "Peter." Prokofiev's musical children's tale then becomes the matrix of Season 3, rather than the "reality" or "history" recorded in Brixby's book, making explicit the fairy tale aspects suggested by the Disney-like storybook opening in S02E09. However, the first sentence of the voice-over narration, clearly referring to the story as a tale ("Each character in this tale is going to be represented by a different instrument of the orchestra"), is contradicted by the first sentence of the disclaimer, still affirming that "This is a true story": in accordance with its continued fascination for quantum paradoxes, the third season describes itself as *both* a tale and a true story.

Episode openings, especially in Season 2, often offer self-reflexive comments on the identity and the status of this TV show that conceives of itself as a film. As is the case with the "storybook opening" of S02E09 – as well as the *Peter and the Wolf* opening of 3.4 – this is not without sometimes dampening the effect of the disclaimer. Already in the first season, the series had broken the televisual codes shared by most drama series when they start an episode. The opening titles of drama television series have been a site of innovation and sophistication over the last 20 years (Hudelet 2009). However in *Fargo* there is no recurring title sequence, or any brief shot of a logo (*à la LOST*), appearing at any moment of the opening sequence, which is always the beginning of the action of the episode. The show proceeds to its own reworking of the credits, not by modernizing the TV models, but by borrowing from the older medium of cinema. The credits themselves appear only at the end of the episode. The text superimposed on the first shots of the episode is the mock disclaimer and then the title. This presentation recalls the beginning of the Coens' film, in which the credits and the film title stood out against the snowy landscape travelled through by a tow truck.

The variations from one episode to the next are sometimes radical: the opening shots range from images of a vehicle on a road evocative of the film *Fargo* to fish swimming in a fish tank to a washing machine being assembled by robots in a factory; the musical theme can be a symphonic piece reminiscent of Carter Burwell's score or a pop song. The latter shifts in the score, in particular, often make apparent the parodic nature of the mock disclaimer, when the seeming seriousness and gravity of the text clash with the cheerfulness of the tune chosen. In these cases, the epic grandeur of the Coens' opening sequence is itself parodied. However since the Coens' cinema is so often parodic, this parody is also a form of homage.

Because the shots and the soundtrack change in each episode, the disclaimer and the title that appear on the screen are the only elements identifying the series. Considering Hawley's statements about the show as a "ten-hour movie," this minimalist choice might at first be understood as a mere concession to televisual norms that were quite unavoidable (each episode has to feature the title of the show and credit the people involved in its creation), with a view to erase as much as possible the sense of a new beginning at the start of each episode and make the informational elements about the show as inconspicuous as possible. The freedom that such a presentation allows is regularly put to use. In the first season, the disclaimer always appears in the first seconds of each episode, but the appearance of the title is sometimes delayed, for up to 13 minutes into the episodes (S01E07; S01E09). The second season introduced greater variations in this regard, sometimes pushing back the appearance of the disclaimer (S02E01 and S02E03) or extending the time between the mention "FX presents" and the title itself (for instance in S02E08). However the result is not one of dilution of the information, on the contrary. Thanks notably to musical effects, the superimposed text is foregrounded, lending considerable presence to these recurring textual elements and distinguishing the opening shots from the remainder of the episode. What is suggested, then, is rather that each episode be viewed as a short film rather than as a part of a televisual whole. Through this significant margin of variation, then, the series seems to flaunt a form of resistance to its own seriality, to the return of the same that defines it, and sheds uncertainty on its own nature. Moreover, these episode beginnings, both because they are different from each other and because they differ from other series' episode openings, put forward the game of resemblance and difference that the series plays with the Coens' 1996 film. In this perspective, each episode, just as it is in the act of reopening the series *Fargo*, appears to be replaying the act of starting the film *Fargo* anew. In the course of its three ten-episode seasons, the series seems to offer 30 different versions of what the beginning of the film could have been like. This experimental dimension also applies to the show itself, which reinvents itself with the beginning of each new episode, experimenting with a range of possibilities of what a recurring title sequence might have looked like but never actually choosing a definitive arrangement of images and sound. In so doing, FX's *Fargo* denies the viewer the ritualistic pleasure and comfort usually granted by the titles in drama series, playing with its own seriality to evade definition and present an ever-changing, protean surface.

The second season frees itself even further from the model provided by the beginning of the 1996 *Fargo*. For instance, the lettering of the disclaimer is now very different from the white letters common to the film and the first season. The words appear on the screen as if being typed on a typewriter – the sound of which can even be heard – a choice evidently related to the storybook opening in episode 9. The beginning of Season 1 is quite an obvious imitation of the opening of the film *Fargo*, both visually, with an extreme long shot of a car arriving from a distance in a snowy landscape, and aurally, with the equally *Fargo*esque musical theme composed by Jeff Russo. The beginning of Season 2, however, is more surprising. First we see the famous roaring lion of the MGM logo, in black and white, before a shot slowly sweeping a battlefield strewn with soldiers' bodies, still in black and white, while a title, "Massacre at Sioux Falls" and credits,

"Starring Ronald Reagan – And Betty LaPlage," announce anything but the show that we intend to watch. The general appearance of the sequence is designed to make us believe that by some mysterious mistake or technical malfunction, we are watching a rerun of an old western, the film of which is even visibly damaged, from the time when Ronald Reagan was a B-movie actor, long before he became the 40th president of the United States. However a few clues give away the trick – the small "Fargo FX" logo appearing after 20 seconds or so in the right-hand corner of the screen; the ridiculous name of the actress co-credited with Reagan; the score that reprises the theme written by Jeff Russo for the series; and, finally, the title itself of this film that turns out to be a forgery, since "Massacre at Sioux Falls" will be identified by assiduous viewers of the first season as an event already mentioned several times by various characters and belonging to their own past.

This false opening also turns out to be a false start. No sooner has the illusion of reality been created than it is broken. First the camera reveals a stately Indian chief, complete with war paint and headdress, surveying the battlefield. Then the actor, instead of delivering his text, starts addressing the film crew on the other side of the camera. We soon understand that they are all waiting for "Dutch," that is, Reagan. "Waiting for Dutch" is the title that was given to the episode, whose Vladimir and Estragon are unmistakably the unnamed actor and the director who joins him in front of the camera. The epic bombast of the opening credits is definitively punctured and gives way to trivial considerations (it is cold; they can't fix the arrows on Reagan) and half-finished sentences. We learn that this is the "actual" battlefield, not that the "Indian" who turns out to be "from New Jersey" seems to care much.

With this beginning, *Fargo* offers a reflexive as well as self-derisive comment on its own relation with cinema – when it poses as a film, it is an old B movie, a stereotypical western, and, even worse, it is the kind of footage that ends up on the cutting room floor. Through these unexpected ontological shifts, from *Fargo* (the series we expected to watch) to "Massacre at Sioux Falls" (the film we are given to watch instead) to "Waiting for Dutch" (the accidental behind-the-scenes recording that we get in the end), the series exposes its true nature as a spectacle that is acted and shot. We are already warned that what will be said to be "true" will not be, and that when we see the "real" Massacre at Sioux Falls, at the end of the season, the bodies lying on the ground will be as dead as the actors freezing and asking for blankets as they lie in various poses in the epic scenery of "Massacre at Sioux Falls'.

This pseudo title sequence is actually the pre-title sequence of the episode. It is followed by a much faster-paced montage of archive footage (Carter's "Crisis of Confidence" speech; serial killer John Wayne Gacy's arrest; petrol shortages) and shots of the series' characters, with the superimposed disclaimer appearing only at this point, and the title itself a while later. The fictitious film entitled *Massacre at Sioux Falls* then becomes part of this flow of televised images and as such brings to the fore the hybrid nature of the series *Fargo*, conceived as a multi-episode film to be aired on TV. In other drama series, the sequence placed before the titles is usually a "teaser" which fulfils its function typically by offering thrilling action, mystery, or simply dialogue and/or images that are significant to the plot. The teaser, which is sometimes a flashback or a flashforward, often ends with a cliff-hanger, a striking event, a meaning-laden revelation, or a surprise. The opening sequence of *Fargo*'s Season 2 may occupy the position traditionally held by the teaser, but it uses none of these devices, and even appears to be an "anti-teaser," offering another illustration of the way Hawley's *Fargo* plays with the conventions of serial narration. This sequence is characterized by its slow pace and the absence of camera movement, with the two-minute-long static shot of the actor joined by the director and the occasional crew member. There is a sense of expectation – everybody is waiting for Reagan – but no particular excitation or anxiety accompanying it. The arrival of "Dutch" is left hanging, but what is created is false suspense rather than the usual exciting cliff-hanger. The characters introduced here will never be seen again. The status of this scene within the series and its diegesis will never be clarified – we will never know whether it is supposed to be a film within the show, perhaps the kind of rerun that Molly or Peggy watch on TV, or a flashback to Reagan's career as an actor. This prologue then presents itself as a gratuitous delay before the action starts, a mere interference undermining the coherence of the narrative whole, even a mistake – and a missed take.

Through this "anti-teaser," however, the series explores alternative ways of linking the pre-title sequence to the remainder of the episode or season: instead of using the liminal position to foreground a passage from the narrative, this introduction of uncertain nature turns out to have an analogical relationship to the story that follows, thereby recalling the practice of the Coen brothers in the opening of *A Serious Man* (2009), a prologue in Yiddish whose characters and setting are apparently disconnected from the main narrative. In *Fargo*'s second-season opening, the title of the Ronald Reagan film, *Massacre at Sioux Falls*, is the name given in the main story to a "historical" event that is supposed to have taken place in 1979 and that is shown at the end of the season. The "celluloid Indian" (Kilpatrick 1999) seen after the fake credits is paralleled by the Native American henchman of the Gerhardt family, Hanzee, who is responsible for the "Massacre at Sioux Falls" and one of its rare survivors. The actor and the director's long wait for Reagan is echoed in the shots of Dodd Gerhardt and Hanzee waiting for Rye Gherhardt that follow the prologue and start the action proper. At the same time, this scene presenting people "waiting for Dutch" announces the series' depiction of the 1979 historical and political context in the United States and the hope raised by Reagan's run for the presidency as the country was going through the "crisis of confidence" described by Carter in the speech cited right at the end of the sequence. Finally, the sense of expectation created by the opening sequence also applies to the arrival of Reagan in the show, as one of the secondary characters. Reagan will appear for the first time in the fifth episode, when he delivers a speech during the presidential campaign. He is portrayed by Bruce Campbell, another B-movie actor famous for his role as Ash Williams, the monster-slaying hero of the horror franchise *Evil Dead*,[13] an intertext that casts Reagan as a slightly comical, not-too-subtle providential man expected to fight off the demons besetting the United States at the end of the 1970s.

Before this moment, however, Reagan's acting career is again alluded to in the fourth episode, in a flashback showing Dodd Gerhardt, then a teenager, committing his first murder, in a cinema during the screening of a (fictional) film entitled *Moonbase Freedom* and, as a shot of the marquee sign informs us, "starring Ronald Reagan." *Moonbase Freedom* continues the pseudo-cinematographic thread initiated at the very beginning of the season. It was created by giving an invented title to a real film, *The Man from Planet X* (dir. Edgar G. Ulmer 1951) (*IMDb* 2015). Some footage from the 1951 science-fiction film can be seen on the cinema screen, showing a woman walking toward a spaceship and then an alien in a spacesuit looking at her. Like the fabricated *Massacre at Sioux Falls*, *Moonbase Freedom* is linked to a theme that runs through the season[14] and announces an event that will take place a few episodes later, when flying saucers appear in the sky above the belligerents at Sioux Falls (in episode 9).[15] As was the case for the western film opening the season, the insertion of this science-fiction film into the series is a way for the show to comment on US cinema and on the way it constantly reinvents American history, producing images that become part of collective memory, thereby hinting at the way the TV show *Fargo* itself uses cinematic devices popular in the seventies (e.g., the split-screen editing) to visually evoke the historical context of the story.

Even if real films starring Reagan are mentioned or alluded to in the dialogues – *Cattle Queen of Montana* (dir. Allan Dwan 1954) and *Bedtime for Bonzo* (dir. Frederick De Cordova 1951)[16] – the Reagan films that are shown are fakes.[17] They are thus pastiches within the larger pastiche constituted by the series itself and reflect the latter's status in relation with the "real" Coen brothers' films. This mirror effect is even stronger in the case of the third fictional film, since the characters do not watch it on a cinema screen but on a television screen. This film, entitled *Operation Eagle's Nest* and supposedly shot in 1942, is watched by Lou Solverson's daughter Molly at the beginning of the season (episode 3) and by Peggy at the end (episode 8), when she and Ed are keeping Dodd prisoner in a log cabin – another allusion to the Coens' *Fargo*, especially as Peggy, like Carl Showalter, fiddles with the TV set to get a clear image on the screen. In the third episode, only the title of the film appears briefly on the TV screen in the Solversons' living room, but the passage shown in episode 8 is much longer and is freed from the frame of the screen within the screen for a few uninterrupted minutes. As the camera moves toward the TV set and gradually makes all elements framing the picture disappear, the grainy, greenish televisual image turns into a flawless black and white. The effect stresses how deeply Peggy is engrossed in the action of the film, while presenting the scene as an apparent digression in much the same way as *Massacre at Sioux Falls*. For a moment, the TV show *Fargo* becomes a black-and-white film, another hint at the series' cinematographic ambitions – and another ambivalent assessment of them. The faux Reagan film both pays homage to the American cinema of the 1940s with its high-quality recreation of black-and-white photography, and ridicules the patriotic stance of Hollywood World War II films with the arrival of the US soldier (presumably played by Reagan), who shoots the SS officer and says, "Take that, you Nazi rat!"

Operation Eagle's Nest is also the theme of a reminiscing by Reagan himself in episode 5, during a conversation with Lou Solverson, who served two tours in the Mekong Delta. In the actor-turned-politician's meandering narrative of "his" war, reality and fiction overlap as he confuses acting with doing, failing to distinguish between the real events of the making of the film and the fictional content of the film. For instance, he names the other actors as if they were real soldiers and the actions he performed as an actor as if they were real military operations:

> Every generation has their time. I remember back in '42, America had just joined the war. I was working on *Operation Eagle's Nest* for Paramount. I got dropped behind enemy lines trying to rescue Jimmy Whitmore and Laraine Day from this SS commando. Bob Stack was on loan from Selznick. That Nazi bastard had us cornered. We were done for, but in the end, with a little American ingenuity, we managed to … No, now wait a minute. Um … Come to think of it, I don't think we made it out of that one.
>
> Or did we? Oh, shit, I can't remember. Well, either way, it was a fine picture.

In the last episode, Peggy experiences a confusion of a similar order, also involving *Operation Eagle's Nest*, when she and a wounded Ed hide from Hanzee in a cold room in a supermarket. When she sees smoke enter the locked room through the air-conditioning unit, she identifies similarities and correspondences between her own desperate situation and a scene from *Operation Eagle's Nest* – the scene we saw her watch on TV in episode 8: "It's just like the movie," she says as images from the film appear in the frame, superimposed on the shots of Peggy.[18] These parallels inspire her with hope: "But they got out! Ed, they got out! They were saved!" And indeed, the sequence of events but also the editing of the shots are reminiscent of the passage from *Operation Eagle's Nest* shown earlier. However the resemblances turn out to be imaginary: when Peggy finally unlocks the door to confront Hanzee, she actually attacks Lou and his colleague, who tell her that there was no smoke and that Hanzee got away. Peggy maintains that "the Indian" was in the building, trying to smoke them out, "just like in the movie," calling to Ed to confirm her story, before realizing that Ed has died. The visual overlap of shots figures the images coming to Peggy's mind as she remembers the film, while also illustrating the way she puts her present predicament and the film characters' story side by side. Ultimately, the superimposition evokes Peggy's confusion between fiction and reality, since she actually re-enacts and re-lives what she saw on TV, unaware that fiction is somehow seeping into her reality, like the smoke she believes is invading the cold room. There is something touchingly ironic about Peggy's identification with a B-movie heroine at that point because one of her main concerns over the course of the season has been to "fully actualize" and she felt she had finally reached that goal when she and Ed kidnapped Dodd Gerhardt and fled from Luverne ("We're actualized," she tells Ed in the car, episode 8). Peggy is a character in search of actuality, who gets caught up in fiction in the end.

The palimpsest of images that characterizes this sequence also points to the intertextual nature of the series, as does Peggy's repeated exclamation that "it's just like (in) the movie," which can be read as a self-reflexive comment of the TV show *Fargo* on its own imitative character. Carter Burwell's theme for the film *Fargo* that can be heard as Peggy is arrested and brought to the police car works as a musical reminder of the connections between the show and the film while also reiterating a type of allusion (the musical quote) that had already been made at the end of the first season. Then this quotation from the Coens' *Fargo* is both intertextual and intra-textual, both paying homage to the film and performing, even as it establishes it, a ritual that finds its meaning in the seriality of the show.

The show is not only "just like" *Fargo* – and so many other Coen brothers films – it is also, in its second season, "just like" the films it fabricated and incorporated. Filmic intertextuality seems to be so vital to the series, to be such a crucial component, that the television drama creates films to quote from and echo. With this intratextuality posing as intertextuality, the TV series positions itself as both originating from and engendering cinema. Its homage to the older art form is part of a totalizing enterprise, a tentacular narrative that annexes cinematic territory.

In the "cold room scene," however, the similarities between the scene from *Operation Eagle's Nest* and Peggy's situation turn out to be partly imaginary, even if the reactivated memories of the film continue to suggest parallels after Peggy's delusion has been revealed, especially between Lou Solverson and the American soldier-savior portrayed by Reagan in the faux WWII movie. There prevails the same sense of uncertainty, of rectification and correction as in Reagan's monologue or the fabricated title sequence at the beginning of the season, even if the tone is entirely serious, even pathetic, in this passage. These memory lapses, these obliterations and revisions, work as (highly controlled) glitches in the well-oiled machine of the serialized narrative. They frustrate the spectators' desire for meaning: "The human mind, aroused by an insistence for meaning, seeks and finds nothing but contradiction and nonsense," says the man who appears to Peggy at the beginning of episode 8. The fake Reagan film clips remain unresolved fragments, unkept promises of more fiction, more stories. They are one of the ways in which the series' narrative expands but also resists expansion. They offer the tantalizing prospect of hidden connections, "Easter eggs" to be unearthed by the patient "forensic-minded" fans (Mittell 2013), both urging them to "drill down to deeper levels" (Mittell 2013) and blatantly thwarting some of their efforts. Characteristically, the DVD bonus feature entitled "The Films of Ronald Reagan with Audio Commentary by Bruce Campbell," a montage of the film clips that appeared throughout the season, is also a forgery: far from delivering behind-the-scenes anecdotes about the actual making of these films for the television series, it is presented as an audio commentary made by Reagan himself during his campaign, in the same vein as his monologue about *Operation Eagle's Nest*: a confused, woolly comment, filled with blunders and trivial details – and is comical at Reagan's expense.

FX's *Fargo* is full of cinema, and even more so in its second season, which not only repeatedly alludes to the film *Fargo* as well as to other films by the Coen brothers and more generally speaking to various film genres, but also features several film clips. The first season ends with the main characters watching the game "Deal or No Deal" on television, but the second season's characters watch films, at the cinema or on television. The mise-en-abyme is symptomatic of the reflexive nature of this season, which regularly offers comments on its own hybridity as a television show conceived as a very long film. In its bidirectional relation to the film *Fargo* and to the Reagan B movies, the series both reproduces and re-produces cinema, using it as a model and source material, while at the same time recreating it and incorporating it into its vast and expanding universe. In many ways, the series is engaged in what could be called "pastiche frenzy": FX's *Fargo* is a pastiche of "pastiche artists" (Robey 2016), and contains numerous pastiches, whose presence only reinforces its Coenesque quality. Hawley seems to have approached his practice as a pasticheur in a way reminiscent of some of Proust's reflections on his own imitative writing: "When we have just finished reading a book, not only do we wish we could continue to live with the characters [...] but our own inner voice, also, which has been disciplined during the entire time of our reading to follow the rhythm of a Balzac or a Flaubert, would like to continue to speak like them" (*Contre Sainte-Beuve*, quoted by Genette 1997, 119). However, the multiplication of pastiches in Hawley's *Fargo* might also be read in Jamesonian terms as postmodern "blank parody" (Jameson 1991, 16) run amok. Ultimately, what preserves the series from this interpretation actually lies in its imitation of the Coen brothers' films: in what Hawley calls "that 'accept the mystery' philosophy that the Coens have built into their work" (Arnold 2014). In the long term provided by the serialized narrative, the various references to cinema do not just play an intertextual, potentially shallow, game. They help to shape and support dramatic tensions that run through the whole series, between reality and fiction; between meaning and absurdity, engaging the viewers in a variety of ways and bringing the television show to experiment with serialized storytelling.

Notes

1 On the involvement of the Coen brothers, Hawley said: "On a day-to-day level, they're not involved. Mostly I try to be as respectful as possible, and keep them in the loop without pressuring them in any way. It's like, here are the scripts and here are the episodes if you want to read or watch them. If you don't, my feelings won't be hurt" (Egner 2015). The filmmakers' (provocative?) declarations about the television series corroborate Hawley's statement: "'We're just not very interested,' Joel Coen says in the latest issue of *Radio Times*. 'I mean, we're perfectly happy with it. We have no problem with it. It just feels divorced from our film somehow' " (Gill 2016).

2 On *Bates Motel* and *Psycho*, see Boni (2016–2017).

3 Pastiche, according to G. Genette's typology, is "the imitation of a style without any satirical intent" (Genette 1997, 25).

4 Hawley himself points out these connections and suggests that they are part of the media "buzz" surrounding the series: " 'I would say if the three movies that influenced Season 1 were *Fargo*, *No Country for Old Men* and *A Serious Man*, this year we are in *Fargo*, *Miller's Crossing* and *The Man Who Wasn't There*', Hawley says. 'So let the Internet speculation begin' " (Porter 2014).

5 A "case-of-the-week" TV series aired in the 1990s in which the sheriff of a small town in Wisconsin solves strange cases.

6 See R. Saint Gelais's definition of transfictionality (*transfictionnalité*) : "une relation de migration (avec la modification qui en résulte presque immanquablement) de données diégétiques" (Saint-Gelais 2011, 10–11).

7 Hawley states that prior knowledge of the film is not necessary: "I don't think you need to watch it before [watching the series], but I think you should watch it because it's a great movie" (Goldberg 2014).

8 The fourth season of *Fargo* was due to premiere on FX in April 2020 but was delayed due to the Covid 19 pandemic.

9 Brixby's book does not reappear in Season 3. However, this season offers new variations involving fictitious books and adaptation in 3.3. Another Barton Fink figure appears in this episode: Thaddeus Mobley, aka Ennis Stussy. He is seen writing in a dingy motel room in Los Angeles, in a flashback about an unfortunate experience he had in Hollywood in the 1970s when he hoped to adapt his science-fiction novel for cinema. An animated adaptation of the novel is actually shown in several parts inserted in the episode when Gloria, Ennis's stepdaughter, reads the book. In comparison to S02E09 then, the distinctions between source and derivative, and between history and fiction, are left intact. Interestingly, too, the audiovisual medium chosen is animation, not live action as was the case of the fake films present in the second season.

10 This framing device was used in the first Disney feature film, *Snow White and the Seven Dwarfs* (1937), and then in numerous other films. See, for instance, the opening of *The Jungle Book* (1967), in which one of the black-and-white illustrations is slowly replaced by the color setting of the film itself. See "Storybook Opening", *TV Tropes* for more examples. According to *TV Tropes*, Disney started this trope.

11 For maps of the Fargoverse created by fans, see: https://www.google.com/maps/d/viewer?mid=13zgc-c7pB0CDfP0izSjXVUQFenQ&hl=en_US&ll=39.2588153603328%2C-96.4786598890625&z=4 ; https://imgur.com/vS6NPSG. Last consultation January 4, 2020.
12 Hills defines hyperdiegesis as "the creation of a vast and detailed narrative space, only a fraction of which is ever directly seen or encountered within the text, but which nevertheless appears to operate according to principles of internal logic and extension" (Hills 2002, 104).
13 The first film of the franchise was *The Evil Dead* (dir. Sam Raimi, 1981). A televised sequel, *Ash vs Evil Dead*, also starring Bruce Campbell, aired on Starz from 2015 to 2018.
14 For instance, in the very first episode, Rye Gerhardt sees strange blue lights in the night sky just before being hit by Peggy's car; in episode 9, the UFO theme is alluded to thanks to a closeup of a small poster showing a flying saucer and the caption "We are not alone" stuck up on the wall of a petrol station.
15 The scene is visibly inspired by the Coens' *The Man Who Wasn't There* (2001), in which the flying saucer's spotlight also singles out the character in a pool of white light. For more on UFOs in FX's *Fargo* and in *The Man Who Wasn't There,* see Meslow (2015).
16 In episode 5.
17 These fictional films imitating the Reagan films are pastiches as well as parodies in some measure since they adopt a more or less emphasized satirical stance toward the type of film they imitate. On parody as "an imitation that is more heavily loaded in satirical or caricatural effect" than pastiche, see Genette 1997, 23.
18 In S03E03, a striking shot also plays with superimposition, when Vivian Lord, the young actress who cons Thaddeus Mobley, seems to materialize out of the footage of a screen test presented on a cinema screen. As she emerges from her seat her filmic image finds itself projected on her body and face, so that her filmic and physical selves overlap for an instant. With its focus on cinema, the flashback to 1975 in S03E03 also appears as a flashback to the predilections of the second season, even borrowing from its aesthetics with split-screen editing.

Works cited

Arnold, Ben. "Fargo Comes to Channel 4: 'This Is Not a TV Series, it's a 10-hour Movie'". *The Guardian,* 04.12.2014. https://www.theguardian.com/tv-and-radio/2014/apr/12/fargo-tv-adaptation-coen-brothers-blessing (accessed 12.12.2018).
Assouly, Julie. "De *Fargo* (Coen, 1996) à *Fargo* saison 1 et 2 (Hawley, 2014–2015)". *Cinema and Seriality Sercia Conference,* conference paper, Paris, 2016.
Boni, Marta. "*Psycho/Bates Motel* : hyperdiégèse et réactivation sélective". *Intermédialités,* 28–29, 2016–2017. http://id.erudit.org/iderudit/1041077ar (accessed 12.12.2018).
Boren, Zachary Davies. "*Fargo* Season 2: Creator Noah Hawley Talks the New Era of American Crime TV". *The Independent,* 10.17.2015. http://www.independent.co.uk/arts-entertainment/tv/fargo-season-2-creator-noah-hawley-talks-the-new-era-of-american-crime-tv-a6697746.html (accessed 12.12.2018).
Couch, Christina. "Death Becomes Him: Noah Hawley on Bringing 'Fargo' to TV". *Get In Media,* June 2014. http://getinmedia.com/articles/film-tv-careers/death-becomes-him-noah-hawley-bringing-fargo-tv (accessed 12.12.2018).

Egner, Jeremy. "Noah Hawley on *Fargo*, Comic Haircuts and Living in the Coen Universe". *The New York Times*, 11.3.2015 http://www.nytimes.com/2015/11/03/arts/television/noah-hawley-on-fargo-comic-haircuts-and-living-in-the-coen-universe.html?_r=0 (accessed 12.12.2018).

"*Fargo* (TV Series), 'Fear and Trembling' (2015), Trivia". *IMDb*, 2015. http://www.imdb.com/title/tt4001070/trivia?ref_=tt_trv_trv (accessed 12.12.2018).

Genette, Gérard. *Narrative Discourse, An Essay in Method*. Translated by Jane E. Lewin. Ithaca, NY: Cornell University Press, 1980. (Originally published in French as "Discours du récit", a portion of *Figures III*. Paris: Editions du Seuil, 1972).

Genette, Gérard. *Palimpsests: Literature in the Second Degree*. Translated by Channa Newman and Claude Doubinski. Lincoln and London: University of Nebraska Press, 1997. (Originally published in French as *Palimpsestes, La Littérature au second degré*. Paris: Editions du Seuil, 1982).

Gill, James. "The Coen Brothers on the Fargo TV series: 'We're Just Not Very Interested'". *Radio Times*, 02.22.2016. http://www.radiotimes.com/news/2016-02-22/the-coen-brothers-on-the-fargo-tv-series-were-just-not-very-interested (accessed 12.12.2018).

Goldberg, Lesley. "FX's *Fargo* Cast, EPs on Film Comparisons, Anthology Format, Courting Billy Bob Thornton". *The Hollywood Reporter*, 01.14.2014. http://www.hollywoodreporter.com/live-feed/fxs-fargo-cast-eps-film-671050 (accessed 12.12.2018).

Hawley, Noah. "*Fargo* Boss Reveals What Ethan Coen Really Thought about the Pilot". *The Hollywood Reporter*, 05.15.2014. http://www.hollywoodreporter.com/news/fargo-boss-reveals-what-ethan-703482 (accessed 12.12.2018).

Hills, Matt. *Fan Cultures*. London and New York: Routledge, 2002.

Hudelet, Ariane. "Un cadavre ambulant, un petit-déjeuner sanglant, et le quartier Ouest de Baltimore : le générique, moment-clé des séries télévisées". *GRAAT On-Line* 6, December 2009. 1–17. http://www.graat.fr/tv01hudelet.pdf (accessed 12.12.2018).

Jameson, Fredric. *Postmodernism, or the Cultural Logic of Late Capitalism*. Durham, NC: Duke University Press, 1991.

Kilpatrick, Jacquelyn. *Celluloid Indians: Native Americans and Film*. Lincoln: University of Nebraska Press, 1999.

Kizu, Kyle. "Noah Hawley AMA: *Fargo* Creator Explains That Unlike the Coens, He's 'Clearly More Talkative'". *IndieWire*, 06.15.2016. http://www.indiewire.com/2016/06/noah-hawley-ama-fargo-creator-difference-coen-bros-1201689220/(accessed 12.12.2018).

Meslow, Scott. "The Truth Is Out There: The UFOs and Aliens on FX's *Fargo*, Explained". *The Week*, 10.19.2015. http://theweek.com/articles/584099/truth-there-ufos-aliens-fxs-fargo-explained (accessed 12.12.2018).

Mittell, Jason. "Film and Television Narrative". In David Herman (ed.), *The Cambridge Companion to Narrative*, Cambridge, MA: Cambridge University Press, 2007. 156–171.

Mittell, Jason. "Forensic Fandom and the Drillable Text". In Henry Jenkins, Sam Ford, and Joshua Green (eds.), *Spreadable Media: Creating Value and Meaning in a Networked Culture*, New York and London: New York University Press, 2013. (enhanced book), http://spreadablemedia.org/essays/mittell/#.WQbrTMYXrIV (accessed 12.12.2018).

Neumann, Birgit, and Nünning, Ansgar. "Metanarration and Metafiction". In Peter Hühn et al. (eds.), *The Living Handbook of Narratology*, Hamburg: Hamburg University, 2014. http://www.lhn.uni-hamburg.de/article/metanarration-and-metafiction (accessed 12.12.2018).

Porter, Rick. "*Fargo* Season 2: EP Noah Hawley Details Where, When and How It's Connected to Season 1". *Screener*, 07.21.2014. http://screenertv.com/blogs/fargo_season_2_spoilers_fx_noah_hawley_keith_carradine_lou_solverson-2014-07/ (accessed 12.12.2018).

Ray, Amber. "*Fargo*: Rounding Up the Easter Eggs in the Series". *Entertainment Weekly*, 06.17.2014. http://ew.com/article/2014/06/17/fargo-film-series-references-season-finale/ (accessed 12.12.2018).

Robey, Tim. "*Hail, Caesar*! Review: 'The Coens' Screwball Stumble'". *The Telegraph*, 03.03. 2016. http://www.telegraph.co.uk/films/2016/04/14/hail-caesar-review-the-coens-screwball-stumble/ (accessed 12.12.2018).

Saint-Gelais, Richard. *Fictions transfuges, La Transfictionnalité et ses enjeux*. Paris: Editions du Seuil, 2011.

"Storybook Opening". *TV Tropes*. http://tvtropes.org/pmwiki/pmwiki.php/Main/StorybookOpening (accessed 12.12.2018).

Series and films cited

American Horror Story. FW, 2011–.
Ash vs Evil Dead. Starz, 2015–2018.
Barton Fink. Joel Coen, 20th C. Fox, 1991.
Bates Motel. A&E, 2013–2017.
Bedtime for Bonzo. Frederick De Cordova, Universal, 1951.
Cattle Queen of Montana. Allan Dwan, RKO, 1954.
Evil Dead. Sam Raimi, Renaissance Pictures, 1981.
Fargo. FX, 2014–.
Fargo. Joel Coen, Gramercy, 1996.
LOST. ABC, 2004–2010.
Man from Planet X, The. Edgar G. Ulmer, United Artists, 1951.
Picket Fences. CBS, 1992–1996.
Psycho. Alfred Hitchcock, Paramount, 1960.
True Detective. HBO, 2014–.

3.3 Screening dreams

Twin Peaks, from the series to the film, back again and beyond[1]

Sarah Hatchuel

In the fictional town of Twin Peaks, somewhere in the northwest of the United States, the body of Laura Palmer (Sheryl Lee), a beautiful 16-year-old girl, is found on the banks of a lake, wrapped in a plastic bag. To tell the secrets of this new Ophelia, David Lynch and Mark Frost's series *Twin Peaks* (ABC 1990–1991; Showtime 2017) combines profound tragedy and trivial burlesque in a story that not only includes dreams but feels like a dream itself. The series generates a kind of quirky malaise, arguably condoning misogynistic fascination for sexually brutalized women and letting the male serial murderer off the hook. Lynch's prequel film, *Twin Peaks: Fire Walk with Me* (1992), which was released a year after the original series was discontinued, dramatizes Laura's very last days. With an approach that combines narratology, intertextuality, and gender studies, this chapter proposes to revisit *Twin Peaks* through the myth of the sacrificed movie star to reveal how the series ideologically and narratively interacts with the prequel film. If the series *Twin Peaks* has broken traditional television codes on the aesthetic and narrative levels, *Fire Walk with Me* innovates on the gender level, as it denounces the mystifying screens created by the original series and its patriarchal ideology. Series that have then been influenced by the seminal show, such as *LOST* (ABC 2004–2010) or *Carnivàle* (HBO 2003–2005), seem to have unfolded Lynch's artistic project by developing explicating or diffracting it. Taking these shows into account will help us build a unified theory on the *Twin Peaks* matrix (the series and the film), in which the cinematic theme of the sacrificed young female star meets a narrative of dreamlike, parallel worlds. Encouraging us to watch the prequel film after the series, then to watch the series in light of the film and of the multiple shows it has influenced, *Twin Peaks* builds an original form of seriality in which cinema and television are both mobilized to engender a never-ending Möbius strip. Just as the characters are trapped in the series' Black Lodge, the viewers are invited to return to a story that demands to be re-watched, re-experienced, and re-interpreted. *Twin Peaks* thus turns seriality into a circular drive in which each turn of the screw digs deeper into the dreamlike fabric of fiction.

Dreaming of stars

Twin Peaks is dreamlike through its surrealistic compositions, its absurd and unexpected situations, its slowness and digressions, its languid and hypnotic music, and its gallery of unusual, eccentric, and sometimes anachronistic characters. Dale Cooper (Kyle MacLachlan), the FBI agent assigned to investigate Laura Palmer's murder, is less interested in scientific facts than in magic and Tibetan methods of intuitive deduction. According to Marine Legagneur, the series occurs "in a space between waking and sleeping, between reality and imagination, a porous interface between two worlds" (Legagneur 2012) where supernatural visions abound.

At the end of the pilot, Sarah Palmer (Grace Zabriskie), Laura's mother, screams in terror as she sees, in a vision, an unknown hand unearthing the heart-shaped pendant that belonged to her daughter. In the second episode,[2] Sarah Palmer is visited by Donna (Lara Flynn Boyle), her daughter's best friend, before experiencing another terrifying vision: Laura's face becomes imprinted on Donna's, suddenly reviving the dead girl, just before a menacing man with long grey hair (who will turn out to be evil Bob) appears crouched by Laura's bed.

This mysterious Bob (Frank Silva) resurfaces in Cooper's dream at the end of episode 3. Cooper first sees a one-armed man, Mike (Al Strobel), who delivers the cryptic stanza: "Through the darkness of future's past/ The magician longs to see/ One chants out between two worlds/ Fire walk with me." Mike divulges that, after meeting God, he cut off his arm to detach himself from his former partner Bob; but Bob is always there, a lurking predator, feeding on fears and pleasures. Bob eventually appears in the dream to promise Mike that he "will kill again." Mike and Bob are both revealed to be parasitic spirits inhabiting the body of their host and feeding on pain and sadness.

Twin Peaks is a dreamlike series not only because it includes sequences of hallucination and magical vision, but because it presents itself openly as a fiction where illusion and reality merge, creating a world of uncertainty and doubt, and playing on the idea of alternate universes and narrative bifurcations where cinematic references abound. For instance, Ben Horne (Richard Beymer), having lost his mind in episode 23, thinks that he is General Lee and imagines that the Confederate army has just won the Civil War. His daughter Audrey (Sherilyn Fenn), who does not want to upset him, disguises herself as Scarlett O'Hara and proposes a version of *Gone with the Wind* where the South is victorious. The characters of *Twin Peaks* thus live as if within a film or a dream.

When Audrey, in episode 3, listens to the music coming from a jukebox – which is also the soundtrack Angelo Badalamenti composed for the series – she begins to dance voluptuously and says, "Isn't this music just too dreamy?" Similarly, in episode 10, Ben Horne's brother asks if this is not all "some kind of strange and twisted dream," and, in episode 12, Donna wonders whether "our dreams are real." Ben visits the brothel he owns in episode 8 and asks to test the new recruit without knowing that she is his own daughter; upon entering the room, he teases the young woman he has yet to recognize and quotes from Shakespeare's *The Tempest*, "Close your eyes. This is such stuff as dreams as made of." The whole fiction thus appears as a midsummer night's dream "governed by libidinal forces [and] unspeakable desires" (Hume 1995, 115).

The series adopts a male gaze on women, offering a catalogue of hetero-sexual men's fantasies: discreet school girls are revealed to be secret pros-titutes; brothels are presented as glamorous places where young girls are dressed up like models; very old men marry teenagers; candidates in the Miss Twin Peaks contest are leered at and appraised by "dirty" old men. *Twin Peaks* is a fiction where *malaise* verges on pedopornography. This specific perverse male gaze does not spare Laura Palmer.

The character of Laura is two-faced: she is the dead young woman in a plastic body bag, offered, like a morbid version of Sleeping Beauty, to a necrophiliac gaze; she is also, in the photograph that punctuates the end of each episode, the beauty queen, all dressed up and made up, immortalized in her ephemeral glow. *Twin Peaks* replays the "Death and the Maiden" motif, Eros and Thanatos combining in an image that freezes the young woman and turns her into an object of worship. Laura is the object that men desire and that women want to imitate or compete with. Through pho-tographs, videos, diaries and testimonies, Laura's absence after her death becomes a form of spectral omnipresence under the desiring and incendiary gazes of viewers who consume and burn their idol (Roche 2010).

Not surprisingly, David Lynch and Mark Frost had first met to work on a film that was to tell the life of Marilyn Monroe, the ultimate sex symbol – one worshipped by the public but whose private life bore the wounds of a stolen childhood. Marilyn's youth was scarred by abandon-ment, sexual assaults perpetrated by people who should have protected her and her mother's refusal to believe her stories of abuse. Frost and Lynch's project did not go through but *Twin Peaks*, the series they made instead, bears its trace in the way the show turns a girl whose reality is that of un-speakable violence, raped intimacy, and tortured sexuality into a glamor-ous star – a girl who is "glowing outside and dying inside" (Lynch quoted in Chion 1998, 168). This reflection on stardom further anchors *Twin Peaks* in the history of cinema and of its myths. Symbolically, the series uses the names of characters we find in Otto Preminger's *Laura* (1944) and Alfred Hitchcock's *Vertigo* (1958). These two films already exposed how cinema creates celluloid goddesses, spectral images of inaccessible stars, engender-ing reverence, desire, and frustration (Thiellement 2010, 11–13). Laura's photograph revisits Gene Tierney's fascinating portrait, while Laura her-self replays the fate of the star sacrificed to fans who adore her but neither know her nor protect her. As Bobby (Dana Ashbrook) shouts in despair at Laura's funeral, "We are all guilty of her death" – a "we" that includes the show's viewers. At the end of episode 9, we see Laura being murdered. In strobe lighting, Laura screams under the blows inflicted by Bob. The images pulsate before our eyes like a heart that will soon stop beating. The stroboscopic light produces quasi-subliminal images that show as much as they hide – a sign that Bob's presence is only a mask, that his "reality" is only intermittent but is compelled to come back in serial form. On screen, Bob serves to screen a reality too sordid to be revealed directly.

Supernatural evil and the denial of incest

A photofit of Bob is drawn according to the visions experienced by Dale Cooper and Sarah Palmer (episode 11). Leland Palmer (Ray Wise), Laura's father, recognizes him as the man he saw when he was a child in his grandfather's house. Bob was a magician who asked him if he wanted to play. The series suggests that Leland was abused as a child – perhaps by his grandfather. Bob appears as a child's imaginary creation to protect himself from the horror of having been raped, but the series is never explicit on this point and maintains the myth of Bob's existence.

Episode 15 unveils Bob behind Leland: Laura's father looks in the mirror and sees the reflection of the monster who inhabits him. After his arrest in episode 17, Leland speaks with Bob's voice: "Oh, Leland, you've been a good vehicle and I've enjoyed the ride." Before dying in his cell, as he painfully realizes the murders he has committed, Leland reveals that Bob wanted to enter Laura's body but failed because she was too strong. In retaliation, he forced Leland to kill her. Since the series imagines that Leland is possessed by an evil spirit that occupies his body and manipulates his mind, the incestuous and abusive father cannot be held responsible for his actions (Hume 1995, 117). If Bob *does* exist, then Leland is innocent and becomes a tragic character. Todd McGowan rightly encourages us to see Bob less as a supernatural entity than as the structural force of patriarchy, a force that unsuccessfully attempts to experience feminine enjoyment (2007, 144–151), but the representation of Bob definitely evolves from the series to the film.

The series first highlights a supernatural Bob and thus a guiltless Leland. Revealingly, when Leland meets Agent Cooper in the Red Room in the last episode, he tells him, "I did not kill anybody." The series thus excuses male violence toward women and displays a world where Laura is no longer there to reveal that she was not only raped by her father and not protected by her mother, but also harassed and coveted by all those who were supposed to help her.

In her diary, Laura recalls a dream in which she wishes to entrust Cooper with the secret of Bob's presence. Her account emphasizes that the words came out of her mouth in a strange and frustrating way. Because Bob's existence is both a secret and a mask, a piece of information that hides the essential missing piece, Laura obviously fails to reveal it. Cooper finally learns what Laura cannot say in a scene where he uses magic to unmask the culprit (episode 17). The vision he then experiences makes Laura's confession finally audible: "My father killed me." Her father. Not Bob.

One of the most important exchanges in the series takes place at the end of episode 17. Leland has just died and Bob seems to have reincarnated into an owl. Albert, the scientific member of the police team, wonders, "Maybe that's all Bob is. The evil that men do." To Sheriff Harry Truman, who has trouble believing in Bob's existence, Agent Cooper responds, "Is it easier to believe that a man would rape and murder his own daughter? Any more comforting?" Sheriff Truman replies, "No." Part of the series' agenda resides in that "No." *Twin Peaks* makes the comforting choice of an evil that, although it inhabits men, fundamentally lies outside of them. If the series uses the supernatural as a denial of reality, the film *Fire Walk with Me* seeks to expose the incestuous truth.

Fire Walk with Me: unmasking the incestuous father

As a prequel to the series, the film focuses on Laura Palmer's last days and paradoxically brings her back to life. The film can hardly be understood without the series but the series is also, retrospectively, illuminated by the film. The series and the film function, in fact, as the two complementary halves of Laura's heart pendant. Many critics have noticed how *Fire Walk with Me* is opposed to the *Twin Peaks* pilot in terms of dramatic situations (Astic 2008, 133). According to David Roche, the script is specifically intended to "frustrate" the expectations of those who know the series (Roche 2010). It has less often been pointed out that the film offers above all an ideological counterpoint allowing Lynch to rewrite the series, freeing himself from his collaboration with Frost to offer a different worldview, in which *Twin Peaks'* extravagant quirkiness gives way to tragedy.

Like the series, the film includes many allusions to dreams. When Cooper steps into his superior's office, he is worried by a dream he has had. Moreover, his colleague Phillip Jeffries (David Bowie) has visions peopled with strange beings who claim to be "living in a dream" and being "only air," like the shadows and spirits that haunt Shakespeare's plays, from *A Midsummer Night's Dream* to *The Tempest*, to symbolize the ephemeral and dreamlike nature of performing arts. But *Fire Walk with Me* mainly shatters the masks and illusions that *Twin Peaks* has built.

If the series encouraged the viewers' fascination for an abused young woman, even offering a glamorous image of despair, the film lets us see the tragedy in its sheer brutality, beyond the dazzling myth. McGowan has explored how the film, by revealing Laura's perspective, her void, and her inability to fully inhabit the contradictory roles that are imposed on her, makes present and "subjectivizes" what remains the absent, though central, object of desire in the series (2007, 131–132). The young woman we discover in the film is less lightheaded and manipulative than sad and fragile; her sexuality is less free than enforced; her life is less ardent and mysterious than dark and traumatized. Behind the Laura/Marilyn of *Twin Peaks* lies the Laura/Norma Jean of *Fire Walk with Me*. *Twin Peaks* is perhaps so much loved by cinephiles because it still contains fantasies of an eroticized star. Where the TV show invites us to worship and emulate the icon (like Donna, who wears Laura's glasses and talks like her), the film refuses to encourage identification with the star: Laura forbids Donna to follow her and to lose herself in a pseudo-romantic and morbid fascination. She tries to deter her from being a fan whose personality dissolves through the admiration of a persona that is *itself* a mask. Similarly, if the series is based on the denial of incest and the idea that Bob controlled Laura's father's body, the film breaks this illusion and reveals, through three crucial sequences, the unfathomable violence a father unleashed on his daughter.

The first sequence exposes the creation of the mask. Laura finds Bob lurking in the family home; she screams, runs outside, and hides. Cowering fearfully on the ground, she then sees her father come out of the house. She cries, "My god! No! No! No!" a reaction that reflects not only shock at the revelation but also an attempt to remain in denial.

Much more clearly than in the series, Bob stands as the mask of a truth that Laura cannot accept because it is too horrifying. Bob symbolizes intergenerational sexual violence as evil, as the male victim becoming predator in turn. He was probably created by Leland as an abused child, then internalized by Laura, to screen trauma and avoid seeing the rapist's true identity. In the film, Laura confides in her friend Harold Smith her fear of passing on evil in turn: "Bob is real! He's been having me since I was twelve. He says he wants to *be* me, or he'll kill me." When Harold holds her in his arms, in an attempt to comfort her, she screams and bares her teeth as if she were going to harm him, before regaining self-control and sobbing desperately. Between tears, fears, laughter, bouts of anger and pain, Laura burns out emotionally. She would rather die than continue the cycle of violence and become an executioner like her father. If, at the end of *Fire Walk with Me*, a shot of Laura lying dead in a sheer plastic body bag establishes the narrative continuity between the film and the series, *Fire Walk with Me* goes beyond this sole morbid image. Instead of ending precisely where the series begins, the film shows us Laura in the Red Room with Dale Cooper. An angel comes down to greet her. Between her joyful tears and sad laughter, the fate of Laura, as a raped and sacrificed icon, ends in a radiant assumption and apotheosis on the altar of our gazes.

In the second crucial sequence, while Bob enters Laura's bedroom through the window and forces himself on her, she shouts, "Who are you?" Behind Bob's face, Laura eventually catches the glimpse of her father's and starts screaming wildly. While the series shows us Bob behind Leland, the film reveals Leland behind Bob. Bob is explicitly denounced as a character created by the child to screen horrible memories and bear the unbearable.

The third sequence takes place when Leland is about to kill his daughter. He has just read her diary and shares his astonishment at seeing Bob mentioned as the rapist on every page: "I always thought you knew it was me," he tells her. In the film, Leland is thus fully aware of his actions. The series pretends to forget this, as if *Twin Peaks* were, like Bob, a screen or a cover-up story. The Red Room is the very area where this narrative spin takes place.

The Red Room: screening clues and the delusion of dreams

At the end of episode 3, Dale Cooper has a dream – a startling oneiric sequence unlike any television had ever shown before – propelling us in a room with red curtains and a floor with a chevron black-and-white pattern. This space seems to yield valuable clues to solve the murder case and confound Laura's murderer (Burkhead 2014, 43–45). The Red Room only includes a couch, a chair, two lamps, and a statue of Venus. This statue becomes a *Venus de Milo* in the last episode, recalling both Mike's severed arm and Laura's arms, bound before she was killed. Through the iconic (mutilated) statue of the goddess of beauty, the series conjures again the motif of a woman who is both eroticized and harmed. With the reference to the mute and armless statue, Laura is not only presented as a new Ophelia but as a new Lavinia, Titus's daughter in *Titus Andronicus*. In Shakespeare's play, Lavinia is raped by Chiron and Demetrius, who then cut out her tongue and cut off her hands to keep her from revealing the crime. In *Twin Peaks*, Laura tries, inside a dream, to reveal to Dale Cooper the truth about the man who raped and murdered her – but she cannot utter a word. To express her pain, she eventually has to resort to a coded narrative, in which a fictional character functions as stand-in for the real-life perpetrator, in a cinematic enactment of the screen memory in the psychoanalytic sense.

Within Laura and Dale's shared dream, an older Cooper is witnessing an amazing scene. Before him, a small man (Michael J. Anderson) – the Man from Another Place in the credits – claps his hands, exclaims, "Let's rock!" and begins a strange swaying dance. This "Let's rock" line also appears on a car's windshield in the movie prequel, creating a time loop: one no longer knows if Cooper recycles in his dreams what he has previously experienced or if the dream actually engenders reality. The small man then sits on the couch where he joins a blond woman who looks exactly like Laura Palmer. Their dialogue, pronounced backward during the filming, is played in reverse so that the lines become intelligible while conveying an uncanny feeling. As Pacôme Thiellement asserts, the scene plays on the cryptographic tradition of pop music and backward recordings (2010, 24).

The woman who looks like Laura puts a finger to the side of her nose, visually signifying that she had a cocaine habit. The small man then says, "I have good news. That gum you like is going to come back in style.

This is my cousin but does not she look almost exactly like Laura Palmer?" When Cooper asks the young woman about her identity, she replies, "I feel like I know her, but sometimes my arms bend back." The small man adds, "She's filled with secrets. Where we're from, the birds sing a pretty song and there's always music in the air." The young woman gets up, kisses Cooper, and whispers in his ear words that we do not hear. Cooper wakes up, convinced that he knows the name of Laura's murderer – a name he quickly forgets, as if it had remained in the world of the dream. When Cooper tells his dream to the police, he remembers being 25 years older. This 25-year gap between the time of the investigation and that of the vision can now be found reflexively in the time that has passed between the end of the first US broadcast in 1991 and the announcement in 2016 that a third season would be released on Showtime, giving the impression that the creators controlled their narrative master plan perfectly. Similarly, in the last episode of the series, Laura Palmer tells Cooper (and the viewers), "I'll see you again in twenty-five years," while the little man says, "When you see me, it will not be me," anticipating a change in the third season's cast and reasserting one of Lynch's favorite themes, that of doublings. As the small man predicts, the release of a third season actually makes the show "come back in style," after having been analyzed, dissected, and chewed like a stick of gum since the 1990s.

The audience has generally taken Cooper's assertions in episode 4 literally: to resolve the criminal case, all you need to do is to break the dream's code. Viewers have been tracking down how each word or gesture in the dream could point to the solution of the puzzle. The coroner confirms the dream's truthfulness when he notices that Laura was tied up with her arms bent back. The young woman "filled with secrets" gradually reveals her drug addiction and her secret sexual encounters. When the police discover a shack in the woods where men used to enjoy Laura's charms, the curtains hanging on the windows recall those of the Red Room. Moreover, the caged Mynah bird and the record player both materialize the "music in the air" and the bird singing "a pretty song" mentioned by the Man from Another Place.

Laura's cousin, Madeleine, comes to visit Sarah and Leland Palmer. Played also by Sheryl Lee, Madeleine is the spitting image of Laura but with brown hair and glasses. As Madeleine adorns a blonde wig and poses as Laura to test Dr. Jacoby's guilt, she becomes her cousin's perfect double and proves again the small man right when he referred to a cousin looking "almost exactly like Laura." Madeleine starts to see Bob in the house (episode 10), falls under Leland's blows (episode 15), and is found in a plastic bag. Tragedy repeats itself as if Laura's murder were an event doomed to replicate itself.

Theories abound regarding Cooper's dreams. He could be receiving messages from a supernatural entity in his sleep, or his intuitions could be so sharp as to enable him to transform his daily experiences into decipherable symbols at night: for instance, before seeing him in his dream in episode 3, Dale had met one-armed Mike in the hospital elevator during the pilot episode (Dolan 1995). Cooper first proves the viewers right when he *himself* reads his dreams as conveyors of clues for the investigation. When he discovers that the murderer was Leland Palmer (episode 17), he is quick to retrospectively list all the dreamlike elements that pointed toward the solution: after Laura's death, Leland had begun to dance as compulsively as the Man from Another Place, and his hair, like Bob's, had gone from black to white overnight.

However, Cooper is misled by tricks and illusions, in the same way as viewers were led to believe that Bob was the real murderer. Because the series is not simply a crime fiction where the completion of the investigation signals the end of the story, the dream sequences are not merely there to guide the FBI agent or the "forensic" spectators (Mittell 2009). As opposed to the dreams in Hitchcock's *Spellbound* (1945), they are not merely texts to be "unlocked." Some elements relate to the police investigation, but others remain opaque, pointing to a lack of meaning and readability. The dreams thus stand as "the antithesis of the classic story where every detail, every sign, serves the organization of events" (Astic 2008, 70) – deceptive leads that play with the viewers' minds, engaging them in a "pure aesthetic experience" (Legagneur 2012). As they deepen and proliferate, the puzzles and riddles end up concealing a greater mystery. In this sense, the beginning of *Fire Walk with Me*, where every detail of Lil's dance is over-interpreted, can be read as a way to denounce excessive decoding instead of simply responding to a poetic experience that points to a forever elusive mystery.

The Red Room as dream-come-true

The series' dreams and visions are ambiguous because their existences lie between the mental and the real. In the last episode, the Red Room proves to be a tangible place that is accessible from a specific location (the circle of the 12 sycamores in the forest) at a specific time (when a number of stars are aligned). In episode 28, we learn that a White Lodge can be opened by love and a Black Lodge by fear. The Red Room seems to stand as the waiting room to the Black Lodge, if not as the Black Lodge itself.

Cooper physically enters the Red Room as he chases Windom Earle (Kenneth Welsh) who has kidnapped Annie Blackburne (Heather Graham), the young woman with whom Cooper has recently fallen in love. His former dream materializes into a real space that keeps replicating itself. More or less identical rooms open on each side of a red-curtained corridor. Cooper enters several rooms or, rather, enters several times into the same room, where the situation changes each time. In one of them, the little man warns him that he took the "wrong way"; in yet another, he pronounces the word "doppelgänger," pointing to the inherent duality in human beings and announcing Cooper's duplication. In this same room, Laura yells under a pulsating light that evokes the moment when she was murdered.

In the next room, Cooper becomes aware that he is bleeding profusely. Following the blood trail he has left behind him, he discovers his own injured and motionless body near that of Caroline, the woman with whom he had had a beautiful love affair until her husband, Windom Earle, shot the lovers. Caroline died and Cooper was badly injured. The Red Room thus appears as an echo chamber where traumatic situations are repeated in variation within a *mise-en-abyme* of fiction. The Red Room thus embodies the very process of seriality, based on both recognition and an *exploration* of repetition, engendering a paradoxically *unique* form of repetition that is specific to each series (Soulez 2011). If a television series may be considered as a narrative, aesthetic, and ideological big bang giving birth to an expanding universe that regularly reformulates and reassesses its origins, the Red Room appears as the literal location where the genesis of *Twin Peaks* takes place. It is the site where the show's narrative potential is revisited, re-examined, and replayed from different angles, questioning what is actually repeated in the series and the film – that is, patriarchal violence against women.

The Red Room and the Media Matrix

The Red Room is a stage between two worlds, where the musical numbers, songs, and dances follow one another in unpredictable ways. It combines live performance (theater, circus) that implies an ephemeral temporality and direct interaction with the public, with the medium of television, which suggests storable images and an indirect, hierarchical relationship between the producers and the viewers. The ethos of theater comes through in the red curtains while the media are symbolized by the stripes on the floor, which recall electricity and radio waves. They are also evoked through the sofa-and-chair layout, which is similar to the set of a television talk show where the host (here, the small man) welcomes the distinguished guests between two musical or commercial breaks (Thiellement 2010, 88–90).

Television is also summoned in *Fire Walk with Me*: the film starts with the static noise of a TV set that implodes during the murder of Teresa Banks, Leland Palmer's first victim. The destroyed TV set signifies both the ending of a character's life and *Twin Peaks'* abrupt cancellation as decided by ABC in 1991. The movie is thus explicitly depicted, metafilmically, as born out of the series' interruption. The cinematic/television divide is here shattered. Paradoxically, cinema seems to be posited as the medium best suited to prolong a television series; but, since the film is narratively situated *before* the story told by the series, television is also conceived retrospectively as the best means to prolong a feature film.

The Red Room's artistic and media matrix is revisited in *Fire Walk with Me* and then diffracted in other series inspired by *Twin Peaks*. The "future's past" chanted by Mike in Cooper's dream may point to the fact that the Red Room exists out of time or all the time. The phrase announces the making of the prequel film – since the viewers of *Fire Walk with Me* already know or even saw what awaits Laura in the future – as well as the reappropriation of the *Twin Peaks* motifs in other series, inviting us to go back to the original show and see it under a new light. The seminal influence that *Twin Peaks* has had on the production of shows in the 1990s, 2000s, and 2010s has engendered a form of intertextuality that verges on seriality, as the story arcs of Laura Palmer and Dale Cooper continue to be revisited, reformulated, and prolonged, but this time outside the series' boundaries.

Shows such as *Battlestar Galactica* (Sci Fi, 2003–2009), *LOST* (ABC, 2004–2010) or *Carnivàle* (HBO, 2003–2005) all include strange initiatory places that are disconnected from time. *Battlestar Galactica* has its opera house where the protagonists find themselves in a dreamlike, out-of-the-world place where different narrative bifurcations are generated and tested. *LOST* has its island, its Church, and its dreamlike flash-sideways that link the characters together and allow them to transcend their pasts. *Carnivàle*,[3] which, like *Twin Peaks*, was interrupted after two seasons, dramatizes the fight between young Ben (an Avatar of Light) and Father Justin (an Avatar of Darkness). The two often meet inside shared dreams where they relive the clash of the previous Avatars (the characters known to us as Scudder and Belyakov). In the dreams, the battles of the First World War and the recurring scene of a chase through a cornfield are shown through flashes that recall the pulsating light in the Red Room. The strobe light embeds secrecy within what is shown and points to a vision that needs to be reconstructed. As for the red curtains, they reappear in the trailer of the mysterious head of the circus, always referred to in the impersonal term "Management"; they close off his bunk from the rest of the trailer, protecting the secret of his identity and, also, as we come to know, his physical deformity. Because *Carnivàle* follows a travelling circus in the United States of the 1930s in an environment that merges economic depression and pre-apocalyptic magic (Du Verger 2012), the show seems to combine John Steinbeck's novel *The Grapes of Wrath* (1930), Todd Browning's film *Freaks* (1932), and the series *Twin Peaks*. The universe of *Carnivàle* in fact diffracts the media mix of the Red Room. Live performances and radio waves become separated and polarized. While *Carnivàle*'s transgressive circus protects, frees, and unites human beings through the ritual of shows where performers and spectators share the same space and time, the radio program hosted by satanic Father Justin offers a magical variation on the real Father Charles Coughlin's evangelical propaganda on the radio in the 1930s and reveals mediation as a hierarchical tool of separation (Thiellement 2015).

In the character of Management, revealed to be the horribly dismembered Belyakov, it is possible to recognize a new version of one-armed Mike; in the evil Scudder, an avatar of infamous Bob; in Father Justin, who passes as a respectable member of the community but is in fact a rapist and a murderer, another Leland Palmer. Samson, the dwarf who runs the circus, appears as a new Man from Another Place, especially since he is played by the same actor. In a sequence that introduces each season, Samson addresses the viewers from a dark space and foretells the eternal struggle of good against evil in a world where magic is still powerful. Like Cooper in the Red Room, he appears older as if he were speaking well after the facts from a timeless no man's land.

The series is therefore presented from the start as a constructed narrative, a fabricated dream that some characters might be aware of. Ben, haunted by his powerful nightmares, tells Samson that he no longer knows what is real and what is not (S01E11) and admits to Sofie, "Sometimes I wonder if this is all a dream" (S02E3). Sofie, Father Justin's daughter, represents the Omega, through whom the End of Times will happen, while Ben, the healing magician, symbolizes Light and Hope. Here again, *Carnivàle* diffracts *Twin Peaks*. Laura Palmer, as the child of the Devil (represented by Leland/Bob), is first akin to Sofie. The two young women are torn between the pure and the impure and are on the verge of becoming evil. But, unlike Sofie, Laura would rather die than become the Omega, because she is also an angel like Ben, who was abandoned by his father and abused by his mother. Laura also spectrally reappears in *Carnivàle*'s young stripper Dora Mae, whose father forces her into prostitution, and who ends up lynched by frustrated and revengeful men. Like Laura, Dora Mae is the victim of those men who rape her and then accuse her of being "defiled" to justify murdering her too, compounding one crime with another. At her funeral, the dead girl's face, seen through a sheer plastic shroud, still displays the word "harlot" that was slashed onto her forehead, bringing back Laura's ghost in a forceful way.

What *Carnivàle* treats in the mode of plurality, *Twin Peaks* presents in the oxymoronic mode, folding opposites within the same character. In a vision, Father Justin can see Ben in a mirror instead of his own reflection (S02E01), but Ben does not *inhabit* Justin in the same way as Bob occupies Leland. Whereas *Carnivàle* portrays two separate opponents (even if the world of dreams brings them together), *Twin Peaks* shows that one's worst enemy is always inside oneself already; every situation, every person, includes an internal opposite.

Laura Palmer and Dale Cooper as world makers

Damon Lindelof, one of the showrunners on *LOST*, has often said he drew his inspiration partly from *Twin Peaks*, a show he watched passionately as a child (Lindelof 2010). *LOST* postulates a dreamlike halfway world (presented in the "flash-sideways" of the last season) between the moment the characters die and the time they really depart to an unknown afterlife. This world, located outside of time, allows the protagonists to remember their past lives, realize they are now dead, and find their friends and loved ones again before "moving on" (Hatchuel 2012). Someone like Desmond has privileged access to this world even during his lifetime. In *LOST*, the characters' encounters and adventures on the island lead to their redemption and the overcoming of their traumas. The postmortem dreamlike dimension is both an individual and collective creation allowing them to experience moments of reunion, giving them the strength and confidence to "let go," and enter the undiscovered country from whose bourn no traveler returns.

In light of these later shows, *Twin Peaks* appears retrospectively as a fiction that never shows its characters' real lives but directly throws the audience into their disorienting flash-sideways, a postmortem dimension filled with mysteries and incongruities. Contrary to *LOST*, this halfway world does not provide the viewers with the keys to understand its status. Moreover, the characters of *Twin Peaks* have not shared a place of transcendence like the island in *LOST*; they have not experienced beautiful encounters to heal their inner wounds and allow them to gradually realize they are now dead. In *Twin Peaks*, the characters can't "let go" and are trapped in a gruesome dimension without any harmonious unity or consistency because it is not their collective creation but rather a form of purgatory. The Red Room that the Man from Another Place once calls "the waiting room" can be seen as the disenchanted equivalent of the Church in *LOST*, in a flash-sideways world that is mainly the creation of two people – Dale and Laura.

In episode 17, a missing page from Laura's secret diary is found. She tells the Red Room dream from her own point of view. While Donna reads Laura's oneiric account, we visualize the dream through Cooper's eyes as he remembers his own experience of it. Both subjectivities combine to create the scene: Laura brings the words, Cooper the images. Laura and Dale seem to (re)produce together the sequence in the Red Room from episode 3 with their own words and memories. Laura describes the room, the red-dressed dwarf and the "old man" to whom she is trying to talk. The "old man" is obviously Cooper, whose name she does not know. She wishes to entrust her secret to him because she thinks "he can help." Cooper appears as Laura's white knight, in whom she can confide because he is a man of ethical integrity and does not consider underage girls as sexual preys (he turns down, for example, Audrey's sexual invitation). The series suggests that Laura's and Cooper's souls can communicate. As in *Battlestar Galactica* or *Carnivàle*, the two "connected" characters share the same dreams and meet in a space of fiction.

The story of *Twin Peaks* thus seems partly to be generated by Laura Palmer from the Red Room limbo or while she is "moving on" at the end of *Fire Walk with Me*. The Red Room again appears as *a machine producing narratives*, recalling Jean-Pierre Esquenazi's definition of television seriality (2015). If *Twin Peaks*' serial formula is based on the creation of different dreamlike worlds reflecting on the abuses against women – an internal regeneration taking place each time the narrative ventures into the

Red Room – the external reformulations in other shows then turn inter-textuality into a form of seriality. Each time *Twin Peaks* is cited explicitly or even spectrally in another fiction, the story of Laura (and, in a sense, of all abused women) is played out again. As the Giant tells Cooper, "It is happening again" (episode 15) at the exact moment when Leland/Bob murders Madeleine, a Laura lookalike, he highlights the fact that *Twin Peaks'* seriality is precisely based on self-referentiality.

As the prequel film concludes, Laura realizes she is dead; she sees the Angel and leaves this world with joy to become a maker of fictions. Laura is the glamorous icon who, sacrificed by a demonic father figure under incendiary gazes and spotlights, then attempts to rebuild herself by re-telling her life. From the space of the film, she contributes to make the series, from which she prefers to disappear so as not to harbor or reproduce evil. She only appears in the form of avatars like Madeleine or in indexical traces such as photographs.

The series is the story she prefers to tell. It is a story in which her father is not fully responsible for his crimes, because Bob forced him to commit them. It is a story that reveals her wish that a perfect knight might have defended her, like Dale Cooper who has *always* been with her in the Red Room – quite simply because Dale Cooper himself might be dead too, and have been dead all along, after having been shot by Windom Earle. This may be the true meaning of his loss of blood in the Red Room and of his seeing his own motionless body alongside his lost love, Caroline. Dale scripts the plot of the series with Laura but, unlike her, does not understand that he died with Caroline. Nevertheless, the postmortem dream that the series is, and which Dale contributes to build, keeps reminding him that he is no longer alive. The allusions to his fatal injury are numerous – in episode 8, he is shot in the belly at close range and left for dead; but Dale, like a writer who wants to continue the story, invents a last-minute bulletproof jacket to deny the evidence. Guy Astic is right to emphasize that the series "can be seen as Dale Cooper's waking dream as well as his sublime and grotesque projection" (2008, 108), but this dream could be a *postmortem* dream generating *multiple cinematic fictions*, as Julien Achemchame (2010, 11; 18) suggests in the case of a later Lynch production, *Mulholland Drive* (2001). Dale is like Malcolm (Bruce Willis) in M. Night Shyamalan's *The Sixth Sense* (1999) or like Jack during *LOST*'s early flash-sideways in the sixth season, when he has not yet accepted his death. Throughout this season, Jack's obsession with his real/fictional status translates in various shots of mirror: Jack keeps scrutinizing his body. The mirror reflections point to the dual reality of the performing role and evoke the figures of identification that actors embody for viewers. In *Twin Peaks*, repeated shots of mirror reflections return to similar questions: Leland, Dale, or Josie (Joan Chen) looks in the mirror to fathom whether they are real or illusions.

If Laura imagines a knight figure in the person of Dale, she is also, reciprocally, created by Dale. In *Fire Walk with Me*, Cooper claims to be certain that the murder of Teresa Banks will recur and predicts that the next victim will be a young blonde woman who is sexually active, takes drugs, and is carrying food at that very moment. As he delivers these words, the film shows us Laura collecting food for charity. In what amounts to a Möbius strip, Dale creates Laura who creates Dale, just as the series engenders its movie prequel that helps us deconstruct the series.

Twin Peaks depicts characters who arrive in the Church/Red Room/ Waiting Room when they are not ready to move to the other side. That is why, in there, they literally run round and round after their own self; or why they exit as a doppelgänger. In the final moments of the series, Bob takes possession of Cooper's soul in exchange for Annie's life. Cooper's two selves run after each other, but the one who exits the Red Room is the evil doppelgänger. Because Cooper could not let go, accept his death, and move on, the evil version of himself returns to the crazy and extravagant dream played out in the town of Twin Peaks. Now the reflection that Cooper sees in his bathroom mirror is Bob. The "good" Cooper, the perfect FBI agent, the knight who was our guide within the story, ultimately fails in his mission. By becoming the "bad guy," he questions the principle of viewer identification with the main character: with Cooper "gone," *Twin Peaks* prompts viewers to take over the initiatory and epiphanic quest on their own (Thiellement 2010, 103–111).

The first two seasons of *Twin Peaks* ends precisely when the hero becomes the villain, anticipating the fact that future series would focus on white male anti-heroes – "Bad Cooper" prefigures Jim Profit, Dexter Morgan, Tony Soprano, Walter White, or Frank Underwood – but this kind of anti-hero would have to wait a decade before being developed on the small screen.

Cooper's replacement by his evil double in the series is simultaneously recalled and anticipated in the prequel film. The second part of *Fire Walk with Me* is the only time we see the characters' "first lives" before they die. Laura wakes up in her room one morning, but paradoxically this awakening marks the beginning of a dream. In bed next to her, she sees a woman she does not know but that viewers recognize as Annie. The latter is covered in blood and says, "My name is Annie, and I've been with Laura and Dale. The good Dale is in the Lodge, and he can't leave. Write it in your diary." Before her death and before Cooper's arrival in Twin Peaks, Laura thus dreams of a future that viewers have already experienced but that she will never live. She appears as the narrative inspiration for Desmond in *LOST*: while she is still alive, she succeeds in communicating, through dreams, with a world outside of time.

By accessing the Other Place in her lifetime, she reveals the Red Room as a *place-time* when everything has already existed and will exist until the loop is broken. The "Missing Pieces" sequences that were left out of *Fire Walk With Me*'s final cut reveal that the dwarf was supposed to ask the following question on two occasions: "Is it future or is it past?" – a question that cannot be answered since, as is revealed at the end of *LOST*'s flash-sideways, "There is no *now* here." In *Twin Peaks: The Return*, broadcast on Showtime in 2017, the question is repeated by Mike and anticipates an ending in which Cooper goes back in time to try and save Laura from being murdered. However, Cooper's attempt only creates yet another loop. The people of Twin Peaks, for one reason or another, all seem stuck in the timeless Red Room, unable to "remember, let go and move on." *Twin Peaks* here evokes the film *The Shining* (dir. Stanley Kubrick, 1980) in which Jack Torrance (Jack Nicholson) appears on a photograph taken in 1921, suggesting that he lived in the Overlook Hotel in a previous life or that he is the prisoner of a parallel dimension with all the ghosts of those who died in the hotel. In the same film, Danny, Jack's young son, repeats the word REDRUM and writes it down on a door. His mother Wendy discovers the meaning of the word when she sees it reflected in a mirror and reads MURDER. In *Twin Peaks* where mirror reflections abound, the Red Room/REDRUM is the place that Laura and the little man, by speaking in reverse, invite us to read as the murder room from which one never emerges unscathed.

Unlike *LOST* that offers a first-life narrative (where the plane crashes) and a second in the shape of a postmortem dream (where the plane does not crash), *Twin Peaks* provides only one layer of the story. Spectators are thus naturally (though probably wrongfully) led to interpret it as real because it is the sole version of the story available to them. However, we should not read *Twin Peaks* as a series where everything is a dream and nothing actually happens. Quite the contrary. The series postulates that this dream-like creation between two worlds actually exists, that the characters really experience it to evolve and understand themselves better. The story implies repetitions in variation until an epiphanic moment is reached for all the characters and spectators, if they have eventually learned how to *see*.

The viewers' experience: Black Lodge or White Lodge?

If, according to Guy Astic, the "Fire" in "Fire Walk with Me" means "the mysteries that consume the people of Twin Peaks [and] the creative fire and passion" (2008, 45) that drives creators David Lynch and Mark Frost, it may also represent, for David Roche, the viewers' creative power to make sense of an aesthetics where the signs are overabundant and imagine the possible paths the fiction could take (Roche 2010). Laura Palmer haunts the residents of Twin Peaks but also the public of the series and prequel film. Like the series it has inspired, *Twin Peaks* has actively involved the audience in the creative process, anchoring the fiction in the very lives of those who watch and wonder about what they see, and ultimately reintroducing some aspects of the performing arts in television fictions where the distance between producers and viewers is usually so great. The show has promoted spectators' interpretive theories through repeated viewings and an actual education of the gaze in a medium that previously seldom encouraged such active participation and reflection on the "responsibility of what we saw and how we saw it" (Hume 1995, 111).

Whereas *LOST*'s flash-sideways present a beautiful dream bringing together the characters' souls one last time, *Twin Peaks* is a tragic nightmare. Whereas *LOST* was able to transcend tragedy toward redemption and reconciliation, the artistic project of *Twin Peaks* does not aim to do so. To date (and maybe forever), *Twin Peaks* compels viewers to wonder if their viewings make them experience a White Lodge or a Black Lodge – the series is perhaps the mysterious Black Lodge itself. On the aesthetic and narrative levels, *Twin Peaks* is a series ahead of its time, straddling several worlds and several possible narratives, which offers, as early as the start of the 1990s, an alternate dream world, but without proclaiming to do so. However, on an ideological and gender level, *Fire Walk with Me* is groundbreaking. In denouncing the cinematic icons' unhappiness and revealing the reality of incest behind the cover-up stories, the 1992 film announces the series of the 2000s, which depict what Hollywood films seldom show. The film foreshadows the enigmatic motto "You understand" hammered by the Guilty Remnants in *The Leftovers* (HBO, 2014–2017),[4] pointing to the fact that we often know very well what we do not want to see.

In all its forms and manifestations – from a daring network TV show, to a feature film disclosing what remained repressed in the first series, to an 18-hour premium cable "limited event" questioning the limits between television and cinema – *Twin Peaks* prolongs its story while always asserting the importance of returning to its past (and re-watching hours of fiction) in order for us to *really* see and understand. This type of transformation that still calls for repeated viewings testifies to a circular and haunted form of seriality as well as to an *anamorphic* quality: each viewing of *Twin Peaks* implies an audiovisual accommodation – a change of perspective nourished by time and by other fictions – that puts new forms and meanings into focus. Cooper and Laura's dream in the Red Room has set in motion a serial and transmediatic machine that has not only contributed to redefining the relations between cinema and television, but also claimed that a series, like a film, can (and sometimes should) be re-watched to perceive its complex and contradictory layers of meaning.

Notes

1 I owe a great debt of gratitude to Monica Michlin and Pacôme Thiellement with whom I discussed several points of this study. A first version of this chapter was published in French in Hatchuel 2015.

2 I consider the pilot as episode 1 and the last episode of Season 2 as episode 30.

3 Created by Daniel Knauf, *Carnivàle* was co-written by Ronald D. Moore, who would become *Battlestar Galactica*'s showrunner. One could almost draw a genealogy of series built on dreams as alternate worlds.

4 In *The Leftovers*, this sentence is uttered by a dying Patti in S01E8 and then written on a poster brandished by Evie in episode S02E10. In a series that

starts with the inexplicable disappearance of 2% of the world's population, these two words, "You understand," point to the manifest incompleteness of the narrative while claiming that the characters and viewers alike are supposed to know – to have always known, in fact – the real meaning of what is being played out in front of their eyes.

Works cited

Achemchame, Julien. *Entre l'oeil et la réalité : le lieu du cinéma* – Mulholland Drive *de David Lynch*. Paris: Publibook, 2010.

Astic, Guy. '*Twin Peaks*' : *les laboratoires de David Lynch*. Pertuis: Rouge Profond, 2008.

Burkhead, Cynthia. *Dreams in American Television Narratives: From 'Dallas' to 'Buffy'*. London; New York: Bloomsbury Academic, 2014.

Chion, Michel. *David Lynch*. Paris: Éditions de l'Étoile, 1998 [1992].

Dolan, Mark. "The Peaks and Valleys of Serial Creativity: What Happened to/on *Twin Peaks*". In David Lavery (ed.), *Full of Secrets: Critical Approaches to* Twin Peaks, Detroit: Wayne State University Press, 1995. 30–50.

Du Verger, Jean. "Melding Fiction and Reality in HBO's *Carnivàle*". *TV/Series* 1, May 2012. https://journals.openedition.org/tvseries/1504 (accessed 01.22.2019).

Esquenazi, Jean-Pierre. "Introduction". In *L'analyse des séries télévisées*, *Écrans* 4 2015-2, 2016. 11–16.

Hatchuel, Sarah. "Lost in *Lost*: Entre quotidien anodin et déstabilisation fantastique, entre réalité alternative et fiction collective". *TV/Series* 1, May 2012. https://journals.openedition.org/tvseries/1032 (accessed 01.22.2019).

Hatchuel, Sarah. *Rêves et séries télévisées : La Fabrique d'autres mondes*. Aix-en-Provence: Rouge Profond, 2015.

Hume George, Diana. "Lynching Women: A Feminist Reading of *Twin Peaks*". In David Lavery (ed.), *Full of Secrets: Critical Approaches to* Twin Peaks, Detroit: Wayne State University Press, 1995. 109–119.

Legagneur, Marine. "*Twin Peaks* : Modernité du conte, conte de la modernité". *TV/Series* 1. May 2012. https://journals.openedition.org/tvseries/1499 (accessed 01.22.2019).

Lindelof, Damon. "Damon Lindelof Discusses the Personal Impact of *Twin Peaks*". *Times Talk Live: Lost*, 2010. https://www.youtube.com/watch?v=jJBNk_Ii8jM (accessed 01.22.2019).

McGowan, Todd. *The Impossible David Lynch*. New York: Columbia University Press, 2007.

Mittell, Jason. "Lost in a Great Story: Evaluation in Narrative Television (and Television Studies)". In Roberta Pearson (ed.), *Reading LOST*, London: I.B. Tauris, 2009. 128–199.

Roche, David. "*Twin Peaks: Fire Walk With Me* (1992) and David Lynch's Aesthetics of Frustration". *Revue Interdisciplinaire Textes & contextes* 5, 2010. http://revuesshs.u-bourgogne.fr/textes&contextes/document.php?id=1103 (accessed 01.22.2019).

Soulez, Guillaume. "La double répétition: structure et matrice des séries télévisées". *Mise au point* 3, 2011. http://map.revues.org/979 (accessed 01.22.2019).

Thiellement, Pacôme. *La Main gauche de David Lynch* : Twin Peaks *et la fin de la télévision*. Paris: Presses Universitaires de France, 2010.

Thiellement, Pacôme. "La société secrète du spectacle". *Les Mots Sont Impor-tants*, January 2015. http://lmsi.net/La-societe-secrete-du-spectacle (accessed 01.22.2019).

Series and films cited

Battlestar Galactica, miniseries. Sci-Fi, 2003.
Battlestar Galactica. Sci-Fi, 2004–2009.
Carnivàle. HBO, 2003–2005.
Freaks. Todd Browning, MGM, 1932.
Gone with the Wind. Victor Flemming, MGM, 1939.
Laura. Otto Preminger, 20th C. Fox, 1944.
The Leftovers. HBO, 2014–2017.
LOST. ABC, 2004–2010.
Mulholland Drive. David Lynch, Universal, 2001.
The Shining. Stanley Kubrick, Warner Bros., 1980.
The Sixth Sense. M. Night Shyamalan, Buena Vista, 1999.
Spellbound. Alfred Hitchcock, United Artists, 1945.
Twin Peaks. ABC, 1990–1991, 2017.
Twin Peaks: Fire Walk with Me. David Lynch, New Line Cinema, 1992.
Twin Peaks: The Return. David Lynch, Showtime, 2017.
Vertigo. Alfred Hitchcock, Paramount, 1958.

Part IV
Meta-serialities

4.1 In-between still and moving pictures

Series and seriality in Stephen Poliakoff's serial drama *Shooting the Past* (1999)

Nicole Cloarec

As Lez Cooke notes in his history of British television drama, what used to be the traditional staple of television drama, namely, the single drama, had all but disappeared from the schedules by the late 1990s while series, serials, and soap operas[1] were steadily increasing.[2] While this trend also marked a shift toward an ever more competitive, market-led broadcasting environment known as the "third age" of British television after the 1990 Broadcasting Act that "usher[ed] in a new deregulated era of multiple channels and new practices" (Cooke 2015, 5), there was growing concern within the industry about the drift toward safer and formulaic productions to the detriment of quality and originality. As Cooke remarks, grievance and alarm were expressed not only from established writers, producers, and directors but also from leading industry figures such as David Liddiment, Director of Television of Programmes at ITV from 1997 to 2002, and Mark Thompson, Controller of BBC 2 from 1996 to 1998, then BBC's Director of National and Regional Broadcasting from 1999 to 2000 and Director of Television at the BBC from 2000 to 2002, whom Stephen Poliakoff convinced into producing – on his own terms – what would be his first serial.

So far Poliakoff had been known primarily as playwright and scriptwriter for television and cinema, and occasionally for directing a few feature films.[3] Not only would he benefit from the dual role of writer and director but he would use the serial format to convey his own personal vision, which is all the more remarkable in a context of series-serial production where what prevail are teams of writers working under producers. Most importantly, Poliakoff refused to conform to mainstream generic and aesthetic codes, and in particular opposing the increasingly fast pace editing and hectic rhythm that characterized television production in the 1990s. Poliakoff himself explains:

> *Shooting the Past* was written as a sort of experiment really. I became very interested in how short scenes had become on television so I thought, right, I will slow television down to the point that it stops … I mean leave scenes so long that they seem ridiculous and try to compel people in that way. (Qtd in Holdsworth 2006, 129)

In an interview in the *Guardian,* the filmmaker recalls how some executives tried to interfere, suggesting strongly he should re-edit the film to quicken its pace, but Poliakoff eventually held his ground and was proved right.[4] *Shooting the Past* drew 2.5 million viewers – while first broadcast against the highly popular American series *24*[5] – and is now considered as Poliakoff's major breakthrough in his career as one of British television's most acclaimed writers and directors.

In this regard, Poliakoff's first television serial may be construed as a manifesto against the prevailing product-line methods of the industry at the time, propounding how serial forms can induce an alternative model of "authored drama" production on television. As a number of critics have noted, Stephen Poliakoff has established himself as "British television auteur par excellence," combining "the writer-led traditions of British theatre and television" with "more recent cinematic conceptions of directors as creator" (Hogg 2010, 437). Likewise, Sarah Cardwell writes:

> The medium of television is the one which has most successfully culti-
> vated Poliakoff's talent as a writer and director, and it is within television
> that he developed distinctive and intriguing thematic preoccupations,
> formal technique and traits of style and mood. (Cardwell 2005, 180)

In this regard, Stephen Poliakoff has taken up the format of the miniseries whose classical British staple is based on the work of an established writer, while refocusing authorial identity on himself as writer and director. He has also fully embraced the miniseries format conceived as an extended television film divided into episodes but with "a clearly defined beginning, a middle and an end,"[6] whereby its type of seriality is devised to serve the development of characters and plot within a completed story. In this respect, television miniseries may also partake of cinematic aesthetics as far as it is produced with narrative and expressive ends that are similar to feature films.[7] However, within the miniseries format, Poliakoff also overtly plays with variations on the notion of series and seriality. If at first sight the drama is devised as a dramatic piece divided into three episodes, thus fitting the definition of a serial drama as multi-part drama "where storyline continues over a number of episodes," it also plays on serial effects characteristic of series, defined as multi-part drama "where stories are resolved within the episode" (Cooke 2015, 187), each part following the same narrative devices of enclosed stories. What is more, through the use of repeated motifs and patterns that are based on expressive montage using series of still photographs, *Shooting the Past* ultimately offers self-reflexive comments on the serial essence of the filmic image. In incorporating still photographs within the television medium, the serial drama both exposes and explores the Kuleshov-like effect of producing meaning through film editing of sequential shots and the power of pictures to build up a narrative and "meet fate" (Godard 1998, 244) when set in montage.

Considering Poliakoff's critique of American influence on British television, it is no small irony that the main storyline of *Shooting the Past* pits an insignificant bunch of English eccentrics resisting foreign intrusion[8] when their workplace, a photographic library, is taken over by American entrepreneurs whose project is to turn the premises into a modern "American business school for the twenty-first century."[9] Poliakoff explained he got the idea for the film from the combination of two real events: one of a collection owned by an English film studio eventually bought over by the George Lucas foundation (Poliakoff 1999); the other of the better-known story of the Hulton collection, unanimously regarded as one of the greatest archives of photojournalism in the world. It started as the photographic archive of the British weekly *Picture Post* and was sold in 1958 to the BBC, which sold it again in 1988 to a cable TV entrepreneur before being acquired by Getty Images in 1996. In both cases, as in *Shooting the Past*,[10] a British archive collection could not survive in its country and ended up in the United States. There is no doubt the Fallon library in the film stands for all public institutions (museums, public organizations like the BBC and libraries, universities) that in the 1980s and the 1990s were placed in jeopardy by new profit-oriented management and neoliberal agendas. As in the later series *Friends and Crocodiles* (2005) for example, Stephen Poliakoff shows a particular concern for analyzing the mutations of British society and the "rampant philistinism of capitalism that had gradually infiltrated British attitudes toward culture and heritage" (Sutton 2016) since the advent of Thatcherism.

Shooting the Past starts with the group of archivists, ensconced in an 18th-century manor house far away from the turmoil of the modern world, welcoming the new owner of the place blissfully unaware that the building and the collection are to be destroyed.[11] The three-part drama relates their struggle to save the collection or at least to find it a new "home." As Oswald, one the main characters, points out, we seem to be on familiar territory, one reminiscent of an old Ealing comedy that follows the struggle of an antiquated group of people to survive in the face of modernity,[12] as in Charles Crichton's *The Battle of the Sexes* (1959) and later spin-offs like *Local Hero* (Bill Forsyth, 1983) or the neo-noirs Mike Figgis's *Stormy Monday* (1988) or Ron Peck's *Empire State* (1987).[13] In all these films the British underdogs eventually manage to win their "enemies" over by either seducing them or through obstinacy and cunning.[14]

However, *Shooting the Past* escapes generic definition: neither pure comedy nor tragedy, neither romance nor detective story, although the story involves seduction, friendship, clues to follow, and secrets to expose.[15] From the start, because the librarians have been given an ultimatum to leave, the drama is placed under the sign of urgency, heralding a race against time and yet it adopts a very slow pace, with theatrical long takes focusing on the actors' performances (one extreme example is provided by the third sequence that lasts no less than 10 minutes 40 seconds) as well as self-reflexive enunciative devices. The whole plot is devoid of any real action and revolves entirely around a series of renegotiations of the initial sales contract that not only has taken place off-screen but has also been purloined, as it were, by Oswald, who is responsible for most of the enunciative framework – more of this later.

The film never makes it clear why Oswald deliberately spirited away the correspondence stipulating the terms of the original contract, which he keeps denying despite evidence to the contrary, but what is certain is that this act triggers off the narrative process, provoking a crisis that forces all parties to reconsider the terms of this missing contract.[16] Each of the three parts is thus devoted to a round of negotiations about the future of the premises and its content, each negotiation being structured around series of interviews and, most importantly, series of photographs. More than their jobs, what the staff want to preserve is the integrity of the archive collection that the Americans intend to dismantle, keeping the "valuable pictures" and disposing of the rest they qualify as "miles and miles of routine pictures [...] of shop fronts and other crap that's in a thousand other collections." Indeed, *Shooting the Past* is undoubtedly a celebration of archive pictures that not only constitute its narrative stake but contribute to shape its décor as well as its visual regime.[17] The film somehow proposes a philosophy of the archive that needs a proper "home" to work as collective memory, echoing Derrida's words in *Mal d'archive* when he foregrounds the necessity of a "home" to allow the constitution of archives, understood as collective memory (Derrida 1995, 13).

Throughout these negotiations, what is actually at stake is the very status and value of the archive pictures in particular and images in general. What is striking is the great diversity of pictures that are shown, some famous,[18] others not, comprising all *genres*, hanging on the walls and on pegs along the aisles, manipulated by the characters with whom we share point-of-view shots or fully inserted into the filmic flow, independent of any subjective point of view.

Each of the three parts revolves around both a minor and a major series of pictures: while each minor series sheds light on the major one,[19] each major series explores one specific type of value that pictures are endowed with. Part 1 thus investigates the testimonial value in a historical perspective. Through the story of a little Jewish girl, Lily Katzman, who miraculously survives the war to end up as a bag lady in south-east London, photographic images testify to the intricacy between personal story and history, illustrating one of Poliakoff's recurring ideas that history is a series of stolen moments captured on film. Paradoxically, Lily's story, however poignant it may be, raises Anderson's distrust as he expresses disapproval of what might be some dubious exploitation: "Going for the heart strings then? [...] A Holocaust story? It won't be difficult to move me ... You've taken an easy route." And Anderson's distrust may well voice the viewer's own suspicion as it soon appears that the filmmaker blends authentic archive pictures with pure fictional ones or uses visual tricks to Photo-shop Lily into actual historical photographs.[20] In part 2, Spig, one of the staff members, suggests using photographs of movie stars and celebrities to highlight the glamorous dimension of the collection. Subsequently Mar-ilyn, the head custodian, tries to convince an advertising agency that her collection contains "ideas for a hundred campaigns" that in a world where images have become so widespread and common, her photographs offer a unique and lasting experience due to their originality or aesthetic quality: "Everything is images now ... images that go straight through you, leaving nothing behind – every evening we see a thousand images on the TV, but hardly any stay with us, they're almost impossible to remember an hour later. But these stay with you ... photos that can haunt the memory ... that you can look at again and again." The agent eventually declines the offer: there are not enough color photographs.

In the end the collection isn't saved thanks to the pictures' intrinsic value, be it their historical content, equating photography and documentary truth, or their formal quality, equating photography and art, but thanks to its spe-cific visual experience, namely, the type of gaze it provokes: when Ander-son is shown photographs of his grandmother that disclose a long-buried family secret, he first proves as skeptical as with Lily's story.[21] He is finally won over when, in the last picture, he sees himself as a baby with his grand-mother Hettie. With this objectified connection between past and present, Anderson is utterly shattered by the discovery of the family secret surround-ing his grandmother's past: "I mean I come to this city – to these buildings here, this weird library – that oughtn't to be here any more – and suddenly, out of nowhere, bang! I have a whole new history." What this last picture suggests is that a photograph always somehow involves its viewer, although it may not *literally* portray him or her. This is also what Oswald implies when he shows Anderson pictures of his hometown and comments, "Do you see yourself? [...] you're there somewhere." Rather than foregrounding a nostalgic view of the past, mummified, as it were, in its irretrievable past-ness, what is highlighted here is the incompleteness of the past that calls for its reappropriation into the viewer's present. In *Le Regard pensif. Lieux et objets de la photographie,* Régis Durand analyzes this specific aptitude of photography to create what Walter Benjamin called "a constellation of the present" (1990, 75). For Georges Didi-Huberman, this specific gaze on photographs that involves its viewer through his/her imagination is first and foremost an epistemological position: "'to comprehend (this history from our place and time), one must *imagine oneself.*' The involvement of the *subject* in *seeing* and *comprehending* is first and foremost the result of an epistemological concern: what is observed cannot be separated from the observer himself" (2003, 198).[22] It now becomes clear why Marilyn is so adamantly opposed to splitting up the collection: what matters is the possibility of making connections between the images. As Arlette Farge in *Le Goût de l'archive* underlines, the archive – here the photographic archive – is never a pure "reflection" of the event or even its "evidence" but some material that needs constant elaboration through its confrontation to other material in a virtual montage (1989, 9). Anderson understands it after hearing Lily's story: "You showed me these – you told me this particular story because these pictures came from all over the collection, right?"[23] Montage proves to be the prerequisite to develop a narrative and "meet fate," to quote Jean-Luc Godard's phrase (1998, 244).

Making connections is one of the central themes in *Shooting the Past*,[24] and it is no accident the photograph that is hanging on the wall just behind Marilyn's desk depicts a switchboard operator. It also accounts for the *mise-en-scène* that Marilyn adopts to tell her stories, leading Anderson from one room to another, stressing the montage was possible only by moving and connecting different elements from different parts of the archive. In so doing, she also structures her own narrative into so many episodes that are conveyed spatially, keeping Anderson – and the viewer – in suspense. A single photograph sets off a search for another and another, until a sequence of images combine into a narrative that conversely triggers the desire for each picture to have it followed by another one, as when Anderson asks whether there is another picture.[25] In this respect, *Shooting the Past* recalls the tale of Scheherazade in the *Arabian Nights* as Marilyn manages to save her collection by multiplying stories.[26] The sequences of photographs have thus a dual regime, forming self-contained stories within the main story, forestalling the outcome while also driving the drama onward.

Most importantly, the insertion of still pictures within the filmic flow raises the question of its impact on the viewing experience itself, what happens to the film when the stilled image becomes "both the pose and pause of film" to quote Raymond Bellour's famous phrase (2002, 115). In other words, the film questions the interplay between still and moving images from a diegetic point of view – as regards history, memory, and identity within the narrative – but also in a discursive perspective, countering the flow that used to define television image[27] with elaborate photographic montage sequences. Through this device, the serial offers "an alternative mode of contemplative engagement with image and storytelling" (Hogg 2010, 438) or, in the words of Amy Holdsworth, "a significant televisual experience designed to haunt the memory" (2006, 131). Indeed, as Raymond Bellour has pointed out, the insertion of photographs in film leads to a paradox: as it inheres in film, the photograph is carried along by the film movement and yet the film seems to be arrested as if to reproduce the hold photography has on its viewer. While it may play an integral part in the narrative, the fascination that photography exerts removes the viewer from the fiction of the film to exacerbate his/her consciousness as a spectator (Bellour 2002, 75–77). Again and again, *Shooting the Past* stresses the act of gazing, with the camera lingering not only over the photographs but also on faces in close ups, thus slowing down the action and producing an embedded chain of looks that ultimately involves the film viewer.

When Marilyn and her colleague Veronica are looking at Anderson who looks at the pictures, no dialogue comes to dilute the intensity of the eye play and only a regular click sound is heard to mimic the shooting of a photograph – and thus the potential arrest of the film strip.

This interplay between stillness and movement and the potential arrest of the image flow is actually dramatized from the onset in the first sequence that starts with the visual aggression of a flash accompanied by the click sound of a camera. This is followed by a long, fairly static, face-to-camera take of Oswald (played by Timothy Spall) who is sitting in an armchair munching crispy food and is explaining that his makeshift apparatus – taking photographs of himself while talking into an old tape recorder – is meant to mimic video-taping:

> First of all, clearly, clearly I don't have a video camera. For the only time in my life it would have helped having one … but it seemed a bit bloody late to buy one, this being the last afternoon of my life. But because I want to leave a record of the extraordinary events that have happened these last few days … I'm talking into this. Ridiculously out of date of course […]. And every now and then I will take a picture of myself. That's not strictly necessary I know but I want to do that. […T]ogether they will form something that can be kept, published, even used by the mass media. Not even – I shouldn't have said that – *must* be used by the mass media. So why the hell should they be interested in a chubby man, wearing a cardy – talking into an old tape machine? […] So why should we care? Or rather why should *you* care?

Though less uncommon today than in the past, the face-to-camera enunciative framework provokes the distancing effect of breaking into the self-contained wholeness of the diegetic world, opening up critical distance on a medium (television) that usually invites viewers to immerse themselves unreservedly. But it also ends up with a direct address ("So why should we care? Or rather why should *you* care?") in the same way as photographs both participate in the narrative and suspend it through the intensified visual hold they have on the viewer. In this respect, Oswald's makeshift apparatus, however preposterous and outmoded, is more than an ironical comment poking fun at the fast-paced rhythm of mainstream productions, mimicking it in a purely artificial way through repeated flashes, as Oswald himself admits, "they [the photographs] are unnecessary of course."

Moreover, Oswald's address opens up a dual temporality first announcing future events ("this being the last afternoon of my life") and then introducing the drama to come as a more classical flashback, triggering the desire to know what will happen against an awareness that it has already happened ("because I want to leave a record of the extraordinary events that have happened these last few days"). From the onset, his narrative stance colludes both a prospective and a retrospective point of view, expanding the present into looking forward and backward at the same time and this extensive present in-between allowing a dual projection is precisely what the visual regime of photography brings to the fore in cinema.[28]

If Marilyn is the storyteller, putting words on the pictures, Oswald is very much like a film director. First he devises some sort of storyboards when making connections between the pictures, as Marilyn points out to Anderson: "You must realize these pictures are all over the collection. Oswald found it of course." Then he is also responsible for manipulating time, allowing all types of play with temporality and teasing cliffhangers. At the end of part 1, after Anderson agrees to give Marilyn more time on condition Oswald should be fired, Oswald is filmed back in his flat face to camera, announcing a reversal of situation: "That's what they think." Then, at the end of part 2, he is left in a suspenseful, life-threatening situation during his suicide attempt but while the camera lingers on his body lying on his bed, we hear his voice observing with wry humor: "I'm quite hungry, you know … Not sure you're really meant to feel like that at that stage." Throughout the drama, Oswald's character embodies elliptic collusions within the filmic enunciation: lines of his introductory address are repeated right at the beginning of part 2, and again in part 3, when Nick listens to his tapes. Each of the first two parts is encompassed within his enunciative frame and part 3, just like the entire series, opens and closes on a close-up of his face looking straight into the camera.[29] Even after his falling into coma, Oswald still manages to control the enunciative framework of the serial, forcing Marilyn to take over and adopt the same face-to-camera address to the viewer. This address is first introduced indirectly when she talks to an unconscious Oswald in a one-way conversation[30] and then becomes direct in the epilogue where Marilyn has taken Oswald's place but with no more self-reflexive devices such as the camera and the tape recorder. He is the only character that provokes flashbacks within his own narrative, as when Marilyn recalls some of the conversations she used to have with him before his suicide attempt. And not only does Oswald manipulate time, he also triggers off virtual scenes that might-have-been, as with the unique subjective flight of fancy, a pseudo flashback at the end when Anderson imagines Oswald in the archive looking for connections, with two alternative versions (one in which Oswald is wearing a security helmet and one in which he is bareheaded).[31] From a narrative point of view, this visualization brings no new element at all, but it definitely contributes to Oswald's characterization as being able to manipulate the imaginative potential of pictures and exploit their combination to create variations within repetitions.

Nowhere is this manipulation of narrative time more potent than at the end of part 2 as it involves the very nature of images. As Oswald is lying on his bed, the camera slowly tracks out to be interrupted by the flashback – literally introduced by a flash – of Oswald taking a photograph of himself, quoting one of the production stills of the beginning of the film. We then see a close-up of Oswald's face from which the camera once again tracks out very slowly before being interrupted again but here and for the next five shots, the production stills of the flashback have turned into black-and-white photographs. Here the film we are watching has been turned into production stills that come to look just like the old photographs of the library collection and are then inserted back into film, into what Philippe Dubois called a *cinématogramme* to refer to the hybrid status of the image in Chris Marker's *La Jetée*: neither simply photographic nor truly cine-matographic but to inverse the notion of the French *photogramme* (a film shot turned into a photograph) into a picture turned into film (2004, 41).

This hybridity or in-betweenness, to quote Bellour's title "L'entre-image," highlights the latent meaning of these images, pointing out the virtual pres-ence of a hidden film running in parallel to the one we are watching. Like production stills, these images, to exist, must negate the very essence of cin-ema as defined by its movement and yet they also reveal it, unveiling some "third" or "obtuse meaning" that Roland Barthes also called the "filmic" (1982, 59), allowing him to assert that the essence of cinema is paradoxi-cally to be found in the still.

Throughout the film, Oswald has been looking for the "third meaning" in pictures, scrutinizing photographs of people who took their own life ("Do we see the clues about what's coming if we stare close enough?") or asking whether one can photograph a lie:

> Sometimes people who break the rules … however irritating … some-times they can do things other people can't. […] Like answering the question – can you photograph a lie? […C]an that moment be frozen, caught there in a photograph? … not like on television programmes … like Nixon lying, where it's the whole general impression … but instead the very moment the lie comes out … can a mute, still image catch that – for ever?

The question is far from rhetorical since Oswald has proved to be an ex-tremely unreliable narrator, refusing in the first place to acknowledge his ini-tial agreement to the terms of the contract. In the epilogue, Marilyn wonders how much Oswald's slowing down is genuine or how much he uses it for his own ends. Truly enough, Oswald cannot stop the flow of time – and of the filmstrip. The last words he manages to utter, in an extremely slow delivery in sharp contrast to the rapid flow of words that he used to speak with, acknowledge this inexorable fact: "We're all hit by changing … things … can't … not able to stop it." Nonetheless, he still manages to slow the film-strip down until it freezes on a close-up of his face in the very last shot of the serial.

In part 3, while looking for the clues left by Oswald to edit Hettie's story, Marilyn uses a TV screen connected to some back-lit table to look at the positive images of old glass plate negatives. The same device is used to zoom in and reframe the photographs, much in the same way as the pictures are reframed throughout the whole serial. Here television is shown to work as a developer, revealing the dialogical relationship between photography and cinema and making possible the series of narrative sutures that the drama constructs from the editing of embedded still photographs into series of narratives. By foregrounding the narrative device of elaborate photographic montage sequences, Poliakoff's serial demonstrates how television image can take on a different aesthetic quality and lingering impact thanks to cinematic effects.[32] As Christopher Hogg summarizes, Poliakoff believes "in foregrounding the intrinsic aesthetic and narrative worth of the televisual image, not as ephemeral byte within a rapid-fire delivery of plot to be instantly forgotten, but as something which deserves the viewer's consideration and appreciation, and which has the potential to linger in the mind" (Hogg 2010, 444). In this respect, *Shooting the Past* is a perfect illustration of Jean-Pierre Esquenazi's definition of "serial art" as an art that necessarily involves time and memory (2010, 136). It is also a consummate demonstration of how "high-end" television drama[33] has been extending the series-serial narrative.

Notes

1 Drama series will be defined here as multi-part drama "where stories are resolved within the episode (on a weekly basis)" and serial drama as multi-part drama "where storyline continues over a number of episodes" (see Cooke 2015, 187). For a history of the term "soap opera" in Great Britain, see Cooke (2015, 89–91).

2 Lez Cooke cites the conclusions of the report commissioned by the Campaign for Quality Television, written by Steven Barnett and Emily Seymour and published in 1999 (entitled *"A Shrinking Iceberg Travelling South..." Challenging Trends in British Television: A Case Study of Drama and Current Affairs*): "The content analysis revealed the extent to which the single play, traditionally the outlet for original drama, had disappeared from the schedule between the late 1970s and late 90s with the number of such productions declining by more than half. Meanwhile, series drama during the same period had increased from 47 per cent of all drama on British television in 1977–8 to 63 percent in 1997–8, while soap operas had increased from 10 percent in the late 1970s to 29 percent in the late 1990s" (2015, 208).

3 Stephen Poliakoff has been writing for the stage since the late 1960s. His debut feature film was *Hidden City* in 1988 (Channel 4).

4 "I wanted to fight the idea that people couldn't concentrate for long, and when it was finished all hell did break loose. By now they did try to tell you how to write, and some relatively junior executives thought it should be cut and made quicker, which would have ruined the whole point of it. I went bananas and eventually won the battle. So it wasn't a question of being invited by the BBC to do what I liked. People did try to interfere, but I resisted them and was ultimately proved right" (Qtd in Wroe 2016).

5 *Shooting the Past* was first broadcast on BBC 2 in January 1999 (Sunday 10, 17 and 24).

6 Francis Wheen argues that "Both soap operas and primetime series [...] cannot afford to allow their leading characters to develop, since the shows are made with the intention of running indefinitely. In a miniseries on the other

hand, there is a clearly defined beginning, a middle and an end, (as in a conventional play or novel) enabling characters to change, mature or die as the serial proceeds. It is for this reason that some television writers who lament the passing of the Golden Age are excited by the possibilities of the miniseries, even if they believe that its potential has not yet been properly exploited" (1985, 35).

7   Although some recent critics have taken issue with the term "cinematic" when applied to TV productions because of its implied demeaning value judgment toward television as a proper object of study (see Mills or Jaramillo in Jacobs and Peacock 2013), I will contend with Robin Nelson that in addition to similar narrative structuring, the technological improvements brought about by digital television in the late 1990s, with wide-screen aspect ratio and better sound and vision qualities, fostered a "cinematic" visual treatment in TV dramas (2011, 22). It is also worth noting that Stephen Poliakoff does not draw any significant distinction between feature film and "film" for television: "The most obvious thing is the size of the image. TV demands swift close-ups and a lot of emphasis. You can give far more information in cinema, especially in a two-shot for example, where you can include much more detail. But I think other differences are arguable" (Adrian Hodges, "Portraying Dark Visions of Today". *Screen International*, 25 December 1982, 12, qtd in Nelson 2011, 194).

8   As regards the celebration of British resilience in the face of adversity, it seems fairly appropriate that some of the first pictures are precisely famous pictures of the Blitz illustrating its "carry-on-as-usual" spirit. This is also made explicit by Oswald's insistence they should have a five-course lunch and act as if nothing had happened.

9   It is also noteworthy that the combined choice of the first names of the two main characters – Marilyn and Oswald – cannot but evoke Marilyn Monroe and Oswald Lee Harvey, two of the most famous and infamous characters in American 20th-century history, thus suggesting America's guilty conscience – or subconscious.

10 In the epilogue, Marilyn tells the resolution of the story: "Mr Anderson – for some reason I hardly ever called him Christopher–Christopher Anderson got an American collection to buy the whole library – they got it cheap, and they didn't want it all–but we persuaded them … We both managed it. So it's still all together. For some other Oswalds to make startling connections between things… reveal other pieces of history… It's saved – *but not in this country of course*" (my emphasis).

11 The first meeting between the staff and the new owners is depicted in terms of a collision between two temporalities: after Marilyn asserts, "there's no need to rush," she keeps asking for how much time she can get within Anderson's "tight schedule," owns up she is "not very used to time pressures like that" before considering all options to "buy" time and begging for more.

12 Talking about Mr. Anderson, the American entrepreneur who wants to erase the 18th-century manor so as to build an "American business school for the 21st century": "He thinks we're pathetic, dusty people who stepped out of an Ealing comedy."

13 In *The Battle of the Sexes*, American businesswoman Angela Barrows is sent to Edinburgh, where she is hired to implement new business methods and is met with the staff's sticking to tradition. In *Local Hero*, an American oil tycoon plans to buy up an entire Scottish village to build a refinery but a local hermit will force the company to negotiate on his terms. Both neo-noirs dramatize the attempts of American shady characters to cash in on contemporary British speculation on real estate and property, Figgis's film in Newcastle, Peck's in London's new Docklands.

14 In *The Maggie* (Alexander Mackendrick, 1954), the Scottish crew of a nearly derelict coal-powered boat manages to safeguard its boat by tricking an American businessman into shipping a valuable load of cargo onboard.

15 Oswald's findings are repeatedly referred to as detective work as in Anderson's comment at the end: "it was a feat of detective and memory work."

16 *Shooting the Past* starts with a misunderstanding as regards the terms of the contract: whereas Marilyn believes the new owner will keep the library as it is, Anderson intends to build new premises and to have the collection destroyed except for the valuable ones. The staff first refuse to split up the collection and hide the valuable pictures in a view to buy more time "to find a home for the collection." Marilyn then accepts to consider the situation provided Anderson visits the collection. After the visit, they strike a new deal whereby the American will be given the valuable pictures on condition he keeps on all the staff that want to stay. At the end of part 1, though, Marilyn denounces the new deal and begs for one more week; Anderson accepts provided Oswald leaves. In part 2, the staff desperately try to find buyers for the collection; they nearly succeed to get an advertising agency interested, but the latter finds there are not enough color photographs. In part 3, Marilyn comes to the conclusion that the only solution is to sell the collection to Anderson. She will eventually convince him to save to collection thanks to Oswald's clues.

17 Poliakoff repeatedly uses depth of field to film the corridors of the library, conveying the feeling of a labyrinthine space, made up of endless aisles and rows, which the camera tracks in or out very slowly as they are empty, ready to let the pictures come alive, as it were.

18 To give but a few examples: the deck of the *Titanic, Grand Central Light* (1930), *Skinny Dippers* (1926) where a policewoman chases naked boys along the Serpentine, *Delivery after Raid* (1940) where a milkman is "doing business as usual" in a London street devastated after a bomb raid, scholars perusing shelves in the bombed-out library of Holland House, movie stars like Elizabeth Taylor, Joan Crawford, Louise Brooks, Joseph Cotton, Lauren Bacall, Bette Davis, Vivian Leigh, Greta Garbo, Sophia Loren, Jean Harlow, Marlene Dietrich, Marilyn Monroe, Virginia Woolf, Tony Hancock.

19 Lily's story is preceded by Anderson's visit of the library with a selection of photojournalistic pictures; Marilyn's "pitch" is introduced by a series of glamorous pictures of movie stars and celebrities; Hettie's story follows a series of pictures depicting 20th-century British Prime Ministers, among which one of Edward Heath conducting an orchestra that gives Marilyn the clue she was looking for (Anderson's grandmother Hettie "eloping" to play in an orchestra).

20 The same device is used with Hettie's story: most are either authentic historical documents or photographs staged for the film, but there are a few photoshopped pictures such as Hettie's face replacing a suffragette's as she is arrested by policemen. Moreover, in the two series, visual tricks are doubled on the soundtrack with implausible sound effects that are meant to reconstruct the atmosphere of the environment depicted in the pictures.

21 "You're building a house of cards." "You have no proof about anything." "I don't believe a word of it–whatever it is." "It all could be bullshit."

22 The author's reflection on the part of the image in History comes from the extreme example of four photographs that were taken in Auschwitz-Birkenau by members of the *Sonderkommando* in August 1944.

23 It is confirmed by Marilyn herself: "You must realize these pictures are all over the collection. Oswald found it of course."

24 Oswald explains in a flashback: "Do you know what I think is wonderful about our lives here? We have a chance to dream ... dream from looking at these pictures ... let the mind float – *make connections* between things, daydreams,

nightdreams. We have space, time, no pressure, the most valuable things on earth." And again in the epilogue, Marilyn comes back to the importance of making connections: "Mr Anderson – for some reason I hardly ever called him Christopher – Christopher Anderson got an American collection to buy the whole library–they got it cheap, and they didn't want it all – but we persuaded them ... We both managed it. So it's still all together. For some other Oswalds *to make startling connections between things ...* reveal other pieces of history" (my emphasis).

25 In part 1, at the end of Lily's stories, Anderson exclaims: "It goes on then? [...] Where is the next picture? Did Oswald find any more?"

26 At the end, Anderson tells Marilyn: "You're great. A great passionate person ... *and a wonderful storyteller*" (my emphasis).

27 The seminal concept of "flow" was coined by Raymond Williams. Drawing an analysis of American and British television, Williams notes that "the central television experience" is "the fact of flow" (Williams 1974).

28 This temporal duality evokes Chris Marker's filmic experimentations, as Philippe Dubois analyzes (2004, 25).

29 Framed by Oswald's enunciation, part 1 leads to a flashback of a single day (from 11 am to around 6 pm) that we come to understand occurred six days before the enunciatory present. Part 2 starts by repeating the beginning of part 1 and lasts six days, ending with Oswald's suicide attempt on the eve of the one-week ultimatum. Part 3 begins when part 2 ended and again covers one day before the epilogue.

30 In one significant passage, Marilyn exclaims: "You left me this teasing message, what can I do, especially with you like this?... I've got to start thinking like you... (slight laugh) God forbid!"

31 "He must have sneaked back here – after he came to see me–and started that little fire – he was in here, in his hard hat; doing his detective work ... no he gave me that hard hat, so it wasn't quite like that."

32 See note 7.

33 This has led Robin Nelson to consider Poliakoff's television production as his most original accomplishment: "Though not wishing to denigrate the theatre and feature film work, in my judgement it is the recent television work that marks the pinnacle of Poliakoff's achievement since all his talents came together to seize the moment of 'high-end' contemporary TV drama. The work makes a particular contribution to the medium by offering an alternative approach to the dominant American model, refashioning the idea of 'authored television drama,' not simply reviving a lost tradition" (2011, 220). For a definition of "high-end" TV drama, see Nelson 2007.

Works cited

Barthes, Roland. *La Chambre claire. Note sur la photographie*. Paris: Cahiers du cinéma/Gallimard/ Seuil, 1980.

Barthes, Roland. *L'Obvie et l'obtus. Essais critiques III*. Paris: Seuil, 1982.

Bellour, Raymond. *L'Entre-Images. Photo. Cinéma. Vidéo*. Paris: Editions de la différence, 2002.

Cardwell, Sarah. " 'Television Aesthetics' and Close Analysis: Style, Mood and Engagement in *Perfect Strangers* (Stephen Poliakoff, 2001)". In John Gibbs and Doug Pye (eds.), *Style and Meaning: Studies in the Detailed Analysis of Film*, Manchester: Manchester University Press, 2005. 179–194.

Cooke, Lez. *British Television Drama. A History*. London: BFI-Palgrave, 2015 [second edition].

Derrida, Jacques. *Mal d'archive*. Paris: Galilée, 1995.

Didi-Huberman, Georges. *Images malgré tout*. Paris: Editions de minuit, 2003.

Dubois, Philippe. "*La Jetée* de Chris Marker ou le cinématogramme de la conscience". In *De la photographie au cinéma, quelles passerelles?*, Ajaccio: Centre régional de documentation pédagogique de Corse, 2004. 17–41.

Durand, Régis. *Le Regard pensif. Lieux et objets de la photographie*. Paris: La Différence, 1990.

Esquenazi, Jean-Pierre. *Les séries télévisées. L'avenir du cinéma?* Paris: Armand Colin, 2010.

Farge, Arlette. *Le Goût de l'archive*. Paris: Le Seuil, 1989.

Godard, Jean-Luc. *Jean-Luc Godard par Jean-Luc Godard II, 1984–1998*. Paris: Cahiers du cinéma, 1998.

Holdsworth, Amy. "Slow Television and Stephen Poliakoff's *Shooting the Past*". *Journal of British Cinema and Television* 3.1, 2006. 128–133.

Hogg, Christopher. "Reevaluating the Archive in Stephen Poliakoff's *Shooting the Past*". *Journal of British Cinema and Television* 16.3, 2010. 437–451.

Jaramillo Deborah. "Rescuing Television from 'the Cinematic': The Perils of Dismissing Television Style". In Jacobs Jason and Peacock Steven (eds.), *Television Aesthetics and Style*, New York: Bloomsbury, 2013. 67–77.

Mills Brett. "What Does It Mean to Call Television Cinematic?". In Jacobs Jason and Peacock Steven (eds.), *Television Aesthetics and Style*, New York: Bloomsbury, 2013. 57–66.

Nelson Robin. *State of Play Contemporary "High-End" TV Drama*. Manchester: Manchester University Press, 2007.

Nelson Robin. *Stephen Poliakoff on Stage and Screen*. London: Bloomsbury, 2011.

Poliakoff, Stephen. Interview. 1999. http://www.pbs.org/wgbh/masterpiece/ archive/programs/shootingthepast/interviews/poliakoff_interview.html (accessed 07.08.2018).

Sutton, Mike. "*Shooting the Past*". BFI Website. http://www.screenonline.org.uk/ tv/id/523425/index.html (accessed 31.03.2020).

Wheen, Francis. *Television: A History*. London: Century, 1985.

Williams, Raymond. *Television, Technology and Cultural Form*. London: Fontana, 1974.

Wroe, Nicholas. "A Life in Drama: Stephen Poliakoff". *The Guardian*, 11.28.2009. https://www.theguardian.com/culture/2009/nov/28/stephen-poliakoff-interview-nicholas-wroe (accessed 07.08.2018).

Films and series cited

24. Fox, 2001–2010.

The Battle of the Sexes. Charles Crichton, Bryanston Films, 1959.

Empire State. Ron Peck, Miracle Films, 1987.

Friends and Crocodiles. Stephen Poliakoff, BBC1, 2006.

Hidden City. Stephen Poliakoff, Channel 4, 1988.

La Jetée. Chris Marker, Argos Films, 1962.

Local Hero. Bill Forsyth, 20th C. Fox, 1983.

The Maggie. Alexander Mackendrick, Ealing Studios, 1954

Shooting the Past. Stephen Poliakoff, BBC, 1999.

Stormy Monday. Mike Figgis, Palace Pictures, 1988.

4.2 "The abominable bride"

Sherlock and seriality

Christophe Gelly

"The Abominable Bride" (Douglas Mackinnon, 2016) is an exceptional installment in a TV series that is itself very original in the way it approaches the adaptation of a classical 19th-century corpus. It has now become common knowledge how the BBC series made the most of a new take on the Victorian subtext by moving the 19th-century Sherlock Holmes into the digital, hyper-technological universe of the 21st century and by pointing the surprising connections between the two worlds in terms of ideology, mythmaking, and investigation methods. To put it in a nutshell, the 21st-century Sherlock uses profiling much the same way the 19th-century original used phrenology and the Lombroso theory. Yet these connections rely very much on a clear separation between the 19th-century model and the 21st-century adaptation – we are supposed to recognize Doyle's creation *in abstentia*, in a new diegetic universe that consistently differs from the original and that never refers to it except through the (often subversive) quotes from the "canon" (i.e., the short stories and novels by Doyle). What the instalment brings is a total reversal of that strategy since the episode is set in the 19th century, at the time of the original publication of the texts. It poses as a "traditional" adaptation of the Holmes canon and cannot thus claim to repeat this introduction of 21st-century technology used to "update" the texts.[1] Moreover, this episode is pointedly presented as a "one shot" installment, an isolated story within the series that is set apart from the general outlook of the BBC series conceived as a modern rereading of Victorian fiction.[2] As such, it plays out its exceptional status as a temporary travel into the "alternative," 19th-century vision of the detective, but it does not purport to establish a long-term relation with that vision. Moreover, the spectators actually learn approximately one hour into the episode that this 19th-century investigation was merely a mental reconstruction by the 21st-century Sherlock of a past case that may help him in the present, so that the past diegetic frame is eventually seen from a distance, from the present-day Sherlock. This is true of the character Sherlock, whom we see at this moment landing in a plane just after the 19th-century Sherlock was confronting Moriarty in his Baker Street lodgings, but this holds true similarly for the whole episode and the series' authors who make a decisive move in this installment by organizing the whole narrative between two different time frames whose interaction provides much of the specific meaning in "The Abominable Bride." This chapter will examine the complex relationship between past and present understood as rooted into the specific treatment of seriality by the series. We shall try to explain what specific use is made of the representation of the past and what this past intrigue means from the 21st-century perspective included in the narrative.

"Alternatively" – 1887, anachrony and time travel

What the episode initially claims to establish is a particular vision of time travel that is akin to the exploration of alternative dimensions of reality – and not simply the "going backward" in time that the narrative pitch seems to rely on. The episode begins with a quick selection from previous seasons in the series, relating noticeably Watson's first meeting with Sherlock, Sherlock's encounter with Irene Adler, Moriarty's death, and Sherlock's apparent suicide, then his coming back to public life. A black screen bearing the word "Alternatively" in white letters then appears, with a calendar going backward in time from 2014 to the 1880s. The narrative then goes back in time to 1895, showing the meeting of Watson, discharged from the Afghanistan war, with Sherlock in the 19th century. After the credit sequence, the story properly speaking begins, at a time when Watson has already been publishing accounts of Holmes's investigation and has become famous for it. Inspector Lestrade calls upon both characters to tell them about the strange case of Emelia Ricoletti, a consumptive bride who fired on passers-by in the street from a balcony before killing herself. She reportedly shot her husband dead later that same evening. Sherlock learns at the morgue from Dr. Hooper that the woman who killed herself, the woman who murdered Mr. Ricoletti, and the body lying in the morgue have all been identified as Emelia Ricoletti. Holmes deduces that these are copycat crimes and that someone is using the legend of Emelia Ricoletti's ghostly survival as a cover-up for his or her own crimes (as proof of that, a number of men are reportedly killed in similar circumstances in and around London). Sometime later, Sherlock's elder brother, Mycroft, suggests to him he should take a case from a certain Lady Carmichael, whose husband Eustace has been terrified by his reception of an envelope containing five orange pips (a death warning common enough in South America especially), and who has witnessed her husband's harassment apparently by a female ghost resembling Emelia Ricoletti. Holmes takes the case and after visiting Sir Eustace, a blatantly chauvinistic man, he sets a trap for the "ghost," but the latter manages to kill her victim and to escape all the same. She leaves on the dead body a label that reads, "Miss me?" a throwback to the question Moriarty used to taunt Sherlock with in the previous episodes in the series. Going back home, Sherlock is confronted by Moriarty in person, who nags at him and then appears to shoot himself but remains alive. At this point the narrative switches forward to the present time, when we find Sherlock landing in a jet and meeting his brother Mycroft, Watson and his wife Mary; we understand that the whole first part of the narrative was in fact a reconstruction in Sherlock's mind (what he calls his "mind palace") of an earlier case that he is trying to solve, the better to understand, it seems, the current situation of Moriarty in the present day. Let us remark incidentally that this insistence from Sherlock on solving a case that is more than a hundred years old points to a specific relation with the past that needs to be examined. Going back to the 19th-century plot, we find again Sherlock – who believes his brief trip to the 21st century was a cocaine-induced hallucination – and follow him to a desecrated church where he and Watson have been called by Mary, Watson's wife, who has secretly been working for Mycroft to uncover the whole mystery. In this church the truth is revealed: the murders were committed by a group of women leagued to punish men who wronged other women by their abusive behavior. The apparent survival of Emelia Ricoletti through death was faked thanks to an elaborate machination that involved the actual killing of another woman, a willing recruit who was dying of an incurable disease and who agreed on sacrificing her life for this feminist cause. Just when Sherlock is accusing Lady Carmichael of being part of this league of murderous women, Moriarty, dressed as a bride, confronts Sherlock and again insults him. Sherlock then "wakes up" in the 21st century and decides to check that Emelia Ricoletti *is* buried in her grave and to ascertain whether the woman whose body was used to simulate Emelia's survival is herself buried under the coffin. Holmes finds only one corpse in the coffin and is just beginning to dig under it, looking for a second corpse, when the first body slowly comes back to life and attacks him. At this point Holmes "awakens" again in the 19th century on a ledge in the Reichenbach Falls, with Moriarty, who fights him and tries to topple him down the precipice, but Watson arrives just on time and kicks Moriarty off the ledge. Eager to go back to the present time, Holmes willingly falls in the precipice, as he feels certain he will survive and reawaken in the 21st century. This is what happens, and we finally see Sherlock in the plane with Mycroft, Watson, and Mary, and ready to face Moriarty once more, or his accomplices whom Moriarty entrusted, Holmes seems to imply, with carrying out his criminal plans after his death. The episode ends with the 19th-century Sherlock sitting in his Baker Street drawing room and explaining to a skeptical John Watson his visions of airplanes and mobile telephones to be invented in the future – as if the whole plot of this episode had been just a construction of the future as imagined by the detective – before looking out the window onto Baker Street in the present day.

Through these constant movements back and forth in time, the narrative of "The Abominable Bride" foregrounds the relation to time – and the potential connections between the past and the present – as an essential topic of the episode. What actually happens at the beginning of the episode is a digest of the previous seasons and adventures of the 21st-century Sherlock, and then we have the presentation of the 19th-century "original" – but what is striking is that this presentation of the 19th-century Sherlock repeats part of what we have just seen at the beginning of the episode, especially concerning the initial meeting between Sherlock and Watson, which is thus told twice, first from a modern-day and then from a contemporary, 1887 perspective. This suggests that the "alternative" quality of the representation is not simply that of a time travel but also – if the same events are repeated – that it refers to another plane of reality in which the same events are taking place in a different diegetic frame. In other words, and more generally, the thematic contents of the whole story (the oppression of women, and the very definition of gender roles that is questioned, as we shall see, by the character of Moriarty) remain the same from one century to the other, even though they are dealt with differently, with due respect for the period aspect the time shift implies. The persistence of the thematic focus from the 19th- to the 21st-century parts of the plot in this episode suggests that each century repeats (differently) the same questions (as to gender roles), hence that the diachronic shift that "colors" the story brings us back to an alternative version of the same world and the same problems. This alternative quality of the 19th-century diegesis is obvious at the outset of the episode that includes a black screen with a calendar going backward and the mention "Alternatively." As a result, the purpose of the episode, especially through the conspicuous comparison between the two meetings between Holmes and Watson, seems to be to examine and "investigate" what grounds such a similarity between the two periods and the two diegetic worlds.[3] This foregrounding of the notion of an alternate universe that both repeats and distorts the initial 21st-century universe of the *Sherlock* series reflexively beckons to the very notion of seriality that lies in the transformability and repetitiveness of an original story universe. It follows that the time travel that Sherlock, the character, goes through in this episode is more than a "transposition" of the series universe back to the 19th century; it constitutes a reflection on the applicability of our thought categories to representations of the past.

The formal devices associated to this time travel are significant of the status of the episode as an alternative take on the "modern-day" Sherlock. The first representation of this time travel appears, as we saw, when at the beginning of the episode we shift from the 21st to the 19th centuries through the figuration of a calendar going backward. But this is only the initial figuration.

Later on, as the 19th-century Sherlock is confronted to the return of Moriarty (dressed as a bride) in the plot (1'16'21), the film uses a blurring of images and sounds to suggest a change in the time frame of the story. This is also the case when Holmes is confronted to Moriarty when he is thinking over the case in his sitting room (59'58) and Moriarty visits him to nag at him after his failure to prevent the murder of Sir Eustace by the ghost of Emelia Ricoletti. What the episode stages in these scenes is the figuration of an earthquake that triggers the passage from one world to another, from one century to another. It is also interesting to examine the way the time shifts are represented within the same period frame. For instance, when the episode figures an ellipsis when Watson and Holmes are travelling on a train toward Sir Eustace's mansion (39'00) we see the image literally turning upside down to reveal the destination of the two characters (Figures 4.2.1–4.2.4). This temporal ellipsis – which beckons to the larger movement of temporal confusion in the film – thus figures the time shifts in the episode as a reversal or another version (turned upside down) of the original reality: in other words as an alternative reality.[4] This suggests again that time travel in "The Abominable Bride" is not merely a matter of going backward in time but of reaching another plane of reality that unfolded not merely at another time but in another, alternative dimension that repeats some events that we are already familiar with (the meeting between Holmes and Watson), and that places these events against a different backdrop in terms of time and context. Of course, not all events from one plot are repeated in the other, and the example of the meeting between the two characters is only an initial stage in the stories that vastly differ from this point onward, but we shall see that a number of issues pertaining to gender relationships appear in both planes of the story and testify to the interconnection between them – one being, again, an alternative vision of the other. The use of this particular mode of transportation in the scene under study is also significant of a slightly ironic take in the episode: the train in the 19th-century story brings a sharp contrast with the only mode of transportation represented in the 21st-century part of the plot, the jet that Sherlock takes off in only to land again after a few minutes' flight, due to his being recalled by his brother Mycroft. The characters in the 19th-century

Figure 4.2.1 The initial stage in the train travel.

Figure 4.2.2 The same image turning around with the Carmichael mansion in the background.

Figure 4.2.3 The superimposition of both images upside down.

plot do travel by cab and train frequently, but the plane travel in the 21st-century plot is only a short roundabout trip and, although a lot of talking is done in the plane, this takes place only when it is landed, so that the conventional vision of the train travel as a pause during which Holmes and Watson "safely" discuss the cases is debunked by this immobility in the plane. This contrast reverses the expected relationship between modern, fast travel and Victorian transportation and suggests that we do not find *all*

Figure 4.2.4 The Carmichael mansion.

the elements from the 19th-century plot in the 21st-century plot, but this contrast only sheds light on the other, more crucial similitudes between both storyworlds, similitudes that are about to be expounded.

The basic definition of the time shift toward an alternative worldview in the episode bears rather obvious connections to the notion of seriality. It relies on the notion that the same story elements can be exploited in markedly different universes – that the key features of a work (whether this is the atmosphere, the main characters, or the narrative structure) may be put to good use in a number of configurations. The time travel effected in "The Abominable Bride" proves that the journey "back" to the 19th century is possible for the "updated" version of the character created by the BBC series at large, despite the popular success of this adaptation that has more or less stabilized this new, technological version as a defining trait of the series. Seriality thus takes the form of a particular assertion by this installment that the time travel from the 21st to the 19th centuries and then back and forth between both historical periods is justified by the quality of *continuum* that exists between both periods. It is essential for instance that the discourse of the Victorian Holmes on the 19th-century women who rebel against chauvinism should be "illustrated" through the editing of various sequences taken from previous episodes in the series, in which the modern-day Sherlock utilizes and exploits the women he meets (1'12'53). This vindication of the same motives – phallocracy, or the inhuman behavior evidenced by Holmes's treatment of fellow human beings at large – in both planes of the story further suggests that the same phenomena that brought about the "female revolution" described in the 19th-century plot are still valid today. This is why we find the same actress, Louise Brealey, playing the role of Molly Hooper (the morgue manager who is forced to dress as a man to ply her trade) and of the pathologist who is repeatedly looked down upon and used by Sherlock in the 21st century. This establishment of thematic connections beyond the time barriers is again typical of the way this episode (and the whole series) envisions the serial quality of the narrative as a *re*-telling of the same story events in a different frame.

Anachronism and time travel are then deeply indebted in this installment to the whole project of Mark Gatiss and Steven Moffat, which is to prove that the story matter can be *reused* and transplanted (both ways, from the past to the present and back to the past) because this exploitation is part of the way a series works to draw benefit from its versatility. This benefit lies in the intertextual enrichment that proceeds from the relation the 21st-century character entertains with his 19th-century counterpart, and from the resonance between the general image of Sherlock in the series with the 19th-century plot topics. The aim is not only to show this re-usability in a critical way—showing for instance how the exploitation of female characters is still topical – but also through the ironical comparison between both contexts. Thus when Watson lights a candle, standing in wait for the ghost of Emelia Ricoletti supposed to have penetrated Sir Eustace's mansion, he says out loud: "After all this is the 19th century" – a funny, reflexive satire of the claim for modernization and updating the BBC series is supposed to be based upon. But apart from this negotiation with the temporal frame that the series is entering, what exactly is the relation of "The Abominable Bride" to the general thematic frame attached both to the previous episodes and to the Victorian representation of the Doylean subtext, and how does that relation fit into a definite approach of seriality?

Seriality and references

"The Abominable Bride" openly reenacts typical Victorian concerns and themes; this is mostly obvious through the two main topics that come to the surface of the 19th-century plot, that is, gender and Gothicism.[5] What I mean to show here is that the episode draws upon references to earlier episodes, as well as to the general outlook of the series, to bring out this reinterpretation of these concerns in a "modern" frame. What happens repeatedly in the episode is an interaction between the Gothic and gendered elements and the return to the 21st-century perspective: when, for instance, Holmes explains away the feminist conspiracy in front of the "hidden army" of women who have participated in Emelia Ricoletti's plot, a conspiracy justified by the revenge they are taking on a chauvinistic society, Moriarty suddenly appears dressed as a bride to counter Sherlock's positivist explanation and to plunge him again in confusion back to his 21st-century throes. This is the way the script plays out the inscription of the Victorian topic in a modern outlook, instilling a 21st-century "queer" thematic into the Victorian plot through Moriarty's disguise, but this is further made sense of if we remember that the topic of gender confusion here reactivates an earlier set of topics revolving around the "bromance" between either Sherlock and Watson or Sherlock and Moriarty – topics that were clearly brought to the forefront in the previous episodes.[6] Gender issues and homoeroticism (which is constantly suggested between Sherlock and Moriarty throughout the series) ought to be considered as separate lines in the plot thematics of the episode since they relate to different representations, chauvinistic behavior on the one hand and male relationships on the other, but their interaction appears in the redefinition of 19th-century stereotypes that "The Abominable Bride" is constantly implementing. The scene where Sherlock misunderstands the words addressed to Watson is a case in point here (1'08'09).

> WATSON: I thought I was losing you. I thought perhaps we were ... neglecting each other
> SHERLOCK: Well, you're the one who moved out.
> WATSON: I was talking to Mary.

This game consisting in integrating homoerotic references comes directly from the previous episodes in the series, but the 19th-century context only serves to enhance their relevance in a world where celibacy raises questions that are perhaps not so salient in the 21st-century context. The transplantation of homoerotic allusions from the 21st-century *Sherlock* into this 19th-century context not only establishes a connection between both storyworlds but also draws on our knowledge of the whole series to recognize these allusions as part of a 21st-century re-reading of the Victorian context. Similarly, the episode includes a hilarious sequence in which Watson tries to probe at the reason(s) why Sherlock is still a bachelor, while they are waiting for the "ghost" of Emelia Ricoletti to make an attempt on Sir Eustace's life (42'53). This scene is funny in itself, yet it takes more significance as it is played out against the background of a time travel to the 19th century in which we surprisingly find the same ambiguity that was obtained in the modern-day adaptation. Sherlock is obviously embarrassed by Watson's query (what the latter calls a "man to man" conversation), and we may understand him if we consider the many innuendoes various characters make in the series about their relationship, innuendoes that are reminded to the spectator in the opening sequence of the episode when we see Mycroft thus summing up their relation: "Since yesterday you've moved in with him and now you're solving crimes together" (00'17);[7] or when we briefly see Watson and Sherlock, the latter naked under a mere sheet, in Buckingham Palace, a scene extracted from *A Scandal in Belgravia* (00'39). Here again, the serial quality adds meaning to the development of characters and of the topics that were featured in the previous episodes, by connecting the 19th-century sequence to a redefinition of our vision of male relationships (including homoeroticism) imbued by the 21st-century *Sherlock*.

This vision enters a direct relationship with the previous representations of homoeroticism that prevailed in the series and which are significantly alluded to here, in a way that reconstructs the meaning of this topic in the series. According to Carlen Lavigne, the series at large articulates an ambivalent discourse on "queerness" in that this topic is brought to the surface repeatedly about Holmes and Watson, only to be disavowed or treated for comic relief solely. The critic relates this treatment to the stereotypes of the "buddy cops" that include but deny (uncomfortably) the possibility of same-sex desire (see Lavigne 2012, 17). What is more significant is that homosexuality is precisely the field wherein Sherlock's mistakes appear blatantly in the whole series, initially in the very first episode in the series, "A Study in Pink," when he wrongly conjectures about Watson's family from the clues borne by his cell phone (the inscription on the phone does not point to Watson's estranged, alcoholic brother but to Watson's lesbian sister) and in "The Great Game" (the third episode in season one) when he meets Jim Moriarty for the first time, posing as a gay lab attendant working with Molly Hooper but really using this pretense to escape Sherlock's insight. Lavigne remarks:

> Questions of sexuality thus twice prove the undoing of Holmes' vaunted detective skills; this disruption of the great detective's otherwise logical deductive process underscores the persistent and tricky ambiguity of *Sherlock*'s queer themes. (2012, 21)

What is remarkable with respect to the connection between "The Abominable Bride" and this previous treatment of the homoerotic topic – or what Lavigne labels "the queer possibility" – is that the 2016 episode also uses a homoerotic scene as a means to derail the apparently smooth chain of deductions by the detective. When Sherlock, in an abandoned church, is explaining how the league of women organized their large-scale revenge on men, Moriarty dressed as a bride comes to interrupt his peroration, and we wonder whether the most disturbing is his return at all or his return in this guise. Once again, the overtly sexual nature of this apparition bypasses the detective's ability to explain and categorize reality, as if the complexity and ambiguity of this reality were too much for his purely logical and normative discourse. This is what Stephen Greer suggests when he explains that sexual "identity" escapes Holmes's grasp because it is not "readable" in the same sense as material reality or social markers:

> in a fictional universe structured on deductions derived from the visible, sexuality is repeatedly shown to frustrate otherwise reliable methods of categorization and knowledge making. It is less the case that being gay "doesn't show" – to recall Dyer – but that the signifiers of sexuality do not signify consistently or exclusively. (2015, 57)

Thus, the interruption that Moriarty causes in the explanatory narrative by Sherlock mirrors the confusion he creates in the detective's mode of approach of reality through the failure of normative sense-making. This shows that the homoerotic topic is used to express a larger question about modern hermeneutic uncertainty that endangers the very practice of investigation since meanings threaten to get "out of control" with the detective. The following extract from "A Study in Pink," the television pilot in the series, broadcast in 2010, includes such a sequence, already commented on by Greer (2015) and Lavigne (2012), and resembling very much the "man to man" conversation between Sherlock and John in the 2016 instalment:

> JOHN: You don't have a girlfriend, then?
> SHERLOCK: Girlfriend? No, not really my area.
> JOHN: Mm. Oh, right. Do you have a boyfriend? Which is fine, by the way.
> SHERLOCK: I know it's fine.
> JOHN: So you've got a boyfriend, then.
> SHERLOCK: No.
> JOHN: Right, okay. Fine. You're unattached. Like me.
> SHERLOCK: John, um ... I think you should know that I consider myself married to my work and while I'm flattered, I'm really not looking for any...
> JOHN: No, I'm ... not asking. No. I'm just saying. It's all fine.
> SHERLOCK: Good. Thank you.

In "The Abominable Bride," the creators Gatiss and Moffat twice relate the narrative interruptions of the 19th-century plot to a meeting with Moriarty (once when Sherlock finds Moriarty in his rooms at Baker Street and witnesses his apparent suicide; once when he meets him in the church where the rebellious women are assembled). These meetings combine narrative discontinuity (we shift from one time frame to another) and either gender crossing elements (Moriarty dressed as a bride) or clearly homoerotic elements (every spectator is bound to remember Moriarty's claim in "The Abominable Bride" before he commits suicide as a way, it seems, to provoke Sherlock: "Dead is the new sexy"). All these clues suggest that the overall treatment of anachronism in the episode serves to enhance how Sherlock's thought processes are destabilized by a topic – sexuality – that eludes his normative worldview. This destabilization is aptly figured by the sudden, brutal discontinuity which is brought to the narrative development each time and which corresponds to the time shifts. The "queer discourse" is then not only meant as a topic but also as a sign marking narrative thresholds, and the crossing thereof, which appears all the more clearly in a plot based on anachronism, that is, time shifts between story levels.[8]

A similar treatment is found concerning the Gothic theme in the sense that it acts as a mediating element between 19th- and 21st-century worldviews. This theme appears through the very connoted plot around the ghost story that is part and parcel of the Ricoletti case – a series of crimes that are seemingly committed by the ghost of an oppressed woman who wished to establish her death as the cornerstone of a movement of revenge against abusive husbands. This plot already constitutes a gendered interpretation of the Gothic cliché of the revenant, but more than that, the Gothic element seems to invade the modern-day plot when Sherlock in the 21st century decides, against all reasonable elements, noticeably voiced by Watson, to look in a churchyard for the corpse of Emelia Ricoletti and of the woman who passed for her when she pretended to commit suicide initially (1'19'50). This scene reinvests the 21st century with a Gothic touch that was first contained within the 19th-century plot and safely maintained apart from the rationalist discourse of Sherlock. When the corpse is unburied it appears in a starkly gruesome shot that spares nothing to the spectator, and Sherlock begins to look for a second corpse underneath the coffin, when suddenly the corpse begins to move. The corpse's attack on Sherlock is suddenly cut and we come back to the 19th century again in a strange scene that reenacts the final confrontation between Holmes and Moriarty in the Reichenbach Falls, except that here Watson is there to save his friend from his arch-enemy. The editing that switches from the 21st-century Gothic scene to a well-known scene from the canon is bound to puzzle the spectators because it leaves the first scene unsolved, incomplete, and suddenly cuts to a scene that ought to be familiar to Doyle readers. This further confusion between the two periods at stake in the episode has another effect apart from mere derailment: it ascribes the Gothic (the resuscitation of Emelia Ricoletti's corpse) to the modern period, *and* it acts out a defusing of the Gothic element by voluntarily and obtrusively *not giving* a denouement to the supernatural line the plot was about to follow, through the cut that brings us back to the 19th century and to the Reichenbach Falls. In other words, the Gothic reference is transplanted to the supposedly rational 21st century and there fails to find an explanation or even a denouement. This game of references to the mindscapes that are usually attributed to the two periods acts out once again on a reversal of the affiliations established beforehand by the series (based on a hyper-rational, technological vision of the 21st-century Sherlock), as if this episode was trying to confuse the extradiegetic spectators through the redefinition of the generic markers that pertain to each period in which the plot unfolds. This redefinition aims at enhancing the apparently inextricable links between the two plots, and to destabilize any set vision of the diegetic features that may distinguish one time frame from the other, so that the episode eventually seems focused on the interpretative uncertainties that affect its worldviews rather than on a definite, "clear" transposition of the series universe back to the 19th century. This is why "The Abominable Bride" as a reflexive *opus* deals with Sherlock's reading method more than with purely thematic interests.

Seeking references, even to generic or cultural markers, is of course a game that it is a little vain to pursue. Only their significance in a wider context can be taken as a sign of the "intent" of the series as a whole. Yet it should be mentioned finally that this episode, through its 19th-century context, offers the possibility to enhance the winks to the spectators who are privy to the jokes and allusions both to the canon and to the previous adaptations of Doyle's stories. Thus it is clear that the plot revolving around Sir Eustace is inspired by Doyle's story "The Five Orange Pips," and once again the colonial context of the initial text is transferred onto a gendered script. Eustace Carmichael teases his wife at breakfast with the following words, just before he receives the ominous orange pips: "And what did your morning threaten my dear? A vigorous round of embroidering? An exhausting appointment to the milliner's?" (31'51). This is clearly a way for the script to realign the character's personality around the topic of male oppression and to widen the scope of the source short story, which revolved around guilt only connected to colonial (mis)deeds. This is an instance in which the allusion to Doyle's text (reflexively) asks the extradiegetic spectators to take in the measure to which the episode is redefining the text along contemporary lines. Other references to the canon appear throughout the episode. Moriarty declares: "There is nothing new under the sun. It has all been done before," which is a quotation from *A Study in Scarlet*, and Mycroft mentioning the Manor House Case brings us back to Doyle's "The Greek Interpreter." The name Ricoletti and the phrase "the abominable wife" appear in "The Musgrave Ritual" in connection with one of the cases solved by Holmes that is never related in the canon and of course the Reichenbach Falls sequence is taken from Doyle's "The Final Problem." But these are mere nods to the wise that are not necessarily meaningful in the thematic network of the episode. To understand their inclusion, we need to assess more generally the metafictional logic of "The Abominable Bride."

The play on the original texts is indeed made openly metafictional when the characters comment on the roles they are given in the short stories, like Mrs. Hudson who complains of not being given enough lines in the published stories or Watson who grudgingly has to bear a moustache so that people recognize him in the street because "the illustrator is out of control" (7'34). These humorous references are also a way of beckoning to the knowing spectator without actually putting any definite sense in this game apart from the humorous metafictional staging of a character discussing his or her own role in the fiction itself. Similarly, the final shot we get is of Holmes smoking a pipe and looking downward at the street – it is a homage to the famous credit sequence of the Granada series (1984–1994)[9] without any definite rereading of this previous adaptation (Figures 4.2.5 and 4.2.6). Ultimately, the Gothic and gendered references in the episode make sense in relation to the playful "updating" of the source text as evinced here. But the meaning in the series of this reshuffling of values (the Gothic being

Figure 4.2.5 Holmes as a second Jeremy Brett.

Figure 4.2.6 The famous Granada credit sequence.

transplanted to the 21st century, for example) lies in the question that is raised about our expectations and positions as 21st-century spectators related to these topics of gender and Gothicism included in a 19th-century rewriting. We may be closer than we think to these 19th-century cultural landmarks. The following development will examine how the episode addresses this issue of spectators' reception.

Distance and spectatorship

The confusion experienced by the spectator stems first and foremost from the anachronistic structure of the episode. We have seen with the example of the exhumation of Emelia Ricoletti's corpse that the shift back and forth between the 19th and the 21st centuries is meant to maintain suspense but also to keep the development of the plot incomplete since the supernatural scene of the resuscitation finds no explanation. A similar openness and confusion is triggered all along the episode through the constant comings and goings between past and present that foreground the un-chronological development of the story/stories and above all that present to the spectator a discontinuous structure. This fragmented, constantly interrupted development is justified from the viewpoint of the story by the fact that the 19th-century plot is supposed to be a recollection by the 21st-century Sherlock, in a thought process that is repeatedly interrupted by the modern-day Watson and Mycroft. A telling example takes place at 1'03'56 when Sherlock in the 21st century is trying to resume his recollection of the past 19th-century case and hears Watson asking him what kind of drug he took ("Which is it today? Morphine or cocaine?"). When he repeats the sentence he thinks he heard, we hear it spoken by Watson in Sherlock's mouth. This is the type of confusion that makes the non-chronological structure of the story deeply unsettling. Moreover, this constant derailment of the narrative from one plane to another reflexively mimics the very structure of the serial consumption of the BBC *Sherlock* – and of any series in fact – by grafting into the structure of the episode the intermittent, discontinuous development of the story that is *the* main defining feature of serial production. Shifting from one time of the story to another, "The Abominable Bride" compels its spectators to become highly aware of the serial mode as a constraint on the continuity of the aesthetic experience.

This constraint is bound to trigger a reflexive distance in the spectator. This is also the case for many other narrative features in the episode that aim at foregrounding the artificial nature of the reconstruction of the past, whether that past refers to the 19th century envisioned from a 21st-century perspective or to the retelling of past criminal events within the 19th-century plot. For instance, when Lestrade exposes the initial events of the criminal case of Emelia Ricoletti, at the moment when he tells how she was shooting at passers-by down her window (12'18), Sherlock interrupts him to ask a question on the time of the events ("When was this?"), which brings us back to the sitting room of Baker Street where this narration is unfolding, but this room is figured within the scene of the criminal recollection itself as a stage from which the characters are discussing the events (Figure 4.2.7). This device was used earlier in the series, noticeably in *A Scandal in Belgravia*. What matters most here in our perspective is again the fact that this metafictional interruption by Holmes – crossing the narrative frontiers, as if the characters in the investigation could interact

Figure 4.2.7 The narrative as metafictional.

with the characters in the crime plot, even those who are dead like Emelia Ricoletti – constitutes not only a throwback to the earlier episodes that feature this device too but also another reflexive comment – somewhat humorous of course – on the fragmented quality of the narration and on the involved time structure that characterizes it. In other words, the series is here flaunting its own quality as a series grounded in intermittence and the encroaching of narrative barriers.

The question that follows naturally is: what can the spectator do with this structure? Do we face a mere game here that is meant to unsettle our expectations of narrative continuity or is there more to it than that? We should remember first that this unsettling quality seems to be the final word of the episode since "The Abominable Bride" ends surprisingly on a last return to the 19th-century frame to stage a quiet conversation by the fireside between Watson and Holmes, in which the whole plot that unfolded in the 21st century is reduced to a mere hypothesis by Holmes about what the future of civilization might look like (1'26'57):

> WATSON: Flying machines, these … er … telephone contraptions? What sort of lunatic fantasy is that?
>
> HOLMES: It was simply my conjecture of what our future world might look like and how you and I might fit inside it.

This sort of sidestepping from any "serious" take on the chronological confusion evidenced in the episode is likely to endanger the whole of the series, since it may justify a definite interruption of it, as co-writer Mark Gatiss recognized.

By having that scene right at the end, where we go back to Victorian London – Victorian Baker Street – and Sherlock explicitly says, "It's an imagined version of what I think the future might be," we have really opened a ridiculous window that the entire series of *Sherlock* might be the drug-induced ravings of the Victorian Sherlock Holmes. Which means we can do absolutely anything. (quoted in Burt 2016)

This fairly negative vision of absolute openness of the narrative development – we can do absolutely anything sounds like a surrender of relevance and sense-making – can be qualified if we refer this feature to what Henry Jenkins, commenting upon Umberto Eco (1985), makes of it in his discussion of cult films. Dealing with Michael Curtiz's *Casablanca*, he writes:

The film needs not be well made, but it must provide resources consumers can use in constructing their own fantasies. [...] And the cult film need not be coherent: the more different directions it pushes, the more different communities it can sustain and the more different experiences it can provide, the better. (2008, 97–98)

In the same line of thought I believe that we should consider the openness of "The Abominable Bride," deeply indebted to its own reflexive staging of its status as part of a series, to justify this type of spectator participation and even fan adhesion[10] that Jenkins describes. This is how the series invites us to "make" our own version of Sherlock, despite his claim: "Nothing made me. I made me" [44'53]. How consistent this vision can be or has to be is not really considered as a relevant question, both from the point of view of fan culture or if we consider the discontinuity that affects the characters' representations.

Seriality is thus treated in "The Abominable Bride" mainly as the staging of cross-references between 19th-century and 21st-century mind-frames, with a view to using the anachronistic structure of the narrative to produce an inextricable combination of both. This not only destabilizes the spectator's experience with numerous narrative interruptions and opens the episode to viewer participation, but it also questions our own capacity to recapture a past context with clarity and without constant intrusions from the present into the past. A telling example of this phenomenon is the fleeting passage where Watson addresses Sherlock in the 19th century in a cab that takes them to the church where Mary is waiting for them, and the image of the 21st-century Watson suddenly appears on screen for a few seconds (1'06'39-Figure 4.2.8). In its implicit discourse on this impossibility to reconnect with a consistent vision of the past, the episode articulates a rather expected, humorous take on the topic of the reconstitution of this past, but it eventually does not purport to address this topic otherwise than as a reconstruction from a contemporary, narratively fragmented perspective.

Figure 4.2.8 21st-century Watson appearing in the 19th-century narrative.

Notes

1 On this feature of the BBC adaptation, see Nicol (2013).
2 It is actually a single episode due to the busy timetable of the two leading actors on the show who could not commit themselves to a whole season for 2016. Thus it is placed very much in the position of the novel *The Hound of the Baskervilles* in the canon, a novel which was published after the fictional death of Holmes with Moriarty but which was supposed to relate an investigation that had happened previous to that death – hence it was a part of, but not a continuation of, the series. The specific status of "The Abominable Bride" is akin to this, although, as we shall see, it is more connected to the previous episodes noticeably through the continuous topic of Moriarty's fate as a link between the various installments.
3 This notion of diegetic worlds refers here simply to the two contexts in which each part of the plot is unfolding – 19th- and 21st-century England – and should not be confused with the notion of "possible worlds" suggested by Umberto Eco in *Lector in Fabula*, which consists in the various redefinition by the readers of the storyworlds in which the characters evolve, a redefinition that is constantly in progress with the development of the plot. In "The Abominable Bride," the stability of each storyworld is remarkable, but the main character Sherlock endangers the barrier between them by constantly crossing it.
4 We should note that this practice of adaptation as a radical redefinition of the initial diegetic universe of the source text fits the understanding of the phenomenon as suggested by L. Hutcheon (2012).
5 See Naugrette (2011) and Porter (2012) on the general topic of references to the source texts in the series.
6 On the topic of homoerotic discourse in the series, see Greer (2015) and Lavigne (2012).
7 The suggestive ending of this quote in the original episode reads as follows: "Might we expect a happy announcement by the end of the week?"

8 Narrative discontinuity seems to be a feature that Gatiss and Moffat meant to give full sway to as the series progressed, since the last episode, entitled "The Final Problem" (2017, S04E03), is entirely based on a set of alternate narratives that ceaselessly interrupt one another, as a sign of Sherlock's hardships experienced in holding the narrative thread all together. This episode stages Sherlock's long-concealed sister Eurus, but Moriarty's role in it is rather limited, and very far from the sexualized connotations that we have noticed in "The Abominable Bride." This is why we will not consider this last episode in the series as directly related to the treatment of homoeroticism in *Sherlock* – although it may be relevant to a study of gender relationships in the series through the character of Eurus.

9 The impact of this series is analyzed in detail in Trembley (1994). See also Gelly (2015).

10 It is interesting to note that this spectator participation was staged in "The Empty Hearse" (2014) when various solutions to Sherlock's possible survival after his confrontation with Moriarty were filmed and integrated into the series in succession in the same sequence before being revealed for what they really were, that is, suggestions by fans of how to move on with the script and justify Sherlock's survival. Not only were these suggestions staged and included into the series but they proceeded from a real-life polling on the BBC site as to how the spectators envisioned the best way of bringing Sherlock to life after the end of Season 2. This is further proof to me that the discontinuous quality of the series is not an obstacle but a motivation for spectator participation. Further material on the fan phenomenon around the Holmes figure is available in the work published by Ue and Cranfield 2014.

Works cited

Burt, Kayti. "Sherlock Creators Tease Season 4, Give Abominable Bride Insight". *Den of Geek*, 02.19.2016 http://www.denofgeek.com/us/tv/sherlock/253100/sherlock-creators-tease-season-4-give-abominable-bride-insight (accessed 01.24.2019).

Eco, Umberto. *Lector in fabula ou la Coopération interprétative dans les textes narratifs*. Paris: Grasset, 1985.

Gelly, Christophe. "*The Hound of the Baskervilles* Revisited: Adaptation in Context". In *The Oscholars: Special Issue on Arthur Conan Doyle*, February 2015. http://oscholars-oscholars.com/doyle/ (accessed 01.24.2019).

Greer, Stephen. "Queer (Mis)recognition in the BBC's *Sherlock*". *Adaptation: The Journal of Literature on Screen Studies* 8.1, 2015. 50–67.

Hutcheon, Linda. *A Theory of Adaptation*. London: Routledge, 2012.

Jenkins, Henry. *Convergence Culture: Where Old and New Media Collide*. New York: NYU Press, 2008.

Lavigne, Carlen. "The Noble Bachelor and the Crooked Man—Subtext and Sexuality in the BBC's *Sherlock*". In Lynette Porter (ed.), *Sherlock Holmes for the 21st Century*, Jefferson, NC and London: Mc Farland, 2012. 13–23.

Naugrette, Jean-Pierre. "*Sherlock* (BBC 2010): un nouveau limier pour le XXIe siècle?" *Etudes Anglaises* 4, 2011. 402–414.

Nicol, Bran. "Sherlock Holmes Version 2.0: Adapting Doyle in the Twenty-First Century". In Sabine Vanacker and Catherine Wynne (eds.), *Sherlock Holmes and Conan Doyle—Multi-Media Afterlives*, Chippenham and Eastbourne: Palgrave Macmillan, 2013. 124–139.

Porter, Lynnette. *Sherlock Holmes for the 21ˢᵗ Century*. Jefferson, NC; London: McFarland, 2012.

Trembley, Elizabeth. "Holmes Is Where the Heart Is: The Achievement of Granada Television's Sherlock Holmes Films". In William Reynolds and Elizabeth Trembley (eds.), *It's A Print—Detective Fiction from Page to Screen*, Bowling Green: Bowling Green State University Popular Press, 1994. 11–30.

Ue, Tom, and Jonathan Cranfield, eds. *Fan Phenomena: Sherlock Holmes*. Bristol: Intellect Books, 2014.

Films, series, and episodes cited

Casablanca. Michael Curtiz, Warner Bros., 1942.

Sherlock. BBC One, 2010–.

"A Study in Pink". *Sherlock*, S01E01. Dir. Paul McGuigan, 07.25.2010.

"The Great Game". *Sherlock*, S01E03. Dir. Euros Lyn, 08.08.2010.

"A Scandal in Belgravia". *Sherlock*, S02E01. Dir. Paul McGuigan, 01.01.2012.

"The Hounds of the Baskervilles". *Sherlock*, S02E02. Dir. Paul McGuigan, 01.08.2012.

"The Reichenbarch Fall". *Sherlock*, S02E03. Dir. Toby Haynes, 01.15.2012.

"The Empty Hearse". *Sherlock*, S03E01. Dir. Jeremy Lovering, 01.01.2014.

"The Abominable Bride". *Sherlock*, S03Special. Dir. Douglas MacKinnon, 2016.

4.3 Subject positions and seriality in *The Good Wife*

Samuel A. Chambers

As an always interdisciplinary, and often alterdisciplinary project, much work in critical television studies implicitly follows the structure of learning, the radical pedagogical practice that Jacques Rancière has recently made famous (again) (Rancière 1991; Bowman 2008; Chambers 2013). For Rancière, learning happens first by learning just one thing by heart or by rote. This might just be our own native language, or it might be a text, any text, whose words we have read over and over again until we *know them*. Once we know one thing, any thing, then we can learn. We *learn* by exploring, by comparing the thing we know with some other thing. And we *teach* by reporting back on what we have learned. This is what I meant in the preface to my book on television when I confessed to my "ignorance" about television and film studies (Chambers 2009). The point was not at all to denigrate the field, or to disqualify myself from building from and participating in that emerging area of inquiry, since indeed I already understood myself as having made a contribution to some of the key work done on television in the post-*Sopranos* age (Chambers 2001, 2003a, 2003b, 2005, 2006a, 2006b; Chambers and Finn 2001; Chambers and Williford 2004; Chambers and Caldwell 2007). Instead I meant to show that rather than simply studying television as a pre-determined object, or as a unique new field of study, I was trying to learn and teach by comparing one thing (a television show) to another (writings in political theory).[1]

This chapter compares *The Good Wife* (*TGW*), a US-network primetime drama, 2009–2016, to Michel Foucault's *The Archaeology of Knowledge* (1972 [1968]) in order to rethink questions of subjectivity and agency, specifically by theorizing norms and normativity. I avoid the rootless abstractions and thin declarations that characterize a great deal of recent work on norms, so as to think about the necessarily broad concepts of subjectivity and normativity within the concrete context of narrative arc, character development, and specific plot examples of *TGW* (Leonard 2017; Orgad 2017). I argue that in order to get a better grip on the very slippery entities that are "norms," we need to return to the less-fashionable but perhaps more roughly textured (more rooted) concept of "subject positions," an idea richly theorized by Foucault long before he himself took up the question of norms directly. *TGW* raises the problematic of subject positions directly in its very title, and over the course of its seven seasons, it recurrently explores that problematic. When read with and through Foucault, *TGW* thereby offers a lens through which to re-envision norms and normativity, and most of all to grasp the possibility of resistance to and subversion of norms.[2]

While the above paragraph describes the general uptake of this project in the context of political theory and queer theory, those arguments all hinge upon something that precedes them, and these prior conditions of possibility will be my central focus here – the primary points I want to prove in my reading of *TGW*. The argument on this front is straightforward, but no less significant: the cultural politics of *TGW* depends upon its serial structure and form. In other words, the seriality of *TGW* makes it possible for the series to do the cultural political work of staging a demonstration of normative forces and mobilizing a critique of normativity. The serial form proves essential. Hence, with one hand I will sketch the outline of an argument about *TGW*'s feminist and queer politics, but with the other I will underscore the crucial importance of the seriality in and of the show.

The Good Wife as "enunciative modality"

The past ten years have seen ratings drop and revenues dwindle on American network television, leading to an intense acceleration of the process by which a new series is canceled; some series no longer make it past the first one or two episodes before the network pulls them from the air, all in search of more viewers.[3] These structural constraints have fed back into the process of creating a new series, leading to numerous shows that now seem to contain all the reasons for watching them packed into the setup, the premise, the pilot, and sometimes even the title of the show; hence we get series like *New Girl*, where the title names an event from the pilot – an event that cannot remain salient past the first portion of the first season. In essence, television series are now required to make their "pitch" to viewers in much the same way as movie pitches have long been conducted in Hollywood, where the entirety of the claims for greenlighting a multimillion-dollar movie budget hinges upon the perfect short-phrase description – "*Speed* on a boat" or "*The Godfather* with Martians."[4]

TGW follows and deepens this trend, but ultimately tweaks it in significant ways. The first scene of the pilot episode encapsulates and embodies the full force of the title of the series. The scene opens in the hallway outside a hotel conference room, with the camera tracking, close-in, the clasped hands of Peter and Alicia Florrick. Circling them from front to back, we follow the couple into the press conference, where Peter announces his resignation as an Illinois County State's Attorney in the face of the scandal over revelations that he had been sleeping with multiple prostitutes. The camera moves from a standard one-shot of Peter, then pans out and slides over to shoot the exact same shot of Peter through the on-screen television monitor;

it then repeats the same move with Alicia, before finally zooming back in to focus on her, standing at the side of her shamed husband. From there the camera lingers with Alicia through to the end of the press conference and back out into the hallway. Once there, Alicia stops short, and when Peter returns to ask her what is wrong, she slaps him – hard – before continuing down the hallway. In total the scene runs for just over three minutes; Alicia never speaks (see Leonard 2014).

The setup for the entire series is completed in the very next scene, set six months later, when we find Alicia lost (literally) on the first day of her new job as an associate attorney, returning to work after 13 years away. A series of Thomas Schlamme-esque walking-and-talking scenes[5] introduce viewers to the law firm's senior partners (Diane Lockhart and Will Gardner) and chief investigator (Kalinda Sharma), along with Alicia's rival as junior associate (Cary Agos) (Smith 2003). More important than these obvious character-establishment snippets is the brief pause in between: when Alicia leaves Diane's office she bumps into the latter's assistant, who is playing a video of Peter's press conference on his office computer. As Alicia stops, the camera reverses from her stunned face in the hallway, to the image of her also stricken visage on the computer screen. This tiny moment, I argue, succinctly and clearly captures the stakes of both the title and overall premise of *TGW*.

It does so through a *mise-en-scène* that demonstrates the constitutive gap (*écart*) between the *concrete individual*, Alicia Florrick (who we see standing anxious in the hallway) and the *subject position*, "the good wife" (which we view in its fixed location on screen). While the literature on subjectivity, "the subject," and "subject positions" proves enormously vast and deep[6] – and frequently full of tensions and contradictions – this moment in the hallway serves as a visual metonym for the fundamental and most important ideas involved. "Alicia Florrick" is flesh and blood, standing before us – where "us" includes both the viewers (through the lens of the camera) and Diane's assistant (the on-screen character) – whereas the subject position "the good wife" appears on and in the frame of a *screen* (see Miller 2017).[7] "The good wife" is precisely a structural location, next to the husband, *silent*, in front of the flashing camera bulbs, and *TGW* as a television series creates the opportunity to explore both the gap that separates and the ties that connect Alicia Florrick to "the good wife."

This scene, itself a microcosm of the series as a whole (Leonard 2014), thereby plays out and exemplifies what Foucault worked so hard to explain with the phrase "discursive relations." Foucault's account has often been misunderstood and frequently mis-represented. He himself was at pains in *The Archaeology of Knowledge* to measure the distance between, on the one hand, his approach, method, and theoretical commitments in his earlier books (Foucault 1970, 1973, 2009), and, on the other, so-called structuralism. Yet with the aid of hindsight it does not seem unfair to say that his rhetorical insistence on the difference between his project and structuralism often failed to draw to the surface with clarity his own epistemological or ontological commitments. In particular, I would argue that at least with respect to Foucault's reception in the UK and North America, his protestations against "structuralism," which most readers assumed to be bad or wrong precisely because it was *determinist*, led them to read his account of "discursive relations" as a form of linguistic idealism.[8] In other words, these readers, perhaps because of certain priming effects produced by Foucault's own response to his French intellectual context, imposed upon Foucault's text the very structure/agency binary that he himself so nicely eschewed or evaded – both in his earlier books and in *The Archaeology* itself.

In the face of these common misconstruals, I would insist that "discursive relations" never be reduced to or conflated with *language*, where that term denotes the mass of words (and their attendant meanings) spoken or written by individual subjects. Indeed, in order to stylize the difference between Foucault's approach and the position of linguistic monism, we might draw a *heuristic* distinction between these two conceptual accounts. "Language" we would thus say is the collection of words that we find in a dictionary – words that can be manipulated by speakers (language *users* as we call them) in order to convey meaning. Language is therefore ideal or symbolic; it denotes ideas or concepts, and while it can be understood to *point to* objects in the world, it is not a material part of the world itself. "Discourse," in stark contrast, is itself a *practice*; it is rule-governed, historical, and absolutely *material*. Therefore, when I claim that "the good wife" is a subject position, or that *TGW* explores and navigates discursive relations, I am absolutely not confining my analysis to the domain of hermeneutics or symbolic analysis.

Foucault himself was usually quite emphatic about these precise points, even if his own terminology was not always perfectly clear. The chapter of *The Archaeology of Knowledge* that specifically deals with the key topic for *TGW* – that is, *subject positions* – carries an unhelpful and potentially confusing title, "The Formation of Enunciative Modalities." Rather than trying to parse the terms that make up the title, it is easier to show that what Foucault really has in mind here is the more direct notion of "subject positions." The chapter opens straightforwardly, with Foucault writing sparsely, "first question: who is speaking?" (Foucault 1972, 50). Foucault then underlines the most basic, yet most important, point, "statements cannot come from anybody" since the "value" and the "efficacy" of those statements "cannot be dissociated from the statutorily defined person who has the right to make them" (Foucault 1972, 51). Here Foucault's claims clearly echo J. L. Austin's famous work on "speech acts," where Austin insists that the "felicity" of a speech act (its success or failure *as an act*) remains tied up with questions of the proper context and the appropriate speaker (Austin 1962, 26). Yet Foucault's focus turns out to be quite different: his concern lies not with isolated speech acts but with the broad ensemble of discursive relations. And this means that unlike Austin, who retained a tight commitment to the subject in the form of the individual speaker, Foucault has his eye on the broader, radical implications of discursive relations for larger questions of social and political theory. As he says early in the text, in one of his many efforts to resist the idea that he is contributing narrowly to "the debate on structure", the book "belongs to that field in which the questions of the human being, consciousness, origin, and the subject emerge, intersect, mingle, and separate" (Foucault 1972, 16).

Foucault always underscores the *separation*. Hence, the "statutorily defined person," referred to in the quote from the preceding paragraph, is not an *actual* person, not a concrete individual but rather a subject position. Later in the chapter Foucault uses this language directly: "the positions of the subject are also defined by the situation that it is possible for him to occupy in relation to the various domains or groups of objects" (Foucault 1972, 52). And above all, these positions are *multiple*. The most important dimension of what Foucault cryptically calls "enunciative modalities" – possibilities for and ways of taking up subject positions so as to make the production of statements possible – is that they can never be traced back or grounded in "the unity of the subject"; rather, they always "manifest his dispersion" (Foucault 1972, 54). Foucault brings the chapter toward its conclusion with a line that strongly supports my heuristic distinction between "language" and "discourse." He writes, "I shall abandon any attempt, therefore, to see discourse as a phenomenon of expression ...; instead, I shall look for a field of regularity for various positions of subjectivity. Thus conceived, discourse is not the majestically unfolding manifestation of a thinking, knowing, speaking subject, but, on the contrary, a totality, in which the dispersion of the subject and *his discontinuity with himself* may be determined" (Foucault 1972, 55, emphasis added).

TGW is a show about the dispersion of "the good wife" and that subject's discontinuity with itself. But this means it is also a show about Alicia Florrick's "dispersion" and her own discontinuity with "the good wife" that she both is and is not – that she can be, and can refuse to be. To say that *TGW* explores discursive relations is to insist that "the good wife" is neither the so-called thing itself (an actual "good" wife) nor merely a meaning (a question of what "good wife" denotes). *TGW* examines concrete discursive practices (examples of which I provide below). Foucault is emphatic here, even if his interpreters[9] over the years have been less so:

> Discursive relations are not [...] internal to discourse: they do not connect concepts or words with one another; they do not establish a deductive or rhetorical structure between propositions or sentences. Yet they are not relations exterior to discourse, relations that might limit it, or impose certain forms upon it, or force it, in certain circumstances, to state certain things. They are, in a sense, at the limit of discourse: they determine the group of relations that discourse must establish in order to speak of this or that object [...]. These relations characterize not the language (*langue*) used by discourse, nor the circumstances in which it is deployed, but discourse itself as a practice. (Foucault 1972, 46, emphasis added)

Now I want to link this Foucauldian reading of *TGW* (and the crucial notion of discourse as a practice) to the broader understanding of norms that this debate broaches. Doing so, as I will show, depends first, and crucially, on capturing the dynamic seriality of the show.

The end as beginning

A certain concept of "seriality" lies at the heart of any theory of norms, just as it centers any understanding of the televisual. The former point has been made repeatedly by theorists of norms, from François Ewald (1990) and Georges Canguilhem (1989), to Foucault. But it has been pressed most forcefully by the widely read recent works of Judith Butler, whose concepts of *performativity* and *resignification* utterly depend upon the idea of repetition. At the core of Butler's project one finds a crucial argument for seriality, in the form of the basic claim that seriality itself proves to be a normative power, because only through repetition do norms attain their worldly material force. And yet, at the same time, it is precisely through a certain sort of repetition (repetition with a difference) that norms can unravel, can be undone just as they have been done (Butler 1999, 2004).

Moving next to the latter point, it might seem trivial to claim that a television *series* is a serial form of art, but the contention remains salient despite sounding redundant. Obviously not all television series embody the same elements of seriality, and in some sense we can observe the extent to which recent changes to the form of television – especially through technological developments that alter the distribution and reception of the medium – have *diminished* its serial aspects. Binge-watching shows through streaming services transforms the serial nature of television, making such shows a bit less like early network television serials and a bit more like long movies or novels (see Mittell 2015). Indeed, recent streaming shows have eschewed the standard 30-minute or 60-minute format entirely: *Gilmore Girls: A Year in the Life* ran as four episodes of 88–102 minutes – leading some critics to describe it as a "telepic" (Petski 2016).[10] Overall, in many contexts and for many people, the rhythm and temporality of television have now changed, with a series consumed over a weekend, rather than lived with and witnessed weekly over many long months. In this context, *TGW* stands out for a number of reasons. The series has now completed a 7-season, 156-episode run, and some have said it will be remembered as the last American network television series to run full 22-episode seasons while garnering critical acclaim and carrying cultural weight (Goldblatt 2016; see Jensen 2016).

And the series aired over precisely the period of time in which the very meaning of "television" and "television series" has been rapidly changing. Here it seems prudent to situate *TGW* in the context of the history of television and also to position its analysis within the terrain of critical television studies – both of which entail considering *TGW* in relation to the "quality television" moniker. A recent special issue of *Television & New Media* devoted to *TGW* makes a strong set of claims about where to locate the series. Here are the framing remarks of the special issue editors:

> Television studies is a historically feminist, and feminized, discipline [...]. From the time the shine wore off the first "Golden Age" of live television in the 1950s [...] until *The Sopranos* in 1999, television was often cast as a "vast wasteland" (see, for example, R. J. Thompson 1996). In recent years [...] quality in the U.S. context has come to narrowly signify subscription-based premium network HBO and the fictional dramatic programming it has influenced: heavily serialized, high production value programs with narratively complex stories, most often centered on a male anti-hero and targeting niche audiences of affluent, highly educated, socially liberal, urban dwelling, mostly white audiences. (Nygaard and Lagerwey 2017, 106–107)

This quote contains a number of significant claims, some of which I wish to underscore and some of which I find problematic and therefore wish to question or contest (or at least reframe).

Unsurprisingly – since so much of my own work on television has operated through the lens of feminist and queer theory – I agree entirely that television studies has been a rich site for important feminist work, and this fact is partially explained by another. Television as an object of scholarly study has surely been denigrated as inferior "low" popular culture, relative to the fields of literary and cinema studies. Nonetheless, it might be overstating the matter to claim that television studies as a scholarly field has itself been "feminized," at least without some evidence to support such a claim. This is a subtle difference in interpretation, but it matters because of the claim that follows. In the quote above, Nygaard and Lagerwey assert that after the first "Golden Age" of television in the 1950s all the way up until *The Sopranos* in 1999 "television was often cast as a 'vast wasteland' "; they cite Thompson (1996), apparently as an *example* of such characterizations; and finally they move on to a description of post-*Sopranos* quality television. In doing so they potentially misrepresent Thompson's work and the history of so-called quality television.[11] The book of Thompson's that they cite was not at all arguing that television was a wasteland; just the opposite, Thompson announced in the very title of his book *Television's Second Golden Age*, what he argued throughout it: that in the 1980s television was a rich ocean of treasures, the site of the (re)emergence of *quality television* (Thompson 1996). More recent (post-*Sopranos*) writings on the quality label base themselves on Thompson's work and then go on to update the debates about quality in the era beyond the one addressed in his now-canonized book (McCabe and Akass 2007). This same period of time has been marked by extensive feminist television criticism (Johnson 2007; Brunsdon and Spigel 2008; Chambers 2009). Moreover, the shows that Thompson places on the "quality" pedestal are not by any stretch all male-centered – for example, *Cagney and Lacey, Moonlighting, St. Else-where*, and *Northern Exposure*. It is doubtless true that for some popular press journalists the meaning of "quality TV" may have narrowed recently to center on the "male anti-hero," and such a phenomenon calls for scrutiny and likely criticism. Yet we still need to ask precisely *for whom* it is that "quality has come to narrowly signify" male-centered premium content? Certainly not for the dozens of television scholars who have published writings on *Buffy the Vampire Slayer* and the rest of the "Whedonverse," or for all those who have contributed to books published on shows like *The L Word, Desperate Housewives, Sex and The City, Ugly Betty*, and the list could go on and on.

The *TGW* special-issue editors describe their work as a "challenge to the masculinization of television studies" (Nygaard and Lagerwey 2017, 108). I happily join them in pushing back against the tendency to align "quality" television with male-centered television, but I worry that they overstate this trend, thereby severing important connections between *TGW* (including their own productive work on *TGW*) and a significant number of *quality* television shows that do not fit the narrow "male anti-hero" mold. As I see it, the "quality" television of the 1980s and then on into the 1990s (the pe-riod Thompson addresses, and the one that immediately follows) undoubt-edly set the stage for *The Sopranos* and all that came after.[12] Rather than claim that *TGW* proves to be an exception to the rule of masculinization, I am more interested in reading *TGW* in the context of its links to recent shows like *The Gilmore Girls, Six Feet Under, Buffy the Vampire Slayer,* and *The West Wing*.[13]

Moreover, by leaning so heavily on the ostensible contrast between *TGW* and the male anti-hero show, the *Television & New Media* special issue misses an opportunity to consider the uniqueness of *TGW* in terms of its se-rial form. This is because most of the third-generation "quality" television series (the ones that Nygaard and Lagerwey cite) appeared in a recognizable and long-standing serial form, broadcast on television at a set, weekly time. When its pilot aired in September of 2009 *TGW* looked just like the dozens of primetime US network dramas that had preceded it over the previous decades; yet when its finale aired in May of 2016, 22-episode shows had grown quite scarce. These structural conditions raised the stakes for the show's seventh and final season, and altered the context in which viewers watched the show.

That is to say, the seventh season of *TGW* was both a standard com-pletion of a US network legal-procedural and at the same time it was the culmination of a series that would be compared to the likes of shows aired on premier cable networks.[14] Unlike premium cable shows or made-for-streaming shows, *TGW* is (one of) the last of an old breed that airs in a fixed (network) time slot, with episodes running across a nine-month season, and (crucially) containing commercials. Millions of viewers of *TGW* thus ac-cessed the show according to a fixed schedule and timetable, stretching out over three seasons of the calendar (hence the American term "season" to refer to what is usually called a "series" in British and European TV). This produces a particular serial rhythm, given voice by the dominant element in television advertising – that is, the ads that push the networks' own shows and never fail to repeat the day and time of the show (in the case of *TGW*, Sunday at 9 pm).[15] Furthermore, the show itself is written and produced according to this same timetable and rhythm, with storylines and characters changing based upon online feedback from fans and from the material realities of actor contracts (see Mittell 2015).[16]

These structural conditions all amplify elements of seriality inherent to the theme and storylines of the show. Since *TGW* is a show about the subject position of "the good wife," over the course of its seven seasons we witness repetition over and over again as the show continually recurs to the theme of the relationship between, on the one hand, *the character* (Alicia Florrick), who changes, grows, experiences success and failure, joy, and heartbreak; and, on the other, *the subject position*, which remains static, structural, fixed. It would be easy to cite dozens of elements of intentional serial repetition in the show: recurring characters, who take on a particularly significant role in a show of *TGW*'s scope (i.e., characters can "come and go" on a 22-episode network series in a way that would prove impossible on an eight- or ten-episode streaming show); recurring tropes, such as surveillance, data privacy, and internet technologies (Hargraves 2017), which allow the show to remain current, connecting the seriality of the show to the seriality of the viewers' lived world; and recurring cases, which play a central role in the basic structure of a legal-procedural (a structure that *TGW* both works within and often revises).

Beyond all of these genuinely significant elements, I want to zero in on what I see as the single most important one. In doing so, I narrow my analysis to Season 7, wherein the series' creators themselves took the occasion of the final season – which, importantly, they knew in advance was the last[17] – to return explicitly to the original groundwork of the show and the themes laid out six years before. Indeed, seriality was so prominent in the minds of the showrunners that they decided to end the series – in the finale, titled, appropriately, "End" – by recreating an almost shot-for-shot repetition of the opening scene of the pilot episode. Just to be clear, especially for those who have not watched the show, the opening scene of the final episode of the series (S07E22) begins just as the opening scene of the pilot did: with Peter and Alicia holding hands and walking through a hotel hallway to enter a press conference – a press conference at which Peter, as he did six years before, will resign his political position, all while Alicia stands silently by his side.

The substance of the scene in terms of plot development can be placed aside, as I want to read the scene for its formal elements, beginning with the following observations. First, the creators were very serious about reconstructing the sets so as to reproduce the same visuals and aesthetics of the pilot, shot more than six years before. Thus, toward the end of the scene, as the press conference breaks up, Alicia and Peter move into a white-brick back hallway (apparently leading underground or to the parking garage); the pilot hallway was distinctively marked by bright red heating and water pipes in the ceiling, which stood out against the stark white bricks. The finale hallway seeks to replicate the industrial white bricks, but it is forced to substitute white cinder blocks (where the pilot had actual bricks). Further, the finale hallway lacks the red-painted pipework of the pilot, and the lower ceiling makes them impossible to add. So the set-makers instead placed red pipes as faux gates or "frames" in the hallway at regular intervals: each frame is three pipes, two running from floor to ceiling along the wall, and one that connects them by running along the ceiling. To be clear, these pipes connect to nothing; close inspection shows they serve no structural function and were almost certainly added to complete the set's overall look, which does indeed effectively resonate with, if not quite replicate, the original pilot hallway. The pipes serve no real purpose beyond aesthetic repetition, but they provide strong evidence for the significance of seriality to the setup and structure of the series finale.

More prominent, and more formally significant than the many details involved to make the finale scene the same as the pilot, are the elements that were specifically chosen to be *different*. The first such difference that matters for my analysis can be located in the framing. The pilot uses a specific framing of shots of Peter and Alicia in order to emphasize the structural location of "the good wife"; hence, when the camera first captures Peter at the podium he fills the main frame almost entirely and he appears in crisp focus; Alicia, in contrast, is pushed as far to the margins of the frame as possible (a shot possible only in widescreen format), and she remains out of focus – a blurry image at the edge of the frame, almost unintelligible as "Alicia Florrick" but still distinctly visible as "the good wife." The framing of the finale contrasts markedly with this *mise-en-scène*; in it, the center of the frame itself remains empty (even more impossible in an earlier age of 4:3 aspect ratios). Neither Peter nor Alicia anchors the frame; each of them is pushed to the edge, where they balance one another, with both in clear focus. Further, in the pilot, Alicia only centers the frame when she is on the "second screen" – that is, when we see her image on the monitor of the camera that is itself shooting the press conference (arguably she only appears in focus *as* "the good wife"). But in the finale Alicia fills the main frame, as the camera loses interest in Peter and lingers on Alicia.

The most important difference emerges in the very opening frames of the finale scene (and thus in the opening frames of the episode); here we see repetition with a difference, where the difference is distinctively and indelibly marked, underlined. As they enter the press conference, Peter and Alicia have switched sides relative to the pilot, with her now on his left. Given the attention to detail in recreating the scene, we might already guess that such a change was not accidental, but the evidence is more than conjectural. Indeed, it would seem that the choice to switch sides was explicit, and that it was made after the scene was shot. This choice was made not in the script or the original shooting, but in editing: Peter clasps Alicia's right hand in his left, but on her hand we see (quite prominently) a wedding ring. Clearly the shot was flipped after the fact, since Alicia has her ring on her left hand throughout the episode (and throughout the series), including immediately before this hallway scene, and immediately after.[18] Indeed, we can see strong evidence here for repetition with a difference: they[19] reshoot the original opening scene not for the purpose of nostalgic repetition but to make visible the transformation from beginning to end – to capture and to symbolize Alicia's altered relationship to the subject position of "the good wife."[20]

I call out this scene for its fabulous example of seriality and intentional framing (and reframing) (cf. Leonard 2014). It shows that a certain kind of specific, carefully planned repetition lies at the heart of the show. The work done by this opening scene of the finale thereby calls to mind Butler's claims about the political potential of seriality, whereby repetition with a difference can produce a challenge to, or subversion of, norms that are usually sustained through silent (undifferentiated) repetition. To develop this last point, I turn to the episode that I read as the ultimate climax of the storyline of the show, and it is an untimely climax since it appears four episodes *prior* to the series finale. Yet, in another untimely move, the repetition that marks the finale proves crucial to my overall reading, just as the seriality of the show does on a more general level: the conditions of the very prominent and self-conscious seriality of the show provide the structural groundwork for what I read as the climax of the show's narrative arc. In other words, the seriality witnessed here, the self-conscious seriality of a show that already embodies a heightened serial form, helps to draw to light and make sense of the cultural politics of the show.

"This is me not caring" – resistance to gender and sexual normativity

As I noted above, *TGW*'s ending took on a larger cultural significance because it was such a prominent, critically well-regarded, high-ratings primetime network drama, in an age in which all of those things appear to be disappearing for good. And it seems clear from the opening episodes of the seventh and final season that the show's writers, creators, and producers were self-aware about the uniqueness of bringing the show to a close. These facts help to explain the odd and interesting turns taken by the show throughout the last season. The opening episodes of Season 7 mark a sort of return to beginnings, both in the sense of having Alicia "start over" and to the extent that the show itself returns to its roots in addressing the relationship between Alicia and "the good wife." Hence the season opens by forcing Alicia to begin again, serving as a lowest-rung lawyer in bond court, while trying to start up her own firm – operating out of her apartment. Breaking from the large corporate firm while stripping away Alicia's status as named partner breathes new air into the show and gives it a new perspective. This altered vision runs the gamut from a very serious look at the plight of those ignored and destroyed by the American criminal justice system all the way to a very playful series of jabs at the status of American millennials.[21]

Season 7 of *TGW* also returns the show to its original context. And by re-making the constituent components of the show at the beginning of the final season the creators of the series are able to devote the last half of the season, particularly the last five episodes, to bringing to conclusion the entire seven-season story arc. In particular, the final five episodes explore the premise and meaning of the show itself: they return directly and with even more focus to the question of the gap that separates, and the ties that link, Alicia Florrick to the subject position of "the good wife." And in the context of concluding the series, these episodes engage with concretely, and explore in some complexity, the subtle relations between norms and normativity – and the question of how or whether to oppose normalizing forces.

I focus my analysis on episode 18 of the final season. Its opening scene brings a certain closure to a key storyline of the entire season: Alicia's flirtation and potential romantic relationship with her investigator – frequently referred to on the show by subject position as "the investigator" – Jason Crouse. The season has recurrently raised and deferred the question of "will they or won't they," and it finally answers that question with the opening shot of this episode: Alicia and Jason in bed, her feet at his head, his at hers, barely covered by a single twisted sheet, and bathed in early dawn light. The shot, framed from above the bed, could not scream "post coitus" more loudly, even if it came with a title. Alicia soon departs for a morning court date, but she insists that Jason stay in her apartment. Her words underscore a subtle series of changes that have been ongoing during the season: the transformation of the Chicago apartment from a space of home and family, where Alicia raised her two children as the good wife, to a place of work, to the private property of Alicia, the individual. Zach, Alicia's oldest, has been off at college and thus absent from the apartment, while Grace, Alicia's youngest, has mainly appeared in the space not as the daughter but as the temporary employee of Alicia, within her new startup law firm. So when Alicia tells Jason, "don't get up, I want to picture you in my bed, all day," she completes this reterritorialization of space.

And she simultaneously also sets up the conflict that drives the episode, since Jason does stay home but only minutes after her departure, Alicia's husband, Peter, lets himself into the apartment to find Jason, in his boxer shorts, coffee mug in hand, coming out of the bedroom. Their exchange – a series of tacit and sometimes explicit expressions of escalating masculinity – is predictable, but Peter's language is telling for the way the scene stages the broader set of structural conflicts, specifically naming subject positions.

PETER: "Is my wife here?"
JASON: "She's in court."
PETER: "You're her investigator?"
JASON: "Yeah."
PETER: [taking one strong step forward, and violently slapping the coffee mug out of Jason's hands] "*We are still married.*"

It is hard to imagine a starker expression of the role of subject positions, because each line from Peter amounts to little more than a reference to these discursive relations: where is *my wife*? … you are *her investigator*? … we are *still married*! Peter's words and actions coalesce into the ultimate expression of the patriarchal claim to the home. But when Peter goes so far as to threaten Jason with real violence, "I should kick your ass," Jason's answer undoes him precisely by revealing the meaninglessness of such violence, "You could try. And then what?" Peter has absolutely no response, since he knows that, ultimately, the husband–wife relation that he has been trying vainly to call on and defend – that relation is itself empty. In this moment, Peter himself is "unmanned" – the title of this episode – in the exact sense that he is "de-husbanded." He has not really been Alicia's husband for quite some time, and the pain of seeing the tangled sheets on the bed is matched and reinforced by the pain of realizing he has no real claim to make as a husband. But Jason does not necessarily know all of this, which explains why, after getting dressed and leaving Alicia's apartment, he ignores her phone calls. Finally Alicia confronts him in person, and Jason explains, again in telling language: "your *husband* came *home* yesterday morning" (my emphasis). Is Peter still Alicia's husband? Is it still his home? Is she still the wife?

Alicia's brief conversation with Jason, along with the delivery of the news of his and Peter's confrontation, triggers Alicia's most pointed, performative, and politically significant act. Despite coming in the middle of the 18th episode of the 22-episode final season, it leads to what I read as the truly climactic scene of the entire series, *TGW*. Alicia marches out of her firm's conference room and strides down the hall with confidence and anger. Given the powers of video editing and the compression of time and space made possible by televisual narrative, it appears as if Alicia walks *directly* from her firm's hallways into the hallways of the governor's office, where, without breaking stride, she interrupts a meeting Peter is having in his office. She throws open the double doors, takes two more decisive strides into the office, and stops. She then, Jed Bartlett style – and in another likely homage to Sorkin's famous "Two Cathedrals" season finale – puts both hands into the pockets of her coat and stares commandingly at Peter. From across the room Peter, flustered, tells her he is busy, but she simply continues to stare. When he then crosses the room for what he hopes will be a quick and quiet conversation, she wastes no time delivering, in palpably measured tone, the decisive line: "I want a divorce."[22]

Thanks to the effects produced by streaming a show (without commercials) that was originally aired on network TV (with commercials), the crucial line is repeated by Alicia with the only pause being a very brief cut to black (the space where the commercial had once been). Thus begins the decisive (yet utterly lopsided) battle between the once-married couple, as Peter tries a series of techniques designed to deflect the full force and implications of the line. First, he asks what's wrong, as if he could merely console her (i.e., "the good wife") in order to undo her decision. But Alicia easily parries; with a lightness in her voice she says, "nothing's wrong," before repeating, "I want a divorce." Then Peter tries to play the I'm-the-governor-card, saying dismissively, while turning to rejoin his meeting, "yeah, well, I'm in the middle of something," and Alicia again outdoes him by mimicking his move and bettering him at it. Lightening her tone even further, while *she turns* to leave the room, she says, "OK, you take care of that; I'll have my lawyer call you."[23] Now Peter begins to panic, follows her out of the room, and turns to anger as his next tactic: "this is about your investigator, isn't it?" Alicia matches his bluster with icy sarcasm, "yes, I would never think of divorcing you unless I had some other man to call my own." Peter looks around nervously, realizing he is losing every round of this bout and that it is happening in full view of everyone. He pulls her into a side office, slams the door, and figuratively drops the gloves, while Alicia literally rolls her eyes and *licks her lips*, truly spoiling for the fight:

> PETER: "I saw him yesterday, walking around in his boxer shorts, like he owned the place."
>
> ALICIA: "Yes. Because *I own the place*, and I told him he was welcome to walk around naked if he wants."
>
> PETER: "And Grace? [Alicia raises her eyebrows questioningly] Oh, you don't give a damn about your daughter."
>
> ALICIA: [laughing and scoffing and bitingly sarcastic] "Yes, I'm an unfit mother. In the divorce you can get full custody for the three weeks before she goes to college."
>
> PETER: [trying out his own sarcasm] "Well this must be true love. ... Again."
>
> ALICIA: [with a look of real pity] "Is that what would upset you most? If I was in love?"
>
> PETER: "What upsets me the most is that you're shoving it in my face."
>
> ALICIA: "I'm not shoving anything. *This is me not caring*. Not caring what people think; what Eli thinks; you think."
>
> PETER: "Or what the FBI thinks. You know I'm about to be indicted, don't you?"
>
> ALICIA: "Peter you're always being indicted. If it weren't today it would be tomorrow. I'll have my lawyer call."

As Alicia opens the door to leave, Peter yells "thanks" loudly for those in the hall to hear. He then slumps down into the small love seat, and the final shot of the scene captures Peter with his hand over his face, eyes staring into the distance. I read it as the tableau of Peter *unmanned,* to again echo the title of the episode; he has been genuinely defeated by Alicia and whoever he now is, he can no longer be the husband and politician with the "good wife" at his side. She's gone.[24] The final frame of the scene thus portrays Peter with the back of his hand across his mouth, staring into the distance – an almost stereotypical *feminine* posture.[25]

This scene demands to be interpreted on multiple levels, since it proves both dense with meaning and complexly multivalent. On the first level it seems straightforwardly obvious that Alicia's thrice-repeated declaration "I want a divorce" functions as a performative speech act; the *announcement* of the desire for and choice of divorce *itself effects* the rejection of the subject position "the good wife." One cannot *want* a divorce and *be* the good wife; put differently, whoever speaks that line is, by definition, not the good wife. This speech act constitutes the climax of the scene, the episode, the season, and the series, because it finally cuts the tether that binds Alicia Florrick to the subject position "the good wife." The dialectic tension that has driven the show for over 150 episodes is now undone, as Alicia has finally decided what she wants, "I want a divorce," and hence who she is – or, at least, who she is *not*. Alicia is not the good wife.

Crucially, however, neither the scene nor the playing out of the relationship between concrete individual and general subject position should or can be reduced to a "choice" that any individual would make. One does not merely *choose* subject positions, and we see this forcefully and repeatedly over the course of the show. Alicia does not have limitless options; she is continually faced with either acting in and as "the good wife," with all the ways in which that subject position enables and constrains her agency, or rejecting or resisting that subject position and thereby facing an uncertain future. Hence, even more important than the performative act, "I want a divorce" is the context for its performance, including the overall scene, the history that leads up to it, and most of all the tone and body language that accompany its delivery. In other words, more significant than Alicia's overt rejection of "the good wife" subject position is the manner in which she rejects it. Alicia's measured calmness throughout the scene – compared, for example, with the barely controllable emotions of the opening scene from the pilot – consistently indicates that Alicia has already thrown off the title "St. Alicia," a title bestowed only upon a subject who is "the good wife." She not only *declares* that she is not the good wife; she *performs* it.

Moreover, her nonverbal cues and her tone and larger affect all serve as a critique of the normativity of "the good wife." All seven seasons of *TGW* attest to the fundamental fact that norms cannot be directly rejected or simply opposed. Yet ultimately Alicia does more than refuse to be "the good wife"; she offers critical resistance to the *normative force* of this subject position. Hence the magnitude, in the climactic scene, of Alicia's sarcasm, of her gay tone, of her mockery – mockery not just of Peter but of "the husband" and therefore of "the good wife." As I have already shown, the scene stages a battle between Peter and Alicia, but it also enacts a critique of the normative force of "the good wife" subject position, as Alicia does more than defeat Peter; she challenges the normalizing force of that enunciative modality.

This second level of critique can be specified, played out, and analyzed at the transition point in their dialogue, the turn from Alicia's claim of propriety and rejection of the household as a family space controlled by the father figure – "I own the place" – to her responses to Peter's attempt to reposition Alicia in a different subject position. When Peter mocks Alicia with the notion of "true love," he is suggesting the frivolity of abandoning her position as powerful wife of the governor only to become, one must imagine, the "girlfriend" or "new wife" of a lowly "investigator." This very attack by Peter provides the opening for Alicia to challenge the larger normative edifice – not only to refuse "the good wife" for herself but also to call into question the normativity of that subject position. This interpretation explains why she looks at Peter with such genuine sadness and *pity*, when she says to him, "Is that what would upset you most? If I was in love?" Peter can only imagine that Alicia would reject her role as wife by reducing her to the naïf who has found "true love." And when Peter says, "again," he refers obliquely but no less forcefully to the sometimes-storybook romance that never really was between Alicia and her once-law-school friend and then boss, Will Gardner. Alicia's pitying response reflects the deep and incisive extent to which she both rejects the subject position of "wife" – doing so soberly, on its own merits – and also refuses the normative and normalizing power of that subject position. The grammar of her response proves absolutely crucial; she says, "if I *was* in love, not if I *were*." The simple past tense conditional "if I was" refuses the future-oriented hypothetical – the *wishful* mood – of the subjunctive ("if I were"). Put differently, Alicia is both refusing the notion that she is divorcing Peter because she is now in love and also rejecting the interpellation of her as someone acting on the basis of a future in which she will one day be in love (see Orgad 2017). The conclusion of their dialogue drives home and underlines this point: when the question of Peter's possible indictment comes up, Alicia *does* use the subjunctive, does imagine a future in which of course Peter will be indicted – "if it *weren't* today it would be tomorrow." Alicia can easily imagine Peter's future criminal indictments, but her rejection of "the good wife" is itself an indictment of the normative force, of the normalizing ideal, of that subject position.

We might call this an "antinormative" force mobilized by the scene, in the very specific sense that it resists or seeks to subvert the *normative and normalizing force* of the subject position "the good wife" as itself a norm of gender, sexuality,[26] and family. In other words, this antinormative force does not reject all norms or presume to evade their territorializing power; rather, it engages with the concrete norms of gender and sexuality and operationalizes a resistance to their hegemony (Chambers 2017; cf. Wiegman and Wilson 2015). Such a specific and circumscribed sense of antinormativity comes through even more strikingly when we look carefully at Peter's penultimate attack combined with Alicia's counter. Peter has already used his seemingly most potent weapon – Alicia being in love – and it missed the mark entirely, so he tries to call on the force of norms of decency, decorum, propriety. Peter: "what upsets me the most is that you're shoving it in my face." Peter's claim here directly and decisively echoes decades of complaints against numerous forms of queer sexuality. Indeed, this sort of statement has long been the go-to line for those who wished to criticize queerness but without appearing openly intolerant or phobic; the idea that gay, lesbian, transgender, and other queer people were "shoving *it*" (their sexuality) in "*our*" (presumptively straight) faces is so commonplace as to be unremarkable. But it is above all a normative and normalizing argument, and it has always been an argument that depends for its critical force upon heteronormativity, and especially upon the unmarked and naturalized nature of heteronormativity. Gay people who declare their sexuality are said to be "shoving it in our faces" only because everyone is presumed to be straight (thanks to the normative force of heterosexuality when it is mobilized, shored up, and enforced by societal traditions, customs, procedures, and laws) (Chambers 2003a; Chambers 2005).

When Peter accuses Alicia of shoving it in his face, he is therefore attempting to call upon the force of normative sexuality to stigmatize her, to render her choices and actions queer. Her response is therefore crucial, because Peter's stigmatizing move gives her the option to claim normality (to claim propriety and decorum), to maintain her status as a proper, *normal*, liberal subject. She opts instead for a more radical queer critique of the normal; she makes an *antinormative* move in the sense described above. First, she takes the wind out of Peter's claim, by saying breezily, "I'm not shoving anything." This simple phrase serves to defuse and undermine the critical claim by showing how empty it is in the first place: those accused of "shoving it in our faces" are usually either just acting the same way straight people do (holding hands or being affectionate in public), or they are explicitly identifying their sexuality – that is, by coming out – only in order to undo the *false assumptions* of the straight world around them. Notice as well how Peter's claim is not just empty in general but utterly false in his particular instance: Alicia shoved nothing in his face; Peter entered her home uninvited, and only at that point did he come face to face with the evidence of her recent sexual behavior.

The *pièce de résistance*, the ultimate subversion of the normative, comes in Alicia's next line: "*this is me not caring.*" One of the most powerful ways of subverting the effort at enforcing a norm is to refuse to recognize its very normative force. Alicia's most potent critique of the normativity of the subject position "good wife" comes not from her deviation from the role that the subject position imposed upon her but from her "not caring" about that very deviation. Her line here resonates with a famous line of Foucault's, where he says that what the straight world may find most disturbing about gay people is not their so-called "deviant" sex acts but the sheer fact of their intimacy and friendship (Foucault 2000; Foucault 2011). Put differently, it is easy to preserve the normative force of heterosexuality by understanding non-heterosexual acts as the thrillingly forbidden margins of the hetero norm, but to see same-sex intimacy, friendship, and love in the everyday – as themselves a part of a new "normal" – *that* would be terribly disturbing and threatening. Translated into language appropriate for the context of *TGW*, we can see that even though it takes the form of violation and indiscretion, marital infidelity is easily assimilable to the normative role of "the good wife." But the idea that Alicia *does not care – that* fact shakes the very foundations of the normative edifice.

For these reasons, the dramatic climax of *TGW* combines a widening of the gap between individual and subject position (indeed, an ultimate refusal of the subject position) with a resistance to and critique of the normativizing and normalizing hegemony of that position. In this way *TGW* explores the distribution of roles, that is, reveals the existence of norms, while also, distinctly but relatedly, offering an antinormative account. There is thus a sometimes latent, but in the end explicit, feminist, and queer politics to the series. Crucially, such a politics depends upon the specific serial form of television, particularly network television. The development of character over seven years and 156 episodes, the consistency of story, and the agonistic negotiation of the relation between individual and subject position would not be possible without this serial form.

Notes

1 Here I closely follow the approach, as described by Ariane Hudelet, that animates the *TV/SERIES* journal: to study television not as an example or reflection of something else but in its own right – which for me means as a cultural artifact as well as a work of art.

2 Elsewhere I argue that such dynamic and active resistance to and subversion of norms must not be confused with the idea of staking out a so-called "antinormative" *position* (Chambers 2017; see Halberstam 2015; cf. Wiegman and Wilson 2015).

3 The structural economic conditions that have given rise to this phenomenon have also given rise to its opposite: the funding, production, and immediate release of a series, available in its entirety, on streaming services such as Netflix, Hulu, or Amazon Video.

4 As discussed below, streaming alters, reverses, or simply disrupts entirely a trend such as this one. Thus we get shows with utterly abstract and non-specific titles, such as Netflix's *Love*, and we see shows change names entirely, such as with UK Channel 4's *Scrotal Recall* reappearing as *Lovesick* on Netflix.

5 The director of *TGW*'s first two episodes, Charles McDougal, clearly had in mind an Aaron Sorkin feel for the show: not only do these office scenes directly

draw from the Schlamme-Sorkin signature made famous in *The West Wing*, but the powerful opening scene also alludes (with its behind-the-shoulders and into-the-lights shot) to the famous Schlamme-directed, Sorkin-written, Season 2 finale, "Two Cathedrals," which closes with President Josiah Bartlet in front of the cameras at a climactic press conference.

6 For example, Ernesto Laclau and Chantal Mouffe write, "our position is clear. Whenever we use the category of 'subject' in this text, we will do so in the sense of 'subject positions' within a discursive structure. Subjects cannot, therefore, be the origin of social relations – not even in the limited sense of being endowed with powers that render an experience possible – as all 'experience' depends on precise discursive conditions of possibility" (Laclau and Mouffe 1985, 115).

7 Of course this is actually a *second* screen, since it appears *within* the screen that we, the viewers, are already watching.

8 In contrast with a material or technological determinism that could be said to deny any significance to human thought or action (thus robbing individuals of agency), linguistic idealism and linguistic monism (mentioned in the text, below) both attribute to language, to speech, or to words, a powerful, vital force. On the one hand, this move overturns structuralism by centering meaning and significance on humans. On the other hand, by making language the true site of agency, linguistic idealism can also – in its own distinct way – be understood as determinist. Hence the desire to emphasize human action can ironically produce a (different sort of) determinist account. On a better reading, Foucault teaches us that the only way to hang on to a meaningful concept of human agency is to see that agency as always embedded within the context of discursive relations.

9 For just one formative example of this type of reading, see the enormously influential work of Dreyfus and Rabinow, who argue that Foucault's anti-Kantian project in the *Archaeology* only winds up replicating Kantian idealism (Dreyfus and Rabinow 1982, 99).

10 There has been a tendency in the popular press to describe this latest "golden age" of television in rather narrow terms as television becoming more "cinematic" or "novelistic." Scholars working on television rightly bristle at this reductivism. Television is doubtless a unique work of art, which calls for its own unique analysis (and hence distinct analytic skills), but uniqueness does not preclude *comparison*. The central point is taken as given in a field like art history, where scholars frequently describe Michelangelo's paintings as "sculptural" and where the concept of "transmediality" proves central to art historical analysis. More pointedly, crucial work has already been done in television by way of comparisons to other art forms: Rhonda Wilcox's now-canonized book on *Buffy* centers on the comparison of *Buffy* to great literature, specifically Melville (Wilcox 2005). And a productive debate has been staged over the extent to which it makes sense to compare *The Wire* to a Victorian novel (DeLyria and Robinson 2011; Scott 2011; Berlatsky 2012; Miller 2012). Returning to my specific point in the text: the recent material transformations in the production and distribution of television have changed it in important ways, and certain (limited) comparisons can help us make sense of those changes. *Breaking Bad*'s long, 16x9 widescreen shots of the New Mexico desert demand to be understood in relation to cinema (a comparative understanding that is not equivalent to reduction). Netflix's *Love* is surely more like a long movie than *TGW*, which is itself much less episodic than *Dragnet* (Mittell 2015).

11 For the record, it was Newton Minow, the chair of the US Federal Communications Committee (FCC) under President Kennedy, who called television a "vast wasteland." *But he did so in 1961.* Thompson cites Minow in order to show how the first "golden age" of television was itself selectively constructed

(partially through accounts of its demise), while himself making the case that a second "golden age" had begun in the 1980s. To be clear, then, contrary to Nygaard and Lagerwey the "vast wasteland" description was neither used by Thompson nor applied (by Minow) to the period from the 1950s to 1999 (Thompson 1996, 25).

12 David Chase made a profound contribution to the *second* "golden age" (with *Northern Exposure*) before he ran the show (*The Sopranos*) that has defined the beginning of the third.

13 Three of these shows have male creators, but I would resist the idea of reducing the potential feminism of a show to the sex of its creator. None of these shows are male-centric and all of them explore complex norms of gender and sexuality. I am also pointing here not just to a set of shows, but to a rich body of literature on those shows, one which consistently cuts against the narrow construction of quality television. As a shorthand here, one could point simply to the lifelong work of David Lavery, for example (Lavery 1994, 2002, 2006; Lavery and Byers 2007).

14 And, indeed, the series finale "End" clearly takes many of its cues from David Chase's (in)famous series finale to the *Sopranos* – ending not with closure but with ambiguity and pregnant futures.

15 Commercials are an essential element in network television seriality, since they routinize and normalize the viewing of 40 minutes of content over a 60-minute period. This routine was first disrupted by the VCR, when viewers used it to develop techniques to "time shift" – a term that sounds like it came out of science fiction – by recording all their shows and watching them both *when* they wanted and *how* they wanted. The latter element means that viewers could skip commercials, and also that they could "binge watch" – a term popularized in the new age of television streaming but a practice that was possible (with a little bit of prior self-denial) long before then.

16 Josh Charles's departure was perhaps the most seismic shift in the show's fictional universe, and its cause obviously lay outside the show itself.

17 On the surface the point seems banal, but it matters a great deal that the culmination of the series was planned in advance, rather than emerging abruptly.

18 Thanks to Rebecca Brown who gets all credit for initially spotting the wedding ring continuity error.

19 With my use of "they" in the text above, and throughout this chapter in my references to choices, intentions, and motivations, I call upon Jason Mittell's excellent theoretical and methodological work with the concept of the "inferred author" (Mittell 2015, 107). Mittell develops this concept out of his own reading of the film studies debate, between Seymour Chatman (1990) and David Bordwell (1985), over the notion of the "implied author," which itself draws from a long tradition of earlier literary theory that had called into question the idea of a governing intentional author – and either decentered that figure entirely (Barthes 1978) or replaced it with the "author function" (Foucault 1984). This is obviously not the space to take up the threads of this dense and complex historical and theoretical debate; rather, I point to Mittell's work as a shorthand methodological explanation for my focus on the *work* that the *text* of the television series accomplishes, rather than analyzing the details of the choices and actions of writers, directors, actors, and producers. There may be an "author" of this text, but it is not any particular producer or director, and to the extent that it even approximates singularity this is because of the work of the reception of the show. To say this is not in any way to deny the monumental importance of the efforts and achievements of the hundreds upon hundreds of individuals that contribute to the creation of the show, and it is certainly not

a refusal to give "credit" to specific writers, producers, directors, or showrunners. However, it is already the job of the Hollywood Foreign Press Association to give out Golden Globes; it is already the job of the Academy of Television Arts & Sciences to give out Emmys; and *TGW* has won *lots* of both, along with a whole host of other accolades from other bodies. It should be the job of the scholar of television to analyze the work as a whole, to do what Mittell says historical poetics does in grasping "innovations" or subversions, "not as creative breakthroughs by visionary artists but at the nexus of numerous historical forces that work to transform norms and possibilities" (Mittell 2015, 5).

20 One other structural difference that I do not analyze here: unlike the pilot scene, the first part of the press conference drops the non-diegetic sound, and for the last half it substitutes vocal popular music for the orchestral strings of the pilot.

21 The associate Diane "mentors" is the starkest example (S07S03), but there are a number of others, including Alicia's own dealings with a millennial who says all the right things, but simply cannot do the job (S07E02)

22 The scene's power also depends upon creative use of non-diegetic sound. As Alicia travels virtually from her conference room to the Governor's office, the theme-based soundtrack of simple orchestral strings marches her along. This is more than simply choosing the right accompaniment for the scene, however: the strings are syncopated with the dialogue, with notes appearing in between Peter's lines "what's going on?" and "Alicia?" so as to dramatically raise the anticipation of the line that Alicia will deliver in response, "I want a divorce."

23 For much more on Alicia's "cagey responses" and also on the power of her silence, see Leonard 2014.

24 Of course, the season itself defers any such climactic conclusions, not just to, but in a way beyond, the season finale that arrives four episodes later. With a criminal indictment truly imminent, Peter asks Alicia to *play* the role of the good wife, to stand by him one more time. And she does so, both throughout his trial, and also at his final press conference when he announces his resignation of the governorship and decision to plead guilty to corruption charges. My reading of episode 18 as the climax therefore renders all the rest as denouement. But really this is not a radical reading and it requires no interpretive stretching, since nothing that happens in those final episodes serves to challenge the reading I give of "Unmanned," and the pivotal significance of Alicia's decision – and announcement thereof – to divorce Peter.

25 Sincere thanks to Monica Michlin for this observation.

26 Notice that the subject position "the good wife" is always already a straight subject; the subject position is therefore decisively situated not only with respect to gender and the family (a "good wife" is a particular kind of woman and mother) but also with respect to sexuality (a "good wife" is not gay and is not queer).

Works cited

Austin, J. L. *How to Do Things with Words*. Cambridge, MA: Harvard University Press, 1962.

Barthes, Roland. "The Death of the Author". In *Image-Music-Text*. Translated by Stephen Heath. New York: Hill and Wang, 1978. 142–148.

Berlatsky, Noah. "*The Wire* Was Really a Victorian Novel". *The Atlantic*, 09.10.2012. https://www.theatlantic.com/entertainment/archive/2012/09/the-wire-was-really-a-victorian-novel/261164/ (accessed 01.24.2019).

Bordwell, David. *Narration in the Fiction Film.* Madison: University of Wisconsin Press, 1985.

Bowman, Paul. "Alterdisciplinarity". *Culture, Theory and Critique* 49.1, 2008. 93–110.

Brunsdon, Charlotte, and Lynn Spigel, eds. *Feminist Television Criticism.* Maidenhead: Open University Press, 2008.

Butler, Judith. *Gender Trouble: Feminism and the Subversion of Identity.* London: Routledge, 1999.

Canguilhem, Georges. *The Normal and the Pathological.* New York: Zone Books, 1989.

Chambers, Samuel. "Language and Politics: Agonistic Discourse and The West Wing". *CTheory*, 11.12.2001. http://www.ctheory.net/articles.aspx?id=317 (accessed 06.24.2020).

Chambers, Samuel. "Telepistemology of the Closet; Or, the Queer Politics of *Six Feet Under*". *Journal of American Culture* 26.1, 2003a. 24–41.

Chambers, Samuel. "Dialogue, Deliberation, and Discourse: The Far-reaching Politics of *The West Wing*". In Peter Rollins and John O'Connor (eds.), *The West Wing: The American Presidency as Television Drama*, Syracuse: Syracuse University Press, 2003b. 83–100.

Chambers, Samuel. "Revisiting the Closet: Reading Sexuality in *Six Feet Under*". In Janet McCabe and Kim Akass (eds.), *Reading* Six Feet Under: *TV to Die For.* London: IB Tauris, 2005. 174–190.

Chambers, Samuel. "Desperately Straight: The Subversive Sexual Politics of *Desperate Housewives*". In Janet McCabe and Kim Akass (eds.), *Reading* Desperate Housewives: *Beyond the White Picket Fence*, London: IB Tauris, 2006a. 61–73.

Chambers, Samuel. "Heteronormativity and *The L Word*: From a Politics of Representation to a Politics of Norms". In Sarah Warn (ed.), *Reading The L Word: Outing Contemporary Television.* London: IB Tauris, 2006b. 81–98.

Chambers, Samuel. *The Queer Politics of Television.* London: IB Tauris, 2009.

Chambers, Samuel. *The Lessons of Rancière.* New York: Oxford University Press, 2013.

Chambers, Samuel. "On Norms and Opposition." *No Foundations: An Interdisciplinary Journal of Law and Justice*, 14, 2017. http://www.nofoundations.com/issues/NoFo14_Chambers.pdf (accessed 06.20.2020)

Chambers, Samuel, and Anne Caldwell. "*24* after 9/11: The American State of Exception". In Steven Peacock (ed.), *Reading* 24: *TV Against the Clock.* London: IB Tauris, 2007. 97–108.

Chambers, Samuel, and Patrick Finn. "Digital Democracy: When Culture Becomes News". *CTheory*, 14, 11.12.2001. https://journals.uvic.ca/index.php/ctheory/article/view/14589 (accessed 06.20.2020)

Chambers, Samuel, and Daniel Williford. "Anti-imperialism in the Buffyverse: A Challenge to the Mythos of Bush as Vampire-Slayer". *Poroi*, 3.2, 2004. https://ir.uiowa.edu/cgi/viewcontent.cgi?article=1040&context=poroi (accessed 06.20.2020)

Chatman, Seymour. *Coming to Terms: The Rhetoric of Narrative in Fiction and Film.* Ithaca, NY: Cornell University Press, 1990.

Delyria, Joy, and Sean Robinson. "'When It's Not Your Turn': The Quintessentially Victorian Vision of Ogden's *The Wire*". *The Hooded Utilitarian*, 03.23.2011.

http://www.hoodedutilitarian.com/2011/03/when-its-not-your-turn-the-quintessentially-victorian-vision-of-ogdens-the-wire/ (accessed 01.24.2019).

Ewald, François. "Norms, Discipline, and the Law". *Representations* 30, 1990. 138–161.

Foucault, Michel. *The Order of Things: An Archaeology of the Human Sciences.* New York: Pantheon Books, 1970.

Foucault, Michel. *Archaeology of Knowledge.* Translated by Alan Sheridan Smith. New York: Pantheon Books, 1972.

Foucault, Michel. *The Birth of the Clinic.* Translated by Alan Sheridan Smith New York: Pantheon Books, 1973.

Foucault, Michel. "What Is an Author?". In *The Foucault Reader.* Translated by Josué V. Harari. New York: Pantheon Books, 1984. 101–120.

Foucault, Michel. "Friendship as a Way of Life". In Paul Rabinow (ed.), *The Essential Works of Michel Foucault, 1954–1984. Subjectivity and Truth Vol. 1,* London: Penguin, 2000. 135–140.

Foucault, Michel. *History of Madness.* Translated by Jonathan Murphy and Jean Khalfa. London: Routledge, 2009.

Foucault, Michel. "The Gay Science". *Critical Inquiry* 37.3, 2011. 385–403.

Goldblatt, Henry. "The Good Wife: EW Series Review". *Entertainment Weekly,* 05.05.2016. https://ew.com/article/2016/05/05/the-good-wife-series-review/ (accessed 06.20.2020)

Halberstam, Jack. "Straight Eye for the Queer Theorist". 2015. https://bullybloggers.wordpress.com/2015/09/12/straight-eye-for-the-queer-theorist-a-review-of-queer-theory-without-antinormativity-by-jack-halberstam/ (accessed 01.24.2019).

Hargraves, Hunter. "To Trust in Strange Habits and Last Calls: *The Good Wife*'s Smartphone Storytelling". *Feminist Media Studies* 14.6, 2017. 115–130.

Jensen, Jeff. "*The Good Wife* Series Finale: EW Review". *Entertainment Weekly,* 05.09.2016.

Johnson, Merri, ed. *Third Wave Feminism and Television: Jane Puts It in Box.* London: IB Tauris, 2007.

Laclau, Ernesto, and Chantal Mouffe. *Hegemony and Socialist Strategy: Towards a Radical Democratic Politics.* London: Verso, 1985.

Lavery, David, ed. *Full of Secrets: Critical Approaches to* Twin Peaks. Detroit, MI: Wayne State University Press, 1994.

Lavery, David, ed. *This Thing of Ours: Investigating* The Sopranos. New York: Columbia University Press, 2002.

Lavery, David, ed. *Reading* Deadwood: *A Western to Swear By.* London: IB Tauris, 2006.

Lavery, David, and Michele Byers, eds. *Dear Angela: Remembering* My So-Called Life. Lexington, KY: Lexington Books, 2007.

Leonard, Suzanne. "Sexuality, Technology, and Sexual Scandal in The Good Wife". *Feminist Media Studies* 14.6, 2014. 944–958.

Leonard, Suzanne. "I May Need You, Peter, but You Sure as Hell Need Me Too": Political Marriages in *The Good Wife* and Beyond". *Television & New Media* 18.2, 2017. 131–146.

McCabe, Janet, and Kim Akass. *Quality TV: Contemporary American Television and Beyond.* London: IB Tauris, 2007.

Miller, Laura. "*The Wire* Is NOT like Dickens". *Salon*. 09.12.2012. https://www.salon.com/2012/09/13/the_wire_is_not_like_dickens/ (accessed 01.24.2019).

Miller, Taylor. "The Fashion of Florrick and FLOTUS: On Feminism, Gender Politics, and 'Quality Television'". *Television & New Media*18.2, 2017. 147–164.

Mittell, Jason. *Complex TV: The Poetics of Contemporary Television Storytelling.* New York: NY Press, 2015.

Nygaard, Taylor, and Jorie Lagerwey. "Broadcasting Quality: Re-centering Feminist Discourse with *The Good Wife*". *Television & New Media* 18.2, 2017. 105–113.

Orgad, Shani. "The Cruel Optimism of *The Good Wife*: The Fantastic Working Mother on the Fantastical Treadmill". *Television & New Media* 18.2, 2017. 165–183.

Petski, Denise. "*Gilmore Girls*' Amy Sherman-Palladino On 'A Year in The Life' Ending; Will There Be More?". 2016. http://deadline.com/2016/12/gilmore-girls-amy-sherman-palladino-a-year-in-the-life-ending-1201862975/ (accessed 01.24.2019).

Rancière, Jacques. *The Ignorant Schoolmaster: Five Lessons in Intellectual Emancipation.* Stanford, CA: Stanford University Press, 1991.

Scott, Cynthia. "HBO or TV: Or How *The Wire* Is Not a Novel." *popmatters*, 02.03.2011. http://www.popmatters.com/feature/133951-hbo-or-tv-or-how-the-wire-is-not-a-novel/ (accessed 01.24.2019).

Thompson, Robert. *Television's Second Golden Age: From* Hill Street Blues *to* ER. Syracuse, NY: Syracuse University Press, 1996.

Wiegman, Robyn, and Elizabeth Wilson. *Queer Theory without Antinormativity.* Durham, NC: Duke University Press, 2015.

Wilcox, Rhonda. *Why Buffy Matters: The Art of* Buffy the Vampire Slayer. London: IB Tauris, 2005.

Series and episodes cited

Breaking Bad. AMC, 2008–2013.

Buffy the Vampire Slayer. The WB, 1997–2001, UPN, 2001–2003.

Cagney and Lacey. CBS, 1982–1988.

Desperate Housewives. ABC, 2004–2012.

Dragnet. NBC, 1951–1959, 1967–1970.

The Gilmore Girls. The WB, 2000–2006, The CW, 2006–2007.

Gilmore Girls: A Year in the Life. Amy Sherman-Palladino and Daniel Palladino, Netflix, 2016.

The Godfather. Francis Ford Coppola, Paramount, 1972.

The Good Wife. CBS, 2009–2016.

"Pilot". *The Good Wife*, S01E01. 2009. Written by Robert King and Michelle King. Directed by Charles McDougal.

"Taxed". *The Good Wife*, S02E04. 2015. Written by Leonard Dick. Directed by Jim McKay.

"Bond". *The Good Wife*, S07E01. 2015. Written by Robert King and Michelle King. Directed by Brooke Kennedy.

"Innocents". *The Good Wife*, S07E02. 2015. Written by Craig Turk. Directed by Luke Schelhaas.

"Unmanned". *The Good Wife*, S07E18. 2016. Written by Tyler Bensinger. Directed by James Whitmore.

"End". *The Good Wife*, S07E22. 2016. Written by Robert King and Michelle King. Directed by Robert King.

The L Word. Showtime, 2004–2009.

Love. Netflix, 2016–2018.

Lovesick. Channel 4, 2014–2015, Netflix, 2015-.

Moonlighting. ABC, 1985–1989.

New Girl. Fox, 2011–2018.

Northern Exposure. CBS, 1990–1995.

Scrotal Recall. Channel 4, 2014–2015, Netflix, 2015-.

Sex and The City. HBO, 1998–2004.

Six Feet Under. HBO, 2001–2005.

The Sopranos. HBO, 1999–2007.

Speed. Jon de Bont, 20th C. Fox, 1994.

St. Elsewhere. NBC, 1982–1988.

Ugly Betty. ABC, 2006–2010.

The West Wing. NBC, 1999–2006.

The Wire. HBO, 2002–2008.

Index

Note: *Italic* page numbers refer to Films and series cites and page numbers followed by "n" denote endnotes.

ABC 10, *15, 52,* 92, *101–2,* 108, 141, 149, 156n6, *158, 176,* 177, 186–7, *195, 256–7*
Ace Drummond, 19–31, *36*
Achemchame, Julien, 190, 194
Action Comics, 22, 25–6, 32n6, 32n9, 33n13–15
adaptation, xi, xii, xiv, 19, 22, 31, 33n12, 70, 91, 103–4, 113, 132, 139, 141, 154, 156n2, 161–2, 173n9, 213, 219–20, 225, 230n1
Adorno, Theodor W. 4
Adventures of Superman, 26, 33n9
A&E 9, *15,* 141, 147, 154, *158,* 159, *176*
aesthetics, xi–xiii, 2–12, 22, 28, 33–4n15, 40, 45–6, 53, 57–8, 64–5, 66n4, 104–5, 108, 115–6, 119n4, 141–2, 147, 149–55, 174n18, 192, 200, 241
agency, 11, 111, 203, 233, 236, 247, 251n8
Akass, Kim 1–2, 55–6, 239
Alberse, Anita 2
Alfie (1966 film), 9, *15,* 122–8, *135*
Alfie (2004 film) 131–3, *135*
Alien (1979–2017 films) 1
Allen, Rob 19
Allied Artists 85, 92
Allrath, Gaby 2
Amazon 2, 6, 67, 250n3
AMC 8, *15, 52,* 54, 61, 65, *75–6, 158, 195, 256*
American Horror Story (FW series, 2011-) 65, *75,* 156n6, 173, *176*
Angelini, Sergio 54

Ant and the Aardvark, The (NBC series, 1969) 95, *101*
anthology 66, 92, 159, 161–2
Apartment, The (1960 film) 81, *101*
Arabian Nights 204
Arkin, Allan 87, 90
Arnold, Ben 159, 163, 172
Arsène Lupin 1, *15*
Ash vs Evil Dead (Starz series, 2015–2018) 174n13, *176*
Askwith, Ivan D. 20
Assouly, Julie 161
Astic, Guy 181, 185, 190, 192
Aumont, Jacques 1
Austin, J. L. 236
auteurism 56, 65
authorized 113
authorship 6, 10, 82, 99, 103, 117–8, 141, 156n4–5, 200, 211n33, 213, 254n19

Bacall, Lauren 210n18
Badalamenti, Angelo 178
Bale, Christian 127
Balio, Tino 33n12, 83, 89–92, 100n2
Balkind, Nicola 104, 107, 113, 177, *133*
Balsam, Martin 152
Barefoot, Guy 19, 22
Barnes, Brooks 107
Barnett, Steven 208n2
Barthes, Roland 207, 252n19
Barton Fink (1991 film) 161, 173n9, *190*
Bass, Saul 33n14
Bates Motel (1987 TV-pilot) 141

Bates Motel (A&E series, 2013–2017)
    9, *15*, 139–58, 159, 173n2, *176*
Battle of the Sexes, The (1959 film) 201,
    209n13, 226
Battlestar Galactica (Sci-Fi series,
    2003–2009) 187, 193n3, *195*
Baughman, James L. 53
Bazin, André 58
BBC xiii, 10–11, *15*, 37, *52*, 76, 100n1,
    100n7, *115*
Beatles, The 84
Becker, Anne 61
Bedtime for Bonzo (1951 film)
    169, *176*
Beethoven, Ludwig von 165
Behrens, Steve 55
Bellour, Raymond 204, 207
Benjamin, Walter 17, 203
Berlatsky, Noah 251n10
Big Little Book 23
Billington, Alex 111
binge-watching 2, 12n4, 66n3, 70, 238,
    252n15
Bischoff, Samuel 12n4
bisexual 126
Black Lodge, The 177, 185, 192–3
Blatty, William Peter 90
Bloch, Robert 139–42, 155
blockbuster xi, 19, 21, 26–8, 33n15,
    66n3, 79, 89, 98, 103
Bomba the Jungle Boy (1949 film)
    85, *101*
Bond 32n5, 84, 91
Boni, Marta 173n2
Bordwell, David 20, 32n7, 59, 86–7,
    252n19
Boren, Zachary Davies 159–60
Bourdaa, Mélanie 104, 116, 119n3
Bourne Identity, The (2002–2016
    films)98
Bowery Boys, The (1914 film) 85, *101*
Bowie, David 181
Bowman, Paul 233
Bradon, Benjamin A. 126
Bray, Christopher 126
Breaking Bad (AMC series, 2008–2013)
    8, 29, 40, 65, 68–9, 144, 251n10
Brennan, Matt 54
British Columbia 148
Broadcasting Act (1990) 199
Brodesser-Akner, Claude 61
Brooks, Louise 210n18
Brooks, Peter 39, 45, 49
Brosnan, Pierce 127

Browning, Todd 201, *209*
Brunsdon, Charlotte 54, 239
Brynner, Yul 92
Bucholz, Horst 97
Buckley, Cara Louise 2, 6
Buckley, Matthew 42
Buffy the Vampire Slayer (The WB
    series, 1997–2001, UPN, 2001–2003)
    69, *75*, 240
Bunch, Sonny 54
Burgess, Anthony 139, 149
Burkhead, Cynthia 183
Burt, Kayti 229
Burwell, Carter 165, 171
Butler, Judith 11, 112–13, 238, 243

Cagney and Lacey (CBS series,
    1982–1988) 240, *256*
Caine, Michael 9, 122–35
Caldwell, Ann 233
Caldwell, John Thornton 2, 62
Campany, David 4
Campbell, Bruce 169, 172, 174n13
Canal+ 67
Canguilhem, Georges 238
Capitol 103–17, 119n8
Capra, Frank 148
Cardwell, Sarah 200
Carnivàle (HBO, 2003–2005) 10, *15*,
    177, 187–9, 193n3
Carr, David 54
Carroll, Noël 60
Casablanca (1942 film) 229, 232
Cast a Giant Shadow (1966 film)
    89, *101*
Cast a Long Shadow (1959 film)
    100n6
Cattle Queen of Montana (1954 film)
    169, *176*
Caughie, John 53
CBS *15*, *52*, 87–8, *101*, *176*, 256–7
Champion, John C. 84
Chan, Charlie 83
Chan, Kenneth 40
Channel 4 xiii, 100n1, 100n4, 100n6,
    101, 208n3, *212*, 250n4, *257*
Chatman, Seymour 252n19
Chibnall, Steve 123, 129–30, 133
Chion, Michel 179
Chordettes, The 149
cinematicity 59–62
cinématogramme 207
Cipriano, Antonio 141–2, 156n5
cliffhanger 20, 22, 24, 67, 144, 206

Clockwork Orange, A (1971 film) 139, 149, *158*
cocaine 183, 215, 227
Coen, Ethan& Joel 10, 132, 159–74
Collins, Suzanne 103, 107, 109, 112, 114, 117, 119n4–*5*
Columbia 26, 28
comic strips 21–3
complex television 5, 56–7
Connery, Sean 127
consumerism *see* consumption
consumption 3–4, 20–1, 103, 105–10, 117
continuity 9, 11, 23–4, 64, 66–8, 80, 100n5, 104, 107, 122, 142, 146, 155, 182, 223, 227–9, 231n8, 237, 252n18
convergence xiii, 2, 4, 6–7, 9, 27, 82, 137, 150
Cooke, Lez 199–200, 208n1–2
Cooper, Gary 148
Coppola, Francis Ford 61, 99, *101*
Cotton, Joseph 210n18
Couch, Christina 159–60
Cowan, Lee 54
Cranfield, Jonathan 231n10
Crary Jonathan 1
Crawford, Joan 210n18
Creeber, Glen 55
Crichton, Charles 201, *212*
Crosby, Bing 146
cross-media 1–3, 9, 19–24, 31
Curtis, Tony 93, 97
Curtiz, Michael 229
Cuse, Carlton 141–2, 156n5
cycle 27, 32n2, 80, 84, 86, 91, 122–7, 130–3, 182–3

Dallas (CBS series, 1978–1991) 41
Damien (A&E series, 2016) 154, *158*
Damone, Vic 93, 97
Darin, Bobby 149
Dasgupta, Sudeep 54
Davis, Bette 210n18
Day, Laraine 170
DC Comics 28–9
Deeley, Michael 123, 129
Delivery after Raid (photograph) 210n18
Delyria, Joy 251n10
Deming, Caren J. 54, 62
Dena, Christy 118n2
Denson, Shane 2, 5, 21, 32n5–6
De Palma, Brian 141, 158

Derrida, Jacques 202
Desperate Housewives (ABC series, 2004–2012) 240, *270*
detective fiction 21, 37, 41, 48, 51n2, 90, 97, 160, 201, 201n15, 211n31, 213, 215, 222–3
Didi-Huberman, Georges 203
Dietrich, Marlene 210n18
Dinehard, Allan 92
discontinuity *see* continuity
Disney 33n13, 34n16, 161–2, 165, 173n10
Disney+ 2
Doctor Zhivago (1965 film) 89, *101*
documentary xiii, 65, 100n1, 100n4–7, 203
Dolan, Mark 185
Donner, Richard 25–7, 32n9, 36, 154
doppelgänger 185, 191
Dracula 32n5
Dragnet (NBC series, 1951–1959, 1967–1970) 251n10, *256*
dream 10, 68, 124, 149, 177–94, 210n24
Dressed to Kill (1980 film) 141, *158*
drugs 144–6, 184, 191, 227, 229
Dubois, Philippe 207, 211n28
Dunleavy, Trisha 2
Dunne, Peter 62
Dunst, Kirsten 164
Durand, Régis 203
Du Verger, Jean 187
DVD 100n4, 111, 128–33, 148, 161–2, 172
Dwyer, Tim 2
Dyer, Richard 110, 222
Dynasty (CBS series, 1981–1989) 41, *52*

Ealing comedy 201, 209n12, *212*
Earp, Wyatt 92
Ebert, Roger 33n10
Eco, Umberto 229
Edgerton, Gary 2, 61
Edwards, Blake *15*, 90, *95*, *102*
Egner, Jeremy 160, 173n1
Ehrin, Kerry 141–2, 156n5
emergent media 60–3
Empire State (1987 film) 201
engagement 3, 6–9, 19–20, 23, 25–6, 30–1, 39–41, 66n3, 70, 112, 151
Epstein, Adam 55–6
Epstein, Michael M. 55
Esquenazi, Jean-Pierre 2, 189, 208

Eternal Sunshine of the Spotless Mind
(2004 film) 98, *101*
Everitt, David 54
Evil Dead (1981 film) 169,
174n13, *176*
Ewald, François 238
Exorcist, The (Fox series, 2016-)
155, *158*

fan activism 116–17
fans 7–8, 11, 20, 29–31, 66n3, 69–71,
104, 107–19, 133, 150–5, 172,
174n11, 179, 182, 231n10, 241
fantasy 41, 66n4, 149, 152, 179, 182,
228–9
Fantomas (series, 1913–1914) 1, *15*
Farge, Arlette 203
Fargo (1996 film) 10, *15*,
159–74, *176*
Fargo (FX series, 2014-) 10, *15*,
159–74, *176*
Farmiga, Vera 143, *147*, 155
feminism 113, 252n13
Feuer, Jane 1
Fiddler on the Roof (1971 film) 81,
89, *101*
Figgis, Mike 201, 209n13, *212*
film noir xii, 41, *65*, 201, 209n13
film serials *see* serials
Fincher, David 65
Firth, Colin 132
Fisher, Mark 98
Fistful of Dollars, A (1964 film)
148, *158*
Forrest, Jennifer 19, 32n2
Forsyth, Bill 201, *212*
Fort Massacre (1958 film) 100n4
Foucault, Michel 11, 233–8,
250–2
Fox *see* 20th C. Fox
franchise 1–2, 8–9, 34n16, 79–84,
97–9, 103–5, 108, 114–19, 139–41,
149–54, 156n2, 169, 174n13
Frankenstein 32n5–6
Freaks (1932 film) 187, *195*
Freeman, Martin 162, 164
Freeman, Matthew 32n4
From Here to Eternity (1953 film)
91, *101*
Frost, Mark 177–82, 192
Fukunaga, Cary 70, 156n6
Fuller Robert 84, 95, 97
Fuller, Bryan 153
Fu Manchu 32n5

Gambit (1966 film) 132, *135*
Gambit (2012 film) 132, *135*
Game of Thrones (HBO series,
2011–2019) xi, 8, *15*, 55, 65
Garbo, Greta 210n18
Gardner, Jared 24
Garland, Judy 149
Gates, Tucker 156n5
Gatiss, Mark 11, 220, 223, 228, 231n8
Gaudreault, André 3, 59
gaze 69, 107–14, 119n6, 179–82,
190–2, 203
Geiger, Jeffrey 59–60
gender xiii, xiv, 10–11, 131–2, 177,
193, 216, 217, 220–1, 223–6, 231n8,
243–9, 252n13, 253n26
gender norms 11, 132, 252n13
Genette, Gérard 162, 164, 172, 173n3,
174n17
genre xii–xiii, 2, 7, 19, 24, 27–8, 34n16,
38, 41, 50n2, 51n4, 56, 65–7, 123,
130, 141, 155, 172, 202
Genz, Stéphanie 112
George, Christopher 84
Gerould, Daniel 50n2
Get Carter (1971 film) 9, *15*, 122–34
Get Carter (2000 film) *15*, 122–34
Gill, James 173n1
Gilmore Girls, The (The WB series,
2000–2007) 240
Gilmore Girls: A Year in the Life (2016
film) 238
Gilmore, James N. 33n12
Gitlin, Todd 2
Gledhill, Christine 38–40, 43, 45, 51n3
Glévarec, Hervé 2
Godard, Jean-Luc 61, 76, 204
Godfather, The (1972 film) 8, 80, 96,
99, *101*, 234
Goldberg, Lesley 143, 160, 163, 173n7
Goldblatt, Henry 238
Golden Age 1, 22, 53–4, 68, 71n1,
129, 148, 159, 209n6, 239, 251n10,
252n11–12, 253n19
Goldman, Eric 144, *147*
Gone with the Wind (1939 film)
178, *195*
Good Wife, The (CBS series,
2009–2016) 11, *15*, 233–57
Gordon, Ian 33n11–12
Gothicism, 220, 226
Gould, Deborah 38
Grand Central Light (photograph)
210n18

Grapes of Wrath, The 187
Graser, Marc 117
Gray, Jonathan 2
Great Escape, The (1963 film) 81, 84, 89, *101*
Greer, Stephen 22–3, 230n6
Guilbert, Georges-Claude 2
Gunfight at Dodge City, The (1958 film) 91, 100n5, *101*
Gunfight at the OK Corral (1957 film) 92, *101*
Guns of the Magnificent Seven (1969 film) 81, 87–9, 95–7, *101–2*
gutter 24–5

hacking 114–16
Hagedorn, Roger 1, 20, 32n3
Halberstam, Jack 250n2
Halloween (1978 film) 141, *158*
Hancock, Tony 210n18
Hannan, Brian 88
Hannibal (NBC series, 2013–2015) 153–5, 156n2, *172*
Hargraves, Hunter 241
Harlow, Jean 210n18
Harris, Richard 156n2
Harvard Business School 85–6
Harvey, Colin B. 104
Harvey, Oswald Lee 209n9
Hawaii (1966 film) 81, 89, 91–2, *101*
Hawaiians, The (1970 film) 92, *101*
Hawes, William 54
Hawks, Howard, 148, *158*
Hawley, Noah 10, 159–65, 172, 173n1–7
Hayward, Jennifer 3, 4, 19, 32n3, 42
HBO (Home Box Office) 8, 10, *15*, *52*, 54, 56, 65, 75, 156n5, *158*, 159, *176*, 177, 187, 193, *195*, 239, *257*
Hearst, William Randolph 22
Heath, Edward 201n19
Henderson, Stuart 79–82, 86, 89–90, 95, 97–9
Heston, Charlton 91–2
heteronormativity 131, 132, 252n13
heterosexuality 127, 249–50
Hey Landlord (NBC series, 1966–1967), 92–3, *101*
Hidden City (1988 film) 208n3, *212*
Higgins, Scott 2, 19, 22, 24
high-brow television 56–9, 66n3
high-end television 208, 211n33
Highmore, Freddy 143, 146, 150, 156n5, 157n6

hijacking *see* hacking 114–16
Hill, George Roy 91, *101*
Hills, Matt 55, 117, 119n9, 164, 174n12
His Girl Friday (1940 film) 148, *158*
Hitchcock, Alfred 9, *15*, 33n14, 122, 139–58
Hobbit, The (2011–2014 films) 1, *15*
Hodges, Adrian 209
Hodges, Mike *15*, 129
Hogg, Christopher 200, 204, 208
Holdsworth, Amy 199, 204
Hollywood xiii, 2, 8, 19, 24–31, 32n7, 50n2, 64, 69, 79–99, 110, 122–34, 170, 173n9, 193, 234, 253n19
homage 147, 161, 165, 170–1, 225, 245
Homeland (Showtime series, 2011-) 144, *158*
homoeroticism 221–3, 230n6, 231n8
homosexual 126, 131
Hooper, Tobe *158*
Hope, Bob 148
Horkheimer, Max 4
Hour of the Gun (1967 film) 92, *101*
House of Cards (Netflix series, 2013–2018) 55, 65, 67, 69
Hudelet, Ariane 250n1
Hulton collection 201
Hulu 2, 6, 54, 250n3
Hume George, Diana 179–80, 193
Hunger Games, The (franchise) 8–9, *15*, 103–135
Hutcheon, Linda 230n4

icon 9, 24, 32n5, 104–18
In The Heat of the Night (1967 film) 8, *15*, 81
Inception (2010 film) 42, *52*
incest 145, 148–51, 180–2, 193
Incredible Hulk, The 20–1, 29–30, 34n16, *36*
Inspector Clouseau (1968 film) 81, 87, 89–90, 97, *101*
integration 79, 82, 98–9, 116
intermediality xi–xiii, 6, 59–62, 70
intertext xii, 4, 10, 30, 61, 129, 141, 162, 169–73, 179, 187, 220
Ipcress File (1965 film) 122, 125–7, 131–2, *135*
Irma La Douce (1963 film) 81, *101*
Iron Horseman, The (NBC, TV Pilot, 1959) 92, 100n5, *101*
Iser, Wolfgang 32n8

Italian Job, The (1969 film) 9, *15*, 122–33, *135*
Italian Job, The (2003 film) 9, *15*, 122–33, *135*
ITV 199

Jacobs, Jason 2, 6, 54, 57, 209n7
Jameson, Fredric 172
Jancovich, Mark 1, 33n12
Jaramillo, Deborah 5, 57, 59, 63, 209n7
Jaws (1975 film) 8, *15*, 80, 99
Jenkins, Henry 2, 29, 32n2, 104, 133, 229
Jenner, Mareike 55
Jensen, Jeff 238
Jess-Cooke, Caroline 31n2, 80
Jetée (La) 216, 211n28
Johnson, Catherine 62
Johnson, Derek 2, 32N2
Johnson, Merri 239
Jones, Stuart Blake 4

Kelleter, Frank 4, 19, 26–7, 31n1, 32n3, 123
Kellison, Catherine 54
Kennedy, George 95, 97
Kerbel, M. 53
Kerr, Paul 1
Key Largo (1948 film) 148, *158*
Kihm, Christophe 12n5
Kilpatrick, Jacquelyn 168
Kipnis, Laura 2
Kizu, Kyle 160
Klein, Amanda Ann 32n2, 125
Klinger, Barbara 128–9, 133
Knick, The (Cinemax series, 2014–2015) 156, *158*
Koos, Leonard R. 19, 32n2
Krampner, Jon 53
Kubrick, Stanley 139, 149, *158*, 192, *195*
Kuleshov effect 200
Kutner, Jerry C. 156n2

Laclau, Ernesto 251n6
Lagerwey, Jorie 239–40, 252n11
Lambert, Josh 20
Landlord, The (1971 film) 92, *101*
Lavery, David 252n13
Lavigne, Carlen 222–3
Law, Jude 127–8, 131–2
Lawrence, Francis *15, 121*
Lawson, Mark 54

Lee Harvey, Oswald 209n9
Legagneur, Marine 178, 185
Leigh, Janet 84
Leigh, Vivian 210n18
Leitch, Thomas 156n3
Lemmon, Jack 93, 97
Leo Burnett Agency, 94
Leonard, Suzanne 233, 235, 243, 253n23
Leopold, Todd 54
lesbian 222, 249
Letourneux, Matthieu 2, 4
Leverette, Marc 2, 6
Levine, Elana 12n2, 54
Levine, Joseph E. 132
Leyda, Julie 5, 31n1
Liddiment, David 199
Life and Legend of Wyatt Earp, The (ABC series, 1955–1961) 92, *101*
Lindelof, Damon 188
Lionsgate *15*, 103–4, 107–8, 113, 115–17, *121*
Lipovetsky, Gilles 5
Littau, Karin 59–60
Local Hero 201, 211n13, *212*
Lodtz, Amanda 2
Logan, Elliot 5, 54
Loock, Kathleen 3, 19, 31n2, 123, 156n3
Lord of the Rings (2001–02–03 trilogy) 91, 97, *101*
Loren, Sophia 210n18
Lost (ABC series, 2004–2010) xiii, 10, *15*, 20, 141, 165, 177, 187–93
Louise, Toni 93, 97
Love (Netflix series, 2016–2018) 251n10, *257*
Lovesick (Netflix series, 2014-) 250n4, *257*
Lucas, George 99, *102*, 201
L Word, The (Showtime series, 2004–2009) 240, *257*
Lynch, David 10, *15, 56*, 61, 65, 149, 177, 179, 181, 184, 190, 192, *195*
Lyons, James 1, 33n12

MacGuffin 144, 151
Mackendrick, Alexander 201n14, *212*
Maclean, Tracy Biga 56, 60
Mad Men (AMC series, 2007–2015) 61, 76
Magnificent Seven, The (1960 film) 8, *15*, 81–2, 84, 87–91, 95–100, *101*

Magnificent Seven, The (CBS series, 1998–2000) 87–8, *101*
Magnificent Seven Ride, The (1972 film) 81, 87–9, 95–6
Man from Planet X, The (1951 film) 169, 176
Man in the Net (1959 film) 100n5
Man of the West (1958 film) 100n5
Man Who Wasn't There, The (2001 film) 173 n4
Mann, Denise 83, 85
Mann, Michael 156n2
Mannoni, Laurent 1
Manovich, Lev 33n15
Maras, Steven 60, 63, 71n7
Marker, Chris 216, 211n28
Marshall, Rick 53
Martin, George R. R. 65
Marvel 1, 28–9, 32n6, 33n13, 34n16, *36*
Mason, Chris 29
Massacre Harbor (1968 film) 94, *101–2*
Massumi, Brian 38
Mast, Gerald 58
Masterson, Bat 92
Matrix, The (1999 film) 91, 97, *101*
Mayer, Ruth 19–20, 22, 32n5–6
Mazzara, Glen 154
McCabe, Janet 1–2, 55–6, 239
MCA 82
McAllister, Matthew P. 1, 33n12
McClarnon, Zahn 164
McCloud, Scott 24
McCrea, Jody 92
McCrea, Joel 92
McDougal, Charles 250n5, 256
McGowan, Todd 180–1
McGregor, Ewan 127
McLean, Gareth 54
McQueen, Steve 95
medium specificity 2–8, 20–25, 53–71, 85, 99, 133, 162, 165, 173n9, 186, 200, 238
Meet John Doe (1941 film) 148, *158*
Meier, Stefan 26
Memento (2000 film) 98, *101*
Meslow, Scott 174n15
metafiction 225, 227
MGM 15, 67, 88, *101*, 123, 135, 166, 195
Midsummer Night's Dream, A 179
Miller, Frank 30, 173n4
Miller, Laura 251n10

Miller, Taylor 235
Miller's Crossing (1990 film) 173n4
Mills, Brett 5, 57, 209n7
Mirisch Company xiii, 8, 79–115
Mirisch, Harold 90
Mirisch, Marvin 94
Mirisch, Walter 80, 85—8, 90, 92, 94, 100n5–7
Missika, Jean-Louis 2, 6
Mittell, Jason 2, 56–9, 151, 163, 172, 185, 238, 241, 251n10, 252–3n19
Moffat, Steven 11, 220, 223, 228, 231n8
Monogram 85–6, *101*
Monroe, Marilyn 90, 179, 209n9, 210n18
Moonlighting (ABC series, 1985–1989) *257*
morphine 227
Motor Psycho (1992 film) 141, *158*
Mouffe, Chantal 251n6
Mulholland Drive (2001 film) 190, *195*
mutation 8, 115, 201

narrative norm 2, 20, 27, 30, 42, 163, 165, 252n15
narratology 2, 10, 177
Naugrette, Jean-Pierre 230n5
NBC 80, 87, 92–3, *101–2*, 147, 153, 156n2, *158*, 256–7
Neale, Steve 50n2
Nelson, Robin 1, 5, 209n7, 211n33
Netflix 2, 6, 12n4, 54, 55n3, 56, 65, 67, 75, 250n3–4, 251n10, *257*
network 2, 4, 11, 12n3, 20, 22, 40–1, 48, 51n4, 55, 61, 82–5, 88, 93, 99, 108, 142, 150, 153–4, 160, 193, 225, 233–4, 238–41, 243, 246–7, 250, 252n15
Neumann, Birgit 163
Newcomb, Horace 53–4
New Girl (Fox series, 2011–2018) 234, *257*
Newman, Michael Z. 12n2, 54
Nicholson, Jack 192
Nicol, Bran 230n1
Nixon, Richard 207
No Country for Old Men (2007 film) 173n4
noir *see* film noir
norm *see* gender norm, narrative norm, social norm
normativity 11, 222–3, 233–4, 238, 243–4, 247–50

Northern Exposure (CBS series, 1990–1995) 240, 252n12, *257*
nostalgia 26, 133, 149
Nünning, Ansgar 163
Nussbaum, Emily 6
Nygaard, Taylor 239–40, 252n11

O'Brien, Hugh 92
Oldman, Gary 127
Olivier, Lawrence 124–5, 132, 134n2
Ollson, Jan 6, 54
Oltean, T. 104
online marketing 70, 71n2, 107–17
opening sequence 7, 10, 20–34, 44, 69, 156n5, 160–9, 173n10, 221, 241–8, 251n5
Operation Eagle's Nest 169–72
operational aesthetics 150–5
Orgad, Shani 233, 248
Organization, The (1971 film) 81, 97, *101*
Ott, Brian L. 2, 6
Owen, Clive 127

package-unit 82–6
Palen, Tim 121
Palmer, R. Barton 32n2
Palomar Pictures International 123, *149*
panopticon 105, 111, 119n4
Paramount Decision 79, 81, 86, 99, *101*, 128, 130, *135*, *158*, *195*
Paramount Pictures *15*, 92, 123
pastiche 149–50, 159–61, 169, 172, 173n3, 174n17
patriarchy 10, 177, 180, 186, 245
Patterson, John 54
Peacock, Steven 2, 6, 54, 57, 209n7
Peck, Ron 201, 209n13, *212*
Peckinpah, Sam 87
Perils of Pauline, The (series, 1914) 1, *15*
Perkins, Anthony 140, 142, 148, 150, *158*
Perkins, Claire 12n5
Peter Loves Mary (NBC series, 1960–1961) 93, 100n5, *102*
Petski, Denise 238
Piazza, Roberta 61
Picket Fences (CBS series, 1992–1996) 160, *176*
Picture Post 201
Pierrot le Fou (1965 film) 61, *76*

pilot 84–5, 87, 92–3, 97, 99, 100n5, *101*–2, 141, 143, 148, 151, 153, 178, 181, 185, 193n2, 223, 234, 240–2, 247, 253n20
Pink Panther Show, The (NBC series, 1969) 92, *102*
Pink Panther, The (1963 film) 8, *15*, 81–2, 89, 90, 84, 97, 99, *102*
Pink Phink, The (1964 film) 95, *102*
Pinter, Harold 132
Poe, Edgar Allan xiv, 152
Poitier, Sidney 87, 89, 97
Poliakoff, Stephen 10, 199–212
police 37, 41–9, 51n2, 70, 97, 155, 160, 165, 171, 181, 184–5, 210n18
Porter, Lynnette 230n5
Porter, Rick 162, 173n4
Porton, Richard 125
preboot 147
preplay 139, 142, 150–5
prequel 1, 10, 99, 141, 142, 144, 146–7, 150–5
Press, Andrea 54
Private Life of Sherlock Holmes (1969 film) 84
Prudhomme, Monique 147
Psycho (1959 novel) 139
Psycho (1960 film) 9, *15*, 139–2, 151, 158, 173n2
Psycho (1998 film) 140, *158*
Psycho II (1982 novel) 140
Psycho II (1983 film) 140, *158*
Psycho III (1986 film) 140, 155, *158*
Psycho IV –The Beginning (1990 film on *Showtime*) 140, *158*
Psycho House (1990 novel) 140, *158*
Psycho Lover (1970 film) 141, *158*
Psycho Sisters (1998 film) 141, *158*
Public Enemy, The (1931 film) 61, 76

Quality television xiii, 1, 3, 29, 55–8, 156, 160, 170, 203, 208, 239–40, 252n13
Quest of the Magnificent Seven 88

Rachmil, Lew 84
Radio Patrol 19, 21–31, *36*
Rancière, Jacques 233
Rat Patrol (ABC series, 1966–1968) 84, 92–4, 99, *102*, 123
Ratner, Brett 156n2
Ray, Amber 160
Reagan, Ronald 167–72, 174n17
Rebello, Stephen 155n1

reboot xiii, 1, 6, 9, 142, 153–5
recycled footage 24
Reeves, Jimmie L. 55
reflexivity 10, 19, 31, 32n6, 56,
    105–6, 161
remake xii–xiii, 1, 9, 19, 31n2, 88, 90,
    122–3, 127–55, 156n2, 160
repetition 3, 10–11, 19, 24, 31, 79, 99,
    105–7, 112–3, 118, 142
replay 10, 19, 139, 142, 150–5, 166,
    179, 186, 150–5, 186, 192, 206,
    238, 241–3
Republic Pictures 24
resignification 113, 238
resistance 104–5, 110–18, 160, 166,
    234, 243, 248–50
Restivo, Angelo 61
Return of the Seven, The (1966 film)
    81, 87–9, 95–6
Rich Man, Poor Man (ABC series,
    1976) 41, 52
Ritchie, Guy 128
Ritchie, Michael 53
River (BBC1 series, 2015) 37–51, 52
Road to Bali (1952 film) 148, *158*
Road to Hong Kong, The (1962 film)
    148, *158*
Road to Morocco (1942 film) 148, *158*
Road to Rio (1947 film) 148, *158*
Road to Singapore (1940 film) 148, *158*
Road to Utopia (1946 film) 148, *158*
Road to Zanzibar (1941 film) 148, *158*
Robey, Tim 172
Robin, Nelson 209n7, 211n33
Robinson, Sean 251n10
Roche, David 179, 181, 192
Rocky IV (1985 film) 69, 76
Rodriguez, Robert 30, *36*
Rogers, Mark C. 55
Roots (ABC series, 1977) 41, 52
Ross, Alex 30
Ross, Gary *15*, 106, *121*
Roth, Tim 127
Round, Julia 24
*Russians are Coming, The Russians are
    Coming, The* (1966 film) 81, *102*
Russo, Jeff 166–7
Ryan, Marie-Laure 104, 118n1
Ryan, Maureen 54

Sachs, Ben 56
Sagal, Boris 84
Saint-Gelais, Richard 160–1, 173n6
Saul, Heather 12n6

Scahill, Andrew 142, 147, 149–51
Schefer, Jean-Louis 64
Scheherazade 204
Schlamme, Thomas 235, 251n5
Scorcese, Martin 61
Scott, Cynthia 251n10
Scrotal Recall (Netflix series, 2014-)
    251n4, *257*
Sellers, Peter 87, 90
Selznick, David 170
sequel xii, 1, 8–9, 19, 26–7, 31n2,
    33n11, 79–100, *102*, 122, 129–31,
    134n4, 139–42, 147, 151, 154,
    156n2–3, 160, 174n13
serial killer 139–57, 167
serials xi, 7, 19, 22–27, 31, 39, 41–2,
    80, 100n1, 199, 238
Serious Man, A (2008 film) 173n4
Serroy, Jean 5
Seven Samurai (1954 film) 90, *102*
Sex and The City (HBO series,
    1998–2004) 240, *257*
Seymour, Emily 208n2
Shaffer, Anthony 124
Shail, Robert 124–6
Shakespeare, William xi–xiv, 179,
    181, 183
Shepherd, Simon 41
Sherlock (BBC1 series, 2010–2017) 11,
    15, 213–32
Shield, The (FX series, 2002–2008)
    154, *158*
Shining, The 192, *195*
Shooting the Past (1999 film) 10, *15*,
    199–212
Shot in the Dark, A (1964 film) 81,
    89–91, 97, *102*
Showrunner 9, 141, 142–6, 150–1,
    156n5, 188, 193n3, 241
Showtime 10, *15*, 54, 140, *158*, 179,
    184, 192, *195*
Shyamalan, M. Night 190, *195*
Silence of the Lambs, The (1991 film)
    154, *158*
Sin City 30, *36*
Singing Detective, The (1986 film)
    59, 76
Six Feet Under (HBO series,
    2001–2005) 240, *257*
Sixth Sense, The 190, *195*
Skinny Dippers (photograph) 210n18
Sleuth (1972 film) 9, *15*, 122–32
Sleuth (2007 film) 122–25, 132–33
Slide, Anthony 53

268   *Index*

Smith, Gerry 54
Smuts, Aaron 58, 71n4
Snead, Elizabeth 148
social norm 38
Soderbergh, Steven 156n5
Some Like it Hot (1959 film) 81, 93, 97, 99, *102*
Sopranos, The (HBO series, 1999–2007) 55, 61, 76, 233, 239–40, 252n12, 252n14, *257*
Sorkin, Aaron 245, 250–1n5
Soulez, Guillaume 186
Spall, Timothy 205
Speed (1994 film) 234, *257*
speed-watching 2, 12n4, 24
Spellbound (1945 film) 185, *195*
Spence, Louise 39, 42, 47
Spider-Man (2002 film) 21, 28, 33n13, *36*
Spider-Man 2 (2004 film) 20–1, 28–30, 33n13, 33n15, *36*
Spigel, Lynn 6, 53, 54, 239
spin-off 20, 80–5, 88, 90, 93, 97, 99, 183, 201
Stack, Robert 170
Staiger, Janet 32n7, 86–7
Stallone, Sylvester 76, 127–30
star 9–10, 84–5, 87–95, 106, 100, 122–5, 127–34, 155, 157n6, 167, 177–85, 203, 210n18
Star Wars (1977 film) 1, 8, 80, 96–9, *102*
Steinbeck, John 187
Stephens, Mitchell 53
Stokes, Jane 60, 63
Stork, Matthias 33n12
Stormy Monday (photograph) 201, *212*
Street, Sarah 123
Stubbs, Jonathan 127
studio system 24, *56*, 65, 82, 86
Sturcken, Frank 53
Sturges, John *15*, 87, 92, 95, *101–2*
subject position 11, 203, 233–53
subversion xiv, 11, 110, 234, 243, 249, 250n2, 253n19
Super Six, The. (NBC series, 1966–69) *102*
superhero 19, 27–9, 33n12–13, 34n15
Superman (1978 film) 19, 21–2, 25–31, 32n4–5, 33n9–11
Superman II (1980 film) 26, 33n11
Suskind, Alex 54
Sutton, David 60, 63, 71n7

Sutton, Mike 201
Sutton, Paul 147

Taradash, Daniel 91
Tarzan 83
Taylor, Aaron 29
Taylor, Elizabeth 210n18
Tempest, The 179, 181
Temporality 67, 147, 186, 205–6, 238
Texas Chainsaw Massacre (1974 film) 156n2, *158*
Thatcherism 201
They Call Me MISTER Tibbs (1970 film) 87, 97, *102*
Thiellement, Pacôme 183, 193n1
Third Man (1949 film) 148, *158*
Thomas Crown Affair, The (1968 film) 81, *102*
Thompson, Derek 54
Thompson, Kirstin 32n7, 59, 82–3
Thompson, Mark 199
Thompson, Robert J. 54, 71n1, 239–40, 251–2n11
Thon, Jan-Noël 104
Thorburn, David 39
Thornton, Billy Bob 164
Thorpe, Vanessa 56
Titoria, Anmol 56
Tomasovic, Dick 33n13
Toys in the Attic (1963 film) 91, *102*
Transamerica 83
transfiction 10, 160–4, 173n6
transmedia xii–xiii, 7–8, 19, 27, 30–1, 32n2, 32n4, 103–19, 193, 251n10
transmedia marketing 103–17
trauma 45, 182, 186, 189
Trembley, Elizabeth 231n9
True Detective (HBO series, 2014-) 51, 59, 76, 156n5, *159*
Trumbo, Dalton 91
Tryon, Chuch 128
Tudor, Andrew 149
TVI, TVII, TVIII, TVIV 55
12 & Holding (2005 film) 141, *158*
24 200, *212*
20th C. Fox *15*, 33n13, *176*, *195*, *212*, *257*
Twin Peaks (ABC series, 1990–91, 2017) 10, *15*, 55n3, 56, 59, 65, 149, 177–95
Twin Peaks: Fire Walk with Me (1992 film) 10, *15*, 177–95
Twin Peaks: The Return (2017 film) 10, 177, 192

Ue, Tom 231n10
Ugly Betty (ABC series, 2006–2010) 240, *257*
Unauthorized 19
United Artists (UA) 81–4, *76*, *101*, *158*, *176*, *195*
Universal Studios 22–4, 36, 87, *101*, 140–1, *158*, *176*, *195*

Van Cleef, Lee *95*, 97
van den Berg, Thijs 19
Van Der Werff, Todd 54, 62
Van Sant, Gus 141, 156n4, *158*
Verevis, Constantine 12n5, 19, 31n2, 80, 129–30, 141, 156n3
Vernet, Marc 112
visual aesthetics 142, 147, 155
Vorel, Jim 54

Wade, Chris 6, 56
Wagner, Jon Nelson 56, 60
Wahlberg, Mark 127, 130
Walking Dead, The (AMC series, 2002–) 154, *158*
Wallach, Eli 95
Warner Bros. *15*, *36*, *52*, *76*, *101*, 128–9, *158*, *195*, 232
Weintraub, Steve 125
Wellman, William 61, *76*
Wells-Lassagne, Shannon 2
Wells, Jessica R. 114
West Side Story (1961 film) 81, 89, *102*

West Wing, The (NBC series, 1999–2006) 240, 251n5, *257*
Wezner, Kelley 119n4
Wheatley, Helen 54
Wheen, Francis 208n6
Whitmore, James 170
Wichita (1955 film) 92–3, 99, 100n5, *102*
Wichita Town (NBC series, 1959–1960) 92–3, 99, 100n6, *102*
Wiegman, Robyn 249, 250n2
Wilcox, Rhonda 251n10
Wilk, Max 53
William Morris Agency, 91
Williams, John 25
Williams, Linda 38–9, 41
Williams, Raymond 211n27
Wilson, Elizabeth 249, 250n2
Wire, The (HBO series, 2002–2008) 40, 55, *76*, 251n10
Wise, Ray 180
Woolf, Virginia 210n18
Wroe, Nicholas 208n4

Yockey, Matt 25–6

Zabunyan, Dork 12n5
Zanger, Anat 133, 141, 151, 156n2
Ziegenhagen, Sandra 20
Zinneman, Fred 91, *101*
ZollerSeitz, Matt 6, 56

Lightning Source UK Ltd.
Milton Keynes UK
UKHW021419180822
407473UK00004B/194